Walter Elliott

The Life of Father Hecker

Walter Elliott

The Life of Father Hecker

ISBN/EAN: 9783337416829

Printed in Europe, USA, Canada, Australia, Japan

Cover: Foto ©Raphael Reischuk / pixelio.de

More available books at **www.hansebooks.com**

FATHER HECKER.

BY

REV. WALTER ELLIOTT.

———•———

NEW YORK:
THE COLUMBUS PRESS.

—

1891.

Nil obstat :

   AUGUSTINUS F. HEWIT,

      Censor Deputatus.

Imprimatur :

   M. A. CORRIGAN,

      Archiepiscopus Neo-Ebor.

AUTHOR'S PREFACE.

THE reader must indulge me with what I cannot help saying, that I have felt the joy of a son in telling the achievements and chronicling the virtues of Father Hecker. I loved him with the sacred fire of holy kinship, and love him still—only the more that lapse of time has deepened by experience, inner and outer, the sense of truth and of purity he ever communicated to me in life, and courage and fidelity to conscience. I feel it to be honor enough and joy enough for a life-time that I am his first biographer, though but a late born child and of merit entirely insignificant. The literary work is, indeed, but of home-made quality, yet it serves to hold together what is the heaven-made wisdom of a great teacher of men. It will be found that Father Hecker has three words in this book to my one, though all my words I tried to make his. His journals, letters, and recorded sayings are the edifice into which I introduce the reader, and my words are the hinges and latchets of its doors. I am glad of this, for it pleases me to dedicate my good will and my poor work to swinging open the doors of that new House of God that Isaac Hecker was to me, and that I trust he will be to many.

WALTER ELLIOTT.

CONTENTS.

INTRODUCTION.

By Most Rev. John Ireland, D.D.,

Archbishop of St. Paul.

LIFE is action, and so long as there is action there is life. That life is worth living whose action puts forth noble aspirations and good deeds. The man's influence for truth and virtue persevering in activity, his life has not ceased, though earth has clasped his body in its embrace. It is well that it is so. The years of usefulness between the cradle and the grave are few. The shortness of a life restricted to them is sufficient to discourage many from making strong efforts toward impressing the workings of their souls upon their fellows. The number to whose minds we have immediate access is small, and they do not remain. Is the good we might do worth the labor ? We cannot at times refuse a hearing to the question. Fortunately, it is easily made clear to us that the area over which influence travels is vastly more extensive than at first sight appears. The eye will not always discern the undulations of its spreading waves ; but onward it goes, from one soul to another, far beyond our immediate ranks, and as each soul touched by it becomes a new motive power, it rolls forward, often with energy a hundred times intensified, long after the shadows of death have settled around its point of departure.

Isaac Thomas Hecker lives to-day, and with added years he will live more fully than he does to-day. His influence for good remains, and with a better understanding of his plans and ideals, which is sure to come, his influence will widen and deepen among laymen and priests of the Church in America. The writing of his biography is a tribute to his memory which the love and esteem of his spiritual children could not refuse ; it is, also, a most important service to generations present and unborn, in whose deeds will be seen the fruits of inspirations gathered from it. We are thankful that this biography has been written by one who from closest converse and most intimate friendship knew Father Hecker so thoroughly. He has given us in his book what we need to know of Father Hecker. We care very little, except so far as details may accentuate the great lines of a life and make them sensible to our obtuse touch, where or when a man was born, what places he happened to visit, what houses he built, or in what circumstances of malady or in what surroundings he died. These things can be said of the ten thousand. We want to know the thoughts and the resolves of the soul which made him a marked man above his fellows and which begot strong influences for good and great works, and if none such can be unfolded then drop the man out of sight, with a " *Requiescant in pace* " engraven upon his tombstone. Few deserve a biography, and to the undeserving none should be given.

If it be permitted to speak of self, I might say that to Father Hecker I am indebted for most salutary impressions which, I sorrowfully confess, have not had in me their due effect ; the remembrance of them, however, is a proof to me of the useful-ness of his life, and its power for good in others. I am glad to have the opportunity to profess publicly my gratitude to him. He was in the prime of life and work when I was for the first time brought to observe him. I was quite young in the ministry, and very naturally I was casting my eye around in search of ideal men, whose footsteps were treading the path I could feel I, too, ought to travel. I never afterwards wholly lost sight of Father Hecker, watching him as well as I could from a distance of two thousand miles. I am not to-day without some experience of men and things, won from years and toils, and I do not alter one tittle my estimate of him, except to make it higher. To the priests of the future I recommend a serious study of Father Hecker's life. To them I would have his biography dedicated. Older men, like myself, are fixed in their ways, and they will not receive from it so much benefit.

Father Hecker was the typical American priest ; his were the gifts of mind and heart that go to do great work for God and for souls in America at the present time. Those qualities, assuredly, were not lacking in him which are the necessary elements of character of the good priest and the great man in any time and place. Those are the subsoil of priestly culture, and with the absence of them no one will succeed in America any more than elsewhere. But suffice they do not. There must be added, over and above, the practical intelligence and the pliability of will to understand one's surroundings, the ground upon which he is to deploy his forces, and to adapt himself to circumstances and opportunities as Providence appoints. I do not expect that my words, as I am here writing, will receive universal approval, and I am not at all sure that their expression would have been countenanced by the priest whose memory brings them to my lips. I write as I think, and the responsibility must be all my own. It is as clear to me as noon-day light that countries and peoples have each their peculiar needs and aspirations as they have their peculiar environments, and that, if we would enter into souls and control them, we must deal with them according to their conditions. The ideal line of conduct for the priest in Assyria will be out of all measure in Mexico or Minnesota, and I doubt not that one doing fairly well in Minnesota would by similar methods set things sadly astray in Leinster or Bavaria. The Saviour prescribed timeliness in pastoral caring. The master of a house, He said, " bringeth forth out of his treasury new things and old," as there is demand for one kind or the other. The apostles of nations, from Paul before the Areopagus to Patrick upon the summit of Tara, followed no different principle.

The circumstances of Catholics have been peculiar in the United States, and we have unavoidably suffered on this account. Catholics in largest numbers were Europeans, and so were their priests, many of whom—by no means all—remained in heart and mind and mode of action as alien to America as if they had never been removed from the Shannon, the Loire, or the Rhine. No one need remind me that immigration has brought us inesti-

mable blessings, or that without it the Church in America would
be of small stature. The remembrance of a precious fact is not
put aside, if I recall an accidental evil attaching to it. Priests
foreign in disposition and work were not fitted to make favorable impressions upon the non-Catholic American population,
and the American-born children of Catholic immigrants were
likely to escape their action. And, lest I be misunderstood, I
assert all this is as true of priests coming from Ireland as from
any other foreign country. Even priests of American ancestry,
ministering to immigrants, not unfrequently fell into the lines of
those around them, and did but little to make the Church in
America throb with American life. Not so Isaac Thomas
Hecker. Whether consciously or unconsciously I do not know,
and it matters not, he looked on America as the fairest conquest for divine truth, and he girded himself with arms shaped
and tempered to the American pattern. I think that it may be
said that the American current, so plain for the last quarter of a
century in the flow of Catholic affairs, is, largely at least, to be
traced back to Father Hecker and his early co-workers. It used
to be said of them in reproach that they were the " Yankee "
Catholic Church ; the reproach was their praise.

Father Hecker understood and loved the country and its
institutions. He saw nothing in them to be deprecated or
changed ; he had no longing for the flesh-pots and bread-stuffs
of empires and monarchies. His favorite topic in book and
lecture was, that the Constitution of the United States requires,
as its necessary basis, the truths of Catholic teaching regarding
man's natural state, as opposed to the errors of Luther and Calvin. The republic, he taught, presupposes the Church's doctrine, and the Church ought to love a polity which is the
offspring of her own spirit. He understood and loved the people
of America. He recognized in them splendid natural qualities.
Was he not right ? Not minimizing in the least the dreadful
evil of the absence of the supernatural, I am not afraid to give
as my belief that there is among Americans as high an appreciation and as lively a realization of natural truth and goodness

as has been seen in any people, and it seems as if Almighty God, intending a great age and a great people, has put here in America a singular development of nature's powers and gifts, both in man and out of man—with the further will, I have the faith, of crowning all with the glory of the supernatural. Father Hecker perceived this, and his mission was to hold in his hands the natural, which Americans extolled and cherished and trusted in, and by properly directing its legitimate tendencies and growth to lead it to the term of its own instincts and aspirations—Catholic truth and Catholic grace. Protestantism is no longer more than a name, a memory. The American has fallen back upon himself, scorning the negations and the doctrinal cruelties of Protestantism as utterly contrary to himself, as utterly unnatural ; and now comes the opportunity of the Catholic Church to show that she is from the God who created nature, by opening before this people her treasures, amid which the soul revels in rational liberty and intelligence, and enjoys the gratification of its best and purest moral instincts. These convictions are the keynote of Father Hecker's controversial discourses and writings, notably of two books, *Aspirations of Nature* and *Questions of the Soul.* He assumed that the American people are naturally Catholic, and he labored with this proposition constantly before his mind. It is the assumption upon which all must labor who sincerely desire to make America Catholic.

He laid stress on the natural and social virtues. The American people hold these in highest esteem. They are the virtues that are most apparent, and are seemingly the most needed for the building up and the preservation of an earthly commonwealth. Truthfulness, honesty in business dealings, loyalty to law and social order, temperance, respect for the rights of others, and the like virtues are prescribed by reason before the voice of revelation is heard, and the absence of specifically supernatural virtues has led the non-Catholic to place paramount importance upon them. It will be a difficult task to persuade the American that a church which will not enforce those primary virtues can enforce others which she herself declares to be higher and more arduous, and as he has implicit confidence in the destiny of his country to produce a high order of social existence, his first test of a religion will be its powers in this direction. This is according to Catholic teaching. Christ came not to destroy, but to perfect what was in man, and the graces and truths of revelation lead most securely to the elevation of the life that is, no less than to the gaining of the life to come. It is a fact, however, that in other times and other countries the Church has been impeded in her social work, and certain things or customs of those times and countries, transplanted upon American soil and allowed to grow here under a Catholic name, will do her no honor among Americans. The human mind, among the best of us, inclines to narrow limitations, and certain Catholics, aware of the comparatively greater importance of the supernatural, partially overlook the natural.

Then, too, casuists have incidentally done us harm. They will quote as our rule of social conduct in America what may have been tolerated in France or Germany during the seventeenth century, and their hair-splitting distinctions in the realm of abstract right and wrong are taken by some of us as practical decisions, without due reference to local circumstances. The American people pay slight attention to the abstract; they look only to the concrete in morals, and we must keep account of their manner of judging things. The Church is nowadays called upon to emphasize her power in the natural order. God forbid that I entertain, as some may be tempted to suspect me of doing, the slightest notion that vigilance may be turned off one single moment from the guard of the supernatural. For the sake of the supernatural I speak. And natural virtues, practised in the proper frame of mind and heart, become supernatural. Each century calls for its type of Christian perfection. At one time it was martyrdom; at another it was the humility of the cloister. To-day we need the Christian gentleman and the Christian citizen. An honest ballot and social decorum among Catholics will do more for God's glory and the salvation of souls than midnight flagellations or Compostellan pilgrimages.

On a line with his principles, as I have so far delineated them, Father Hecker believed that if he would succeed in his work for souls, he should use in it all the natural energy that God had given him, and he acted up to his belief. I once heard a good old priest, who said his beads well and made a desert around his pulpit by miserable preaching, criticise Father Hecker, who, he imagined, put too much reliance in man, and not enough in God. Father Hecker's piety, his assiduity in prayer, his personal habits of self-denial, repel the aspersion that he failed in reliance upon God. But my old priest—and he has in the church to-day, both in America and Europe, tens of thousands of counterparts—was more than half willing to see in all outputtings of human energy a lack of confidence in God. We sometimes rely far more upon God than God desires us to do, and there are occasions when a novena is the refuge of laziness or cowardice. God has endowed us with natural talents, and not one of them shall be, with His permission, enshrouded in a napkin. He will not work a miracle, or supply grace, to make up for our deficiencies. We must work as if all depended on us, and pray as if all depended on God.

God never proposed to do by His direct action all that might be done in and through the Church. He invites human co-operation, and abandons to it a wide field. The ages of most active human industry in religious enterprises were the ages of most remarkable spiritual conquests. The tendency to overlook this fact shows itself among us. Newman writes that where the sun shines bright in the warm climate of the south, the natives of the place know little of safeguards against cold and wet. They have their cold days, but only now and then, and they do not deem it worth their while to provide against them: the science of calefaction is reserved for the north. And so, Protestants, depending on human means solely, are led to make the most of them ; their sole resource is to use what they have ; they are the anxious cultivators of a rugged soil. Catholics, on the contrary, feel that God will protect the Church, and, as Newman adds, " we sometimes forget that we shall please Him best, and get most from Him, when, according to the fable, we put our shoulder to the wheel, when we use what we have by nature to the utmost, at the same time that we look out for what is beyond nature in the confidence of faith and hope." Lately a witty French writer pictures to us the pious friends of the leading Catholic layman of France, De Mun, kneeling in spiritual retreat when their presence is required in front of the enemy. The Catholic of the nineteenth century all over the world is too quiet, too easily resigned to "the will of God," attributing to God the effects of his own timidity and indolence. Father Hecker rolled up his sleeves and "pitched in" with desperate resolve. He fought as for very life. Meet him anywhere or at any time, he was at work or he was planning to work. He was ever looking around to see what might be done. He did with a rush the hard labor of a missionary and of a pastor, and he went beyond it into untrodden pathways. He hated routine. He minded not what others had been doing, seeking only what he himself might do. His efforts for the diffusion of Catholic literature, THE CATH-OLIC WORLD, his several books, the Catholic tracts, tell his zeal and energy. A Catholic daily paper was a favorite design to which he gave no small measure of time and labor. He anti-cipated by many years the battlings of our temperance apostles. The Paulist pulpit opened death-dealing batteries upon the saloon when the saloon-keeper was the hero in state and church. The Catholic University of America found in him one of its warmest advocates. His zeal was as broad as St. Paul's, and whoever did good was his friend and received his support. The walls of his parish, or his order, did not circumscribe for him God's Church. His choice of a patron saint—St. Paul—reveals the fire burning within his soul. He would not, he could not be idle. On his sick-bed, where he lay the greater part of his latter years, he was not inactive. He wrote valuable articles and books, and when unable to write, he dictated.

He was enthusiastic in his work, as all are who put their whole soul into what they are doing. Such people have no time to count the dark linings of the silvery clouds; they realize that

God and man together do not fail. Enthusiasm begets enthusiasm. It fits a man to be a leader; it secures a following. A bishop who was present at the Second Plenary Council of Baltimore has told me that when Father Hecker appeared before the assembled prelates and theologians in advocacy of Catholic literature as a missionary force, the picture was inspiring, and that the hearers, receiving a Pentecostal fire within their bosoms, felt as if America were to be at once converted. So would it have been if there had been in America a sufficient number of Heckers. He had his critics. Who ever tries to do something outside routine lines against whom hands are not raised and whose motives and acts are not misconstrued? A venerable clergyman one day thought he had scored a great point against Father Hecker by jocosely suggesting to him as the motto of his new order the word "Paulatim." The same one, no doubt, would have made a like suggestion to the Apostle of the Gentiles. Advocates of "Paulatim" methods have too often left the wheels of Christ's chariot fast in the mire. We rejoice, for its sake, that enthusiasts sometimes appear on the scene. The missions of the early Paulists, into which went Father Hecker's entire heart, aroused the country. To-day, after a lapse of thirty or thirty-five years, they are remembered as events wherever they were preached.

His was the profound conviction that, in the present age at any rate, the order of the day should be individual action—every man doing his full duty, and waiting for no one else to prompt him. This, I take it, was largely the meaning of Father Hecker's oft-repeated teaching on the work of the Holy Ghost in souls. There have been epochs in history where the Church, sacrificing her outposts and the ranks of her skirmishers to the preservation of her central and vital fortresses, put the brakes, through necessity, from the nature of the warfare waged against her, upon individual activity, and moved her soldiers in serried masses; and then it was the part and the glory of each one to move with the column. The need of repression has passed away. The authority of the Church and of her Supreme Head is beyond danger of being denied or obscured, and each Christian soldier may take to the field, obeying the breathings of the Spirit of truth and piety within him, feeling that what he may do he should do. There is work for individual priests, and for individual laymen, and so soon as it is discovered let it be done. The responsibility is upon each one ; the indifference of others is no excuse. Said Father Hecker one day to a friend : " There is too much waiting upon the action of others. The layman waits for the priest, the priest for the bishop, and the bishop for the pope, while the Holy Ghost sends down to all the reproof that He is prompting each one, and no one moves for Him." Father Hecker was original in his ideas, as well as in his methods ; there was no routine in him, mental or practical.

I cannot but allude, whether I understand or not the true intent of it, to what appears to have been a leading fact in his life : his leaving an old-established religious community for the purpose of instituting that of the Paulists. I will speak so far of this as I have formed an estimate of it. To me, this fact seems to have been a Providential circumstance in keeping with all else in his life. I myself have at this moment such thoughts as I imagine must have been running through his mind during that memorable sojourn in Rome, which resulted in freeing him from his old allegiance. The work of evangelizing America demands new methods. It is time to draw forth from our treasury the " new things " of the Gospel ; we have been long enough offering " old things." Those new methods call for newly-equipped men. The parochial clergy will readily confess that they cannot of themselves do all that God now demands from His Church in this country. They are too heavily burdened with the ordinary duties of the ministry : instructing those already within the fold, administering the sacraments, building temples, schools, and asylums—duties which must be attended to and which leave slight leisure for special studies or special labors. Father Hecker organized the Paulist community, and did in his way a great work for the conversion of the country. He made no mistake when he planned for a body of priests, more disciplined than usually are the parochial clergy, and more supple in the character of their institute than the existing religious orders.

We shall always distinguish Isaac Thomas Hecker as the ornament, the flower of our American priesthood—the type that we wish to see reproduced among us in widest proportions. Ameliorations may be sought for in details, and the more of them the better for religion ; but the great lines of Father Hecker's personality we should guard with jealous love in the formation of the future priestly characters of America.

THE LIFE OF FATHER HECKER.

CHAPTER I.

CHILDHOOD.

TOWARDS the close of the eighteenth century a German clockmaker named Engel Freund, accompanied by his wife and children, left his native town of Elberfeld, in Rhenish Prussia, to seek a new home in America. There is a family tradition to the effect that his forefathers were French, and that they came into Germany on account of some internal commotion in their own country. The name makes it more probable that they were Alsatians who quietly moved across the Rhine, either when their province was first ceded to France, or perhaps later, at the time of the Revocation of the Edict of Nantes, in 1685. When Engel Freund quitted Germany the disturbing influences of the French Revolution may have had a considerable share in determining his departure. He landed at New York in 1797 and established himself in Hester Street, between Christie and Forsyth.

His wife, born Ann Elizabeth Schneider, in 1764, was a native of Frankenburg, Hesse Cassel. She became the mother of a son and several daughters, who attained maturity and settled in New York. As his girls grew into womanhood and married, Engel Freund, who was a thrifty and successful tradesman in his prime, dowered each of them with a house in his own neighborhood, seeking thus to perpetuate in the new the kindly patriarchal customs of the old land.

To the New-Yorker of to-day, or, indeed, to any reputable and industrious immigrant, the notion of settling a family in Hester Street could not seem other than grotesque. It is now the filthy and swarming centre of a very low population. The Jewish pedlar *par éminence* lives there and thereabouts. Signs painted in the characters of his race, not of his accidental na-

tionality, abound on every side. Here a synagogue occupies the
story above a shop; there Masonic symbols are exhibited between the windows in a similar location. Jewish faces of the
least prepossessing type look askance into eyes which they
recognize as both unfamiliar and observant. Women, unkempt
and slouchy, or else arrayed in dubious finery, brush against one.
At intervals fast growing greater the remains of an extinct domes-
ticity and privacy still show themselves in the shape of old-fashioned brick or wooden houses with Dutch gables or Queen
Anne fronts, but for the most part tall tenement-houses, their
lower stories uniformly given up to some small traffic, claim exclusive right of possession. The sidewalks are crowded with the
stalls of a yet more petty trade; the neighborhood is full of unpleasant sights, unwholesome odors, and revolting sounds.

But the Hester Street of seventy years ago and more was
another matter. When a canal flowed through Canal Street, and
tall trees growing on either side of it sheltered the solid and
roomy houses of retired merchants and professional men, Hester
Street was a long way up town. Seven years before the subject of the present biography was born, that elegantly propor-
tioned structure, the City Hall, which had then been nine years
a-building, was finished in material much less expensive than had
been intended when it was begun. Marble was very dear, reasoned the thrifty and far-sighted City Fathers of the day, and
as the population of New York were never likely to settle to
any extent above Chambers Street, the rear of the hall would be
seen so seldom that this economy would not be noticeable.
What is now Fourteenth Street was then a place given over to
market-gardens. Rutgers Street, Rutgers Place, Henry Street,
were fashionable localities, and the adjacent quarter, now so mal-
odorous and disreputable, was eminently respectable. Freund's
daughters, as they left the parental roof for modest houses of his
gift close by, no doubt had reason to consider themselves abundantly fortunate in their surroundings.

One of these daughters, Caroline Sophia Susanna Henrietta
Wilhelmina, born in Elberfeld on the 2d of March, 1796, was
still a babe in arms at the time of the family emigration. She
was a tall, fair, handsome girl, not long past her fifteenth birthday when she became a wife. Her husband, John Hecker, was
nearly twice her age, having been born in Wetzlar, Prussia, May
7, 1782. He was the son of another John Hecker, a brewer by

trade, who married the daughter of a Colonel Schmidt. Both parents were natives of Wetzlar. Their son learned the business of a machinist and brass-founder, and emigrated to America in 1800. He was married to Caróline Freund in the Old Dutch Church in the Swamp, July 21, 1811. He died in New York, in the house of his eldest son, July 10, 1860.

Events proved John Hecker to have been equally fortunate and sagacious in his choice of a wife. At the time of their marriage he was thrifty and well-to-do. At one period he owned a flourishing brass-foundry in Hester Street, and during his early married life his prosperity was uninterrupted. But before many years had passed his business declined, and from one cause and another he never succeeded in re-establishing it. This misfortune, occurring while even the eldest of the sons was still a lad, might easily have proved irreparable in more senses than one. But the very fact that the ordinary gates to learning were so soon closed against these children caused the natural tendency they had toward knowledge to impel them all the more strongly in that shorter road to practical wisdom which leads through labor and experience. The Hecker brothers were all hard at work while still mere children, and before John, the eldest, had attained to legal manhood, they had fixed the solid foundations of an enduring prosperity, and all need of further exertion on the part of their parents was over for ever.

Isaac Thomas Hecker, the third son and youngest child of this couple, was born in New York at a house in Christie Street, between Grand and Hester, December 18, 1819, when his mother was not yet twenty-four. He survived her by twelve years only, she dying at the residence of her eldest son's widow in 1876, in the full possession of faculties which must have been of no common order. From her, and through her from Engel Freund, who was what is called "a character," Father Hecker seems to have derived many of his life-long peculiarities. "I never knew a son so like his mother," writes to us one who had an intimate acquaintance with both of them for more than forty years. She adds:

"Mrs. Hecker was a woman of great energy of character and strong religious nature. Her son, Father Hecker, inherited both of these traits, and there was the warmest sympathy between them. He was her youngest son, her baby, she called him, but with all her tender love she had a holy veneration for his character as priest.

"She deeply sympathized with him through the trials and anxieties that were his in his search after truth, and when his heart found rest, and the aspirations of his soul were answered in the Holy Catholic Church, her noble heart accepted for him what she could not see for herself.   She said to a lady who spoke to her on the subject and who could not be reconciled to the conversion of a daughter : ' No, I would not change the faith of my sons.   They have found peace and joy in the Catholic Church, and I would not by a word change their faith, if I could.'

"She had a very earnest temperament, and what she did she did with all her heart.   The last years of her life she was a great invalid, but from her sick room she did wonders.   Family ties were kept warm, and no one whom she had loved and known was forgotten.   The poor were ever welcome, and came to her in crowds, never leaving without help and consolation.   She had a very cheerful spirit, and a bright, pleasant, and even witty word for every one.

"But the strongest trait in her character was her deeply religious nature. With the Catholic faith it would have found expression in the religious life, as she sometimes said herself.   The faith she had made her most earnest and devout, according to her light."

Mrs. Georgiana Bruce Kirby,* who spent a month at the house in Rutgers Street just after Isaac finally returned from Brook Farm, when Mrs. Hecker was in the prime of middle life, speaks of her as

"a lovely and dignified character, full of ' humanities.'   She was fair, tall, erect, a very superior example of the German house-mother.   Hers was the controlling spirit in the house, and her wise and generous influence was felt far beyond it.   She was a life-long Methodist, and took me with her to a ' Love Feast,' which I had never witnessed before."

To the good sense, good temper, and strong religious nature of Caroline Hecker her children owed, and always cordially acknowledged, a heavy, and in one respect an almost undivided, debt of gratitude.   Neither Engel Freund nor John Hecker professed any religious faith.   The latter was never in the habit of attending any place of worship.   Both were Lutheran so far as their antecedents could make them so, but neither seems to have practically known much beyond the flat negation, or at best the simple disregard, of Christianity to which Protestantism leads more or less quickly according as the logical faculty is more or less developed in those whose minds have been fed upon it. However, there was nothing aggressive in the attitude of either toward religious observance.   The grandfather especially seems to have been a "gentle sceptic," an agnostic in the germ, affirming nothing beyond the natural, probably because all substantial ground for supernatural affirmations seemed to him to be cut

* *Years of Experience.*   G. P. Putnam's Sons.   1887.

away by the fundamental training imparted to him. He was a
kindly, virtuous, warm-hearted man, with a life of his own which
made him incurious and thoughtful, and singularly devoid of prejudices. When his daughter Caroline elected to desert the
Reformed Dutch Church in which the family had a pew, and to
attach herself to another sect, he had only a jocular word of
surprise to say concerning her odd fancy for "those noisy Methodists." He had a true German fondness for old ways and settled customs, and to the end of his days spoke only his own
vernacular.

"Why don't you talk English?" somebody once asked him
toward the close of his life.

"I don't know how," he answered. "I never had time to
learn."

"Why, how long have you been here?"

"About forty years."

"Forty years! And isn't that time enough to learn English
in?"

"What can one learn in forty years?" said the old man, with
an unanswerable twinkle.

Between him and the youngest of his Hecker grandchildren
there existed a singular sympathy and affection. The two were
very much together, and the little fellow was allowed to potter
about the workshop and encouraged to study the ins and outs
of all that went on there, as well as entertained with kindly talk
that may at first have been a trifle above his years. But he was
a precocious child, shrewd, observant, and thoughtful. It was in
the old watchmaker's shop that the boy, not yet a dozen years
old, and already hard at work helping to earn his own living,
conceived the plan of making a clock with his own hands and
presenting it to the church attended by the family, which was
situated in Forsyth Street between Walker and Hester. The
clock was finished in due time and set up in the church, where
it ticked faithfully until the edifice was torn down, some forty
years later. Then it was returned to its maker in accordance
with a promise made by the pastor when the gift was accepted.
In 1872 the opening number of the third volume of *The
Young Catholic* contained a good engraving of it, accompanied
by a sketch descriptive of its career. Although Father Hecker
did not write the little story, it is so true both to fact and to
sentiment that we make an extract from it. The clock hung in

the Paulist sacristy for about ten years. Then, for some reason, it was taken to the country house of Mr. George Hecker, where it was accidentally destroyed by fire :

"There were points of resemblance in my own and my boy maker's nature. In him, regularity, order, and obedience were fixed principles ; and with us both, Time represented Eternity. As the days of his young manhood came his pursuits and tastes in life changed. Deep thought took possession of his mind, and with it a tender love for souls and a heart-hungriness for a further knowledge of what man was given a soul for, and the way in which he was to save it. As these thoughts were maturing in his mind I often noticed his troubled look. One Sunday in particular, he lingered behind the congregation and stood before me, with a new expression in his keen gray eye ; and amid the silence of the deserted aisles he thus apostrophized me : 'Farewell, old friend ! fashioned by these hands, thou representest Truth, the eternal. What man is ever seeking, through me thou hast found. Here I stand, not man's but God's noblest work, as yet not having repaid my Maker with one act of duty or of service. Thou hast faithfully performed thy mission ; henceforth I labor to perform mine.' With a grave and sad look my boy maker, now a young man, left me. I felt then that we had looked our last upon each other in this place ; but little did either of us dream of where, when, and how we would meet again. For thirty-five years I labored on unchanged, though I must own to having had some ailments now and then. About this period of my existence I overheard straggling remarks, as the worshippers passed out of the church, which led me to conclude that some change was contemplated, and my suspicions were confirmed by the rector proposing from the pulpit the erection of a new church edifice in another part of the city, to be fashioned after a more modern style of architecture. . . . In accordance with the promise made my boy maker, I was to go back to him. My heart bounded at the prospect. Never in all those years had I seen him. . . .

"In a short time I learned that the author of my existence, after many hard struggles and trials, had at last found truth and light, peace and rest, in the bosom of the Holy Catholic Church. He had returned, when he found me, from the Plenary Council of 1867. He is now a priest, and the head of a religious community. Need I assure those who have been interested in my history that I also have found a home in the same community, where I am consecrated to its use? I am no longer alone now ; I am busy from morning until night, helping to regulate the movements of the community. There is not an hour in the day when I do not see my boy maker. We have established sympathies in common ; I call him to prayers, to his meals, to his matins, and to his rest. Many a time, when he finds me alone, he gives me some spiritual reading, or says aloud some prayers. Every time I strike, he breathes an aspiration of love and thanksgiving. In short, we have found our glorious mission in our new birth. We are both apostles : I represent Time ; he preaches of Eternity."

There can be little doubt, however, that the chief formative influence in the Hecker household was that which came directly through the mother. Young as she was when an unduly heavy share of the domestic burdens fell to her portion, she took it up with courage and bore it with dignity and fidelity. What aid her father could give her was doubtless not lacking, but we may well suppose that, as age crept on Engel Freund, his business began to slip away from him into younger hands. He was probably no longer in a position to endow daughters or to undertake the education of grandchildren. What is certain is that Caroline Hecker's boys, after very brief school-days, were put at once to hard work. What decided their choice of an occupation is not so sure, but in all probability they consulted with their mother and then took the common-sense view that as there is a never failing market for food staples, even poverty, if mated with diligence and sagacity, may find there a fair field for successful enterprise. John, the eldest, upon whom the mother soon began to rely as her right hand, went to learn his trade as a baker with a Mr. Schwab, whose shop was on the corner of Hester and Eldridge Streets. George, who was some three or four years younger, as the only girl, Elizabeth, came between them, presently followed his brother to the same business.

As for Isaac, whom hard necessity, or, more probably, a mistaken thrift, likewise forced away from school when not much more than ten years old, his earliest ventures bear a curious symbolic likeness to his latest. He earned his first wages in the service of a religious periodical, the Methodist publication still known as *Zion's Herald*, whose office was situated in Crosby Street near Broadway. From there he went to learn a trade in the type foundry in Great Thames Street. But as it was already apparent that the family road to prosperity was identical with that chosen by his elder brothers, we find him working away beside them in the bake-house by the time he was eleven. They had already established the bakery in Rutgers Street, between Monroe and Cherry, where the family lived for so many years. They had another shop in Pearl Street, to which Isaac used to carry bread every morning.

This was a part of his life to which he was fond of recurring in his last years. "Thanks be to God!" he said on the first day of 1886, "how hard we used to work preparing for New Year's Day! Three weeks in advance we began to bake New Year's cakes—flour, water, sugar, butter, and caraway seeds. We never could make enough. How I used to work carrying the bread around in my baker's cart! How often I got stuck in the gutters and in the snow! Sometimes some good soul, seeing me unable to get along, would give me a lift. I began to work when I was ten and a half years old, and I have been at it ever since."

And again, a few days later, as a poor woman carrying a heavy basket passed him in the street, he said to the companion of his walk : "I have had the blood spurt out of my arm carrying bread when I was a baker. A lady asked me once for a hundred dollars to help her send her only son to college. I answered her that my mother had four children and got along without begging, and that I would not exchange one year of those I spent working for several at college."

Less than a month before his death he fell into conversation with a newsboy on the corner near the Paulist church in Fifty-ninth Street. "It interested me very much," he said afterwards. "I found out that he is one of five little brothers, and their mother is a widow. She is trying to bring them up, poor thing ! It reminds me of my own mother."

It is plain that there could not have been much room for formal study in a life of hard physical labor, so soon begun and so unremittingly continued during the years usually given up to school work. An ordinary boy, placed in such circumstances, would doubtless have grown up ignorant and unformed. But while none of the Hecker boys was quite of the ordinary stamp, Isaac was distinctly *sui generis* and individual. He has said of himself that he could remember no period of his life when he had not the consciousness of having been sent into the world for some especial purpose. What it was he knew not, but expectation and desire for the withheld knowledge kept him pondering and self-withdrawn. Once in his childhood he was given over for death with a bad attack of confluent small-pox, and his mother came to his bedside to tell him so. "No, mother," he answered her, "I shall not die now. God has a work for me to do in the world, and I shall live to do it."

Such instruction as Isaac obtained before beginning to earn his own bread was given him in Ward School No. 7. A Dr. Kirby was then its principal, and the time was just previous to the introduction of the present system. The schools were not entirely free, a small payment being required from the parents for each pupil, to supplement the grant of public funds. No doubt the boy, who had an ardent thirst for knowledge, regretted his removal from his desk more deeply than he was at the time willing to express. Still, it may be questioned whether he ever had any natural aptitude for close, continuous book-work, at least on ordinary and prescribed lines. He was "always studying," indeed, as he sometimes said in speaking of his early life, but the thoughts of other men, whether written or spoken, do not seem to have been greatly valued by him, except as keys which might help him to unlock those mysteries of God and man, and their mutual relations, which tormented him from the first. He was to the last an indefatigable reader, but yet it would be true to say that he was never either a student or a scholar in the ordinary sense. It is a curious question as to how a thorough education might have modified Father Hecker. It is possible—nay, as the reader may be inclined to believe with us as the story of his inner life goes on, it is even probable—that the more he was taught by God the less he was able to receive from men.

It is certain, however, that he seriously regretted and soon set himself to rectify the deficiencies of his early training. This was one of the reasons which took him to Brook Farm. In the first entry of the earliest of his diaries which has been preserved he thus speaks of his hidden longing after knowledge. He was twenty-three when these sentences were written, and he had been at Brook Farm for several months :

"If I cast a glance upon a few years of my past life, it appears to me mysteriously incomprehensible that I should be where I am now. I confess sincerely that, although I have never labored for it, still, something in me always dreamed of it. Once, when I was lying on the floor, my mother said to my brother John, without anything previously being spoken on the subject, and suddenly, in a kind of unconscious speech, 'John, let Isaac go to college and study.' These words went through me like liquid fire. He made some evasive answer and there it ended. Although to study has always been the secret desire of my heart from my youth, I never felt inclined to open my mind to any one on the subject. And now I find, after a long time, that I have been led here as strangely as possible."

His childhood seems to have been a serious one. In recurring to it in later life, as he often did, he never spoke of any games or sports in which he had shared, nor, in fact, of any amusements before the time when he began to attend lectures and the theatre. It was the childhood of what we call in America a self-made man—one in which the plastic human material is rudely dealt with by circumstances. His mother taught him his prayers, the schoolmistress his letters, necessity his daily round of duties, and for the rest he was left very much to himself and to that interior Master of whose stress and constraint upon him he grew more intimately conscious as he grew in years. The force of this inward pressure showed itself in many ways. Outwardly it made his manner undemonstrative, and fixed an intangible yet very real barrier between him and his kindred, even when the affection that existed was extremely close and tender. From infancy he exhibited that repugnance to touching or being touched by any one which marked him to the end. Even his mother refrained from embracing him, knowing this singular aversion. She would stroke his face, instead, when she was pleased with him, and say, "That is my kiss for you, my son."

The mutual respect for each other's personalities shown in this closest of human relations was characteristic of the entire family, as will be seen later, when the nature of the business connections between Isaac and his brothers has to be considered. Far from weakening the natural ties, or impairing their proper influence, it seems to have strengthened and perfected them. Asked once towards the close of his life how it was that he had never used tobacco in any form, he answered : "Mother forbade it, and that was enough for George and me. I was never ruled in any way but by her affection. That was sufficient." The parallel fact that he never in his life drank a drop of liquor at a bar or at any public place was probably due to a similar injunction. The children were brought up, too, with exceedingly strict ideas about lying and stealing, and all petty vices. Throughout the family there prevailed an extreme severity on such faults. "I have never forgotten," said Father Hecker, "the furious anger of an aunt of mine and the violent beating she gave one of my cousins for stealing a cent from her drawer. That training has had a great and lasting effect upon my character."

In such antecedents and surroundings it is easy to see the source of that abiding confidence in human nature, and that love for the natural virtues which marked Father Hecker's whole career. They had kept his own youth pure. He had been baptized in infancy, however, as the children of orthodox Protestants more commonly were at that period than at present, and in all probability validly, so that one could never positively say that nature in him had ever been unaided by grace in any particular instance. It is the conviction of those who knew him best that he had never been guilty of deliberate mortal sin. One of these writes :

"During all the intimate hours I spent with him, speaking of his past life he *never once said that he had been a sinner* in a sense to convey the idea of mortal sin. And on the other hand he said much to the contrary ; so much as to leave no manner of doubt on my mind that he had kept his baptismal innocence. He was deeply attached to an edifying and religious mother ; he was at hard work before the dawn of sensual passion, and his recreation, even as a boy, was in talking and reading about deep social and philosophical questions, and listening to others on the same themes. He expressly told me that he had never used drink in excess, and that he had never sinned against purity, never was profane, never told a lie ; and he certainly never was dishonest.

"The influence of his mother was of the most powerful kind. He told me that the severest punishment she ever inflicted on him was once or twice (once only, I am pretty sure) to tell him that she was angry with him ; and this so distressed him that he was utterly miserable, sat down on the floor completely overcome, and so remained till she after a time relented and restored him to favor. Such a relationship is quite instructive in reference to the original innocence of his life."

CHAPTER II.

YOUTH.

IT has been said already, in speaking of Father Hecker's childhood, that he had been consciously under the influence of supernatural impressions from a very early period. It seems probable, therefore, that at least during the few years which preceded his juvenile plunge into politics he must have been devout and prayerful, though doubtless in his own spontaneous way. Such were his mother's characteristics, and we find her son writing to her, when his aspirations after the perfect life had led him to the threshold of the church, that she, of all persons, ought most to sympathize with him, for he is about doing that which will aid him to be what she has always desired to see him. But his devotions probably bore small resemblance to those of the ordinary religiously minded boy, either Catholic or Protestant. He has said that often at night, when lying on the shavings before the oven in the bake-house, he would start up, roused in spite of himself by some great thought, and run out upon the wharves to look at the East River in the moonlight, or wander about under the spell of some resistless aspiration. What does God desire from me? How shall I attain unto Him? What is it He has sent me into the world to do? These were the ceaseless questions of a heart that rested, meanwhile, in an unshaken confidence that time would bring the answer.

But these were early days, days when the influence of his mother, never wholly shaken off, was still dominant and pervasive in all that concerned him. There came a period, however, beginning in all likelihood about his fourteenth, and lasting until his twentieth year or thereabouts, in which he certainly lost hold on all distinctively Christian doctrines. With such a mind as his, and such a training, this was almost inevitable. His intellect, while it hungered incessantly after supernatural truth, kept nevertheless a persistent hold upon the verities of the natural order, and could not rest until it had synthetized them into a coherent whole. That was his life-long characteristic. During the years of painful ill health which preceded his death, he often said that he was unlike the Celt, who takes to the supernatural as if by instinct. "But I am a Saxon and cling to the earth," he would say; "I want an explicit and satisfactory reason why any innocent pleasure should not be enjoyed." He attributed this to his racial peculiarities. Others may differ with him and credit it to his nature, taken in its human and rational integrity. Furthermore, he was always singularly independent and self-poised. He could not endure being hindered of anything that was his, except by an authority which had legitimated to his intelligence its right to command. He could obey that readily and entirely, as his life from infancy clearly witnesses ; but he never knew a merely arbitrary master.

Such a nature, fed on the mingled truth and error characteristic of orthodox Protestantism, was certain to reject it sooner or later, impelled by hunger for the whole Divine gift of which that teaching contains fragments only. The soul of Isaac Hecker was one athirst for God from the first dawn of its conscious being. Upon Him, its Creator and Source, it never lost hold, and never ceased to cry out for Him with longing and aspiration, even during that bitter and protracted period of his youth when his mind, entangled in the maze of philosophic subjectivism, seemed in danger of rejecting theism altogether. But the underpinning of his faith, so far as that professed to be Christian and to come by hearing—to have an intellectual basis, that is—began to slip away almost as soon as he left his mother's knee. It is possible that very little stress was ever laid upon distinctively Christian doctrines in her teaching. To adore God the Creator, to listen to His voice in conscience, to live honestly and purely as in His sight—the heritage she transmitted to him probably contained little more than this. Like most others reared in heresy who afterwards attain to the true knowledge of the Incarnation, he had to seek for it with almost as great travail of mind as if he had been born a pagan. It cannot be too strongly insisted on, however, that his struggles were merely intellectual, and, when they began to take a definite turn, shaped themselves into the natural result of a metaphysic as repugnant to common sense as it is to Christian philosophy. To this fact, so important in certain of its bearings, we have ample testimony in the private diaries kept before his conversion, from which we shall make extracts later on. They find a later confirmation in some most interesting memoranda, jotted down, after conversation with him at intervals during the last years of his life, by one whom he admitted to an unusually close intimacy.

He was always singularly reserved concerning matters purely personal; his confidences, when they touched his own soul, seldom seemed entirely voluntary, and were quickly checked. Occasionally they were taken by surprise, as when the course of talk insensibly turned toward internal ways; and again they were deliberately angled for with a hook so well concealed that it secured a prize before he was aware. From these notes we shall here make a few quotations bearing on the point made above—*i.e.*, that his difficulties prior to his entrance into the church were neither moral nor spiritual, but intellectual. Of him, if of any man, it was always true that his heart was naturally Christian. The first of these extracts, bearing as it does on a topic constantly in his thoughts, affords a good enough example of what was meant in saying that his confidences were sometimes taken by surprise:

"There are some for whom the predominant influence is the external one, authority, example, precept, and the like. Others in whose lives the interior action of the Holy Spirit predominates. In my case, from my childhood God influenced me by an interior light and by the interior touch of His Holy Spirit."

At another time he said:

"While I was a youth, and in early manhood, I was preserved from certain sins and certain occasions of sin, in a way that was peculiar and remarkable. I was also at the same time, and, indeed, all the time, conscious that God was preserving me innocent with a view to some future providence. Mind, all this was long before I came into the church."

And again:

"Many a time before my conversion God gave me grace to weep over those words: 'And all those who love His coming.' I did not believe in His coming, but I loved it honestly and longed to believe it. I had learned much of the Bible from my mother and had read it often and much myself."

This consciously supernatural character of his inner life from the first, should be kept closely united in the reader's mind with that other idea of his adhesion to "guileless nature" which was such a favorite theme with Father Hecker. No one could be more emphatic than he in asserting the necessity of the supernatural for the attainment of man's destiny. How could it be otherwise, when he considered that destiny to be the elevation of man above all good merely human, and by means far beyond the compass of his natural powers? Still, this was undoubtedly a conclusion of his riper years, a result arrived at after a certain

intense if not very prolonged experience in contemporary Uto-
pias, in futile endeavors to raise man above his own level while
remaining on it, whether by socialistic schemes or social politics.

In an article called "Dr. Brownson and the Workingman's
Party Fifty Years Ago," published in *The Catholic World*
of May, 1887, Father Hecker has himself made some interesting
references to his experiences in the latter field, and upon these
we shall draw heavily for our own account of this period of his
life, supplementing them with whatever bears upon the subject
in the memoranda already referred to.

Concerning the inception of this party, to which all three of
the young Heckers belonged in 1834, we have a better statement in Dr. Brownson's *Convert* than we know of elsewhere.
Brownson was for a time actively interested in it, and in 1829
established a journal in support of its principles somewhere in
Western New York. From him we learn that it was started in
1828 by Robert Dale Owen, Robert L. Jennings, George H.
Evans, Fanny Wright, and a few other doctrinaires, foreign-born
without exception, in the hope of getting control of political
power so as to use it for establishing purely secular schools.
Their advocacy of anti-Christian and free-love doctrines had so
signally failed among adult Americans that the slower but surer
method of educating the children of the country without religion
had dawned upon them as more certain to succeed.

"We hoped," writes Dr. Brownson, "by linking our cause with the ultra-
democratic sentiment of the country, which had had from the time of Jefferson
and Tom Paine something of an anti-Christian character ; by professing ourselves the bold and uncompromising champions of equality ; by expressing a
great love for the people and a deep sympathy with the laborer, whom we represented as defrauded and oppressed by his employer ; by denouncing all pro-
prietors as aristocrats, and by keeping the more unpopular features of our plan
as far in the background as possible, to enlist the majority of the American
people under the banner of the Workingman's party ; nothing doubting that,
if we could once raise that party to power, we could use it to secure the adoption
of our educational system."

This party, however, both as an engine in politics and as a
fitting embodiment of his private views, Dr. Brownson soon abandoned. He was not truly radical, in the evil sense of that word, —
at any period of his career, and the theories of the leaders soon
became insupportable to his moral sense. But he remained true
to the cause of the workingmen while abandoning the organiza-

tion which assumed to voice their needs and their wishes. Probably these more ulterior aims of their leaders were never fully appreciated by the rank and file of those who followed them. Yet the genesis of the present purely secular school system, against whose workings and results nearly all Christian denominations are too late beginning to protest, is clearly traceable to the propaganda carried on half a century ago by men and women whose only half-veiled warfare against Christianity, property, and marriage was then an offence in the nostrils of our people at large. It is fair to predict that this generation, or another which shall succeed it, will yet have the good sense to regret, and the courage to atone for, the fact that hatred to the Catholic Church, and a desire to cripple her hands where her own children were concerned, should have been a more powerful agent in dragging them and theirs into the abyss of secularism than was their love of Christianity in deterring them from it.

Father Hecker's account of his own youthful connection with the " Workingman's Democracy," although written with the direct intention of placing his estimate of Dr. Brownson on record, has too many strictly autobiographic touches in it to be here omitted. Such passages, bearing on long past personal history, are fewer than we could wish them among his papers, published or unpublished. The five articles on Dr. Brownson, beginning in *The Catholic World* of April, 1887, and concluding in November of the same year, contain almost the only matters relative to his personal history which he ever put into print. Concerning the party, of which Dr. Brownson says that he had ceased to be a recognized leader at this time, although he still threw his influence as a speaker into all its projects for social reform, Father Hecker writes :

" We called ourselves the genuine Democracy, and in New York City were for some years a separate political body, independent of the ' regular ' Democracy, and voting our own ticket. I have before me the files of our newspaper organ, the *Democrat*, the first number of which appeared March 9, 1836, published by Windt & Conrad, 11 Frankfort Street. In its prospectus the *Democrat* promises to contend for ' Equality of Rights, often trampled in the dust by Monopoly Democrats,' to battle ' with an aristocratic opposition powerful in talent and official entrenchment, and mighty in money and facilities for corruption.' ' In the course of this duty it will not fail fearlessly and fully to assert the inalienable rights of the people against ' vested rights ' and ' vested wrongs.' It claims to be the ' instructive companion ' of the mechanics' and workingmen's leisure, ' the promotion of whose interests will ever form a leading feature of the *Democrat*.' And in the editorial salutatory it speaks thus :

" ' We are in favor of government by the people. Our objects are the restoration of equal rights and the prostration of those aristocratical usurpations existing in the state of monopolies and exclusive privileges of every kind, the products of corrupt and corrupting legislation. . . . At this moment we are the only large nation on the face of the earth where the mass of the people govern in theory—where they may govern in reality, if they will—where the real taxes of government, although too heavy, are but trifling, and where a majority of the population depend on their own labor for support; yet such is the condition of that large class that the fruits of their toil are inadequate to sustain themselves in comfort and rear their families as the young citizens of a republic ought to be reared.

" ' . . . He is very shortsighted, however, who thinks that a majority of the people, where universal suffrage exists, will submit long to a state of toil and mendicity. The majority would soon learn to exercise its political rights, and command its representatives to carry the laws abolishing primogeniture and entails one step further, and stop all devises of land and prohibit it from being an article of sale. (In a foot-note of the editorial:) We actually heard these and several such propositions discussed by a number of apparently very intelligent mechanics, after the adjournment of a meeting called to consider the subject of wages, rents, etc.'

" At that time the main question was the condition of the public finances, and our agitation was directed chiefly against granting charters to private banks of circulation. We condemned these as monopolies, for we were hostile to all monopolies—that is to say, to the use of public funds or the enjoyment of public exclusive privileges by any man or association or class of men for their private profit."

We interrupt our direct quotation from this article in order to relate one of the humors of the period, so far as these brothers were concerned, in the words of the late Mr. George Hecker:

"When we were bakers the money in common use was the old-fashioned paper issued by private banks under State charters. We were regularly against it. So we bought a hand printing-press and set it up in the garret of our establishment. All the bills we received from our customers, some thousands sometimes every week, we smoothed out and put in a pile, and then printed on their backs a saying we took from Daniel Webster (though I believe it was not quite authentic): 'Of all the contrivances to impoverish the laboring classes of mankind, paper money is the most effective. It fertilizes the rich man's field with the poor man's sweat.' They tried to punish us for defacing money, but we beat them. We didn't deface it; we only printed something on the back of it. Isaac and I often worked all night putting up handbills for our meetings, for in those days there were no professional bill-posters."

Father Hecker's acquaintance with Dr. Brownson, which had so powerful an effect upon his future career, began in 1834, when Brownson was invited to lecture in New York in favor of the principles and aims of this party. Isaac was then in his fifteenth year. Among the conversations recorded in the memoranda we find this reference to their earliest interview :

> "I first met Dr. Brownson in New York, in our house. I was then reading the Washington *Globe*, Benton's speeches, Calhoun's, etc. The elder Blair was its editor ; its motto was, 'The world is governed too much '—a motto in whose spirit there could be no great movement except in the way of revolution. After the establishment of the American Government the principle expressed in that motto could only be abandoned or pushed into revolution and anarchy.
>
> "I put this question to Brownson : 'How can I become certain of the objective reality of the operations of my soul?' He answered : 'If you have not yet reached that period of mental life, you will do so before many years.'
>
> "It is a great humiliation for me to admit that I was ever in a state in which I doubted the actual validity of the testimony of my own faculties, and the reality of the phenomena of my mental existence. I had begun my mental life in politics, and in a certain sense in religion ; but to my philosophical life I was yet unborn."

In the article on the "Workingman's Party," already quoted from, Father Hecker, after mentioning that Dr. Brownson continued to lecture before the New York members of the party for several years, goes on as follows :

> "If it be asked why a man like Dr. Brownson, a born philosopher, should have thus busied himself with the solution of the most practical of problems by undertaking to abolish inequality among men, the answer is plain. The true philosopher will not confine himself to abstract theories. But, furthermore, Brownson at this epoch of his life had lost his grip on the philosophy that leads men to trust in a supernatural happiness to be enjoyed in a future state ; and the man who does not look to the hope of a future state of beatitude for the chief solace of human misery must look to this life as its end. If a man does not seek beatitude in God he seeks it in himself and his fellow-men—in the highest earthly development of our better nature if he becomes a socialist of one school, and in the lusts of the animal man if he becomes a socialist of the brutal school. The man who has any sympathy in his heart and is not guided by Catholic ethics, if he reasons at all on public affairs, will become a socialist of some school or other. Says Dr. Brownson in *The Convert*, p. 101 :

> "'The end of man, as disclosed by my creed of 1829, is obviously an earthly end, to be attained in this life. Man was not made for God, and destined to find his beatitude in the possession of God his Supreme Good, the Supreme Good itself. His end was happiness—not happiness in God, but in the possession of the good things of this world. Our Lord had said, 'Be not anxious as to what ye shall eat, or what ye shall drink, or wherewithal ye shall be clothed ; for after all these things do the heathen seek.' I gave Him a flat denial, and said, Be

anxious ; labor especially for these things, first for yourselves, then for others. Enlarging, however, my views a little, I said, Man's end for which he is to labor is the well-being and happiness of man in this world—is to develop man's whole nature, and so to organize society and government as to secure all men a paradise on the earth. This view of the end to labor for I held steadily and without wavering from 1828 till 1842, when I began to find myself tending unconsciously towards the Catholic Church.'

" The reader will have seen by the extracts given that we were a party full of enthusiasm. I was but fifteen when our party called Dr. Brownson to deliver the lectures above mentioned. But my brothers and I had long been playing men's parts in politics. I remember when eleven years of age, or a year or two older, being tall for my years, proposing and carrying through a series of resolutions on the currency question at our ward meetings. As our name indicates— ' Workingman's Democracy '—we were a kind of Democrats. As to the Whig party, it received no great attention from us. At that time its chances of getting control of this State or of the United States were remote. Our biggest fight was against the ' usages of the party' as in vogue in the so-called regular Democracy embodied in the Tammany Hall party. This organization undertook to absorb us when we had grown too powerful to be ignored. They nominated a legislative ticket made up half of their men and half of ours. This move was to a great extent successful ; but many of us who were purists refused to compromise, and ran a stump ticket, or, as it was then called, a rump ticket. I was too young to vote, but I remember my brother George and I posting political handbills at three o'clock in the morning ; this hour was not so inconvenient for us, for we were bakers. We also worked hard on election day, keeping up and supplying the ticket booths, especially in our own ward, the old Seventh. I remember that one of our leaders was a shoemaker named John Ryker, and that we used to meet in Science Hall, Broome Street.

" If this was the high state of my enthusiasm, so was it that of us all. Our political faith was ardent and active. But if we had been tested on our religious faith we should not have come off creditably ; many of us had not any religion at all. I remember saying once to my brother John that the only difference between a believer and an infidel is a few ounces of brains. . . . We were a queer set of cranks when Dr. Brownson brought to us his powerful and eloquent advocacy, his contribution of mingled truth and error. He delivered his first course of lectures in the old Stuyvesant Institute in Broadway, facing Bond Street – the same hall used a little afterwards by the Unitarian Society while they were building a church for Mr. Dewey in Broadway opposite Eighth Street, the very same society now established in Lexington Avenue, with Mr. Collyer as minister. The subsequent courses were delivered in Clinton Hall, corner of Nassau and Beekman, the site now occupied by one of our modern mammoth buildings. I forget how much we were charged admission, except that a ticket for the whole course cost three dollars. There was no great rush, but the lectures drew well and abundantly paid all expenses, including the lecturer's fee. The press did not take much notice of the lectures, for the Workingman's party had no newspapers expressly in its favor, except the one I have already quoted from. But he was one of the few men whose power is great enough to advertise itself. Wherever he was he was felt. His tread was heavy and he could make way for himself.

" Dr. Brownson was then in the very prime of manhood. He was a handsome man, tall, stately, and of grave manners. His face was clean-shaved. The first likeness of him that I remember appeared in the *Democratic Review.* It made him look like Proudhon, the French Socialist. This was all the more singular because at that time he was really the American Proudhon, though he never went so far as ' *La propriété, c'est le vol.*' As he appeared on the platform and received our greeting he was indeed a majestic man, displaying in his demeanor the power of a mind altogether above the ordinary. But he was essentially a philosopher, and that means that he could never be what is called popular. He was an interesting speaker, but he never sought popularity. He never seemed to care much about the reception his words received, but he exhibited anxiety to get his thoughts rightly expressed and to leave no doubt about what his convictions were. Yet among a limited class of minds he always awakened real enthusiasm—among minds, that is, of a philosophical tendency. He never used manuscript or notes; he was familiar with his topic, and his thoughts flowed out spontaneously in good, pure, strong, forcible English. He could control any reasonable mind, for he was a man of great thoughts and never without some grand truth to impart. But to stir the emotions was not in his power, though he sometimes attempted it; he never succeeded in being really pathetic.

"It must be remembered that although Dr. Brownson was technically classed among the reverends, he was not commonly so called. It may be said that he was still reckoned among the Unitarian ministry, owing mostly to his connection with Dr. Channing, of Boston, who took a great interest in the Workingman's party. But I do not think he was advertised by us as reverend or publicly spoken of as a clergyman. He may have been yet hanging on the skirts of the Unitarian movement. But his career had become political, and his errand to New York was political. He had given up preaching for some years, and embarked on the stormy waves of social politics, and had by his writings become an expositor of various theories of social reform, chiefly those of French origin. So that the dominant note of his lectures was not by any means religious, but political. He was at that time considered as identified with the Workingman's party, and came to New York to speak as one of our leaders. The general trend of his lectures was the philosophy of history as it bears on questions of social reform. At bottom his theories were Saint-Simonism, the object being the amelioration of the condition of the most numerous classes of society in the speediest manner. *This was the essence of our kind of Democracy.* And Dr. Brownson undertook in these lectures to bring to bear in favor of our purpose the life-lessons of the providential men of human history. Of course, the life and teachings of our Saviour Jesus Christ were brought into use, and the upshot of the lecturer's thesis was that Christ was the big Democrat and the Gospel was the true Democratic platform !

"We interpreted Christianity as altogether a social institution, its social side entirely overlapping and hiding the religious. Dr. Brownson set out to make, and did make, a powerful presentation of our Lord as the representative of the Democratic side of civilization. For His person and office he and all of us had a profound appreciation and sympathy, but it was not reverential or religious; the religious side of Christ's mission was ignored. Christ was a social Democrat, Dr. Brownson maintained, and he and many of us had no other religion but the social theories we drew from Christ's life and teaching; that was the meaning of Christianity to us, and of Protestantism especially."

In penning the reminiscences just given Father Hecker probably had in mind the whole period lying between his fourteenth year and his twenty-first. In the autumn of 1834, when he first made acquaintance with Orestes Brownson, Isaac Hecker was not yet fifteen, while the reform lecturer was in his early thirties. But the boy who began at once, as he has told us, to put philosophical questions, and to seek a test whereby to determine the validity of his mental processes, was already well known to the voters of his ward, not merely as an overgrown and very active lad, always on hand at the polling booths, and ready for any work which might be entrusted to a boy, but also as a clear and persuasive speaker on various topics of social and political reform.

Politics of the kind into which the young Heckers threw themselves so ardently were not very different in their methods fifty years ago from what they are to-day. Reform politics are always the reverse of what are called machine politics. The meetings of which Father Hecker speaks were spontaneous gatherings of determined and earnest men, young and old, held sometimes in public halls, sometimes, when elections were close at hand, in the open street. Often they were dominated by leaders better able to formulate theories than to bring about practical remedial measures. The inception of all great parties has something of this character. It generally happens that principles are dwelt upon with an exclusive devotion more or less prejudicial to immediate practical ends. This is why young men, and even striplings, provided they are energetic and persuasive, will be listened to with attention at such eras. Men are seeking for enlightenment, and hence views are taken for what they seem to be worth rather than out of respect for the source they spring from. Imagine, then, this tall, fair, strong-faced boy of fourteen, mounted, perhaps, on one of his own flour-barrels, dogmatizing the principles of social democracy, posing as a spontaneous political reformer before a crowded street full of men twice and thrice his years, but bound together with him by the sympathies common to the wage-earning classes. It is true that Isaac Hecker and his brothers, of whom the eldest had but recently attained to the dignity of a voter, although still poor and hard-working, had already, by virtue of sheer industry and pluck, passed over to the class of wage-payers. But they were not less ardent reformers after than before that transition. Isaac, at all events, was consistent and unchanged throughout his life in the political principles he adopted among the apprentices and journeymen of New York over half a century ago. There was little room for vulgar self-conceit in a nature so frank and sincere as his. What he had to learn, as well as what he had to teach, always dwarfed merely personal considerations to their narrowest dimensions in his mind. Hence his impulsive candor, the clearness of his views, and the straightforward simplicity of his speech at once attracted notice, and although so young, he went speedily to the front in the local management of his party. In the article already quoted from, he tells us that after 1834 the managers left all future engagements of lecturers to his brother John and himself. It was doubtless this fact which led directly to that lasting and fruitful intimacy with Dr. Brownson which then began. His was the strongest purely human influence, if we except his mother's, which Isaac Hecker ever knew. And these two were on planes so different that it is hardly fair to compare them with each other.

CHAPTER III.

A BRIEF consideration at this point of a certain permanent tendency of Father Hecker's mind will be of present and future
value to the student of his life. It has been said already that he
never changed the principles he had adopted as a lad among the
apprentices and journeymen of New York; principles which, for
all social politics, he summarized in the homely expression, "I am
always for the under dog." Thus, in the article quoted in the
preceding chapter, he had the right to say of himself and his
associates :

"We were guileless men absorbed in seeking a solution for
the problems of life. Nor, as social reformers at least, were we
given over to theories altogether wrong. The constant recurrence
of similar epochs of social agitation since then, and the present
enormous development of the monopolies which we resisted in
their very infancy, show that our forecast of the future was not
wholly visionary. The ominous outlook of popular politics at the
present moment plainly shows that legislation such as we then
proposed, and such as was then within the easy reach of State
and national authority, would have forestalled difficulties whose
settlement at this day threatens a dangerous disturbance of public order."

We dwell on his political consistency, however, only because
it affords an evidence of that unity of character which was always
recognized in Father Hecker by those who knew him best.
Change in him, in whatever direction it seemed to proceed,
meant primarily the dropping off of accidental excrescences.
There was nothing radical in it. What he once held with the
settled allegiance of his intelligence he held always, adding to or
developing it further as fast as the clouds were blown away
from his mental horizon. From the standpoint of personal experience he could fairly criticise, as he did in conversation some
few years before his death, Cardinal Newman's dictum that "conversion is a leap in the dark." "I say," he went on, "that it
is a leap in the light." "*Into* the light, but through the dark,"
was suggested in reply.

"No," he answered. "If one arrives at a recognition of the

truth of Catholic doctrine through one or other form of Protestant orthodoxy, then the difficulties of ordinary controversy will indeed leave him to the very end in the dark. But if he comes to the Church through the working and the results of natural reason, it is light all the way, and to the very end. I had this out with Cardinal Newman personally, and he agreed that I was right."

It is true that his views were rectified when he entered the Church, and that when once in it he was ever acquiring new truth and new views of truth. But his character never changed. He was a luminous example of the truth of the saying that the child is father to the man, so often apparently falsified by experience. Boy and man, the prominent characteristic of his mind was a clear perception of fundamentals and a disregard of non-essentials in the whole domain of life. To reverse a familiar maxim, " Take care of the dollars and the cents will take care of themselves," might describe his plan of mental economy. To the small coin of discussion in any field of inquiry he paid little attention. One who knew him many years has often heard him say, " Emphasize the universal always."

He was a teacher by natural vocation. No sooner was he satisfied that he knew anything of general moment than he felt pressed to impart his knowledge. Contact with him could never be simply for acquaintance' sake ; still less for an idle comparison of views. While no man could be more frank in the admission of a lack of data on which to base an opinion in matters of fact, or a lack of illumination on affairs of conduct or practical direction, when such existed, yet to be certain was, to him, the self-luminous guarantee of his mission to instruct. But until that certainty was attained, in a manner satisfactory to both the intellectual and the ethical sides of his nature, he was silent.

As a priest, though he undertook to teach anybody and everybody, yet he could seldom have given the impression of desiring to impose his personal views, simply as such. His vital perception that there can be nothing private in truth shone through his speech too plainly for so gross a misconception to be easily made by candid minds. The fact is that the community of spiritual goods was vividly realized by him, and in good faith he credited all men with a longing like his own to see things as they really are. As he had by nature a very kindly

manner, benignant and cheerful, the average man readily submitted to his influence. In his prime he was always a most successful and popular preacher and lecturer, from the combined
effect of this earnestness of conviction and his personal magnetic
quality. Men whose mental characteristics resembled his became,
soon or late, his enthusiastic disciples, and as to others, although
at first some were inclined to suspect him, many of them ended
by becoming his warm friends.

It is in this light that we must view the precocious efforts of
the young politician. Nothing was further from his thoughts at
any time than to employ politics as a means to any private end.
Although we have already quoted him as saying that he always
felt bound to demand some good reason why he should not use
all things lawfully his, and enjoy to the full every innocent pleasure, yet that demand was made solely in the interests of human
freedom, never in that of self-indulgence. He seems to have
been ascetic by nature—a Stoic, not an Epicurean, by the very
make-up of his personality. The reader will see this more clearly
as we pass on to the succeeding phases of Father Hecker's
interior life. But we cannot leave the statement even here without explaining that we use the word ascetic in its proper sense,
to connote the rightful dominance of reason over appetite, the
supremacy of the higher over the lower; not the jurisdiction of
the judge over the criminal. In his case, during the greater part
of his life, the adjustment of the higher and lower, the restraint
he placed upon the beast in view of the elevation due to the
man, was neither conceived nor felt as punitive. We shall see
later on how God finally subjected him to a discipline so corrective as to be acknowledged by him as judicial.

Isaac Hecker threw himself into public questions, then, because,
being a workman, he believed he saw ways by which the working classes might be morally and socially elevated. He wanted
for his class what he wanted for himself. To get his views into
shape, to press them with all his force whenever and wherever
an opportunity presented itself, was for him the inescapable consequence of that belief. Like his great patron, St. Paul, "What
wilt Thou have me to do?" was always his first question after
his own illumination had been granted. There is a note in the
collection of private memoranda that has been preserved, in which,
alluding to the painful struggles which preceded his clear recognition that the doctrines of the Catholic Church afforded the

adequate solution of all his difficulties, he says that his interior sufferings were so great that the question with him was "whether I should drown myself in the river or drown my longings and doubts in a career of wild ambition." Still, to those who knew him well, it is impossible to think of him as ever capable of any ambition which had not an end commensurate with mankind itself. To elevate men, to go up with them, not above them, was, from first to last, the scope of his desire. The nature of his surroundings in youth, his personal experience of the hardships of the poorer classes, his intercourse with radical socialists, together with the incomplete character of the religious training given him, made him at first look on politics as a possible and probable means to this desirable end. But he was too sensibly impelled by the Divine impulse toward personal perfection, and too inflexibly honest with himself, not to come early to a thorough realization, on one hand of the fact that man cannot, unaided, rise above his natural level, and, on the other, that no conceivable amelioration of merely social conditions could satisfy his aspirations. And if not his, how those of other men?

One thing that becomes evident in studying this period of Isaac Hecker's life is the fact that his acquaintance with Dr. Brownson marks a turning-point in his views, his opinions, his whole attitude of mind toward our Lord Jesus Christ. Until then the Saviour of men had been represented to him exclusively as a remedy against the fear of hell; His use seemed to be to furnish a Divine point to which men might work themselves up by an emotional process resulting in an assurance of forgiveness of sin and a secure hope of heaven. Christianity, that is to say, had been presented to him under the form of Methodism. The result had been what might have been anticipated in a nature so averse to emotional excitement and possessing so little consciousness of actual sin. Drawn to God as he had always been by love and aspiration, he was not as yet sensible of any gulf which needed to be bridged between him and his Creator; hence, to present Christ solely as the Victim, the Expiatory Sacrifice demanded by Divine Justice, was to make Him, if not impossible, yet premature to a person like him. Meantime, what he saw and heard all around him, poverty, inequality, greed, shiftlessness, low views of life, ceaseless and poorly remunerated toil, made incessant demands upon him. These things he knew by actual contact, by physical, mental, and moral experience, as a man knows by touch and taste and smell. Men's sufferings, longings, struggles, disappointments had been early thrust upon him as a personal and most weighty burden; and the only relief yet offered was the Christ of emotional Methodism. To a nature more open to temptation on its lower side, and hence more conscious of its radical limitations, even this defective presentation of the Redeemer of men might have appealed profoundly. But Isaac Hecker's problems were at this time mainly social; as, indeed, to use the word in a large sense, they remained until the end. Now, Protestantism is essentially unsocial, being an extravagant form of individualism. Its Christ deals with men apart from each other and furnishes no cohesive element to humanity. The validity and necessity of religious organization as a moral force of Divine appointment is that one of the Catholic principles which it has from the beginning most vehemently rejected. As a negative force its essence is a protest against organic Christianity. As a positive force it is simply men, taken one by one, dealing separately with God concerning matters strictly personal. True, it is a fundamental verity that men must deal individually with God; but the external test that their dealings with Him have been efficacious, and their inspirations valid, is furnished by the fact of their incorporation into the organic life of Christendom. As St. Paul expresses it: "For as the body is one, and hath many members; and all the members of the body, whereas they are many, are yet one body, so also is Christ. For in one Spirit were we all baptized into one body, whether Jews or Gentiles, whether bond or free, and in one Spirit have we all been made to drink."*

It is plain, then, that a religion such as Protestantism, which is unsocial and disintegrating by virtue of its antagonistic forces, can contribute little to the solution of social problems. Even when not actively rejected by men deeply interested in such problems, it is tolerably sure that it will be practically ignored as a working factor in their public relations with their fellows. Religion will remain the narrowly personal matter it began; chiefly an affair for Sundays; best attended to in one's pew in church or at the family altar. Probably it may reach the shop, the counter, and the scales; not so certainly the factory, the mine, the political platform, and the ballot. If Christianity had never presented itself under any other aspect than this to Isaac

---

* 1 Cor. xii. 12, 13.

Hecker, it is certain that it would never have obtained his allegiance. Yet it is equally certain that he never rejected Christ under any aspect in which He was presented to him.

Even concerning the period of his life with which we are now engaged, and in which we have already represented him as having lost hold of all distinctively Christian doctrines, we must emphasize the precise words we have employed. He "lost hold"; that was because his original grasp was weak. While no authoritative dogmatic teaching had given him an even approximately full and definite idea of the God-man, His personality, His character, and His mission, the fragmentary truths offered him had made His influence seem restrictive rather than liberative of human energies. Yet even so he had not deliberately turned his back upon Him, though his tendency at this time was doubtless toward simple Theism. He had begun to ignore Christianity, simply because his own problems were dominantly social, and orthodox Protestantism, the only form of religion which he knew, had no social force corresponding to its pretensions and demands.

Now, upon this state of mind the teaching of Dr. Brownson came like seed upon a fallow soil. Like that which preceded it, it erred rather by defect than by actual or, at any rate, by wilful deviation from true doctrine. Isaac Hecker met for the first time in Orestes Brownson an exponent of Jesus Christ as the great Benefactor and Uplifter of the human race in this present life. Dr. Brownson has himself given a statement of the views which he held and inculcated between 1834 and 1843—which includes the period we are at present considering—and it is so brief and to the point that we cannot do better than to quote it:

"I found in me," he writes (*The Convert*, p. 111), "certain religious sentiments that I could not efface; certain religious beliefs or tendencies, of which I could not divest myself. I regarded them as a law of my nature, as natural to man, as the noblest part of our nature, and as such I cherished them; *but as the expression in me of an objective world, I seldom pondered them.* I found them universal, manifesting themselves, in some form, wherever man is found; but I received them, *or supposed I received them*, on the authority of humanity or human nature, and professed to hold no religion except that of humanity. I had become a believer in humanity, and put humanity in the place of God. The only God I recognized was the divine in man, the divinity of humanity, one alike with God and with man, which I supposed to be the real meaning of the Christian doctrine of the

Incarnation, the mystery of Emmanuel, or God with us—God manifest in the flesh. There may be an unmanifested God, and certainly is; but the only God who exists for us is the God in man, the active and living principle of human nature.

"I regarded Jesus Christ as divine in the sense in which all men are divine, and human in the sense in which all men are human. I took him as my model man, and regarded him as a moral and social reformer, who sought, by teaching the truth under a religious envelope, and practising the highest and purest morality, to meliorate the earthly condition of mankind; but I saw nothing miraculous in his conception or birth, nothing supernatural in his person or character, in his life or doctrine. He came to redeem the world, as does every great and good man, and deserved to be held in universal honor and esteem as one who remained firm to the truth amid every trial, and finally died on the cross, a martyr to his love of mankind. As a social reformer, as one devoted to the progress and well-being of man in this world, I thought I might liken myself to him and call myself by his name. I called myself a Christian, not because I took him for my master, not because I believed all he believed or taught, but because, like him, I was laboring to introduce a new order of things, and to promote the happiness of my kind. I used the Bible as a good Protestant, took what could be accommodated to my purpose, and passed over the rest, as belonging to an age now happily outgrown. I followed the example of the carnal Jews, and gave an earthly sense to all the promises and prophecies of the Messias, and looked for my reward in this world."

The passages we have italicized in this extract may go to show how far Dr. Brownson himself was, at this period, from being able to give any but the evasive answer he actually did give to the searching philosophical questions put by his youthful admirer. But it is not easy, especially in the light of Isaac Hecker's subsequent experiences, to overestimate the influence which this new presentation of our Saviour had upon the development of his mind and character. For reasons which we have tried to indicate by a brief description of some of his life-long interior traits, the ordinary Protestant view, restricted and narrow, which represents Jesus Christ merely as the appointed though voluntary Victim of the Divine wrath against sin, had been pressed upon him prematurely. Now He was held up to him, and by a man who was in many ways superior to all other men the boy had met, as a great personality, altogether human, indeed, but still the most perfect specimen of the race; the supremely worshipful figure of all history, whose life had been given to the assertion of the dignity of man and the equality of mankind. That human nature is good and that men are brethren, said Dr. Brownson, was the thesis of Christ, taught throughout His life, sealed by His death. The Name which is above all names became thus in a new sense a watchword, and the Gospels a treasury for that social apostolate to which Isaac Hecker had already devoted himself with an earnestness which for some years made it seem religion enough for him.

So it has seemed before his time and since to many a benevolent dreamer. Though the rites of the humanitarian cult differ with its different priests, its creed retains everywhere and always its narrow identity. But that all men are good, or would be so save for the unequal pressure of social conditions on them, is a conclusion which does not follow from the single premise that human nature, inasmuch as it is a nature and from the hand of God, is essentially good. The world is flooded, just at present, with schemes for insuring the perfection and happiness of men by removing so far as possible all restraints upon their natural freedom ; and whether this is to be accomplished with Tolstoï, by reducing wants to a minimum and abolishing money ; or by establishing clubs for the promotion of culture and organizing a social army which shall destroy poverty by making money plenty, appears a mere matter of detail—at all events to dreamers and to novelists. But to men who are in hard earnest with themselves, men who "have not taken their souls in vain nor sworn deceitfully," either to their neighbor or about him, certain other truths concerning human nature besides that of its essential goodness are sure to make themselves evident, soon or late. And among these is that of its radical insufficiency to its own needs. It is a rational nature, and it seeks the Supreme Reason, if only for its own self-explication. It is a nature which, wherever found, is found in the attitude of adoration, and neither in the individual man nor in humanity at large is there any Divinity which responds to worship.

It is impossible to say just when Isaac Hecker's appreciation of this truth became intensely personal and clear, but it is easy to make a tolerable approximation to the time. He went to Brook Farm in January, 1843, rather more than eight years after his first meeting with Dr. Brownson. It was by the advice of the latter that he made this first decisive break from his former life. From the time when their acquaintance began, Isaac appears to have taken up the study of philosophy in good earnest, and to have found in it an outlet for his energies which insensibly diminished his absorption in social politics. We have a glimpse of him kneading at the dough-trough with Kant's *Critique of Pure Reason* fastened up on the wall before him, so that he might lose no time in merely manual labor. Fichte and Hegel succeeded Kant, all of them philosophers whose mother-tongue was likewise his own, and whose combined influence put him farther off than ever from the solution of that fundamental doubt which constantly grew more perplexing and more painful. We find him hiring a seat in the Unitarian Church of the Messiah, where Orville Dewey was then preaching, and walking every Sunday a distance of three miles from the foot of Rutgers Street, "because he was a smart fellow, and I enjoyed listening to him. Did I believe in Unitarianism? *No! I believed in nothing.*"

His active participation in local politics did not continue throughout all these years. His belief in candidates and parties as instruments to be relied on for social purification received a final blow very early—possibly before he was entitled to cast a vote. The Workingmen had made a strong ticket one year, and there seemed every probability of their carrying it. But on the eve of the election half of their candidates sold out to one of the opposing parties. What other results this treachery may have had is a question which, fortunately, does not concern us, but it dispelled one of the strongest of Isaac Hecker's youthful illusions. He continued, nevertheless, to prove the sincerity with which his views on social questions were held, by doing all that lay in his power to better the condition of the men in the employment of his brothers and himself. After he passed his majority his interest in the business declined rapidly, and it is impossible to doubt that one of the chief reasons why it did so is to be sought in his changing convictions as to the manner in which business in general should be carried on.

Although in accepting Christ as his master and model he had as yet no belief in Him as more than the most perfect of human beings, yet, even so, Isaac Hecker's sincerity and simplicity were too great to permit him to follow his leader at a purely conventional distance. "Do you know," he said long afterwards, "the thought that first loosened me from the life I led ? How can I love my fellow-men and yet get rich by the sweat of their brows ? I couldn't do it. You are not a Christian, and can't call yourself one, I said to myself, if you do that. The heathenish selfishness of business competition started me away from the world."

If he had received a Catholic training, Isaac Hecker would soon have recognized that he was being drawn toward the practice of that counsel of perfection which St. Paul embodies to St. Timothy in the words : " Having food and wherewith to be covered, with these we are content."* Could he have sought at this time the advice of one familiar with internal ways, he must have been cautioned against that first error to which those so drawn are liable, of supposing that this call is common and imperative, and can never fail to be heard without some more or less wilful closing of the ears. Though the Hecker brothers were, and ever continued to be, men of the highest business integrity, and though there existed between them a cordial affection, which was intensified to an extraordinary degree in the case of George and Isaac, yet the unfitness of the latter for ordinary trade grew increasingly evident, and to himself painfully so. The truth is, that his ideas of conducting business would have led to the distribution of profits rather than to their accumulation. If he could make the bake-house and the shop into a school for the attainment of an ideal that had begun to hover, half-veiled, in the air above him, he saw his way to staying where he was ; but not otherwise.

In the autumn of 1842 there came upon him certain singular intensifications of this disquiet with himself and his surroundings. In the journal begun the following spring, he so frequently and so explicitly refers to these occurrences, now speaking of them as " dreams which had a great effect upon my character "; and again, specializing and fully describing one, as something not dreamed, but seen when awake, " which left an indelible impress on my mind," weaning it at once and for ever from all possibility of natural love and marriage, that the integrity of any narrative of his life would demand some recognition of them. His own comment, in the diary, will not be without interest and value, both as bearing on much that follows, and as containing all that need be said in explanation of the present reference to such experiences :

* 1 Timothy vi. 8.

"*April* 24, 1843.— . . . How can I doubt these things? Say what may be said, still they have to me a reality, a practical good bearing on my life. They are impressive instructors, whose teachings are given in such a real manner that they influence me whether I would or not. Real pictures of the future, as actual, nay, more so than my present activity. If I should not follow them I am altogether to blame. I can have no such adviser upon earth; none could impress me so strongly, with such peculiar effect, and at the precise time most needed. Where my natural strength is not enough, I find there comes foreign aid to my assistance. Is the Lord instructing me for anything? I had, six months ago, three or more dreams which had a very great effect upon my character; they changed it. They were the embodiment of my present in a great degree. Last evening's was a warning embodiment of a false activity and its consequence, which will preserve me, under God's assistance, from falling. . . . I see by it where I am; it has made me purer."

In addition to these peculiar visitations, and very probably in consequence of them, Isaac's inward anxieties culminated in prolonged fits of nervous depression, and at last in repeated attacks of illness which baffled the medical skill called to his assistance. Towards Christmas he went to Chelsea to visit Brownson, to whom he partially revealed the state of obscurity and distress in which he found himself. Brownson, who had been one of the original promoters of the experiment in practical sociology at West Roxbury, advised a residence at Brook Farm as likely to afford the young man the leisure and opportunities for study which he needed in order to come to a full understanding with himself. He wrote to George Ripley in his behalf, and later undertook to reconcile the Hecker household with Isaac's determination to go thither.

It was during his stay at Chelsea that Isaac first began plainly to acquaint his family with the fact that his departure meant something more important than the moderately prolonged change of scene and circumstances which they had recognized as essential to his health. We shall make abundant extracts from the letters which begin at this date, convinced that his own words will not only afford the best evidence of the strength of the interior pressure on him, but will show also its unique and constant bent.

Our purpose is to show, in the most explicit manner possible, first, how irresistibly he was impelled toward the celibate life and the practice of poverty ; and second, that in yielding to this impulse, he was also drawn away from his former view of our Saviour, as simply the perfect man, to the full acceptance of the supernatural truth that He is the Incarnate God.

It is at this period of Father Hecker's life that we first meet with a positive interference of an extraordinary kind in the plans and purposes of his life.   Many men who have outlived them, and settled down into respectable but in nowise notable members of society, have felt vague longings and indefinite aspirations toward a good beyond nature during the " Storm and Stress " period of their youth.   The record of their mental struggles gets into literature with comparative frequency, and sometimes becomes famous.   It has always a certain value, if merely as contributing to psychological science ; but in any particular instance is of passing interest only, unless it can be shown to have been instrumental in shaping the subsequent career.   The latter was the case with Father Hecker.   The extraordinary influences already mentioned continued to dominate his intelligence and his will, sometimes with, oftener without, explicit assignment of any cause. It is plain enough that, up to the time when they began, he had looked forward to such a future of domestic happiness as honest young fellows in his position commonly desire.   " He was the life of the family circle," says one who knew the Hecker household intimately ; " he loved his people, and was loved by them with great intensity, and his going away must have been most painful to him as well as to them."

On this point the memoranda, so often to be referred to, contain some words of his own to the same purport.   They were spoken early in 1882 : " You know I had to leave my business— a good business it was getting to be, too.   I tell you, it was agony to give everything up—friends, prospects in life and old associates ; things for which by nature I had a very strong attachment.   But I could not help it ; I was driven from it.   I wanted something more ; something I had not been able to find. Yet I did not know what I wanted.   I was simply in torment."

The truth is that, while he had always cherished ideals higher than are usual, still they were not such as need set him apart from the common life of men.   But now he became suddenly

averse from certain pursuits and pleasures, not only good in themselves, but consonant to his previous dispositions. The road to
wealth lay open before him, but his feet refused to tread it. He
was invincibly drawn to poverty, solitude, sacrifice ; modes of life
from which he shrank by nature, and which led to no goal that
he could see or understand. There is no name so descriptive of
such impulses as supernatural.

CHAPTER IV.

LED BY THE SPIRIT.

THE earliest of the letters so fortunately preserved by the affection of Isaac Hecker's kindred is addressed to his mother, from Chelsea, and bears date December 24, 1842. After giving some details of his arrival, and of the kindly manner in which he had been received, he writes : *

"But as regards your advice to write my thoughts to you, that is an impossibility which I cannot govern or control. This ought not to be so, but so it is. Am I to blame ? I feel not. And what if I could tell ? It might be only a deep dissatisfaction which could not be made intelligible, or at least not be felt as it is felt by me. Let us be untroubled about it. A little time, and, I hope, all will pass away, and I be the same as usual. We all differ a little, at least in our characters; hence there is nothing surprising if our experiences should differ. I feel that a little time will be my best remedy, which I trust we will await without much anxiety. Resignation is taught when we cannot help ourselves. Take nothing I have said discouragingly. Turn fears into hopes and doubts into faith, and we shall be better if not happier. There is no use in allowing our doubts and fears to control us ; by fostering them we increase them, and we want all our time for something better and higher."

Two days later he writes more fully, and this letter we shall give almost entire :

"*Chelsea, December* 26, 1842.—BROTHERS : I want to write to you, but what is the use of scrawling on paper if I write what I do not feel—intend ? It is worse than not writing. And yet why I should be backward I don't know. The change that I have undergone has been so rapid and of such a kind ; that may be the reason. I feel that as I now am perhaps you cannot understand me. I am afraid lest your conduct would be such that under present circumstances I could not stand under it. Do not misunderstand me. If I have ever appreciated anything in my life, it is the favor and indulgent treatment you have shown me in our business. I know that I have never done an equal share

---

* We have corrected some slight errors of orthography and punctuation in these early letters. They were of the sort to be expected from a self-trained youth, as yet little used to the written expression of his thoughts. They soon disappear almost entirely.

in the work which was for us all to do. I have always been
conscious of this. I hope you will receive this as it is written,
for I am open. Daily am I losing that disposition which was
attributed to me of self-approval. . . . There is no reason why
I should distrust your dispositions toward me but my own feelings, and it is these that have kept me back, that and the change
my mind is undergoing. This is so continuous, and at the same
time so firmly fixed, that I am unable to keep back any longer.
I had hopes that my former life would return, so that I would
be able to go on as usual, although this tendency has always
been growing in me. But I find more and more that it is not
possible. I would go back if I could, but the impossibility of
that I cannot express. To continue as I am now would keep me
constantly in an unsettled state of health, especially as my future
appears to be opening before me with clearness. I say sincerely
that I have lost all but this one thing, and how shall I speak it?
My mind has lost all disposition to business; my hopes, life, existence, are all in another direction. No one knows how I tried
to exert myself to work, or the cause of my inability. I was
conscious of the cause, but as it was supposed to be a physical
one, the reason of it was sought for, but to no purpose. In the
same circumstances now I should be worse. When I say my
mind cannot be occupied as formerly, do not attribute it to my
wishes. This is what I fear; it makes me almost despair, makes
me feel that I would rather die than live under such thoughts. I
never could be happy if you thought so. My future will be my
only evidence. *My experience, which is now my own evidence,
I cannot give you.* To keep company with females—you know
what I mean—I have no desire. I have no thought of marrying, and I feel an aversion to company for such an end. In my
whole life I have never felt less inclined to it. If my disposition
ran that way, marrying might lead me back to my old life, but
oh! that is impossible. To give up, as I have to do, a life which
has often been my highest aim and hope, is done with a sense
of responsibility I never imagined before. This, I am conscious,
is no light thought. It lies deeper than myself, and I have not
the power to control it. I do not write this with ease; it is done
in tears, and I have opened my mind as I have not done before.
How all this will end I know not, but cannot but trust God. It
is not my will but my destiny, which will not be one of ease
and pleasure, but one which I contemplate as a perpetual sacri-

fice of my past hopes, though of a communion I had never felt. Can I adopt a course of life to increase and fulfil my present life? I am unable to give this decision singly. You will, I hope, accept this letter in the spirit I have written it. I speak to you in a sense I never have spoken to you before. In this letter I have opened as far as I could my inmost life. My heart is full and I would say a great deal more. Truly, a new life has opened to me, and to turn backward would be death. Not suddenly has it undergone this change, but it has come to that crisis where my decision must be made; hence am I forced to write this letter. For its answer I shall wait with intense anxiety. Hoping you will write soon, my love to all.—ISAAC."

The next letter, though addressed to his brothers, was apparently intended for the whole family, and begins with more than Isaac's customary abruptness:

" *Chelsea, December* 28, 1842.—I will open my mind so that you can have the materials to judge from as well as myself. I feel unable to the task of judging alone correctly. I have given an account of my state of mind in my former letter, but will add that what is there said describes a permanent state, not a momentary excitement. You may think that in a little time this would pass away, and I would be able to resume my former life ; or, at least, you could so adapt things at home that although I should not precisely occupy myself as then, still it might be so arranged as to give me that which I feel necessary in order to live somewhat contented.

" I am sorry to say I can in no way conceive such an arrangement of things at home. Why ? I hate to say it, yet we might as well come to an understanding. I have grown out of the life which can be received through the accustomed channels of the circle that was around me. I am subject to thoughts and feelings which the others had no interest in ; hence they could not be expressed. There can be no need to tell you this—you all must have seen it. How can I stop my life from flowing on? You must see the case I stand in. Do not think I have less of the feelings of a brother and a son. My heart never was closer, not so close as it is now to yours. . . .

" Do not think this is imagination ; in this I have had too much experience. The life that was in me had none to commune with, and I felt it was consuming me. I tried to express this in different ways obscurely, but it appeared singular and no one understood me. This was the cause of my wishing to go away, hoping I would either get clear of it or something might turn up, I knew not what. One course was advised by the doctor, and you all thought as he did—that was to keep company with the intention of getting married. This was not the communion that I wanted or that was congenial to my life. Marrying would not, I am convinced, have had any permanent effect. It was not that which controlled me, then or now. It is altogether different; it is a life in me which requires altogether different circumstances to live it. This is no dream; or, if it is, then have I never had such reality. . . .

"When I wrote last it struck me I might secure what I need at Brook Farm, but that would depend greatly upon how you answer my letter. If you do as perhaps you may, I will go and see whether I could be satisfied and how it is, and let you know.

"So far had I written when your letter came. . . . You appear to ask this question: What object have you in contemplation? *None further than to live a life agreeable to the mind I have, which I feel under a necessity to do.*"

"*Chelsea, December* 30, 1842.—TO MOTHER: I am sorry to hear that you feel worried. My health is good, I eat and sleep well. That my mind is not settled, or as it used to be, is no reason to be troubled, for I hope it is not changing for the worse, and I look forward to brighter days than we have seen in those that are gone. I was conscious my last letter was not written in a manner to give you ease; but to break those old habits of our accustomed communion was to me a serious task, and done under a sense of duty, to let you know the cause of the disease I was supposed to labor under. That is past now, and I hope we shall understand each other, and that our future will be smooth and easy. The ice has been broken. That caused me some pain but no regret, and instead of feeling sorrow, you will, I hope, be contented that I should continue the path that will make me better."

Concerning Isaac Hecker's residence at Brook Farm, which was begun about the middle of the following January, we shall have more to say hereafter. At present our concern is chiefly with those explanations of his conduct and motives which the anxieties of his family continually forced him to attempt. There is, however, among the papers belonging to this period one which, although found with the letters, was evidently so included by mistake, and at some later date. It is an outpouring still more intimate than he was able to make for the enlightenment of others, and is the first vestige of a diary which has been found. But it seems plain that his longing for what he continually calls "communion," and the effort to divine the will of Providence in his regard, must frequently have urged him to that introspective self-contemplation so common to natures like his before their time for action has arrived. We make some brief extracts from this document which illustrates, still more plainly than any of the letters, the fact that the interior pressure to which he was subjected had for its uniform tendency and result his vivid realization of the Incarnation of God in Jesus Christ. It is written in a fine, close hand on a sheet of letter-paper, which it entirely covers, and bears date January 10, 1843 :

"Could I but reveal myself unto myself! What shall I say? Is life dear to me? No. Are my friends dear to me? I could suffer and die for them, if need were, but yet I have none of the old attachment for them. I would clasp all to my heart, love all for their humanity, but not as relatives or individuals. . . . Lord, if I am to be anything, I am, of all, most unfit for the task. What shall I do? Whom shall I cry to but Him who has given me life and planted this spirit in me? Unto Thee, then, do I cry from the depths of my soul for light to suffer. If there is anything for me to do, why this darkness all around me? I ask not to be happy. I will forego, as I always had a presentiment I must do, all hopes which young men of my age are prone to picture in their minds. If only I could have a ray of light on my present condition! O Lord! open my eyes to see the path Thou wouldst have me walk in. . . .

"Jan. 11.—True life is one continuous prayer, one unceasing aspiration after the holy. I have no conception of a life insensible to that which is not above itself, lofty. I would not take it on myself to say I have been 'born again,' but I know that I have passed from death to life. Things below have no hold upon me further than as they lead to things above. It is not a moral restraint that I have over myself, but it is such a change, a conversion of my whole being, that I have no need of restraint. Temptations still beset me—not sensual, but of a kind which seek to make me untrue to my life. If I am not on my guard I become cold. May I always be humble, meek, prayerful, open to all men. Light, love, and life God is always giving, but we turn our backs and will not receive. . . .

"Who can measure the depths of Christ's suffering—alone in the world, having that which would give life everlasting, a heaven, to those who would receive it, and yet despised, spit upon, rejected of men! Oh! how sweet must it have been to His soul when He found even one who would accept a portion of that precious gift which He came to the world to bestow! Well could He say, 'Father, forgive them; they know not what they do.' He would give them life, but they would not receive. He would save them, but they rejected Him. He loved them, and they despised Him. Alas! who has measured even in a small degree the love of Christ and yet denied His superiority over man! His love, goodness, mercy are unbounded. O Lord! may I daily come into closer communion with Thy Son, Jesus Christ."

On the 22d of February he addresses both of his parents in reply to a letter sent by his brother John, detailing some of their troubles on this head. He writes:

"It is as great a difficulty for me to reconcile my being here with my sense of duty towards you, . . . Since I must speak, let me tell you that I have at present no disposition to return. Neither are the circumstances that surround me now those which will give me contentment; but I feel that I am here as a temporary place, and that by spring something will turn up which I hope will be for the happiness of us all. What it will be I have not the least idea of now. It is as impossible for me to give you an explanation of that which has led me of late as it would be for a stranger. All before me is dark, even as that is which leads me now and has led me before. One sentiment I have which I feel I cannot impart to you. It is that I am controlled. Formerly I could act from intention, but now I have no future to design, nothing in prospect, and *my present action is from a present cause,* not from any past. Hence it is that while my action may appear to others as designed, to me it is unlooked-for and unaccountable. I do not expect that others can feel this as I do. I am tossed about in a sea without a rudder. What drives me onward, and where I shall be driven, is to me unknown. My past life seems to me like that of another person, and my present is like a dream. Where am I? I know not. I have no power over my present, I do not even know what it is. Whom can I find like myself, whom can I speak to that will understand me?

" This makes me still, lonely ; and I cannot wish myself out of this state. I have no will to do that—not that I have any desire to. All I can say is that I am in it. What would be the effect of necessity on me, I know not, whether it would lead me back or lead me on. My feeling of duty towards you is a continual weight upon me which I cannot throw off—it is best, perhaps, that I cannot. All appears to me as a seeming, not a reality. Nothing touches that life in me which is seeking that which I know not."

To George Hecker.—*"Brook Farm, March* 6, 1843.—What was the reason of my going, or what made me go? The reason I am not able to tell. But what I felt was a dark, irresistible influence upon me that led me away from home. What it was I know not. What keeps me here I cannot tell. It is only when I struggle against it that a spell comes over me. If I give up to it, nothing is the matter with me. But when I look to my past, my duty toward you all, and consider what this may lead me to, and then attempt to return, I get into a state which I cannot speak of. . . .

" By attempt to return I mean an attempt to return to my old life, for so I have to call it—that is, to get clear of this influence. And yet I have no will to will against it. I do not desire it, or its mode of living, and I am opposed to its tendency.

" What bearing this has upon the question of my coming home you will perceive. As soon as I can come, I will. If I should do so now, it would throw me back to the place from which I started. Is this fancy on my part ? All I can say is that if so the last nine or ten months of my life have been a fancy which is too deep for me to control."

After paying his family a visit in April, he writes to them on his return :

" *Brook Farm, April* 14, 1843.—Here I am alone in my room once more. I feel settled, and begin to live again, separated from everything but my studies and thoughts, and the feeling of gratitude toward you all for treating me so much better than I am aware of ever having treated you. May I ever keep this sense of obligation and indebtedness. My prayer is, that the life I have been led to live these few months back may prove to the advantage of us all in the end. I sometimes feel guilty because I did not attempt again to try and labor with you. But the power that kept me back, its hold upon me, its strength over me, all that I am unable to communicate, makes my situation appear strange to others, and to myself irreconcilable with my former state. Still, I trust that, in a short period, all things will take their peaceful and orderly course."

To George Hecker.—"*Brook Farm, May* 12, 1843.—How much nearer to you I feel on account of your good letter you cannot estimate—nearer than when we slept in the same bed. Nearness of body is no evidence of the distance between souls, for I imagine Christ loved His mother very tenderly when He said, 'Woman, what have I to do with thee?'"

"I have felt, time and again, that either I would have to give up the life that was struggling in me, or withdraw from business in the way that we pursue it. This I had long felt, before the period came which suddenly threw me involuntarily out of it. Here I am, living in the present, without a why or a wherefore, trusting that something will shape my course intelligibly. I am completely without object. And when occasionally I emerge, if I may so speak, into actual life, I feel that I have dissipated time. A sense of guilt accompanies that of pleasure, and I return inwardly into a deeper, intenser life, breaking those tender roots which held me fast for a short period to the outward. In study only do I enter with wholeness; nothing else appears to take hold of my life." . . . "I am staying here, intentionally, for a short period. When the time arrives" (for leaving) "heaven knows what I may do. I am now perfectly dumb before it. Perhaps I may return and enter into business with more perseverance and industry than before; perhaps I may stay here; it may be that I shall be led elsewhere. But there is no utility in speculating on the future. If we lived as we should, we would feel that we lived in the presence of God, without past or future, having a full consciousness of existence, living the 'eternal life.' . . .

"George, do not get too engrossed with outward business. Rather neglect a part of it for that which is immortal in its life, incomparable in its fulness. It is a deep, important truth: 'Seek first the kingdom of God, and then all things will be added.' In having nothing we have all."

To Mrs. Hecker.—"*Brook Farm, May* 16, 1843.—Dear Mother: You will not take it unkind, my not writing to you before ? I am sure you will not, for you know what I am. Daily I feel more and more indebted to you for my life, especially when I feel happy and good. How can I repay you? As you, no doubt, would wish me to—by becoming better and living as you have desired and prayed that I should, which I trust, by Divine assistance, I may.

"Mother, I cannot express the depth of gratitude I feel toward you for the tender care and loving discipline with which you brought me up to manhood. Without it, oh! what might I not have been ? The good that I have, under God, I am conscious that I am greatly indebted to thee for ; at times I feel that it is thou acting in me, and that there is nothing that can ever separate us. A bond which is as eternal as our immortality, our life, binds us together and cannot be broken.

"Mother, that I should be away from home at present no doubt makes you sorrowful often, and you wish me back. Let me tell you how it is with me. The life which surrounds me in New York oppresses me, contracts my feelings, and abridges my liberty. Business, as it is now pursued, is a burden upon my spiritual life, and all its influence hurtful to the growth of a better life. This I have felt for a long time, and feel it now more intensely than before. And the society I had there was not such as benefited me. My life was not increased by theirs, and I was gradually ceasing to be. I was lonely, friendless, and without object in this world, while at the same time I was conscious of a greater degree of activity of mind in another direction. These causes still remain. . . .

" . . . I feel fully conscious of the importance of making any change in my life at my present age—giving up those advantages which so many desire ; as well as the necessity of being considerate, prudent, and slow to decide. I am aware that my future state here, and hence hereafter, will greatly depend upon the steps I now take, and therefore I would do nothing unadvised or hastily. I would not sacrifice eternal for worldly life. At present I wish to live a true life, desiring nothing external, seeing that things external cannot procure those things for and in which I live. I do not renounce things, but feel no inclination for them. All is indifferent to me—poverty or riches, life or death. I am loosed. But do not on this account think I am sorrowful ; nay, for I have nothing to sorrow for. Is there no bright hope at a distance which cheers me onward and beckons me to speed ?

I dare not say. Sometimes I feel so—it is the unutterable. Yet I remain contented to be without spring or autumn, youth or age. One tie has been loosened after another; the dreams of my youth have passed away silently, and the visions of the future I then beheld have vanished. I feel awakened as from a dream, and like a shadow has my past gone by. With the verse at the bottom of the picture you gave me, I can say :

> " ' Oh ! days that once I used to prize,
> Are ye for ever gone ?
> The veil is taken from my eyes,
> And now I stand alone.'

" But I would not recall those by-gone days, nor do I stand alone. No ! Out from this life will spring a higher world, of which the past was but a weak, faint shadow."

CHAPTER V.

AT BROOK FARM.

THE famous though short-lived community at West Roxbury, Massachusetts, where Isaac Hecker made his first trial of the common life, was started in the spring of 1841 by George Ripley and his wife, Nathaniel Hawthorne, John S. Dwight, George P. Bradford, Sarah Sterns, a niece of George Ripley's, Marianne Ripley, his sister, and four or five others whose names we do not know. In September of the same year they were joined by Charles A. Dana, now of the New York *Sun*. Hawthorne's residence at the Farm, commemorated in the *Blithedale Romance*, had terminated before Mr. Dana's began. The Curtis brothers, Burrill and George William, were there when Isaac Hecker came. Emerson was an occasional visitor; so was Margaret Fuller. Bronson Olcott, then cogitating his own ephemeral experiment at Fruitlands, sometimes descended on the gay community and was doubtless " Orphic " at his leisure.

The association was the outcome of many discussions which had taken place at Mr. Ripley's house in Boston during the winter of 1840-41. Among the prominent Bostonians who took part in these informal talks were Theodore Parker, Adin Ballou, Samuel Robbins, John S. Dwight, Warren Burton, and Orestes Brownson. Each of these men, and, if we do not mistake, George Ripley also, presided at the time over some religious body. Mr. Ballou, who was a Universalist minister of much local renown, was, perhaps, the only exception to the prevailing Unitarian complexion of the assembly.

The object of their discussions seems to have been, in a general way, the necessity for some social reform which should go to the root of the commercial spirit and the contempt for certain kinds of labor so widely prevalent ; and, in a special way, the feasibility of establishing at once, on however small a scale, a co-operative experiment in family life, having for its ulterior aim the reorganization of society on a less selfish basis. They probably considered that, a beginning once made by people of their stamp, the influence of their example would work as a quickening leaven. They hoped to be the mustard-seed which, planted in a congenial soil, would grow into a tree in whose branches all the birds of the air might dwell. It was

The Young Transcendentalist.

(From a daguerreotype.)

the initial misfortune of the Brook-Farmers to establish themselves
on a picturesque but gravelly and uncongenial soil, whose poverty
went very far toward compassing the collapse of their undertaking.

Not all of the ministers whose names have just been mentioned were of one mind, either as to the special evils to be
counteracted or the remedies which might be tentatively applied.
Three different associations took their rise from among this hand-
ful of earnest seekers after better social methods. Mr. Ballou,
who headed one of these, believed that unity and cohesion could
be most surely obtained by a frank avowal of beliefs, aims, and
practices, to which all present and future associates would be
expected to conform. Mrs. Kirby, whose interesting volume *
we have already quoted, says that the platform of this party
bound them to abolitionism, anti-orthodoxy, women's rights,
total abstinence, and opposition to war. They established themselves at Hopedale, Massachusetts, where, so far as our knowledge
goes, some vestige of them may still remain, though the analo-
gies and probabilities are all against such a survival. A second
band of "come-outers," as people used to be called in that day
and region, when they abandoned the common road for reasons
not obviously compulsory, went to Northampton in the same
State, and from there into corporate obscurity.

Mr. Ripley's scheme was more elastic, and if the money
basis of the association had been more solid, there seems no
reason on the face of things why this community at Brook
Farm might not have enjoyed a much longer lease of life. It
seems to have left a most pleasant memory in the minds of
all who were ever members of it. In matters of belief
and of opinion no hard-and-fast lines were drawn at any
point. In matters of conduct, the morality of self-respecting
New-Englanders who were at a farther remove from Puritanic
creeds than from Puritanic discipline, was regarded as a sufficient
guarantee of social decorum. Of the earliest additions to the
co-operative household, a sprinkling were already Catholic ;
others, including the wife and the niece of the founder, afterwards became so. Some attended orthodox Protestant churches ;
the majority were probably Unitarians. Discussion on all subjects appears to have been free, frank, and good-tempered.

There was no attempt made at any communism except that
of intellectual and social gifts and privileges. There was a

* *Years of Experience.* New York : G. P. Putnam's Sons. 1887.

common table, and Mrs. Kirby has given us some attractive glimpses of the good feeling, and kindly gayety, and practical observance of the precept to "bear one another's burdens" which came into play around it. For many months, as no one could endure to have his equal serve him, and all were equals, there was a constant getting up and down at table so that each might help himself. Afterwards, when decline had already set in, so far as the material basis of the undertaking was concerned, and those who had its success most at heart had begun to study Fourier for fruitful suggestions, the first practical hint from that quarter resulted in Mr. Dana's organizing "a group of servitors." These, writes Mrs. Kirby, * comprised "four of the most elegant youths at the community — the son of a Louisiana planter, a young Spanish hidalgo, a rudimentary Free-Soiler from Hingham, and, if I remember rightly, Edward Barlow (the brother of Francis). These, with one accord, elected as chief their handsome and beloved teacher. It is hardly necessary to observe that the business was henceforth attended to with such courtly grace and such promptness that the new *régime* was applauded by every one, although it did appear at first as if we were all engaged in acting a play. The group, with their admired chief, took dinner, which had been kept warm for them, afterwards, and were themselves waited upon with the utmost consideration, but I confess I never could get accustomed to the new regulation."

The watchword of the place was fraternity, not communism. People took up residence at Brook Farm on different terms. Some paid a stipulated board, and thus freed themselves from any obligatory share in either domestic or out-door labor. Others contributed smaller sums and worked out the balance. Some gave labor only, as was the case with Mrs. Kirby, then Georgiana Bruce, an English girl of strong character. She says she agreed to work eight hours a day for her board and instruction in any branches of study which she elected to pursue. As an illustration of the actual poverty to which the community were soon reduced, and, moreover, of the low money value they set on domestic labor, we give another characteristic passage from her book. The price of full board, as we learn from a bill sent by Mr. Ripley to Isaac Hecker after the latter's final departure from the Farm, was five dollars and fifty cents a week:

* *Years of Experience,* pp. 178, 179.

" When a year had elapsed I found my purse empty and my wardrobe much the worse for wear. As I was known to be heartily interested in the new movement, my case was taken under consideration, and, with the understanding that I was to add two more hours to my working day, I was admitted as *bona-fide* member of the association (which included only a dozen), and was allowed to draw on the treasury for my very moderate necessities. Forty dollars a year would cover these, writing-paper and postage included. The last item was no unimportant one, as each letter cost from ten to fifty cents, and money counted for more then than now.

" I should explain that for the whole of one winter there remained but two bonnets fit for city eyes among six of us. But the best of these was forced on whomever was going to town. As for best dresses, a twenty-five cent delaine was held to be gorgeous apparel. The gentlemen had found it desirable to adopt a tunic in place of the more expensive, old-world coat " *

The income of the association was derived from various sources other than the prices paid for board. There was a school for young children, presided over by Mrs. Ripley, assisted by various pupil-teachers, who thus partially recompensed the community for their own support. Fruit, milk, and vegetables, when there were any to spare, were sent to the Boston markets Now and then some benevolent philanthropist with means would make a donation. No one who entered was expected to contribute his whole income to the general purse, unless such income would not more than cover the actual expense incurred for him. When Isaac Hecker went to West Roxbury the establishment included seventy inmates, who were distributed in several buildings bearing such poetical names as the Hive, the Eyrie, the Nest, and so on. The number rose to ninety or a hundred before he left them, but the additions seem occasionally to have been in the nature of subtractions also, taking away more of the cultivation, refinement, and general good feeling which had been the distinguishing character of the place, than they added by their money or their labor.

Isaac Hecker was never an actual member of that inner community of whose aspirations and convictions the Farm was intended as an embodiment. He entered at first as a partial boarder, paying four dollars a week, and undertaking also the

* *Years of Experience,* p. 132.

bread-making, which until then had been very badly done, as he
writes to his mother. It should be understood that whatever was
received from any inmate, either in money or labor, was accepted
not as a mere return for food and shelter, but as an equivalent
for such instruction as could be imparted by any other member
of the collective family. And there were many competent and
brilliant men and women there, whose attainments not only quali-
fied them amply for the tasks they then assumed, but have since
made them prominent in American letters and journalism. Mr.
Ripley lectured on modern philosophy to all who desired an
acquaintance with Spinoza, Kant, Cousin, and their compeers.
George P. Bradford was a thorough classical scholar. Charles A.
Dana, then fresh from Harvard, was an enthusiast for German
literature, and successful in imparting both knowledge and enthusiasm to his pupils. There were classes in almost everything
that any one cared to study. French and music, as we learn
from one of Isaac's letters home, were what he set himself to at
the first. The latter was taught by so accomplished a master as
John S. Dwight, who conducted weekly singing-schools for both
children and adults.

To what other studies Isaac may have applied himself we
hardly know. It will be noticed that Mr. George William Curtis,
in the kindly reminiscences which he permits us to embody in
this chapter, says that he does not remember him as "especially
studious." The remark tallies with the impression we have
gathered from the journal kept while he was there. His mind
was introverted. Philosophical questions, then as always, interested
him profoundly, but only in so far as they led to practical results.
It might be truer to say that philosophy was at no time more
than the handmaid of theology to him. At this period he was
in the thick of his struggle to attain certainty with regard to the
nature and extent of the Christian revelation, and what he sought
at Brook Farm was the leisure and quiet and opportunity for
solitude which could not be his at home. "Lead me into Thy
holy Church, which I now am seeking," he writes as the final
petition of the prayer with which the first bulky volume of his
diary opens. With the burden of that search upon him, it was
not possible for such a nature as his to plunge with the unreserve
which is the condition of success into any study which had no
direct reference to it. We find him complaining at frequent intervals that he cannot give his studies the attention they demand.

Nor were his labors as the community baker of long continuance. They left him too little time at his own disposal, and in a short time he became a full boarder, and occupied himself only as his inclinations directed.

It may occur to some of our readers to wonder why a man like Brownson, who was then fast nearing the certainty he afterwards attained, should have sent a youth like Isaac Hecker to Brook Farm. It must be remembered that Brownson's road to the Church was not so direct as that of his young disciple, nor so entirely free in all its stages from self-crippling considerations. As we shall presently see, by an abstract of one of his sermons, preached in the spring of 1843, which was made by Isaac Hecker at the time, Brownson thought it possible to hold all Catholic truth and yet defer entering the Church until she should so far abate her claims as to form a friendly alliance with orthodox Protestantism on terms not too distasteful to the latter. He was not yet willing to depart alone, and hoped by wait-ing to take others with him, and he was neither ready to renounce wholly his private views, nor to counsel such a step to young Hecker. He was in harmony, moreover, with the tolerant and liberal tendency which influenced the leading spirits at Brook Farm. Although he never became one of the community, he had sent his son Orestes there as a pupil, and was a frequent visitor himself. Their aims, as expressed in a passage which we subjoin from *The Dial* of January, 1842, were assuredly such as would approve themselves to persons who fully accepted what they believed to be the social teaching of our Lord, but who had not attained to any true conception of the Divine authority which clothes that teaching :

"Whoever is satisfied with society as it is ; whose sense of justice is not wounded by its common action, institutions, spirit of commerce, has no business with this community ; neither has any one who is willing to have other men (needing more time for intellectual cultivation than himself) give their best hours and strength to bodily labor to secure himself immunity therefrom. . . . Everything can be said of it, in a degree, which Christ said of His kingdom, and therefore it is believed that in some measure it does embody His idea. For its Gate of Entrance is strait and narrow. It is, literally, a pearl *hidden in a field.* Those only who are willing to lose their life for its sake shall find it. . Those who have not the faith that the princi-

ples of Christ's kingdom are applicable to this world, will smile
at it as a visionary attempt."

Brook Farm has an interest for Catholics because, in the
order of guileless nature, it was the preamble of that common
life which Isaac Hecker afterwards enjoyed in its supernatural
realization in the Church. It was a protest against that selfishness of the individual which is highly accentuated in a large
class of New-Englanders, and prodigiously developed in the
economical conditions of modern society. Against these Isaac
had revolted in New York; at Brook Farm he hoped to find
their remedy. And in fact the gentle reformers, as we may
call these West Roxbury adventurers into the unexplored
regions of the common life, were worthy of their task though
not equal to it. There is no doubt that in small numbers and
with a partial surrender of individual prerogatives, well-meaning
men and women may taste many of the good things and be
able to bear some of the hardships of the common life. But to
compass in permanent form its aspirations in this direction, as
in many others, nature is incompetent. The terrible if wonderful
success of Sparta is what can be attained, and tells at what cost.
The economy of the bee-hive, which kills or drives away its
superfluous members, and the polity of Sparta, which put the
cripples and the aged to death, are essential to permanent success in the venture of communism in the natural order. "Sweetness and light" are enjoyed by the few only at the sacrifice of
the unwholesome and burdensome members of the hive.

Brook Farm, however, was not conceived in any spirit of
cruelty or of contempt of the weaker members of humanity; the
very contrary was the case. Sin and feebleness were capable,
thought its founders, of elimination by the force of natural virtue.
The men and women who gathered there in its first years were
noble of their kind; and their kind, now much less frequently
met with, was the finest product of natural manhood. Of the
channels of information which reach us from Brook Farm, and
we believe we have had access to them all, none contains the
slightest evidence of sensuality, the least trace of the selfishness
of the world, or even any sign of the extravagances of spiritual
pride. There is, on the other hand, a full acknowledgment of
the ordinary failings of unpretentious good people. Nor do we
mean to say that they were purely in the natural order—who
can be said to be that? They were the descendants of the

baptized Puritans whose religious fervor had been for generations at white heat. They had, indeed, cut the root, but the
sap of Christian principle still lingered in the trunk and branches
and brought forth fruit which was supernatural, though destined
never to ripen.

Christ was the model of the Brook-Farmers, as He had
become that of Isaac Hecker. They did not know *Him* as well
as they knew His doctrine. They knew better what He said
than why He said it, and that defect obscured His meaning and
mystified their understandings. That all men were brethren was
the result of their study of humanity under what they conceived
to be His leadership ; that all labor is honorable, and entitled to
equal remuneration, was their solution of the social problem.
While any man was superfluously rich, they maintained, no man
should be miserably poor. They were reaching after what the
best spirits of the human race were then and now longing for,
and they succeeded as well as any can who employ only the
selvage of the Christian garment to protect themselves against
the rigors of nature. Saint-Simon was a far less worthy man than
George Ripley, but he failed no more signally. Frederic Ozanam, whose ambition was limited in its scope by his appreciation of both nature and the supernatural, succeeded in establishing a measure of true fraternity between rich and poor
throughout the Catholic world.

There can be no manner of doubt that although Father
Hecker in after life could good-naturedly smile at the singu-
larities of Brook Farm, what he saw and was taught there had
a strong and permanent effect on his character. It is little to
say that the influence was refining to him, for he was refined
by nature. But he gained what was to him a constant corrective
of any tendency to man-hatred in all its degrees, not needed by
himself, to be sure, but always needed in his dealing with others.
It gave to a naturally trustful disposition the vim and vigor of
an apostolate for a cheerful view of human nature. It was a
characteristic trait of his to expect good results from reliance
on human virtue, and his whole success as a persuader of men
was largely to be explained by the subtle flattery of this trustful attitude towards them. At Brook Farm the mind of Isaac
Hecker was eagerly looking for instruction. It failed to get even
a little clear light on the more perplexing problems of life, but
it got something better—the object-lesson of good men and

women struggling nobly and unselfishly for laudable ends. Brook Farm was an attempt to remove obstructions from the pathway of human progress, taking that word in the natural sense.

Even afterwards, when he had known human destiny in its perfect supernatural and natural forms, and when the means to compass it were in his possession and plainly competent for success, his memory reproduced the scenes and persons of Brook Farm in an atmosphere of affection and admiration, though not unmingled with amusement. He used not infrequently to quote words heard there, and cite examples of things done there, as lessons of wisdom not only for the philosopher but also for the ascetic. He was there equipped with the necessary external guarantee of his inner consciousness that man is good, because made so by his Creator—inclined indeed to evil, but yet a good being, even so inclined. Nothing is more necessary for one who is to be a teacher among a population whose Catholicity is of blood and family tradition as well as of grace, than to know that there is virtue, true and high in its own order, outside the visible pale of the Church. Especially is this necessary if Catholics in any age or country are to be fitted for a missionary vocation. That this is the vocation of the Church of his day was Isaac Hecker's passionate conviction. He was able to communicate this to Catholics of the old stock as well as to influence non-Catholics in favor of the Church ; perhaps even more so. More than anything else, indeed, Brook Farm taught him the defect of human nature on its highest plane ; but it taught him also the worthiness of the men and women of America of the apostle's toil and blood. The gentle natures whom he there knew and learned to love, their spirit of self-sacrifice for the common good, their minds at once innocent and cultivated, their devotion to their high ideal, the absence of meanness, coarseness, vulgarity, the sinking of private ambitions, the patience with the defects of others, their desire to establish the communism of at least intellectual gifts—all this and much more of the kind fixed his views and affections in a mould which eminently fitted him as a vessel of election for apostolic uses.

Before passing to the study of Isaac Hecker's own interior during the period of his residence at Brook Farm, it is our pleasant privilege to communicate to our readers the subjoined charming reminiscence of his personality at the time, from one who was his associate there :

" *West New Brighton, S. I.,* February 28, 1890.—DEAR SIR : I fear that my recollections of Father Hecker will be of little service to you, for they are very scant. But the impression of the young man whom I knew at Brook Farm is still vivid. It must have been in the year 1843 that he came to the Farm in West Roxbury, near Boston. He was a youth of twenty-three, of German aspect, and I think his face was somewhat seamed with small-pox. But his sweet and candid expression, his gentle and affectionate manner, were very winning. He had an air of singular refinement and self-reliance combined with a half-eager inquisitiveness, and upon becoming acquainted with him, I told him that he was Ernest the Seeker, which was the title of a story of mental unrest which William Henry Channing was then publishing in the *Dial.*

" Hecker, or, as I always called him and think of him, Isaac, had apparently come to Brook Farm because it was a result of the intellectual agitation of the time which had reached and touched him in New York. He had been bred a baker, he told me, and I remember with what satisfaction he said to me, ' I am sure of my livelihood because I can make good bread.' His powers in this way were most satisfactorily tested at the Farm, or, as it was generally called, ' the Community,' although it was in no other sense a community than an association of friendly workers in common. He was drawn to Brook Farm by the belief that its life would be at least agreeable to his convictions and tastes, and offer him the society of those who might answer some of his questions, even if they could not satisfy his longings.

" By what influences his mind was first affected by the moral movement known in New England as transcendentalism, I do not know. Probably he may have heard Mr. Emerson lecture in New York, or he may have read Brownson's *Charles Elwood,* which dealt with the questions that engaged his mind and conscience. But among the many interesting figures at Brook Farm I recall none more sincerely absorbed than Isaac Hecker in serious questions. The merely æsthetic aspects of its life, its gayety and social pleasures, he regarded good-naturedly, with the air of a spectator who tolerated rather than needed or enjoyed them. There was nothing ascetic or severe in him, but I have often thought since that his feeling was probably what he might have afterward described as a consciousness that he must be about his Father's business.

" I do not remember him as especially studious. Mr. Ripley had classes in German philosophy and metaphysics, in Kant and Spinoza, and Isaac used to look in, as he turned wherever he thought he might find answers to his questions. He went to hear Theodore Parker preach in the Unitarian Church in the neighboring village of West Roxbury. He went into Boston, about ten miles distant, to talk with Brownson, and to Concord to see Emerson. He entered into the working life at the Farm, but always, as it seemed to me, with the same reserve and attitude of observation. He was the dove floating in the air, not yet finding the spot on which his foot might rest.

"The impression that I gathered from my intercourse with him, which was boyishly intimate and affectionate, was that of all ' the apostles of the newness,' as they were gayly called, whose counsel he sought, Brownson was the most satisfactory to him. I thought then that this was due to the authority of Brownson's masterful tone, the definiteness of his views, the force of his 'understanding,' as the word was then philosophically used in distinction from the reason. Brownson's mental vigor and positiveness were very agreeable to a candid mind which was speculatively adrift and experimenting, and, as it seemed to me, which was more emotional than logical. Brownson, after his life of varied theological and controversial activity, was drawing toward the Catholic Church, and his virile force fascinated the more delicate and sensitive temper of the young man, and, I have always supposed, was the chief influence which at that time affected Hecker's views, although he did not then enter the Catholic Church.

"He was a general favorite at Brook Farm, always equable and playful, wholly simple and frank in manner. He talked readily and easily, but not controversially. His smile was singularly attractive and sympathetic, and the earnestness of which I have spoken gave him an unconscious personal dignity. His temperament was sanguine. The whole air of the youth was that of goodness. I do not think that the impression made by him forecast his career, or, in any degree, the leadership which he afterwards held in his Church. But everybody who knew him at that time must recall his charming amiability.

"I think that he did not remain at Brook Farm for a whole year, and when later he went to Belgium to study theology at the seminary of Mons he wrote me many letters, which I am sorry to say have disappeared. I remember that he labored with friendly zeal to draw me to his Church, and at his request I read the life and some writing of St. Alphonse of Liguori. Gradually our correspondence declined when I was in Europe, and was never resumed ; nor do I remember seeing him again more than once, many years ago. There was still in the clerical figure, which was very strange to me, the old sweetness of smile and address ; there was some talk of the idyllic days, some warm words of hearty good will, but our interests were very different, and, parting, we went our separate ways. For a generation we lived in the same city, yet we never met. But I do not lose the bright recollection of Ernest the Seeker, nor forget the frank, ardent, generous, manly youth, Isaac Hecker.

"Very truly yours,
"GEORGE WILLIAM CURTIS."

CHAPTER VI.

THE private journals from which we are about to quote so largely were an unhoped-for addition to the stock of materials available for Father Hecker's biography. Until after his death not even their existence, still less the nature of their contents, was suspected. With the exception of two important documents, one written while he was in Belgium, in obedience to the requirements of his director; the other in Rome, for the consideration of the four venerable religious whose advice he sought before founding his community, no records of his interior life have been discovered which are at all comparable in fulness to those made during the eighteen months which preceded his admission to the Church. In his years of health and strength he lived and worked for others; and in those weary ones of illness which followed them, he thought and wrote and suffered, but apparently without making any deliberate notes of his deeper personal experience.

On those of our readers whose acquaintance with Father Hecker dates, as our own does, from his intensely active and laborious prime, these revelations of the period when he was being passively wrought upon and shaped for his work by the hand of God, may produce an effect not unlike that we have been conscious of in studying the greater mass from which our extracts are taken. They will, perhaps, be struck, in the first place, by the unexpectedly strong witness they bear to the wholly interior and mystical experience of the man. They testify, moreover, to the real and objective character of that leading which he was constrained to follow; and not only that. They do so in a way which furnishes a convincing reply to a very plausible doubt as to whether the narrow and uncongenial surroundings of his early life might not, by themselves, be sufficient to explain the discontent of a poetic and aspiring nature such as his.

He was at Brook Farm when that community was at its pleasantest. The shadow of care and the premonition of failure were, indeed, already looming up before those who bore the chief responsibilities of the undertaking, but the group by virtue of whose presence it became famous had hardly begun

to dwindle. And besides those whose names have since become
well known, there were others, young, gay, intelligent, and well
bred, acquaintance and familiarity with whom were in many ways
attractive to a susceptible youth like Isaac Hecker. What impression he made upon the circle he entered, how cordially he
was received and held in high esteem, our readers already
know. And if he gave pleasure, he received it also. At first
the new circumstances were a little strange and embarrassing to
him. After a fortnight, or thereabouts, we find him noting that
he is "not one of their spirits. They say 'Mr. Hecker' in
a tone they do not use in speaking to each other." But the
strangeness soon wore off, and he yielded to the influence of the
place with a wholeness which would have been entire but for
the stronger drawing which never let him free.

On this point, too, the witness of the journal is peremptory.
So it is as to the unity and consistence of his interior experiences from first to last. Child, and boy, and man, there was
always the same ardent sincerity of purpose in him, the same
docility to the Voice that spoke within, the same attitude toward "the life that now is" which Mr. Curtis, in the letter
given in the preceding chapter, has described, with so fine an
insight, as one of reserve and observation. "He was the dove
floating in the air, not yet finding the spot on which his foot
might rest," writes Mr. Curtis of Isaac Hecker at that period
of his youth when his surroundings and companions were for
the first time, and very possibly for the last, wholly congenial
to his natural inclinations. And again: "There was nothing
ascetic or severe in him; but I have often thought since that
his feeling was probably what he might have afterward described as a consciousness that he must be about his Father's
business."

These words are significant testimony to the nobility of the
impression made on others by Father Hecker's personality in
early manhood. Even if our only addition to such scanty
knowledge of his life at Brook Farm as could be gathered from
his own conversations in later years were this happily-touched
sketch, it could hardly be more interesting than it is. But, fortunately, it does not stand alone. Its fine recognition of the lofty
purity of his nature is everywhere borne out by the unpremedi-
tated and candid self-revelations of the diary. Their characteristic trait is everywhere aspiration—a sense of joy in elevation

above the earthly, or a sense of depression because the earthly
weighs him down. Then come eager glances of inquiry in
every direction for the satisfaction of his aspirations, little by little narrowing down to the Catholic Church, wherein the dove of
Mr. Curtis's image was finally to rest his foot for ever. And in
all this he scarcely at all mentions a dread of the Divine wrath
as a motive for his flight. It is not out of the city of destruction,
but toward the celestial city that he goes. He is drawn by
what he wants, not hounded by what he fears. Always there is
the reaching out of a strong nature toward what it lacks—a
material for its strength to work on, a craving for rational joy,
coupled with an ever-increasing conviction that nature cannot
give him such a boon. Men who knew Father Hecker only in
his royal maturity, sometimes cavilled at his words of emphatic
faith in guileless nature; but they had only to know him a
little better to learn his appreciation of the supernatural order,
and his recognition of its absolute and exclusive competency to
satisfy nature's highest aspirations. Reading these early journals,
we have constantly recalled the later days when he so often,
and sometimes continually, repeated, "Religion is a boon!" No
one could know that better than he who had so deeply felt
the want it satisfies.

The diary was begun in the middle of April, 1843, when
Isaac had just returned to Brook Farm after a fortnight spent at
home. It opens with a prayer for light and direction, which is
its dedication to the uses not only of an earnest but a religious
seeker. He addresses himself directly to God as Father, not
making either appeal or reference to our Lord. But there is in
it an invocation to those "that are in heaven to intercede and
plead" for him, which recalls the fact, so often mentioned by
him, that it was the teaching of the Catechism of the Council
of Trent on the Communion of Saints which cleared away his
final clouds and brought him directly to the Church. There is
a note, too, among his later papers, in which, speaking of the
phenomena of modern spiritualism, he says that the same longing for an assurance of personal immortality which leads so
many into that maze of mingled truth and error, had a great
share in disposing his mind to accept the authoritative doctrine
of the Church, which here as elsewhere answered fully the
deepest longings of his soul.

We shall not attempt to follow the chronological order of

the journal with exactness, but in making our extracts shall pursue the order of topics rather than of time. By the middle of April the question of the Church had presented itself so unmistakably to Isaac Hecker, as the necessary preliminary to further progress—to be settled in one way or another, either set definitely aside as unessential or else accepted as the adequate solution of man's problems, that his struggles for and against it recur with especial frequency. Faber has said somewhere that the Church is the touchstone of rational humanity, and that probably no adult passes out of life without having once, at least, been brought squarely face to face with it and made to understand and shoulder the tremendous responsibility which its claims impose. There would be no need of a touchstone if there were no alloy in human nature, no feebleness in man's will, no darkness in his understanding. Were that the condition of humanity, the call to the supernatural order would be simply the summons to come up higher, its symbol a beacon torch upon the heights. As it is, the path may be mistaken. He whose feet have been set in it from birth by Christian training may wilfully forsake it. He whose heart is pure and whose aspirations noble, may be so surrounded by the mists of inherited error and misapprehension that the light of truth fails to penetrate them when it first dawns. The road is always strait which leads any son of Adam to supernal joy in conscious union with his Creator, even when his will is good and his desire unfeigned.

We shall find, therefore, that Isaac Hecker's struggles were many and painful before he fully recognized and attained the necessary means to the end he craved. They were characteristic also. He was looking for the satisfaction of his rational aspirations rather than for the solution of historical problems, although his mind was too clear not to see that the two are inextricably bound up together. But inasmuch as at the period of which we are writing, which was that of the Oxford Tracts, controversy turned mainly on questions of historical continuity and of Divine warrant in the external revelation of holy Scripture, it follows that he, and such as he, must have taken a lonely and unfrequented road towards the truth. Every time he looked at the Church he was greeted with the spectacle of unity and uniformity, of discipline and order. These are elements which always have been, and probably always will be, most attractive to the

classes called educated, to men seeking for external notes of
truth, flying from disorder, fearful of rebellion. But to Isaac
Hecker, the only external note which deeply attracted him was
that of universal brotherhood. If he were to bow his knee with
joy to Jesus Christ, it would be because all, in heaven and earth
or hell, should one day bend in union with him.

It takes an intimate knowledge of Catholicity to perceive the
interior transformation of humanity by its supernatural aids. On
the one hand, the influence of Isaac Hecker's Brook Farm surroundings was to persuade him to confide wholly in nature, which
there was very nearly at its unaided best. On the other hand, the
treasures of Catholicity for the inner life were hidden from him.
Religion, in his conception of it—in the true conception of it—
must be the binding of all things together, natural and supernatural. Hence we find him at times complaining that the
Church is not sufficient for *his wants.* If it were not personal
in its adaptation to him, it was little that it should be historical this, hierarchical that, or biblical the other. It must be his
primarily, because he cannot live a rational and pure life without it. An ordinarily decorous life, if you will; free from lust
or passion, and without gross unreason, but nevertheless tame, un-
progressive, dry and unproductive, without any absolute certainty
except that of the helplessness of man. Such a life seemed to
him hardly more than a synonym for death. "The fact is," as
he writes on a page now lying before us, "I want to live every
moment. I want something positive, living, nourishing. I negative only by affirming."

The earliest entry in this diary has been already quoted in
the first chapter of the present biography. On its second page
occurs the following account of his impressions while in church
on Easter Sunday :

"*Monday, April* 17, 1843.—Yesterday I went to the Catholic
church at West Roxbury. It was Easter Sunday. The services
were, to me, very impressively affecting. The altar-piece represented Christ's rising from the tomb, and this was the subject-
matter of the priest's sermon. In the midst of it he turned and
pointed to the painting, with a few touching words. All eyes
followed his, which made his remarks doubly affecting. How
inspiring it must be to the priest, when he is preaching, to see
around him the Saviour, and the goodly company of martyrs,
saints, and fathers! There may be objections to having paintings

and sculptures in churches, but I confess that I never enter a
place where there is either but I feel an awe, an invisible influence, which strikes me mute. I would sit in silence, covering
my head. A sanctified atmosphere seems to fill the place and to
penetrate my soul when I enter, as if I were in a holy temple.
'Thou standest in a holy place,' I would say. A loud word,
a heavy footstep, makes me shudder, as if an infidel were dese-
crating the place. I stand speechless, in a magical atmosphere
that wraps my whole being, scarcely daring to lift my eyes. A
perfect stillness comes over my soul; it seems to be soaring on
the bosom of clouds."

"*Tuesday, April* 18.—I confess that either the Church is not
sufficient for my wants or I have not seen it in its glory. I
hope it may be the latter. I do not want to say it, but I
must own that it fills me no more. I contemplate it, I look at
it, I *comprehend* it. It does not lead me to aspire. I feel that
either it has nothing to give, or that what it has is not that
for which my soul is aching I know it can be said. in reply
that I cannot know what the Church has until I am in communion with it ; that it satisfies natures greater than mine ; that
it is the true life of the world; that there is no true spirituality
outside of it, and that before I can judge it rightly my life
must be equal to it in purity and elevation. Much more might
be said. But, after all, what is it ? The Catholic shows up the
Anglican ; the Anglican retorts with an accusation of corruption,
and even a want of purity ; the Protestant, the Presbyterian,
claim their own mission at the expense of consistency and good
logic. . . .

"The whole fact, I suppose, is that if there is anything in
Succession, Tradition, Infallibility, Church organism and form, it is
in the Catholic Church, and our business will be to stop this
controversy and call an Ecumenical Council which shall settle
these matters according to the Bible, Tradition, and the light of
the Church."

There is a touch of unconscious humor in the final paragraph which clamored for quotation. But it was plainly written
in profound earnest.

"*Thursday, April* 20.—My soul is disquieted, my heart aches.
. . Tears flow from my eyes involuntarily. My soul is
grieved—for what ? Yesterday, as I was praying, the thought
flashed across my mind, Where is God ? Is He not here ? Why

prayest thou as if He were at a great distance from thee ? Think
of it. Where canst thou place Him—in what locality ? Is He
not here in thy midst ? Is His presence not nearest of all to
thee ? Oh, think of it ! God is here. . . .

"Am I impious to say that the language used in Scripture
for Christ's expresses the thoughts of my soul ? Oh, could we
but understand that the kingdom of heaven is always *at hand*
to the discerner, and that God calls upon all to ' Repent, for ye
shall not all disappear until it shall open. This generation shall
not pass away.'"

Then follows a page of philosophizing on time and eternity,
immensity and space, and "monads who may develop or fulfil
their destiny in other worlds than this," a reminiscence, perhaps,
of the lectures on such topics at which Mr. Curtis says Isaac
used to "look in," hoping to "find an answer to his questions."
Such speculations are a trait throughout the diary, though they
are everywhere subordinate to the practical ends which dominantly interest him. A day or two later comes a passage,
already given in a preceding chapter, in reference to certain
prophetic dreams which it has been given him to see realized.
And at once this follows :

"*April* 24, *Noon.*—The Catholic Church alone seems to satisfy
my wants, my faith, life, soul. These may be baseless fabrics,
chimeras dire, or what you please. I may be laboring under a
delusion. Yet my soul is Catholic, and that faith responds to my
soul in its religious aspirations and its longings. I have not
wished to make myself Catholic, but that answers on all sides
to the wants of my soul. It is so rich, so full. One is in
harmony all over—in unison with heaven, with the present,
living in the natural body, and the past, who have changed.
There is a solidarity between them through the Church. I do
not feel controversial. My soul is filled."

From this point he speedily recedes. By the next day he is
"lost almost in the flesh"; "fallen into an identity with my
body," and notes that for some time he has "done little in study,
but feel that I have lived very much." What hinders him
he supposes to be "contemplating any certain amount of study
which I ought to accomplish—looking to it as an end. Why
should I not be satisfied when I am living, growing? Did
Christ and His apostles study languages ? I have the life—is
not that the end ? "

"*April* 28.—What shall I say? Am I wrong? Should I submit and give myself up to that which does not engage my whole being? To me the Church is not the great object of life. I am now out of it in the common meaning. I am not subject to its ordinances. Is it not best for me to accept my own nature rather than attempt to mould it as though it were an object? Is not our own existence more than this existence in the world?

"I read this morning an extract from Heine upon Schelling which affected me more than anything I have read for six months. The Church, says Schelling in substance, was first Petrine, then Pauline, and must be love-embracing, John-like. Peter, Catholicism; Paul, Protestantism; John, what is to be. The statement struck me and responded to my own dim intuitions. Catholicism is solidarity; Protestantism is individuality. What we want, and are tending to, is what shall unite them both, as John's spirit does—and that in each individual. We want neither the authority of History nor of the Individual; neither Infallibility nor Reason by itself, but both combined in Life. Neither Precedent nor Opinion, but Being—neither a written nor a preached Gospel, but a living one. . . .

"It is only through Christ we can see the love, goodness, and wisdom of God. He is to us what the telescope is to the astronomer, with this difference: He so exalts and purifies us that our subject becomes the power to see. The telescope is a medium through which the boundaries of our vision are enlarged, but it is passive. Christ is an active Mediator who begets us if we will, and gives us power to see by becoming one with Him."

"*May* 3.—We all look upon this world as suits our moods, assimilating only such food as suits our dispositions—and no doubt there is sufficient variety to suit all. . . . Every personality individualizes the world to himself, not subjectively but truly objectively. . . . Every individual ought, perhaps, to be satisfied with his own character. For it is an important truth of Fourier's that attractions are in proportion to destinies. Fear in proportion to hope, pain in proportion to pleasure, strength in proportion to destiny, etc. But it is mysterious that we know all this. 'Man has become as one of us.' We are all dead.

"Ah, mystic! dost thou show thyself in this shape? But now, being dead, shall we receive life and immortality (for I imagine immortality the solidarity of life—*i. e.*, the union of the two lives, here and heaven) through Jesus Christ, the Son of the living God, and so lose 'the knowledge of good and evil.' 'For as in Adam all died, so shall ye all be made alive through Jesus Christ.' The effect of the fall was literally the knowledge of good and evil. God knows no evil, and when we become one with Him, through the Mediator, we shall regain our previous state. Knowledge is the effect of sin, and is perhaps destined to correct itself. Consciousness and knowledge go together. Spontaneity and life are one. Knowledge is no gain, for it gives nothing. I can only know what has been given through spontaneity. Spontaneity is unity, one; knowledge is division of being. If Adam had not been separated he would doubtless not have sinned. 'The woman that Thou gavest me said unto me, Eat, and I did eat.' Still, through the seed of the woman, which will be the union restored, is the serpent to be bruised."

"*May* 4.—The real effect of the theory of the Church is to isolate men from the outward world, withdraw them from its enjoyments, and make them live a life of sacrifice of the passions. This is one statement. Another would be this: All these things can and should be enjoyed, but in a higher, purer, more exalted state of being than is the present ordinary condition of our minds. The only opposition to them arises when the soul becomes sensual, falls into their arms, and becomes lost to higher and more spiritual objects. . . .

"All is dark before me, impenetrable darkness. I appear to live in the centre. Nothing seems to take hold of my soul, or else it seeks nothing. Where it is I know not. I meet with no one else around me. I would that I could feel that some one lived in the same world that I now do. Something cloudy separates us. I cannot speak from my real being to others. There is no mutual recognition. When I speak, it is as if a burden accumulated round me. I long to throw it off, but I cannot utter my thoughts and feelings in their presence; if I do, they return to me unrecognized. Shall I ever meet with one the windows of whose soul will open simultaneously with mine?"

On the first Sunday of May Isaac went into Boston to hear Brownson preach, and a day or two later made the subjoined shrewd comments on the sermon in a letter to his mother:

"*May* 9, '43.—His intention is to preach the Catholic doctrine and administer the Sacraments. How many of them, I suppose, depends on circumstances. He justifies himself on the ground that he that is not against us is for us, and that in times of exigency, and in extraordinary cases, we may do what we could not be excused for doing otherwise. And he thinks by proclaiming the Catholic faith and repudiating the attempt to build up a Church, that in time the Protestant world will become Catholic in its dispositions, so that a unity will be made without submission or sacrifice. Under present circumstances it would be impossible, even if the Protestant churches should be willing to unite with the Catholic, that the Catholic could even supply priests for forty millions of Protestants, the Protestant priests being most of them married, etc.

"I confess the sermon was wholly unsatisfactory to me, uncatholic in its premises, and many of his arguments and facts chimerical and illusive. If you grant that the Roman Catholic Church is the true Church, there is, to my thought, no stopping-place short of its bosom. Or even if it is the nearest to the truth, you are under obligations to join it. How any one can believe in either one of those propositions, as O. A. B. does, without becoming a Catholic in fact, I cannot conceive. This special pleading of exceptions, the necessity of the case, and improbable suppositions, springs more, I think, from the position of the individual than from the importance or truth of the arguments made use of. Therefore I think he will give up in time the ground upon which he now supports his course—not the object but his position. . . . I have bought a few Catholic books in Boston which treat upon the Anglican claims to Catholicity, and I think I can say, so far, I never shall join a Protestant Church—while I am not positive on the positive side, nor even in any way as yet decided."

CHAPTER VII.

STRUGGLES.

THE citations thus far made from Isaac Hecker's youthful diary, although penned at Brook Farm, bear few traces of that fact. They might have been written in a desert for all evidence they give of any special influence produced upon him by personal contact with others. It is not until the middle of May, 1843, that he begins to make any reference to his actual surroundings.

Before following him into these more intimate self-confidences, and especially before giving in his own words an account of that peculiar occurrence which so permanently affected his future, some preliminary remarks seem necessary.

It has been said already, in an earlier chapter of this biography, that but for some special intervention of Divine Providence, it is more than probable that Isaac Hecker would have led the ordinary life of men in the world, continuing, indeed, to cherish a high ideal of the duties of the citizen of a free country, but pursuing it along well-beaten ways. There is no doubt that, unless some such event as he has narrated, or some influence equivalent to it in effect, had supernaturally drawn him away, he would of his own volition have sought what he was repeatedly advised to seek by his most attached friends, a congenial union in wedlock. He was naturally susceptible, and his attachments were not only firm, but often seemed obstinate. Of celibacy he had, up to this time, no other idea than such as the common run of non-Catholics possess. At home, indeed, when afterwards pressed to seek a wife, he had answered, truly enough, though holding fast to his secret, that he " had no thought of marrying and felt an aversion to company for such an end." And again he writes to his mother, anxious and troubled for his future, that the circle which surrounded him in New York oppressed and contracted him, and abridged his liberty. There was no one in it who " increased his life."

But at Brook Farm he met some one, as is revealed by his diary and correspondence, who deeply attracted him, and who might have attracted him as far as marriage had he not already received the Holy Spirit's prevenient grace of virginity. That is to say, he found " a being," to use his impersonal term, whose name and identity he is careful to veil, awkwardly enough at times with misleading pronouns, whose charm was so great as to win from him what would have been, in his normal state, a marital affection. But he was no longer normal. Although still beyond the visible pale of that garden of elect souls, God's holy Church, he was already transformed by the quickening grace which "reaches from end to end mightily and orders all things sweetly." Our next quotations afford explicit proof on this point:

"*Tuesday, May* 16.—Life appears to be a perpetual struggle between the heavenly and the worldly.

"Here at Brook Farm I become acquainted with persons who have moved in a higher rank in society than I—persons of good education and fine talents; all of which has an improving influence on me. And I meet with those to whom I can speak, and feel that, to a great degree, I am understood and responded to. In New York I am alone in the midst of people. I am not in any internal sense *en rapport* with them.

"I suppose the reason why I do not, in my present state, feel disposed to connect myself with any being, and would rather avoid a person whom I was conscious I might or could love, is that I feel my life to be in a rapid progress, and that no step now would be a permanent one. I am afraid the choice I would have made some time since (*if there had not been something deeply secret in my being which prevented me*) would now be very unsatisfactory. I feel conscious there could not have been an equal and mutual advance, because the natures of some are not capable of much growth. And I mistrust whether there would not have been an inequality, hence disharmony and un-happiness.

"To be required to accept your past is most unpleasant. Perhaps the society with which I was surrounded did not afford a being that unified with mine own. And I have faith that there are spiritual laws beneath all this outward framework of sight and sense, which will, if rightly believed in and trusted, lead to the goal of eternal life, harmony of being, and union with God. So I accept my being led here. Am I superstitious or egoistic in believing this? This is, no doubt, disputed territory. Have we any objective rule to compare our faith with which would give us the measure of our superstition? How much of to-day would have seemed miraculous or superstitious to the past ? I confess I have no rule or measure to judge the faith of any man.

" The past is always the state of infancy. The present is an eternal youth, aspiring after manhood ; hoping wistfully, intensely desiring, listfully listening, dimly seeing the bright star of hope in the future, beckoning him to move rapidly on, while his strong heart beats with enthusiasm and glowing joy. The past is dead. Wish me not the dead from the grave, for that would be death re-enacted. . . .

" Oh, were our wishes in harmony with heaven, how changed would be the scenes of our life ! . . . This accordance would be music which only the angels now hear—too delicate for beings such as we are at present. List ! hast thou not heard in some bright moment a strain from heaven's angelic choirs ? Oh, yes ! In our sleep the angels have whispered such rich music, and the soul being then passive, we can hear. And the pleasure does not leave us when passion and thought take their accustomed course.

" O man ! were thy soul more pure, what a world would open to thy inner senses ! There would be no moment of thy existence but would be filled with the music of love. The prophet said : ' In that day my eyes were opened.' And behold what he saw ! He *saw* it. Could we but hear ! The word of the Lord is ever speaking—alas ! where is one that can hear ? Where are our Isaiahs, our Ezekiels, our Jeremiahs ? Oh ! thou shrunken-visaged, black, hollow-eyed doubt ! hast thou passed like a cloud over men's souls, making them blind, deaf, and dumb ? Ah, ha ! dost thou shudder ? I chant thy requiem, and prophets, poets, and seers shall rise again ! I see them coming. Great heaven ! Earth shall be again a paradise, and God converse with men ! "

The next entry is undated, but it was probably made on the last day of May. It has served to fix the proximate time of the illness and disquiet which led to his first withdrawal from business and home.

" *Wednesday.*—About ten months ago—perhaps only seven or eight—I saw (I cannot say I dreamed ; it was quite different from dreaming ; I was seated on the side of my bed) a beautiful, angelic being, and myself standing alongside of her, feeling a most heavenly pure joy. It was as if our bodies were luminous and gave forth a moon-like light which sprung from the joy we experienced. I felt as if we had always lived together, and that our motions, actions, feelings, and thoughts came from one centre. When I looked towards her I saw no bold outline of form, but an angelic something I cannot describe, though in angelic shape and image. *It was this picture that has left such an indelible impression on my mind.* For some time afterward I continued to feel the same influence, and do now so often that the actual around me has lost its hold. *In my state previous to this vision I should have been married ere this, for there are those I have since seen who would have met the demands of my mind.* But now this vision continually hovers over me and prevents me, by its beauty, from accepting any one else; for I am charmed by its influence, and conscious that, should I accept any other, I should lose the life which would be the only one wherein I could say I live."

Those of our readers who are either versed in mystical theology or who have any wide knowledge of the lives of the Church's more interior saints, with neither of which Isaac Hecker had at this time any acquaintance, will be apt to recall here St. Francis of Assisi and his bride, the Lady Poverty, the similar occurrences related by Henry Suso of himself, and the mystic espousals of St. Catharine. We have in this relation not only the plainly avowed reason why he accepted the celibate life, even before entering the Church or arriving at any clear understanding of his duty to do so, but we have something more. Not yet certain of his own vocation, the dream of a virginal apostolate, including the two sexes, had already absorbed his yearnings, never again to be forgotten. Neither priest nor Catholic, save in the as yet unrevealed ordinance of God, he was no longer free to invite any woman to marriage, no matter how deeply he might be sensible of her feminine attraction. The union of souls? Yes; for uses worthy of souls. The union of bodies? No; that would only clip his wings and narrow his horizon. Thenceforward the test of true kinship with him could only be a kindred aspiration after union in liberty from merely natural trammels, in order to tend more surely to a supernatural end.

This may seem to some a strange beginning to a life so simply and entirely set apart from the active, or, at least, public union of the sexes in apostolic labors. Strange or not, the reader will see it to be more true as this biography proceeds, and its writer is not conscious of any reluctance to make it known. Such an integral supernatural mission to men was what he ever after desired and sought to establish, though he only attained success on the male side. We cannot deny that this diary, surprising to us in many ways, was most so in this particular, although in this particular we found the explanation of many words spoken by Father Hecker in his maturity and old age, words the most sober and the most decided we ever heard from him. He never for an hour left out of view the need of women for any great work of religion, though he doubtless made very sure of his auditor before unveiling his whole thought. He never made so much as a serious attempt to incorporate women with his work, but he never ceased to look around and to plan with a view to doing so. Among the personal memoranda already mentioned are found evidences of this so direct, and corroborated by such recent facts, that they cannot be used until the lapse of time shall have made an extension of this life as well possible as necessary.

"*June* 1.—One cannot live a spiritual life in the world because it requires so much labor to supply food and clothing that what is inward and eternal has to be given up for the material and life in time. If one has to sustain himself at Brook Farm without other means to aid him, he must employ his strength to that degree that he has no time for the culture of the spiritual. I cannot remain and support myself without becoming subject to the same conditions as existed at home. I cannot expect them to be willing to lessen their present expenses much for the sake of gaining time for spiritual culture; nor do I see how I can at home live with my relatives and have the time which I require. I see no way but to give up the taste for fine clothing and variety in food. I would prefer the life of the monastery to that of the external world. The advantages for my being are greater. The harmony of the two is the full and perfect existence; but the spiritual should always be preserved at the expense of the other, which is contrary to the tendency of the world, and perhaps even to that of this place. I would prefer going hungry in body than in soul. I am speaking against neither, for I believe in the fulness of life, in amply supplying all its wants; but the kingdom of God is more to me than this world. I would be Plato in love, Zeno in self-strength, and Epicurus in æsthetics; but if I have to sacrifice either, let Epicurus go."

"*June* 12.—At times I have an impulse to cry out, 'What wouldst Thou have me to do?' I would shout up into the empty vault of heaven : 'Ah, why plaguest Thou me so ? What shall I do ? Give me an answer unless Thou wilt have me consumed by inward fire, drying up the living liquid of life. Wouldst Thou have me to give up all ? I have. I have no dreams to realize. I want nothing, have nothing, and am willing to die in any way. What ties I have are few, and can be cut with a groan.'"

"*Monday, June* 26.—Solomon said, after he had tasted all the joys of the world, 'Vanity of vanities, all is vanity.' I, my friend, who have scarcely tasted any of the pleasures of the world, would say with Solomon, 'All is vanity.' I see nothing in which I can work. All are vanities, shadows ; beneath all there is nothing. Great God ! what is all this for ? Why torment and pain me so ? Why is all this action a profanity to me ? And even holiness, what is it ?

"Oh ! I am dumb; my soul is inarticulate. There is that in me which I would pour out. Oh ! why is it that the noblest actions of humanity speak not to my soul ? All life is inadequate—but not in the sense of the world. I would joyfully be silent, obscure, dead to all the world, if this alone which is in me had life. I ask not for name, riches, external conditions of delight or splendor. No; the meanest of all would be heaven to me, if this inward impulse had action, lived itself out. But no; I am imprisoned in spirit. What imprisons ? What *is* imprisoned ? Who can tell ?

"You say, good adviser, 'You must accept things as they are—be content to be ; have faith in God ; do that work which your hands find to do.' Good ; but it is taken for granted we know what things are—which is the question. 'Be content to be.' Be what ? 'Have faith in God.' Yes. 'Work ?' Yes ; but how ? Like others. But this is not work to me; it is death ; nay, worse—it is sin ; hence, damnation—and I am not ready to go to hell yet. *Your* work gives *me* no activity; and to starve, if I must, is better than to do the profane, the sacrilegious labor you place before me. I want God's living work to do. My labor must be a sermon, every motion of my body a word, every act a sentence. My work must be devotional. I must feel that I am worshipping. It must be music, love, prayer. My field must be the kingdom of God. Christ must reign in all. It must be Christ doing in me, and *not me*. My life must be poetical, divine. Head, heart, and hands must be a trinity in unity; they must tone in one accord. My work must be work of inspiration and aspiration. My heart cannot be in heaven when my head and hands are in hell. I must feel that I am building up Christ's kingdom in all that I do. To give Christ room for action in my heart, soul, and body is my desire, my aim, purpose, being. . . .

"It is not he who goes to church, says his prayers, sings psalms, says 'Lord, Lord,' who is in God and establishing His kingdom. No; it is he who is doing it. The earth is to be His kingdom, and your prayers must be deeds, your actions music ascending to heaven. The Church must be the kingdom of God in its fulness. . . .

"Are we Christians if we act not in the spirit in which Christ acted? Shall we say: 'What shall we do?' Follow the spirit of Christ which is in you. 'Unless ye are reprobates, ye have it in you.' 'Be ye faithful, as I am,' said Jesus. 'Love one another as I have loved you.' Take up your cross and follow Him. Leave all, if the Spirit leads you to leave all. Do whatever it commands you. There will be no lack of action. Care not for the world; give up wealth, friends, those that you love, the opinions of all. Be willing to be despised, spit upon, crucified. Be silent, and let your silence speak for you."

It is plain that what Isaac Hecker is here condemning is the life of the world, wholly ordinary in its aims and motives. It is not to be understood as a condemnation of the common lot of men, or of that life in itself. It was only as he saw it over against his own vocation to something higher that it became repulsive, nay guilty *to him*. Nor was he even yet so settled in his view of the contrasted worth of the two careers between which he had to choose, as to be quite free from painful struggles. In the entry made on the day preceding this outburst, he once more recurs to the subject of marriage:

"*Monday Evening, June 26.*—This evening the same advice that has been given me before, first by the doctor who attended me, next by my dearest friend, was given me again by a man who now resides here."

"*Tuesday Morning, June 27.*—Rather than follow this advice, I would die. I should be miserable all my life. Nay, death before this. These men appear to me as natural men, but not in the same life as mine. They are older, have more experience and more judgment than I, perhaps; but considering the point of view from which their judgment is formed, their advice does not appear to be the counsel for me. I never can, nor will, save my health or life by such means. If that is the only remedy, then unremedied must I remain.

"But the cause of my present state of mind is not what they suppose. It is deeper, higher, and, O God! Thou knowest what it is! Wilt Thou give me hope, strength, guidance?" . . .

"*Friday, June 29.*—Am I led by something higher to the life to which I am tending? Sometimes I think it is most proper for me to return home, accept things as they are, and live a life like others—as good, and as much better as possible. If I can find one with whom I think I can live happily, to accept such a one, and give up that which now leads me.

"My friends would say this is the prudent and rational course—but it appears this is not mine. That I am here is one evidence that it is not mine. A second is that I struggled against what led me here as much as lay in my power, until I became weak, sick, and confined to my bed. Farther than that I could not go.

"They tell me that if I were married it would not be so with me. I will not dispute this, although I do not believe it. But, my good friends, that is the difficulty. To marry is to me impossible. You tell me this is unnatural. Yes, my brethren, it may be unnatural, but how shall I be natural? Must I commit that which in my sight is a crime, which I feel would make me miserable and be death to my soul? 'But this is foolish and one-sided in you. You are wrong-minded. You will lose your health, your youthful joy, and the pleasure which God has, by human laws, designed you to enjoy. You should give up these thoughts and feelings of yours and be like those around you.'

"Yes, my friends, this advice I accept with love, knowing your kindness to me. But, alas! I feel that it comes from such a source that I cannot receive it."

"*July* 5.—My brother George has been here; he stayed three days. He told me he had often talked with my brother John about living a life higher, nobler, and more self-denying than he had done. It appears from his conversation that since I left home they have been impressed with a deeper and better spirit. To me it is of much interest to decide what I shall do. I have determined to make a visit to Fruitlands. To leave this place is to me a great sacrifice. I have been much refined in being here.

"To stay here—to purchase a place for myself—or to go home. These are questions about which I feel the want of some friend to consult with. I have no one to whom I can go for advice. If I wish to be self-denying, one would say at home is the best, the largest field for my activity. This may be true in one sense. But is it wise to go where there are the most difficulties to overcome? Would it not be better to plant the tree in the soil where it can grow most in every direction? At home, to be sure, if I have strength to succeed, I may, perhaps, do the most good, and it may be the widest sphere for me. But there are many difficulties which have such a direct influence on one to injure, to blight all high and noble sentiments, that I fear to encounter them, and I am not sure it is my place. Perhaps it would be best for me not to speculate on the future, but look to Him who is above for wise direction in all that concerns my life. Sacrifices must be made. I must expect and accept them in a meek, humble, and willing spirit."

CHAPTER VIII.

FRUITLANDS.

WHAT influenced Isaac Hecker to leave Brook Farm, a place so congenial in many ways to his natural dispositions, was, plainly enough, his tendency to seek a more ascetic and interior life than he could lead there. The step cost him much, but he had received all that the place and his companions could give him, and his departure was inevitable.

His next move in pursuit of his ideal took him to Fruitlands. This was a farm, situated near Harvard, in Worcester Co., Massachusetts, which had been bought by Mr. Charles Lane, an English admirer of Amos Bronson Alcott, with the hope of establishing on it a new community in consonance with the views and wishes of the latter. Perhaps Fruitlands could never, at any stage of its existence as a corporate home for Mr. Alcott's family and his scanty following of disciples, have been truly described as in running order, but when Isaac Hecker went there, on July 11, 1843, it was still in its incipiency. He had paid the Fruitlanders a brief visit toward the end of June, and thought that he saw in them evidences of "a deeper life." It speaks volumes for his native sagacity and keen eye for realities, that less than a fortnight's residence with Mr. Alcott should have sufficed to dispel this illusion.

Bronson Alcott seems to have been by nature what the French call a *poseur;* or, as one of his own not unkindly intimates has described him, "an innocent charlatan." Although not altogether empty, he was vain; full of talk which had what was most often a false air of profundity; unpractical and incapable in the ordinary affairs of life to a degree not adequately compensated for by such a grasp as he was able to get on the realities that underlie them; and with an imposing aspect which corresponded wonderfully well with his interior traits. That, in his prime, his persuasive accents and bland self-confidence, backed by the admiration felt and expressed for him by men such as Emerson, and some of the community at Brook Farm, should have induced an open-minded youth like Isaac Hecker to take him for a time at his own valuation, is not strange. The truth is, that it was one of Father Hecker's life-long traits to prove all things, that he might find the good and hold fast to it. There was an element of justice in his make-up which enabled him to suspend judgment upon any institution or person, however little they seemed to deserve such consideration, until he was in a condition to decide from his own investigations. We shall see, later on, how he tried all the principal forms of Protestantism before deciding upon Catholicity, strong as his tendency toward the Church had become. We have never known any other man who, without exhibiting obstinacy, could so steadfastly reserve his judgment on another's statement, especially if it were in the nature of a condemnation.

When Isaac Hecker first made his acquaintance, Mr. Alcott had but recently returned from England, whither he had gone on the invitation of James P. Greaves, a friend and fellow-laborer of the great Swiss educator, Pestalozzi. Mr. Alcott had gained a certain vogue at home as a lecturer, and also as the conductor of a singular school for young children. Among its many peculiarities was that of carrying "moral suasion" to such lengths, as a solitary means of discipline, that the master occasionally publicly submitted to the castigation earned by a refractory urchin, probably by way of reaching the latter's moral sense through shame or pity. This was, doubtless, rather interesting to the pupils, whether or not it was corrective. Mr. Alcott's peculiarities did not stop here, however, and Boston parents, when he began to publish the *Colloquies on the Gospels* which he held with their children, concluded, on the evidence thus furnished, that his thought was too "advanced" to make it prudent to trust them longer to his care. Miss Elizabeth P. Peabody, since so well known as an expositor of the Kindergarten system, had been his assistant. She wrote a *Record of Mr. Alcott's School* which attracted the attention of a small band of educational enthusiasts in England. They gave the name of "Alcott House" to a school of their own at Ham, near London, and hoped for great things from the personal advice and presence of the "Concord Plato." He was petted and fêted among them pretty nearly to the top of his bent; but his visit would have proved a more unalloyed success if the hard Scotch sense of Carlyle, to whom Emerson had recommended him, had not so quickly dubbed his vaunted depths deceptive shallows.

On his return he was accompanied by two Englishmen who seemed to be like-minded with himself, a Mr. H. G. Wright and Mr. Charles Lane, both of whom returned within a year or two to their own country, wiser and perhaps sadder men. Lane, at all events, who was a simple and candid soul for whom Isaac Hecker conceived a long-enduring friendship, sunk all his private means irrevocably in the futile attempt to establish Fruitlands on a solid basis. To use his own words in a letter now at our hand, though referring to another of Mr. Alcott's schemes, his little fortune was "buried in the same grave of flowery rhetoric in which so many other notions have been deposited."

Lying before us there is an epistle—Mr. Alcott's most ordinary written communications with his friends must have demanded that term in preference to anything less stately—in which he has described his own ideal of what life at Fruitlands ought to be. No directer way of conveying to our readers a notion of his peculiar faculty of seeming to say something of singular importance occurs to us, than that of giving it entire. Though found among Father Hecker's papers, it was not addressed to him but to one of his most-valued Brook Farm associates :

"*Concord, Mass., February* 15, 1843.—DEAR FRIEND : In reply to your letter of the 12th, I have to say that as until the snow leaves the ground clear, the Family cannot so much as look for a locality (which then may not readily be found), it seems premature to talk of the conditions on which any association may be formed.

" Nevertheless, as human progress is a universally interesting subject, I have much pleasure in communicating with you on the question of the general conditions most conducive to that end.

" I have no belief in associations of human beings for the purpose of making themselves happy by means of improved outward arrangements alone, as the fountains of happiness are within, and are opened to us as we are preharmonized or consociated with the Universal Spirit. This is the one condition needful for happy association amongst men. And this condition is attained by the surrender of all individual or selfish gratification—a complete willingness to be moulded by Divinity. This, as men now are, of course involves self-renunciation and retrenchment ; and in enumerating the hindrances which debar us from happiness, we shall be drawn to consider, in the first place, ourselves ; and to entertain practically the question, Are we prepared for the giving up all, and taking refuge in Love as an unfailing Providence ? A faith and reliance as large as this seems needful to insure us against disappointment. The entrance to Paradise is still through the strait gate and narrow way of self-denial. Eden's avenue is yet guarded by the fiery-sworded cherubim, and humility and charity are the credentials for admission. Unless well armed with valor and patience, we must continue in the old and much-trodden broad way, and take share of the penalties paid by all who walk thereon.

"The conditions for one are conditions for all. Hence there can be no parley with the tempter, no private pleas for self-indulgence, no leaning on the broken reed of circumstances.

"It is not for us to prescribe conditions; these are prescribed on our natures, our state of being—and the best we can do, if disqualified, is either to attain an amended character, or to relinquish all hopes of securing felicity.

"Our purposes, as far as we know them at present, are briefly these:

"First, to obtain the free use of a spot of land adequate by our own labor to our support; including, of course, a convenient plain house, and offices, wood-lot, garden, and orchard.

"Secondly, to live independently of foreign aids by being sufficiently elevated to procure all articles for subsistence in the productions of the spot, under a regimen of healthful labor and recreation; with benignity towards all creatures, human and inferior; with beauty and refinement in all economies; and the purest charity throughout our demeanor.

"Should this kind of life attract parties towards us—individuals of like aims and issues—that state of being itself determines the law of association; and the particular mode may be spoken of more definitely as individual cases may arise; but, in no case, could inferior ends compromise the principles laid down.

"Doubtless such a household, with our library, our services and manner of life, may attract young men and women, possibly also families with children, desirous of access to the channels and fountain of wisdom and purity; and we are not without hope that Providence will use us progressively for beneficial effects in the great work of human regeneration, and the restoration of the highest life on earth.

"With the humane wish that yourself and little ones may be led to confide in providential Love,

"I am, dear friend, very truly yours,
"A. BRONSON ALCOTT."

It must be admitted that there is something delightful in the *naïveté* of this undertaking to be "sufficiently elevated to live independently of foreign aids," after first getting "the *free use* of a spot of land, . . . including, *of course*, a convenient plain house, and offices, wood-lot, garden, and orchard." Establishments which would tolerably approximate to this description, and to the really essential needs of its prospective founder, have long existed in every civilized community. There are certain restrictions placed upon their inmates, however, and Mr. Alcott's desire was to make sure of his basis of earthly supplies, while left entirely free to persuade himself that he had arrived at an elevation which made him independent of them. Still, though "a charlatan," it must not be forgotten that he was "an innocent" one. He was plainly born great in that way, and had no need to achieve greatness in it. As Father Hecker said of him long afterwards, "Diogenes and his tub would have been Alcott's ideal if he had carried it out. But he never carried it out." Diogenes himself, it may be supposed, had his ideal included a family and an audience as well as a tub, might finally have come to hold that the finding of the latter was a mere detail, which could be entrusted indifferently to either of the two former or to both combined. Somebody once described Fruitlands as a place where Mr. Alcott looked benign and talked philosophy, while Mrs. Alcott and the children did the work. Still, to look benign is a good deal for a man to do persistently in an adverse world, indifferent for the most part to the charms of "divine philosophy," and Mr. Alcott persevered in that exercise until his latest day. "He was unquestionably one of those who like to sit upon a platform," wrote, at the time of his death, one who knew Alcott well, "and he may have liked to feel that his venerable aspect had the effect of a benediction." But with this mild criticism, censure of him is well-nigh exhausted. There was nothing of the Patriarch of Bleeding Heart Yard about him except that "venerable aspect," for which nature was responsible, and not he.

Fruitlands was the caricature of Brook Farm. Just as the fanatic is the caricature of the true reformer, so was Alcott the caricature of Ripley. This is not meant as disparaging either Alcott's sincerity or his intelligence, but to affirm that he lacked judgment, that he miscalculated means and ends, that he jumped from theory to practice without a moment's interval, preferred to be guided by instinct rather than by processes of reasoning, and deemed this to be the philosopher's way.

In the memoranda of private conversations with Father Hecker we find several references to Mr. Alcott. The first bears date February 4, 1882, and occurs in a conversation ranging over the whole of his experience between his first and second departures from home. We give it as it stands:

"Fruitlands was very different from Brook Farm—far more ascetic."

" You didn't like it ? "

" Yes; but they did not begin to satisfy me. I said to them : ' If you had the Eternal here, all right. I would be with you.' "

" Had they no notion of the hereafter ? "

" No ; nothing definite. Their idea was human perfection. They set out to demonstrate what man can do in the way of the supremacy of the spiritual over the animal. ' All right,' I said, ' I agree with you fully. I admire your asceticism; it is nothing new to me ; I have practised it a long time myself. If you can get the Everlasting out of my mind, I'm yours. But I know' (here Father Hecker thumped the table at his bedside) ' that I am going to live for ever.' "

" What did Alcott say when you left ? "

" He went to Lane and said, ' Well, Hecker has flunked out. He hadn't the courage to persevere. He's a coward.' But Lane said, ' No ; you're mistaken. Hecker's right. He wanted more than we had to give him.' "

Mr. Alcott's death in 1888 was the occasion of the reminiscences which follow :

" *March* 5, 1888.—Bronson Alcott dead ! I saw him coming from Rochester on the cars. I had been a Catholic missionary for I don't know how many years. We sat together. ' Father Hecker,' said he, ' why can't you make a Catholic of me ? ' ' Too much rust here,' said I, clapping him on the knee. He got very angry because I said that was the obstacle. I never saw him angry at any other time. He was too proud.

" But he was a great natural man. He was faithful to pure, natural conscience. His virtues came from that. He never had any virtue beyond what a good pagan has. He never aimed at anything more, nor claimed to. He maintained that to be all.

" I don't believe he ever prayed. Whom could he pray to ? Was not Bronson Alcott the greatest of all ? "

" Did he believe in God ? "

" Not the God that we know. He believed in the Bronson Alcott God. He was his own God."

" You say he was Emerson's master : what do you mean by that ? "

" He taught Emerson. He began life as a pedler. The Yankee pedler was Emerson's master. Whatever principles

Emerson had, Alcott gave him. And Emerson was a good pupil; he was faithful to his master to the end.

"When did I know him first? Hard to remember. He was the head of Fruitlands, as Ripley was of Brook Farm. They were entirely different men. Diogenes and his tub would have been Alcott's ideal if he had carried it out. But he never carried it out. Ripley's ideal would have been Epictetus. Ripley would have taken with him the good things of this life; Alcott would have rejected them all."

"How did he receive you at Fruitlands?"

"Very kindly, but from mixed and selfish motives. I suspected he wanted me because he thought I would bring money to the community. Lane was entirely unselfish.

"Alcott was a man of no great intellectual gifts or acquirements. His knowledge came chiefly from experience and instinct. He had an insinuating and persuasive way with him—he must have been an ideal pedler."

"What if he had been a Catholic, and thoroughly sanctified?"

"He could have been nothing but a hermit like those of the fourth century—he was naturally and constitutionally so odd. Emerson, Alcott, and Thoreau were three consecrated cranks: rather be crank than president. All the cranks look up to them."

Beside these later reminiscences we shall now place the contemporary record of his impressions made by Isaac Hecker while at Fruitlands. Our first extract, however, was written at Brook Farm, a few days before going thither:

"*July* 7, 1843.—I go to Mr. Alcott's next Tuesday, if nothing happens. I have had three pairs of coarse pants and a coat made for me. It is my intention to commence work as soon as I get there. I will gradually simplify my dress without making any sudden difference, although it would be easier to make a radical and thorough change at once than piece by piece. But this will be a lesson in patient perseverance to me. All our difficulties should be looked at in such a light as to improve and elevate our minds.

"I can hardly prevent myself from saying how much I shall miss the company of those whom I love and associate with here. But I must go. I am called with a stronger voice. This is a different trial from any I have ever had. I have had that of leaving kindred, but now I have that of leaving those whom I love from affinity. If I wished to live a life the most gratifying to me, and in agreeable company, I certainly would remain here. Here are refining amusements, cultivated persons—and one whom I have not spoken of, one who is too much to me to speak of, one who would leave all for me. Alas! him I must leave to go."

In this final sentence, as it now stands in the diary and as we have transcribed it, occurs one of those efforts of which we have spoken, to obliterate the traces of this early attachment. "Him" was originally written "her," but the *r* has been lengthened to an *m*, and the *e* dotted, both with a care which overshot their mark by an almost imperceptible hair's-breadth. If the nature of this attachment were not so evident from other sources, we should have left such passages unquoted; fearing lest they might be misunderstood. As it is, the light they cast seems to us to throw up into fuller proportions the kind and extent of the renunciations to which Isaac Hecker was called before he had arrived at any clear view of the end to which they tended.

"*Fruitlands, July* 12.—Last evening I arrived here. After tea I went out in the fields and raked hay for an hour in company with the persons here. We returned and had a conversation on Clothing. Some very fine things were said by Mr. Alcott and Mr. Lane. In most of their thoughts I coincide; they are the same which of late have much occupied my mind. Alcott said that to Emerson the world was a lecture-room, to Brownson a rostrum.

"This morning after breakfast a conversation was held on Friendship and its laws and conditions. Mr. Alcott placed Innocence first; Larned, Thoughtfulness; I, Seriousness; Lane, Fidelity.

"*July* 13.—This morning after breakfast there was held a conversation on The Highest Aim. Mr. Alcott said it was Integrity; I, Harmonic being; Lane, Progressive being; Larned, Annihilation of self; Bower, Repulsion of the evil in us. Then there was a confession of the obstacles which prevent us from attaining the highest aim. Mine was the doubt whether the light *is* light; not the want of will to follow, or the sight to see."

"*July* 17.—I cannot understand what it is that leads me, or what I am after. Being is incomprehensible.

"What shall I be led to? Is there a being whom I may marry and who would be the means of opening my eyes? Sometimes I think so—but it appears impossible. Why should others tell me that it is so, and will be so, in an unconscious way, as Larned did on Sunday last, and as others have before him? Will I be led home? It strikes me these people here, Alcott and Lane, will be a great deal to me. I do not know but they may be what I am looking for, or the answer to that in me which is asking.

"Can I say it? I believe it should be said. Here I cannot end. They are too near me; they do not awaken in me that sense of their high superiority which would keep me here to be bettered, to be elevated. They have much, very much. I desire Mr. Alcott's strength of self-denial, and the unselfishness of Mr. Lane in money matters. In both these they are far my superiors. I would be meek, humble, and sit at their feet that I might be as they are. They do not understand me, but if I am what my consciousness, my heart, lead me to feel—if I am not deceived—why then I can wait. Yes, patiently wait. Is not this the first time since I have been here that I have recovered myself? Do I not feel that I have something to receive here, to add to, to increase my highest life, which I have never felt anywhere else?

"Is this sufficient to keep me here? If I can prophesy, I must say no. I feel that it will not fill my capacity. O God! strengthen my resolution. Let me not waver, and continue my life. But I am sinful. Oh, forgive my sins! What shall I do, O Lord! that they may be blotted out? Lord, could I only blot them from my memory, nothing would be too great or too much."

"*July* 18.—I have thought of my family this afternoon, and the happiness and love with which I might return to them. To leave them, to give up the thought of living with them again—can I entertain that idea? Still, I cannot conceive how I can engage in business, share the practices, and indulge myself with the food and garmenture (*sic*) of our home and city. To return home, were it possible for me, would most probably not only stop my progress, but put me back.

"It is useless for me to speculate upon my future. Put

dependence on the spirit which leads me, be faithful to it; work, and leave results to God. If the question should be asked me, whether I would give up my kindred and business and follow out this spirit-life, or return and enjoy them both, I could not hesitate a moment, for they would not compare—there would be no room for choice. What I do I must do, for it is not I that do it; it is the spirit. What that spirit may be is a question I cannot answer. What it leads me to do will be the only evidence of its character. I feel as impersonal as a stranger to it. I ask, Who are you? Where are you going to take me? Why me? Why not some one else? I stand amazed, astonished to see myself. Alas! I cry, who am I and what does this mean? and I am lost in wonder."

"*Saturday, July* 21.—Yesterday, after supper, a conversation took place between Mr. Alcott, Mr. Lane, and myself; the subject was my position with regard to my family, my duty, and my position here. Mr. Alcott asked for my first impressions as regards the hindrances I have noted since coming here. I told him candidly they were: 1st, his want of frankness; 2d, his disposition to separateness rather than win co-operators with the aims in his own mind; 3d, his family, who prevent his immediate plans of reformation; 4th, the fact that this place has very little fruit on it, while it was and is their desire that fruit should be the principal part of their diet; 5th, my fear that they have too decided a tendency toward literature and writing for the prosperity and success of their enterprise.

"My relations with my family are very critical at this period —more so than they have ever been. It is the crisis of the state we have been in for this past year. If God gives me strength to be true to the spirit, it is very doubtful how far those at home will be willing to second it. I have written them a letter asking for their own aims and views of life, and I am anxious for their answer. The question of returning is not a wilful one with me, for it is the spirit which guides me. If it can live there, I go back. If not, I am governed and must follow where it leads, wherever that may be."

The letter referred to in this entry of the diary is too long, and covers too much ground already traversed, to be quoted in full, but it contains some striking passages. It was written at Fruitlands, July 17, '43. After inquiring with his customary

directness what are their aims in life and what they are doing
to attain them, he goes on to say :

"Although the idea or aim which each one aspires toward
and tries to realize will be colored by his own peculiar tendencies, still, in substance, in practice, they will agree if they are
inspired by the self-same spirit."

Here we have the practical good sense which reined in and
directed Isaac Hecker throughout his life, making it finally impossible for him not to see and recognize the visible Church,
notwithstanding his mystical tendency, his want of thorough
education, and his birthright of heresy.

Again he writes :

"There are all the natural ties why we should not be
separated, and no reasons why we should, unless there exists
such a wide difference in the aims we seek to realize that it
would be injurious or impossible for us to live in family, in unity,
in love. I do not believe this difference exists, but if it does, and
we are conscious of being led by a higher spirit than our own,
we should and would sacrifice all that hinders us from the divine
calling. That demands implicit, uncompromising obedience. It
speaks in the tone of high authority. The dead must bury their
dead. That which offends it must be got rid of at all costs, be
it wife, parents, children, brothers, sisters, or our own eye
or hand. I do not contemplate a sacrifice of either of these ;
still, it is well to consider whether, if such a demand should be
made of us, we are in such a state of mind that we would be
willing to give one or all up, if they should stand in the way
of our progress toward God. . . .

"If you desire to continue the way of life you *have* and do
now lead, be plain, frank, and so express yourselves explicitly. If
not, and you have any desire or intention in your minds to alter
or make a radical change in your external circumstances for the
sake of a higher, better mode of life, be equally open, and let
me know all your thoughts and aspirations which are struggling
for expression, for real life. . . .

"We have labored together in union for material wealth ;
can we now labor in the same way for spiritual wealth ? If
there are sufficient points of accord in us in this higher life, we
must come together and live in harmony. Since my departure

from home there has been a change in my mind, or, perhaps more truly, a sudden and rapid growth in a certain direction, the germs of which you must have heretofore perceived in my conduct and life. On the other hand, I suppose there has been a progress in your minds, and I feel that the time has arrived when we should see where we are, so that we may either come together or separate. Our future relation cannot be a wilful one. It must be based on a unity of spirit, for the social, the humane instincts cannot bind us together any longer. . . . Have we the spiritual as well as the natural brotherhood? this is the question which deeply concerns us now. . . . I do not know what the spirit has done for you since my departure. If it has led you as it has led me, there is no reason why I should be amongst strangers by birth, although not altogether strangers in love . . . Think seriously upon your answer. Act true. Life is to me of serious import, and I feel called upon to give up all that hinders me from following this import wherever it may lead. But do not let this influence you in your judgments. We have but a short life to live here, and I would offer mine to some worthy end: this is all I desire. My health is very good. I am still at Fruitlands, and will remain here until something further happens. Accept my deepest love."

While waiting for an answer to this letter, the diary shows how continuously Isaac's mind was working over this problem of a final separation from his kindred. It seems probable that it was, on the whole, the deepest emotional one that he had to solve. Both filial duty and natural affection were strong sentiments with him. One notices in these letters how courteous and urbane is the tone he uses, even when insisting most on the necessity which lies upon him to cut all the ties which bind him. This was a family trait. In a letter written to us last September in answer to a question, Mr. Charles A. Dana incidentally refers to a visit he paid Isaac Hecker at his mother's house. "It was a very interesting family," he writes, "and the cordiality and sweetness of the relations which prevailed in it impressed me very greatly."

The entry we are about to quote opens with an odd echo from a certain school of mysticism with which Isaac about this time became familiar:

"*July* 22, 1843.—Man requires a new birth—the birth of the feminine in him.

"The question arises in my mind whether it is necessary for me to require the concurrence of my brothers in the views of life which now appear to demand of me their actualization.

"Can I not adopt simple garmenture and diet without their doing so? Must I needs have their concurrence? Can I not leave results to themselves? If my life is purer than that of those around me, can I not trust to its own simple influence?

"But if there is a great difference of spirit, can we live together? Does not like seek like? In money matters things must certainly be other than they have been. We must agree that no accounts shall be kept between ourselves, let the consequences be what they may. I would rather suffer evils from a dependence on the spirit of love than permit that of selfishness to exist between us. I ask not a cent above what will supply my immediate, necessary wants. . . They may demand ten times more than I, and it would be a happiness to me to see them use it, even if I thought they used it wrongfully. All the check I would be willing to employ would be that of love and mutual good feeling. If I remain as I now am, I shall require very little, and that little would be spent for the benefit and help of others.

"*July* 23.—I will go home, be true to the spirit with the help of God, and wait for further light and strength. . . . I feel that I cannot live at this place as I would. This is not the place for my soul. . . My life is not theirs. They have been the means of giving me much light on myself, but I feel I would live and progress more in a different atmosphere."

On the 25th of July Isaac finally departed from Fruitlands, and after remaining for a few days at Brook Farm, he returned to his home in New York. Before following him thither, it may be well to give at once such further references to this period of his life as are contained in the memoranda. The following extract is undated:

"*A propos* of Emerson's death, Father Hecker said: 'I knew him well. When I resolved to become a Catholic I was boarding at the house of Henry Thoreau's mother, a stone's-throw from Emerson's at Concord.'"

"What did Thoreau say about it?"

" ' What's the use of your joining the Catholic Church? Can't you get along without hanging to her skirts ? ' I suppose Emerson found it out from Thoreau, so he tried his best to get me out of the notion. He invited me to tea with him, and he kept leading up to the subject and I leading away from it. The next day he asked me to drive over with him to the Shakers, some fifteen miles. We stayed over night, and all the way there and back he was fishing for my reasons, with the plain purpose of dissuading me. Then Alcott and he arranged matters so that they cornered me in a sort of interview, and Alcott frankly developed the subject. I finally said, ' Mr. Alcott, I deny your inquisitorial right in this matter,' and so they let it drop. One day, however, I was walking along the road and Emerson joined me. Presently he said, ' Mr. Hecker, I suppose it was the art, the architecture, and so on in the Catholic Church which led you to her ?' ' No,' said I ; ' but it was what caused all that.' I was the first to break the Transcendental camp. Brownson came some time after me.

" Years later, during the war, I went to Concord to lecture, and wanted Emerson to help me get a hall. He refused.

" Alcott promised that he would, but he did not, and I think Emerson dissuaded him. After a time, however, a priest, a church, and a congregation of some six or seven hundred Catholics grew up in Concord, and I was invited to lecture, and I went. The pastor attended another station that Sunday, and I said the Mass and meant to give a homily by way of sermon. But as I was going to the altar, all vested for the Mass, two men came into my soul : one, the man who lived in that village in former years, a blind man, groping about for light, a soul with every problem unsolved ; the other a man full of light, with every problem solved, the universe and the reason of his existence known as they actually are. Well, there were those two men in my soul. I had to get rid of them, so I preached them off to the people. Some wept, some laughed, all were deeply moved. That night came the lecture. It rained pitchforks and pineapples, but the hall, a large one, was completely filled. Multitudes of Yankees were there. Emerson was absent, but Alcott was present. I had my lecture all cut and dried. 'Why I became a Catholic ' was the subject. But as I was about to begin, up came those two men again, and for the life of me I couldn't help firing them off at the audience, and with remarkable effect.

Next day I met Emerson in the street and we had a little talk together. None of those men are comfortable in conversation with an intelligent Catholic. He avoided my square look, and actually kept turning to avoid my eyes until he had quite turned round! Such men, confronted with actual, certain convictions are exceedingly uncomfortable. They feel in subjection to you. They cannot bear the steadfast glance of a man of certain principles any better than a dog can the look of his master. Like a dog, they turn away the head and show signs of uneasiness."

From the memoranda, also, we take this reminiscence of George Ripley, the man whom Father Hecker loved best of all the Transcendental party:

"*January* 23, 1885.—Seeing my perplexity at Brook Farm, George Ripley said, 'Mr. Hecker, do you think we have not got true religion? If you think so, say so. If you have views you think true, and which we ought to have, let us hear them.' I answered, 'No; I haven't the truth, but I am trying to get it. If I ever succeed, you will hear from me. If I don't, you never will. I am not going to teach before I am certain myself. I will not add myself to the list of humbugs.'

"Ripley was a great man; a wonderful man. But he was a complete failure. I loved him dearly, and he knew it, and he loved me; I know well he did. When I came back a Redemptorist from Europe, I went to see him at the *Tribune* office He asked me, 'Can you do all that any Catholic priest can do?' 'Yes.' 'Then I will send for you when I am drawing towards my end.'

"Indeed, if one could have gone to Ripley, at any time in his later years, and said, 'You will never return again to the society of men,' and persuaded him it was true, he would have said at once, 'Send for Father Hecker or some other Catholic priest.' I am persuaded that the fear of facing his friends hindered George Ripley from becoming a Catholic. He sent for me when taken down by his last illness, but his message was not delivered. As soon as I heard that he was ill I hastened to his bedside, but his mind was gone and I could do nothing for him."

And now, having given so fully such of his own impressions as remain of the persons and places which helped to shape Father Hecker in early manhood, we will terminate the record of this period with two letters, one from each community, which were written him soon after his return to New York. No words of our own could show so well the hearty affection and implicit trust which he awakened and returned:

" *Brook Farm, September* 18, 1843.—MY DEAR FRIEND : I was rejoiced to hear from you, though you wrote too short a letter. Your beautiful fruit, enough to convert the direst sceptic to Grahamism, together with the pearled wheat, arrived safely, although a few days too late to be in perfectly good order. We distributed them to all and singular, men, women, and children, who discussed them with great interest, I assure you ; many, no doubt, with silent wishes that no good or beautiful thing might ever be wanting to you. I am glad to learn that you are so happy in New York, that you find so much in your own mind to compensate for the evils of a city environment, and that your aspirations are not quenched by the sight of the huge disorders that daily surround you. I hardly dare to think that my own faith or hope would be strong enough to reconcile me to a return to common society. I should pine like an imprisoned bird, and I fear I should grow blind to the visions of loveliness and glory which the future promises to humanity. I long for action which shall realize the prophecies, fulfil the Apocalypse, bring the new Jerusalem down from heaven to earth, and collect the faithful into a true and holy brotherhood. To attain this con-summation so devoutly to be wished, I would eat no flesh, I would drink no wine while the world lasted. I would become as devoted an ascetic as yourself, my dear Isaac. But to what end is all speculation, all dreaming, all questioning, but to advance humanity, to bring forward the manifestation of the Son of God ? Oh, for men who feel this idea burning into their bones ! When shall we see them ? And without them, what will be phalanxes, groups and series, attractive industry, and all the sublime words of modern reforms ?

"When will you come back to Brook Farm ? Can you do without us ? Can we do without you ? But do not come as an amateur, a self-perfectionizer, an æsthetic self-seeker, willing to suck the orange of Association dry and throw away the peel. Oh ! that you would come as one of us, to work in the faith of a divine idea, to toil in loneliness and tears for the sake of the kingdom which God may build up by our hands. All here, that is, all our old central members, feel more and more the spirit of devotedness, the thirst to do or die, for the cause we have at heart. We do not distrust Providence. We cannot believe that what we have gained here of spiritual progress will be lost through want of material resources. . At present, however, we are in great straits. We hardly dare to provide the means of keeping warm in our pleasant nest this winter.

"Just look at our case. With property amounting to $30,-000, the want of two or three thousands fetters us and may kill us. That sum would free us from pecuniary embarrassment, and for want of that we work daily with fetters on our limbs. Are there not five men in New York City who would dare to venture $200 each in the cause of social reform, without being assured of a Phalanx for themselves and their children for ever? Alas! I know not. We are willing to traverse the wilderness forty years; we ask no grapes of Eshcol for ourselves; we do not claim a fair abode in the promised land; but what can we do, with neither quails nor manna, with raiment waxing old, and shoes bursting from our feet?

"Forgive me, my dear Isaac, for speaking so much about ourselves. But what else should I speak of? And who more sympathizing with our movement than yourself?

"Do not be surprised at receiving this letter so long after date. Not less than four times have I begun it, and as often have been interrupted. Pray write me now and then. Your words are always sweet and pleasant to my soul. Believe me, ever yours truly, GEORGE RIPLEY."

"*Harvard, Mass., November* 11, 1843.—DEAR FRIEND: Your kind letter of the 1st came duly to hand, and we are making arrangements to enjoy the benefit of your healthful bequest.

"Please to accept thanks for your sympathy and the reports of persons and things in your circle. They have interested me much, but I am about to make you the most incongruous return conceivable. For pleasure almost unqualified which you have conferred on me, I fear I shall trouble you with painful relations; in return for a barrel of superfine wholesome wheat-meal, I am going to submit to you a peck of troubles. Out of as many of these as you lovingly and freely can, you may assist me; but, of course, you will understand that I feel I have no claim upon you. On the contrary, indeed, I see that I run the hazard of forfeiting your valued friendship by thus obtruding my pecuniary concerns into our hitherto loftier communings. You know it to be a sentiment of mine that these affairs should never be obtruded between æsthetic friends, but what can one do in extremity but to unburden candidly to the generous?

"When I bought this place, instead of paying the whole $1,800, as I wished, $300 of my money went to pay old debts with which I ought to have had nothing to do; and Mrs. Alcott's brother, Samuel J. May, joined his name to a note for $300, to be paid by instalments in two years. And now that the first instalment is due, he sends me word that he declines paying it.

As all my cash has been expended in buying and keeping up the affair, I am left in a precarious position, out of which I do not see the way without some loveful aid, and to you I venture freely to submit my feelings. Above all things I should like to discharge at once this $300 note, as unless that is done the place must, I fear, fall back into individuality and the idea be suspended. Now, if as much cash is loose in your pocket, or that of some wealthy friend, there shall be parted off as much of the land as will secure its return, from the crops alone, in a few years; or, I would sell a piece until I can redeem it; or, I would meet the loan in any other secure way, if I can but secure the land from the demon usury. This mode seems to me the *most* desirable. But I could get along with the instalment of $75, and would offer like security in proportion. Or, if you can do it yourself, and would prefer the library as a pledge, you shall select such books as will suit your own reading and would cover your advance in cash any day you choose to put them up to auction, if I should fail to redeem them. Or, I would give my notes of hand that I could meet by sales of produce or of land. If I had the benefit of your personal counsel, we could contrive something between us, I am sure, but I have no such aid about me. The difficulty in itself is really light, but to me, under present circumstances, is quite formidable. If at your earliest convenience you acquaint me with your mind, you will much oblige.

" I have another trouble of a personal nature. I suffer already this winter from the inclemency of the weather, so much that my hands are so chapped that I can scarcely hold the pen. If I could find employment in a more southern position that would support me and the boy, and leave a little to be applied to the common good, I would undertake it. I think I could at the same time be of some mental and moral service to the people where I might be located.

"Another trouble. Young William has been very ill for the last month, brought on, I believe, by excessive work. He is still very weak, and has not sat up for three weeks.

" All these, besides sundry slighter plagues, coming upon me at once, have perhaps a little disconcerted my nerves, and the advice and assistance of a generous friend at such a juncture would be indeed serviceable. If the journey were not so long and so costly I would ask you to come. Be assured that whatever may be your decision in any of these relations, my esteem for you cannot be thereby diminished. My only fear is that such encroachments on your good nature will reduce your estimation of, dear friend, yours most sincerely,

CHARLES LANE.

" Regards to the Doctor and all friends. The Shakers have kindly inquired for you, and they still take much interest in our life. Have you seen the last *Dial?* The *Present* is good, but surely not good enough. I hope to write a more universal letter in response to your next, for which I wait."

Poor Lane, failing to find any equally confiding and generous friend to shoulder with him the personal debts of the founder of Fruitlands, was compelled at last to let the farm " lapse into individuality" and to see " the idea suspended." In his next and "more universal letter" he announces that the experiment is ended in consequence of Mrs. Alcott's refusal to remain on the place through the winter. Lane went over to the neighboring Shaker community, and from there to England, where Father Hecker met him during his own residence at Clapham, after his ordination. His letters followed Father Hecker for several years, and breathe always the same unselfishness, the same simple trust in human goodness, and the same fondness for speculations on "the universal."

CHAPTER IX.

SELF-QUESTIONINGS.

NOT finding any solution of his spiritual difficulties at either Fruitlands or Brook Farm, Isaac Hecker turned his face once more toward the home from which he had departed nearly a year before. He expected little from this step, but his state of mind was now one in which he had begun to anticipate, at any turn, some light on the dispositions of Providence in his regard which might determine his course for good and all. And, meantime, as patient waiting was all that lay in his own power, it seemed the wisest course to yield to the solicitations of his kindred and abide results in his own place. He did not go there at once, however, after quitting Alcott's community, but returned to Brook Farm for a fortnight. His journal during this period offers many pages worthy of transcription.

It is possible that we have readers who may deem us too copious in our quotations from this source. But, if wearisome to any, yet they are necessary to those for whom this Life is especially written. The lessons to be learned from Father Hecker are mainly those arising from the interaction between God's supernatural dealings with him, and his own natural characteristics. This fact, moreover, is typical as well as personal, for the great question of his day, which was the dawning of our own, was the relation of the natural man to the regenerating influences of Christianity. This being so, it is plain to our own mind that no adequate representation of the man could be made without a free use of these early journals. They seem to us one of the chief Providential results of the spiritual isolation of his youth. He was in a manner driven to this intimate self-communing, on one hand by his never-satisfied craving for sympathetic companionship, and on the other by his complete unacquaintance with a kind of reading which even at this point might have shed some light upon his interior difficulties. In later years he enjoyed, in the study of accredited Christian mystics, that kind of satisfaction which a traveller experiences who, after long wanderings in what had seemed a trackless desert, obtains a map which not only makes his whole route plain, but assures him that he did not stray from well-known paths even during his times of most extreme bewilderment.

That the diary has the character we here claim for it, and is not the mere ordinary result of a morbid and aimless introspection, is plainly shown by the speedy cessation of excessive self-analysis on Father Hecker's part, after he had actually reached the goal to which he was at this period alternately sweetly led and violently driven. But it is also shown by the deep humility which is revealed precisely by this sharp probing of his interior. Though he felt himself in touch with God in some special way, yet it was with so little pride that it was his profound conviction, as it remained, indeed, throughout his life, that what he had all had or might have. But the study of his interior thus forced upon him was far from a pleasing task. "It is exceedingly oppressive to me to write as I now do," we find him complaining; "continually does myself appear in my writing. I would that my *I* were wholly lost in the sea of the Spirit—wholly lost in God."

We preface the subjoined extract from the diary with the remark that Father Hecker's reading of signs of the Divine will in men and events often brought him to the verge of credulity, over which he was prevented from stepping by his shrewd native sense. Though he insisted all his life on interpreting them as signal flags of the Divine wisdom, this did not hinder him from gaining a reputation for sound practical judgment:

"*Brook Farm, July* 31, 1843.—Man is the symbol of all mysteries. Why is it that all things seem to me to be instinct with prophecy? I do not see any more individual personalities, but priests and oracles of God. The age is big with a prophecy which it is in labor to give birth to."

"My experience is different now from what it has been. It is much fuller; every fibre of my being seems teeming with sensitive life. I am in another atmosphere of sentiment and thought. . . . I have less real union and sympathy with *her*, and with those whom I have met much nearer heretofore. It appears as if their atmosphere was denser, their life more natural, more in the flesh. Instead of meeting them on my highest, I can only do so by coming down into my body, of which it seems to me that I am now almost unconscious. There is not that sense of heaviness, dulness, fleshliness, in me. I experience no natural desires, no impure thoughts, nor wanderings of fancy. Still, I feel more intensely, and am filled to overflowing with love, and with desire for union. But there is no one to meet me where I am, and I cannot meet them where they are."

All his life Father Hecker was on the lookout for the great human influences which run across those of religion, either to swell their volume or to lessen their force. These are mainly the transmissions of heredity, and the environments that are racial, temporal, epochal, or local. This enduring tendency is foreshadowed in the following extracts:

"*August* 2, 1843.—I have been thinking much of late about the very great influence which nationality and the family progenitors have upon character. Men talk of universality, impartiality, many-sidedness, free judgment, unbiased opinion, and so on, when in reality their national and family dispositions are the centre and ground of their being, and hence of their opinions. They appear to be most themselves when they show these traits of character. They are most natural and earnest and at home when they speak from this link which binds them to the past. Then their hearts are opened, and they speak with a glow of eloquence and a peculiar unction which touch the same chord in the breasts of those who hear them. It is well for man to feel his indebtedness to the past which lives in him and without which he would not be what he is. He is far more its creature than he gives himself credit for. He reproduces daily the sentiments and thoughts of the dim and obscure before. There are certain ideas and aspirations which have not had their fulfilment, but which run through all men from the beginning and which are continually reproduced. There is a unity of race, called Humanity; one of place, called Nationality; one of birth, called Kindred; one of affinity, called Love and Friendship. By all these we are greatly influenced. They all make their mark upon the man."

"The faculties which take cognizance of the inner world have been awakened in only a few of the human race, and these, to distinguish them, have been called prophets, miracle-workers, Providential men, seers, and poets. Now, their privilege is that of all men in a greater or less degree, just as is the case with regard to the faculties which relate to the outward world. For when men in general were as ignorant about the exterior world as they now are about the interior, the men of science, the astronomers, the mathematicians, the founders of the arts, were held to be miraculous, gods, and they were deified. What any one man (and this is a most comfortable and cheering thought) has been or has done, all men may in a measure be or do, for each is a type, a specimen of the whole human race. If it is said in reply, 'These miracles or great acts, which you hold as actual, are mere superstitious dreams,' I care not. That would be still more glorious for us, for then they are still to be performed, they are in the coming time, these divine prophetic instincts are yet to be actualized. The dreams of Orpheus, the inspired strains of the Hebrew bards, and, above all, the prophecies of Christ, are before us. The divine instincts will be realized as surely as there is a God above who inspires them. It is the glory of God that they should be so; it is His delight. This world must become heaven. This is its destiny ; and our destiny, under God, is to make it so. Prophecy is given to encourage and nourish our hopes and feed our joys, so that we may say with Job, 'I know that although worms shall eat this flesh, and my bones become dust, yet at the latter day I shall see my Redeemer face to face.' "

The sentences which follow can be paralleled by words taken from all who have truly interpreted the doctrine of Christ by their lives or their writings:

" To him that has faith all things are possible, for faith is an act of the soul; thy faith is the measure of thy power."

" If men would act from the present inspiration of their souls they would gain more knowledge than they do by reading or speculating."

" No man in his heart can ask for more than he has. Think of this deeply. God is just. We have what we ought to have, even according to our own sense of justice."

" The desire to love and be beloved, to have friends with whom we can converse, to enter society which we enjoy—is it not best to deny and sacrifice these desires ? It may be said that, gratified, they add to life, and the question is how to increase life, not how to diminish it. But by denying them, would not our life gain by flowing in a more heavenly direction ? "

" We are daily feeding the demons that are in us by our,

wicked thoughts and sinful acts ; these are their meat and drink. I make them gasp sometimes. My heart laughs quite merrily to think of it. When I am hungry, and there is something tempting on the table, hunger, like a serpent, comes creeping up into my throat and laps its dry tongue with eagerness for its prey, but it often returns chagrined at its discomfiture."

"That which tempts us we should deny, no matter how innocent it is in itself. If it tempts, away with it, until it tempts no more. Then partake of it, for it is then only that you can do so prudently and with temperance."

"All our thoughts and emotions are caused by some agent acting on us. This is true of all the senses and the spiritual faculties. Hence we should by all possible means purify and refine our organism, so that we may hear the most delicate, the sweetest, the stillest sounds and murmurings of the angels who are about us. How much fuller and richer would be our life if we were more acutely sensitive and finely textured ! How many exquisite delights nature yields which we are not yet aware of ! What a world surrounds us of which none but holy men, prophets, and poets have had a glimpse ! "

"The soul is a plate on which the senses daguerreotype indelibly pictures of the outer world. How cautious should we be where we look, what we hear, what smell, or feel, or taste ! And how we should endeavor that all around us should be made beautiful, musical, fragrant, so that our souls may be awakened to a divine sense of life without a moment's interruption ! "

"O God, be Thou my helper, my strength and my redeemer! May I live wholly to Thee ; give me grace and obedience to Thy Spirit. May all self be put from me so that I may enter into the glorious liberty of the sons of God. Awaken me, raise me up, restore me, O Jesus Christ, Lord, Heavenly King ! "

In reading what next follows it must be remembered that at the time when it was written Isaac Hecker had absolutely no knowledge of Catholic mystical theology. It is since that day that English-speaking Catholics have had access to the great authorities on this subject through adequate translations. But what little he had learned from other sources, combined with his own intuitional and experimental knowledge of human capabilities for penetrating the veil, had already furnished him with conclusions which nothing in his devoted study of Catholic mystical writers forced him to lay aside :

"Belief in the special guidance of God has been the faith of all deeply religious men. I will not dispute the fact that some men are so guided, but will offer an explanation of it which seems to me to reconcile it with the regular order of laws established by God. My explanation would be that this guidance is not a miraculous power, specially bestowed upon some men, but merely a higher degree of ordinary divine guidance. Our ordinary life is inspired ; the other is only a higher degree of what is common to all. The evil which arises from the contrary opinion is this : men who have received a higher degree of insight believe that it is a special miraculous gift, and that all they may say is infallibly true, whereas they still retain their own individuality though raised to a purer state of being. They have not been so raised in order to found new sects, or to cause revolutions, but to fulfil the old, continue and carry it on as far as they have been given light to do so. In forming new sects they but reproduce their own individualities with all their errors. So Swedenborg did, and Wesley, men of modern times who were awakened in a greater degree than the mass of their fellows. Their mistake lay in their attempt to make universal ends out of their individual experiences. In the ordinary state no man does this, but these, being lifted a little above the mass, became intoxicated. The only one, so far as I have read, who has had humility equal to his inspiration was Jacob Boehmen. Luther, Calvin, Fox, Penn, Swedenborg, Wesley, had self in view. Selfism is mixed with their universalism. None has spoken truth so pure and universal as Boehmen. He is the most inspired man of modern times. He had more love and truth than all the other mystics put together, and fewer faults than either one of them taken singly."

CHAPTER X

IT was the middle of August, 1843, when Isaac Hecker once more took up his residence with his family in New York. His first endeavor was to sink back again as far as possible into the old routine of business.

"To-morrow I commence to work," he writes on the evening of his return. "My interior state is quiet and peaceful. I have not met any one yet. My dear mother understands me better than any one else. How far business will interfere with my inner life remains to be seen. O Lord! help me to keep my resolution, which is not to let the world enter my heart, but to keep it looking toward Thee! My heart has been in a constant prayerful state since I have been at home. It is busy in its own sanctuary, its own temple, God. O Lord! preserve it."

One of the first noteworthy things revealed by the diary—which from this time on was kept with less regularity than before—is that Isaac not only maintained his abstemious habits after his return, but increased their rigor. For a robust man, working hard for many hours out of every twenty-four, and deprived of all the pleasant relaxations, literary, conversational and musical, to which he had been accustoming himself for many months, the choice of such a diet as is described in the following sentences was certainly extraordinary:

"*August* 30.—If the past nine months or more are any evidence, I find that I can live on very simple diet—grains, fruit, and nuts. I have just commenced to eat the latter; I drink pure water. So far I have had wheat ground and made into unleavened bread, but as soon as we get in a new lot, I shall try it in the grain."

He had evidently at this time a practical conviction of the truth of a principle which, in after years, he repeated to the present writer in the form of a maxim of the transcendentalists: "A gross feeder will never be a central thinker." It is a truth of the spiritual no less than of the intellectual order. A little later we come upon the following profession of a vegetarian faith, which will be apt to amuse as well as to edify the reader:

"*Reasons for not eating animal food.*

"It does not feed the spirit.

"It stimulates the propensities.

"It is taking animal life when the other kingdoms offer sufficient and better increment.

"Slaughter strengthens the lower instincts.

"It is the chief cause of the slavery of the kitchen.

"It generates in the body the diseases animals are subject to, and encourages in man their bestiality.

"Its odor is offensive and its appearance unæsthetic."

The apprehension under which he had labored, that city life would present many temptations which he would find it difficult to withstand, appears to have been unfounded. Some few social relaxations he now and then permitted himself, but they were mostly very sober-toned. "Last evening I attended a Methodist love-feast," is his record of one of these. "In returning I stopped at the ward political meeting." Then he notes that although the business he follows is especially full of temptations—as no doubt it was to a man keeping so tight a rein over his most natural and legitimate appetites—he feels deeply grateful that, so far, he has had no need to fear his being led away. "What yet remains?" he adds. "My diet is all purchased and all produced by hired labor. I suppose that slave labor produces almost all my dress. And I cannot say that I am rightly conditioned until all I eat, drink, and wear is produced by love."

It was a vivid recollection of these early efforts after an ascetic perfection which had neither guide nor definite plan, which prompted the following vigorous self-appreciation, made by Father Hecker two years before his death. He had been speaking of some of his youthful experiments in this direction, and ended with an amused laugh and the ejaculation,

"Thank God! He led me into the Catholic Church. If it hadn't been for that I should have been one of the worst cranks in the world."

Here are two expressions taken from the diary of a permanent fact of Father Hecker's individuality. They help to explain why he was misunderstood by many in later years:

"Men have fear to utter absurdities. The head is sceptical of the divine oracles of the heart, and before she utters them she clothes them in such a fantastic dress that men hear the words but lose the life, the thought."

"We often act to be understood by the heart, not by the head; and when the head speaks of its having understood, we deny its understanding. It is the secret sympathy of the heart which is the only response that is looked for. Speech is cold, profane."

This must recall, to those who were intimate with Father Hecker, how often he arrived at his own convictions by discussing them with others while they were yet but partially formed. It is a custom with many to do so, mind assisting mind, negation provoking affirmation, doubt vanishing with the utterance of the truth. In Father Hecker's case his perfect frankness led him, when among his own friends, to utter half-formed ideas, sometimes sounding startling and erroneous, but spoken with a view to get them into proper shape. At such times it required patience to know just what he meant, for he never found it the easiest to employ terms whose meaning was conventional.

By the first of September such faint hopes as Isaac had entertained of adapting himself to the conditions of his home in New York were well-nigh dissipated. But a certain natural timidity, joined with the still complete uncertainty he felt as to what his true course should be, made him dissemble his disquiet so long as it was bearable. After a month or two, by a mutual agreement between his brothers and himself which exonerated him from much of the manual labor which they still shared with the men in their employment, he devoted himself to an occupation more accordant to his mind. He set to work to make single beds and private rooms for the workmen, contriving various conveniences and means of occasional solitude for them, and in other ways doing all in his power to achieve for them the privileges he found so necessary for himself. Of these efforts we get occasional glimpses in the diary. But it is, in the main, devoted to more impersonal and larger topics, and the facts of his daily employment, as just given, have been gained from other sources

"*September* 1.—There are two ways in which the spirit may live itself out. One is to leave all these conditions, purchase a spot of ground, and live according to its daily dictates. The other is to make these conditions as harmonic as possible by giving the men" (workmen) "an associative interest in the accumulations of our associative labor. Both extremes require renunciation of property and of self. Love, universal love is the ruler, and only by it can the spirit find peace or be crowned with the highest happiness."

"The mystery of man's being, the unawakened capacities in him, we are not half aware of. A few of the race, the prophets, sages, and poets, give us a glimpse of his high destiny. Alas! that men should be on the borders of such mighty truths and stand as blind and dumb as lower animals before them!"

"Balaam sometimes, but ignorantly, utters true prophecies. A remark I heard to-day leads me to say this. Speaking of diet a man said: 'Why, what do you intend? At last you will have men to live on God.' We must become God-like, or God-full. Live as He lives, become one with Him. Until we are reconciled with our Father we are aliens, prodigals. Until we can say, My Father and I are one, we have not commenced to be. We must fulfil what the Apostle said (and it means, perhaps, more than we commonly imagine): 'In God we live and move and have our being.'"

"The deeper and more profound a truth is, the less proof can you give in its support."

"*September* 8.—On the evening of the 6th I went to see the French Opera Company in Auber's 'Black Domino.' It did not please me as well as some music I have heard, though parts of it were very beautiful. The hymns of the nuns were very sweet. The thought occurred to me that if the Church does not provide religious gratifications for the true wants of humanity, she must be silent if men feed them profanely. It is because the Church has not done her duty that there are so many secular societies for Reformation, Temperance, and so on. The Church has provided for the salvation of the sinner's soul by means of spiritual acts, such as prayer, penance, the Eucharist

and other sacraments. But now she must provide terrestrial
sacraments for the salvation and transfiguration of the body."

"We should strive constantly to actualize the ideal we perceive. When we do realize all the beauty and holiness that we
see, we are not called to deny ourselves, for then we are living
as fully on all sides as we have capacity to do. Are we not in
this state? Then, if we are sincere, we will give up lower and
unnecessary gratifications for the sake of the ideal we have in
view.

"I would die to prove my immortality."

"At times we are called to rely on Providence, to be im-
prudent and reckless according to the wisdom of the world. So
I am willing to be thought. Each of us has an individual character to act out, *under the inspiration of God*, and this is the
highest and noblest we can do. We are forms differing from one
another, and if we are acting under the inspirations of the Highest, we are doing our uttermost; more the angels do not. What
tends to hinder us from realizing the ideal which our vision sees
must be denied, be it self, wealth, opinion, or death."

"The Heart says, 'Be all that you can.' The Intellect says,
'When you are all that you can be—what then?'"

"Infinite love is the basis of the smallest act of love, and
when we love with our whole being, we are in and one
with God."

"Increase thy love by being true to that thou hast if thou
wouldst be nearer to God."

"To love is to lose one's self and gain God. To be all in
love is to be one with God."

"When the Spirit begets us, we are no more; the Spirit is,
and there is nothing else."

"There is much debauchery in speaking wilfully.
"Every act of self is sin, is a lie.
"The Spirit will lead you into solitude and silence if it has
something to teach you.
"You must be born again to know the truth. It cannot be
inculcated.

"To educate is to bring forth, not to put in. To put in is death ; to flow out is life."

Lest the reader may have got an impression, from any of the extracts already given, that Isaac Hecker was puffed up by the pride of his own innocence, we transcribe what follows. It shows that he did not fall under the Apostle's condemnation: " If we say that we have no sin, we deceive ourselves, and the truth is not in us." It was written on the last Sunday of September, and, after this long outpouring of confession, longing, and weakness, the diary was not again resumed for nearly a month. The desire expressed in its second paragraph for the kind of spiritual refreshment which in after years he so often enjoyed under the name of a "retreat," seems noteworthy.

" *September* 24, 1843.—The human heart is wicked above all things. The enemy of man is subtle and watchful beyond conception. Instead of being on the way of goodness, I am just finding out the wickedness of my nature, its crookedness, its impurity, its darkness. I want deep humility and forgetfulness of self. I am just emerging out of gross darkness and my sight is but dim, so that my iniquities are not wholly plain to my vision.

" At present I feel as if a week of quiet silence would be the means of opening more deeply the still flowing fountains of divine life. I would cut off all relations but that of my soul with the Spirit—all others seem intrusions, worldly, frivolous. The inpouring of the Spirit is checked by so much attention to other than divine things. In the bustle and noisy confusion its voice is unheard.

" I feel that one of my greatest weaknesses, because it leads me to so much sin, is my social disposition. It draws me so often into perilous conversations, and away from silence and meditation with the Spirit. Lately I have felt almost ready to say that good works are a hindrance to the gate of heaven. Pride and self-approbation are so often mixed with them. I feel that nothing has been spoken against the vain attempt to trust in good works which my soul does not fully accord with. This is a new, a very new experience for me."

The foregoing must be understood in the sense of good works hindering better works. Isaac Hecker felt his noblest as-

pirations to be, for the moment at any rate, towards solitude
and the passive state of prayer; and in this he was hindered by
the urgency of his zeal for the propagation of philanthropic
schemes and his great joy in communing with men whom he
hoped to find like-minded with himself. The time came when
he was able to join the two states, the inner purifying the outer
man and directing his energies by the instinct of the Holy Spirit.
This entry goes on as follows :

"By practice of our aspirations, ideals, and visions, we convert them into real being.

"We should be able to say, 'Which of you convinceth me
of sin?' before we are fit to preach to others in such a way
that our preaching may have a practical effect upon society.

"Did all our efforts flow into realizing the teachings of
the Spirit, we should do much more good and be greater in
the sight of God than we are now by so much speaking and
writing. But let us be watchful that the pride of good works
does not take the place of that of speaking and writing.

"By our sins and many weaknesses we are prevented from
entering the Promised Land, and must die just in sight of it.
Instead of being humble, willing, and self-denying in our youth,
and being led by the Spirit of God, we keep on in the spirit
of the world and give all the substance of our being to its
service. And when we are nearly worn out we flee to God, and
die, perhaps, in sight of heaven, instead of having been among
its inhabitants, living in it upon earth, in the full bloom of our
youthful joy of life. . . .

"The Lord has been good to me and my heart is filled
with His warm love. Blessed be Thou, O God! for Thou hast
given me a taste of Thy sweetness. Thou hast given me gratitude and thankfulness and an overflowing heart of praise. I
would stand still and shout and bless God. It is God in us that
believes in God. Without the light of God we should be in
total darkness, and He is the only source of light. The more
of God we have in us, the more we see beyond us.

"Thy inspiration, O God! is love and wisdom. In Thee
they are one, as light and warmth are in the fire.

"Thou art the true, eternal food of life, and he that has
tasted Thee can never be at rest until he is wholly filled with
Thee. Lord, when we are without Thee we are lost, dead, in

darkness.   It is in and by Thy presence that we live and move
and have our being.

" Ever more, O Lord, increase Thy Spirit in us until between
us there is no more we or Thee, but Thou, O Father, art all !

" Like the fixed light in a crystal which flashes back the light
of the sun, so does the soul of man reflect God.

" A good life consists in passive as well as active virtues.

" O Lord, so fill me that nothing shall be left but Thee, and
I may be no more."

One would be tempted to believe that none but a master in
the spiritual life could have written the sentences which immediately follow this outburst of love and praise.   Yet remember
that Isaac Hecker was not yet twenty-four, and that he knew
nothing of the ways of the Spirit except what the Spirit Himself had directly taught him :

" The reason why men are perplexed and in darkness about
their being and the questions which their being often asks, is not
that these are insoluble, but that the disposition and spirit in
which a solution is attempted is so contrary to that in which they
may be solved, that they appear as hidden mysteries.

" When we come together to converse, it should be to learn
from each other what good we can and ought to do, and so
mingle the brightness of one with the dimness of the other.
Our meetings should be such that we should go away feeling
that God had been with us and multiplied our blessings.   The
question should be, ' Brother, can you teach me the way of the
Lord in a more perfect manner than that in which I tread it,
so that my soul may be increased and God abide in me more
and more ? '   Oh ! he is my brother, my master, who leads me
to do more and more good and to love and live more of God.
He that does not increase my heart in love or my mind in true
godly wisdom, is unprofitable and negatively injurious to me.

" Wilfulness locks up while willingness " (docility) " unlocks
the portal to the divine mysteries of God.   I would not attempt to solve a mystery by intellect, but by being."

" *October* 17.—It is some time since I have written in this
book.   All my spare time has been occupied in writing letters to
my friends, meditating, feeling, arranging matters with my brothers
regarding our relations with each other, and attending to the

business. I have had little time to read and to visit my friends. Since I have written my feelings have become more definite, my thoughts clearer and more distinct, and my whole mind more systematic. . . .

"The settlement which has been made with my brothers gives me the opportunity of doing what my spirit has long demanded of me. This afternoon I have been working on their bedroom, making it larger and more pleasant for their minds. This is the first movement I have made toward ameliorating their condition. I hope that God will give me strength to continue."

"*October* 18.—I feel this afternoon a deep want in my soul unsatisfied by my circumstances here, the same as I experienced last winter when I was led from this place. It is at the very depth of my being. Ah, it is deeply stirred! Oh, could I utter the aching void I feel within! Could I know what would fill it! Alas! nothing that can be said, no, nothing, can touch the aching spot. In silence I must remain and let it ache. I would cover myself with darkness and hide my face from the light. Oh, could I but call upon the Lord! Could I but say, Father! Could I feel any relationship!"

"*November* 3.—All things considered, could I, under any circumstances, have more opportunities for self-culture and for doing good than I have in my present position?

"For one thing, there is too much demand on me for physical action. My heart and head have not their share of time. But when I consider, I am at a loss to know how we can possibly diminish our business in any way without a still greater demand on us for physical labor in consequence of diminishing it.

"Yesterday afternoon I went alone in my bedroom and I was led to pray, and to think what more I can do for the friends around me than I now do. This morning I arose and prayed, and felt determined not to let any outward event disturb my inward life; that nothing should ruffle my inward peace, and that this day should be one of interior life, let come what would.

"Often I think of my past life and my present with such a strength of emotion that I would cry aloud, 'O Heaven help me from my course! This is not the life I would lead, but how shall I change it? O Lord! wilt Thou guide me and lead me, no matter what pain or distress I may have to pass through, to the true path Thou wouldst have me go in ? Oh ! I thank Thee for all Thou hast in any way inflicted on me ; it has been to me the greatest blessing I could have received. And, O Lord ! chasten me more, for I need it. How shall I live so that I may be the best I can be under any conditions? If those in which I now am are not the best, where shall I go or how shall I change them ? Teach me, O Lord ! and hear my humble prayer.'"

The following account of his curious inner experiences tells of the positive interference of God and His angels, supplementing the calmer moods in which Isaac longed for and struggled towards the settled condition only to be attained after his entering the Church.

"*November* 5.—How is it and why is it that I feel around me the constant presence of invisible beings who affect my sensibility, and with whom I converse, as it were, in thought and feeling, but not in expression ? At times they so move me that I would escape them, if I could, by running away from where I am. I can scarcely keep still ; I feel like beating, raving, and grasping what I know not. Ah ! it is an unearthly feeling, and painfully afflicts my heart. How to get rid of it I do not know. If I remain quietly where I am, by collecting its scattered rays it burns more deeply into my soul, bringing forth deep sighs, groans, and at times demanding all my energy to repress an unnatural howl.

"How shall I escape this? By remaining here and trying to bear it, or by travelling ? · To do the latter has often occurred to me of late. By such a cause I was driven from home last winter. What the result will be this time I cannot tell ; but if I did know, I would not wait, as I did then, until it came on me with such power as to be torturing in the extreme. Ah, what nervous strength and energy I feel at such times ! If I speak of it to my brothers, they cannot understand me, never having had the same experience. My timidity, which does not wish to be thought of as desiring anything extra on account of my life, makes me bear it until it is unendurable. Hence I am silent so long as it does not speak for itself, which extremity might be prevented were circumstances other than they are. Since they are not, let it be borne with, say strength and resignation united with hope. 'Tis this that is fabled in Prometheus and Laocoön—and how well fabled, too."

It is significant that after every extraordinary disturbance, such as the above, he experienced the impulse to study the credentials of claimants in the outer religious world, the envoys of the Deity to man ; and this especially concerning the Catholic Church. He goes on at once to say :

"Of late I have felt more disposed to look into church matters than for six months past. Last evening I made a visit to the Rev. Mr. Haight " (an Episcopal clergyman) " and conversed with him about that subject for an hour and a half. We differed very little in our opinions. If the Church of Rome has fallen into corruptions from her over-warmth, the Anglican has neglected some of her duties through her coldness. And if the Anglican receives the first five or six councils as legitimate and rejects the Council of Trent as not a full one, still, as an individual, I think Rome did not establish or enjoin anything in those decrees" (the Tridentine) " which was not in harmony with the Spirit of Christ, the Scriptures, and tradition. But the Anglican thinks she has, and hence, in his judgment, they are unwarrantable and unnecessary."

"*November* 15.—How does Jesus commune with Humanity through the Church? Does He now commune with the Church ? Was the life given by Him to His immediate disciples all that has been given and transmitted to us, or does He now commune with the visible Church ? And how ? He promised to be with His disciples even unto the end of the world, to send the Comforter who should lead them into all truth, and to intercede for us with the Father. The Church holds that its sacraments and forms are the visible means for communing with the invisible— that grace is imparted through them to the worthy receiver. Is it true that such grace is imparted ? If it is, it will be shown by its fruits. Contrast the Catholic who believes most in the sacraments with the Quaker who does not believe in them at all as religious or moral forces. Certainly, if the sacraments have any beneficial effect, it should be shown in the contrast between those who totally deny their efficacy and those who religiously believe in them. Now, does this show what one would naturally expect to flow from faith in the sacraments ?

"*November* 20.—I feel in better health than I have ever had, both mind and body, having at the same time an increased sensitiveness, so that the touch of any one I cannot bear. Also, I am conscious of a more constant spiritual communion. I feel more vividly and distinctly the influence and presence—spiritual presence—of others.

"I lie down in my bed at night with the same feelings with which I rise in the morning. I anticipate as much from one as from the other. The events, emotions, and thoughts which come in my sleep are as much a part of my real life as those of the day. Waking and sleeping are two forms of existence. To me the latter state is full of interest and expectation. The two states mutually act upon each other. . . .

"Hope, Faith, Wish, are the presentiments of sight, the evidences of becoming sight to the senses. They are the fore-runners of vision. It is by them we know. . . .

"To believe is to see, not with the senses but with the higher faculties of the soul, reason, imagination, hope. . . .

"I believe that every faculty may be elevated to the state of prophecy.

"Reasoning is faith struggling with doubt."

CHAPTER XI.

THAT "movable feast," Thanksgiving Day, gave Isaac occasion for making this examination of conscience at five o'clock in the morning :

"When I cast my eyes back, it seems to me that I have made some progress—that I have grown somewhat better than I was. Thoughts, feelings, and passions which were active in my bosom, and which, in truth, were not to be well-spoken of, have given place, I hope, to a better state of mind.

"How am I now actualizing my spiritual life? It would be hard for me to answer at this moment. Am I less wilful? Do I sacrifice more than I did? Am I more loving? I am afraid that I am doing nothing more than I did ; and therefore I took up this book to give an account of myself.

"Study occupies the best part of my time most generally. I recite lessons in Latin and in German every day, and now intend to study English grammar again. Then I read considerable, and write letters to my friends. All this, added to the hours I have to spend in business, leaves me not sufficient time to meditate ; and there is no opportunity here for me to go into a retired, silent place, where I can be perfectly still, which is what has the most internal effect on me, and the best and most lasting. Two things I should and must do for my own soul's sake : speak less, and think less of my friends. To do this will give me a retired place and an opportunity for silence in the midst of all that is around me.

"I feel that I am not doing anything to ameliorate the social condition of those around me who are under my influence and partial control. Just now there seems a stand-still in this direction. The Spirit promises to teach us in all things : what more would it have me do in this way? What should be my next step? My mind has been partially drawn away from this by the present poor state of business, which keeps us cramped in our funds.

"I fear that to take less food than I now do would injure my health—else I should fast often.

"To-day let me put in practice the two above-mentioned duties : silence, and less thought upon my friends.

"And now, O God! if Thou helpest not I shall be worse than before. Heavenly Father, as the flower depends on the light and warmth of the sun for its grace and beauty, so, and much more, do I depend on Thee for life and progress. O Lord! from the depths of my heart I would implore Thee to aid me in all good intentions. My heart overflows with its fulness of gratitude for what Thou hast done for me, and I know Thou wilt not shorten Thy hand. Thy beauty, Thy loveliness, O God! is beyond our finite vision, far above our expression. Lord, all I can utter is, Help my weakness."

"*December* 2, 1843.—My heart, these two days back, has been filled with love. Oh, had I some one to whom I could unbosom myself! There is a something that affects my heart which is invisible, and to me strange."

Here he seems to intend the literal, physical heart, making it the scene, at the same time, of a spiritual emotion. On the same day he writes :

"I will not feed my body with impure food—is it not of infinitely more importance that I should not feed my spirit with deeds of impurity? By this I mean my gaining a living by making and selling articles which, in my judgment, are injurious, being luxurious and altogether unnecessary. Should I cease from doing that which is contrary to my spirit, what else should I do? O Lord, enlighten Thou my path!"

With what zeal he still persisted in the practice of bodily mortification this entry bears witness :

"*December* 6.—Day before yesterday I fasted and took a cold shower-bath. My diet is apples, potatoes, nuts, and unleavened bread. No water—scarcely a mouthful a week."

Then follow some thoughts on the solidarity of humanity, which retards individual progress by weighting each with the burdens of all others. He finds in this an explanation of the truth that our Lord took all the sins of men upon Himself and suffered for them on the cross. The blind ingratitude with which this sacrifice has been repaid cuts him with anguish, from which he rises into this cry of love and adoration :

" O Lord! my heart is choked from the utterance of its depth of thankfulness. O dear Christ! O sweet Christ! O loving Christ! oh, more than brother, friend! oh, more than any other being can be! O Son of God! oh, Thou who showest forth the pure love of God! oh, Thou inexpressible Love! draw me nearer Thee, let me feel more of Thy purity, Thy love! Oh, baptize me with Thy Spirit and loosen my tongue that I may speak of Thy love to men! Oh, it cannot be spoken of, nor can our hearts feel its great-ness. God! what is Thy mercy that Thou sufferest us to live? Our ingratitude is too great to be uttered. Lord, I am silent, for who can speak in Thy presence? O Father! O Love! O Loving-kindness! My heart could fly away!"

On his birthday, December 18, 1843, having finished his twenty-third year, he puts down an account of conscience in the form of prayers and aspirations to God, breathing a deep sense of humility, expressing regret for his inactivity, his lack of gratitude for favors both spiritual and temporal, and adding a fervent appeal for more light and greater courage. In almost every entry of any length in the diary during this period he complains of his lack of solitude and of the means of obtaining it. His mind, after arriving home, was tossed with many interior distresses which he could not com-municate to his brothers, nor even to his mother, with any hope of assuagement, but which silence and solitude enabled him to soothe by prayer. On the last day of the year he reverts to the great changes which 1843 had witnessed in his soul, and which, he says, were accompanied by bitter anguish. Twelve months before he had been with his " dear friend, O. A. Brownson, filled with an unknown spirit, driven from home by it, and like one intoxicated, not knowing who I was or wherefore I was so troubled "—then to Brook Farm, and to Fruitlands, and back again in New York for the previous five or six months, the same spirit still in sovereign mastery over him, and, " though regulated, none the less powerful." He says that he is not so restless nor his mind so chaotic, but that he still has a pain at heart which he declares to be almost unbearable, joined to some nervous excitability.

Meantime, besides trying to employ himself actively in the business of the Hecker Brothers, he recited lessons daily in both German and Latin, and read much, chiefly on topics suggested by the difficulties with which his life was beset, such as philosophy, religious controversy, and the graver sorts of poetry, of which that of Goethe made a deep impression on him. The melancholy unrest and longing which such poetry embodies sunk into his very heart. Often it gave perfect expression to his own doubting and distressed state of soul. He also found some relaxation in an occasional visit to the theatre and heard nearly all the lectures given in the city. One of the dreams of his life, the amelioration of the social condition of the working people, he found himself unable to actualize in any appreciable degree. It is evident that his brothers shared his philanthropic views; but when it came to set practically to work there was a lack of harmony. John Hecker was for attaining the object by stricter discipline, treating the men rather as servants; while " we," says Isaac, speaking of himself and George, "took the side of treating them with kindness, and, as far as possible, as brethren." In truth, it was evidence of nobility of character in these three brothers that they could so much as dream of actualizing so radical a social reform in but one establishment amidst so many in ardent business competition with each other. It may be said in passing that the practical charity of the Hecker Brothers continued to do credit to the spirit which originally prompted their attempts at social reform. During a period of general distress some years since they distributed bread free, sending their own wagons around the city for the purpose.

No small part of Isaac's distress arose from what the diary calls the ugliness, vulgarity, and discord everywhere to be met with in his daily round of duties. He had one refuge from this in his domestic life—a pleasant, pure, and peaceful home; and another in the inner chamber of his soul, better fitted every day to be a sanctuary to which he could fly for solace. But his heart fairly bled for the vast mass of men and of women about him, only a few of whom had such an outer refuge, and perhaps fewer still the inner one. This sympathy he felt his life long. He ever blamed the huge accretion of law and customs and selfishness which is called society for much of this misery of men, this hindrance to a fair distribution of the goods of this world, this guilty permission on the part of the fortunate few of the want and dirt and ugliness and coarseness which are the lot of almost the whole race of man. Yet he was not blind to individual guilt. Right here in his diary, after lamenting his enforced inability to succor human misery, he says that some words dropped by the workmen in conversation with him cause him to record his conviction that suffering and injustice, together with

the deprivation of liberty, are due to one's own fault as well as
to that of others:

"Every evil that society inflicts upon me, the germ of it is
my own fault; in proportion as I free myself from my vices will
I free myself from the evils which society inflicts upon me. Be
true to thyself and thou canst not be false to any one. Be true
to thyself, and it follows as night follows day that others cannot
be false to thee."

Of course this panacea offers only an inward healing, for none
more readily admitted than he who wrote these sentences that in
externals the true heart is often the first victim of the malice
of the false heart.

Ever and again we find in the diary reflections on the general
aspect of religion. The Protestant churches seemed to him to
fail to meet the aspirations of the natural man; that is the burden
of his complaint against them all. Some, like the Unitarians, did
but offer man his best self, and hence added nothing to humanity, while humanity at its best ceaselessly condemned itself as in-
sufficient. This insufficiency of man for himself, Calvinistic and
Lutheran Protestantism in their turn condemned as a depravity
worthy of the deepest hell, making man a wretch maimed in his
very nature so cruelly and fatally as to be damned for what he
could not help being guilty of. Meantime the Catholic Church
was seen by Isaac Hecker as having elements the most attractive.
It recognized in man his native dignity; it saw in him a being
made God-like by the attribute of reason, and called him to a
state infinitely more God-like by a supernatural union with Christ.
It understood his weakness, pitied it, and knew how to cure it.
True, there are passages here in which his impatience with the
public attitude of the Church betrays that his view of it was yet
a distant one; they show, also, an undue concentration of his gaze
upon social evils. "The Church is a great almoner," he says,
"but what is she doing to ameliorate and improve the circumstances of the poorer and more numerous classes? She is more
passive than active." "Instead of the Church being in the head
and front of advancement, suffering martyrdom for Christ, she is
in a conservative relation with society." Yet he adds: "We
speak of the Church as she is exhibited by her bishops and clergy,
and only in this sense."

Isaac Hecker's renewed experiment of engaging in business
and following at the same time the lead of the peremptory Spirit

within him soon proved a failure. He complains, though not as
bitterly as the year before when he felt the first agony of this
suffering, that the greater part of his true life is lost in his present
position—the thoughts, feelings, studies which are of supreme value
to him, getting entrance into his mind almost by stealth, while,
at the same time, he is not of much use in the business and of little
benefit to others in any way. On March 10 he wrote to Brownson
that he was going to give up business totally and finally, and
asked his advice about a course of study "for the field of the
Church," not having yet fully settled as to whether it should be
"the Roman or the Anglican." Upon his determination to withdraw from the secular affairs of life he experienced "such peace,
calmness, and deep, settled strength and confidence" as never before. "I feel the presence of God," he writes, "wherever I am.
I would kneel and praise God in all places. In His presence I
walk and feel His breath encompass me. My soul is borne up by
His presence and my heart is filled by His influence. How thankful ought we to be! How humble and submissive! Let us lay our
heads on the pillow of peace and die peacefully in the embrace
of God."

Brownson answered his letter with one of encouragement to
carry out his purpose. Yet, there was a pang; Isaac laments
"the domestic comforts, the little offices of tender love" which
he should lose by going from home. And well he might, for
tender love may well describe the bond uniting the dear old
mother and her three noble sons. The present writer had no
personal acquaintance with John Hecker, but we never heard his
name mentioned by Father Hecker except with much affection.
George always seemed to us something like a perfect man. He
especially it was who all his life gave his entire unselfish love to
his brother Isaac. The reader has noticed, we hope, that there
has been no mention so far in the diary of difficulty in obtaining
money for the expenses of his various journeyings and for his
support when absent from home. The two brothers in New
York appear to have held these pilgrimages in search of the
truth in such reverence as to make Isaac their partner, only in a
higher sense than ever before. And George Hecker, especially,
seemed throughout his life to continue Isaac a member of his
great and rich firm, lavishing upon his least wish large sums of
money, and these not only for his strictly personal expenditure,
but for any cause whatever he might have at heart.

CHAPTER XII.

THE MYSTIC AND THE PHILOSOPHER.

BEFORE summarizing and conveniently arranging Isaac Hecker's reasons for becoming a Catholic and narrating the accompanying incidents, we give the following profession of faith in the authority of the Spirit speaking within. It was written in the diary in the midst of his preparations for his baptism, and is an early witness of a permanent characteristic of Father Hecker's life. It is, besides, a fitting introduction to the description of his state of mind when he entered the Church, showing better than anything we have found what kind of man became a Catholic in Isaac Hecker.

"Man is a mystic fact.

"What is most interior is ever mystical, and we should ever be in the centre of the circle of the mystic life.

. " We must unfold the mystical in all our expressions, actions, thoughts, and motions.

"It is the mystic life only which can fully interest man. This is deeper than all conditions, behind all organs, faculties, and functions.

"We must listen to those who speak to us in the interior world, and hear the mystic man speak through us.

"The mystic man is ever youthful, fresh, and new.

"The mystic sphere is the kingdom of heaven within.

"I can neither study nor sit down and read for any length of time. The inner man will not permit me. Ever he calls me from it to meditate and enjoy his presence.

"He says: I am all. Ask of me and I will give you more than has been written—more than you can ever find or dig out by study.

"Be my spokesman—this is your office. Submit to me—this is your glory. I have taken up my abode in you on condition that you will be faithful and submissive.

"You have no business to ask of me what I am going to set you about. I am, and you know it—and this is enough for you to know.

"This is my condition of remaining with you—that you entertain me, and me alone, and no other on any pretext whatsoever.

I am all, and this suffices. You have nothing to say, to do, or to be troubled about. Do only as I bid you, follow what I tell you, and be still.

"If you neglect me in any way, or forget me for any other object, now that you have enjoyed my confidence, love, and blessing, I will not abide with you any longer.

"I want all your time and to speak all that is to be said. You have no right to speak a word—not a word—of your own. You are not your own. You have given yourself up to me, and I am all. I will not leave you unless you leave me first, and even then I shall ever be the nearest to you, but you will not know it.

"I am your Friend; the One who loves you. I have discovered myself to you and will do so yet more. But the condition of so doing requires from you even more faith, tenderness, and submissiveness.

"Nothing is so real, so near, so full of enjoyment as I am to you, and you cannot leave me without giving up the greater for the less.

"I talk to you at all times and am near you at all seasons, and my joy is to be in your presence, to love you and to take delight in this love I bestow upon you. I direct your pen, speech, thought, and affections, though you know it not sensibly. But you shall know more clearly who I am, and all respecting me, if you but comply with my requirements. You need not fear: you cannot make any mistakes if you submit to be guided by me."

Isaac Hecker had now tried every form of philosophy. Whoever sailed with Brownson on that voyage which ended on the shores of Catholic truth, had explored the deep seas and sounded the shoal waters of all human reason; and young Hecker had been Brownson's friend and sympathizer since the years of his own earliest mental activity. Pantheism, subjectivism, idealism, and all the other systems were tried, and when at last he was convinced that *Life is Real* it was only after such an agony as must attend the imminent danger of fatal shipwreck.

He had, meantime, given a fair trial to philanthropy. Theoretically and practically, Isaac Hecker loved humanity; to make men happy was his ever-renewed endeavor; was, in truth, the condition on which his own happiness depended. For years this view of his life-task alternated with his search for exact answers to the questions his soul asked about man's destiny hereafter; or, one might rather say, social questions and philosophical ones borrowed strength from each other to assail him till his heart throbbed and his brain whirled with the agony of the conflict.

In a series of articles in *The Catholic World* published in 1887, and before referred to, Father Hecker called Dr. Brownson's road to the Church the philosophical road. Finding that doctrines which his philosophical mind perceived to answer the deepest questions of the soul were taught only in one society, and there taught with authority, he argued validly that that society could lay claim to the right to teach. From the doctrine to the teacher, from the truth to the external authority that teaches it, is an inference of sound reason. This applies to Father Hecker's case also, for he was of a bent of mind truly philosophical, and he has placed on record the similarity of his philosophical difficulties with those of Brownson. But in addition to philosophical questions, and far more pressing, were to Isaac Hecker the problems arising from the mystical occurrences of which his soul was the theatre. Were these real?—that is, were they more than the vagaries of a sensitive temperament, the wanderings of a sentimental imagination, or, to use Father Hecker's own words, "the mere projections into activity of feelings entirely subjective; mystical impulses towards no corresponding objective realities, or, at any rate, with objects which it is not possible to bring into the field of the really knowable? Some will admit that religious feeling is as much a verity as any other part of human consciousness, affirming, however, the subjectivity of all purely spiritual life; and no more can be said, they insist, for the principles, metaphysical and logical, with which they are associated in the spiritual life of man. Now, such a theory never leaves the soul that is governed by reason at rest. The problem ever and again demands solution: are these yearnings, aspirations, unappeased desires, or religious feelings—the ruling traits of the noblest men and women—are they genuine, real, corresponding to and arising from the reality of certain objects external to the soul? I think that in the solution of this problem Dr. Brownson fought and won his greatest victory; at any rate, it was to me the most interesting period of his life. No wonder, since I had the same battle to fight myself, and it was just at this epoch that I came into closest contact with him. We fought this battle shoulder-to-shoulder."—*Catholic World*, October, 1887, pp. 5–6.

Brownson's heavy heart was due to philosophical difficulties, and Isaac Hecker's to the same; but in addition the latter had a mystical experience to which Brownson was at that time, certainly, a stranger, and, as far as we know, he remained so; and these mystical difficulties demanded settlement far more imperatively than did the philosophical ones. Isaac Hecker's inner life must have an external adjunct of divine authority. Such aspirations of the soul for present union with God in love as he had, are more peremptory in demanding satisfaction than those of the logical faculty in demanding the ascertainment of the certain truth. Philosophy outside the Church is to the searcher after truth what St. Paul said the Law was to the Jews, a schoolmaster; but, to a soul in the condition of Isaac Hecker, the Holy Spirit is a spouse demanding union. Both Brownson and himself were men true to their convictions, courageous and unselfish. They were both firmly determined to have the truth and to have the whole of it, whether spoken *ex cathedra* in the divine court of the innermost soul, or *ex cathedra* by the supreme authority of God in the organism of the Christian Church. "Brownson was firmly persuaded," says Father Hecker, "and so am I, that the great fault of men generally is that they deem the life of their souls, thoughts, judgments, and convictions, yearnings, aspirations, and longings to be too subject to illusion to be worthy their attentive study and manly fidelity; that even multitudes of Catholics greatly undervalue the divine reality of their inner life, whether in the natural or supernatural order."

The philosophical difficulty was far less serious than the spiritual one. To the philosopher the fundamental truths of human reason are established as objective realities by processes common to every sane mind, and are backed by the common consent of men; and this is true also of the prime verities of ethics. But when a man finds himself subject to secret influences of the utmost power over him, able to cast him off or to hold him, to sicken his body and distress his soul, extending his views of the truth by flashes of light into vistas that seem infinite, making his love of right an ecstasy, his sympathy for human misery a passion, controlling his diet and his clothing, ordering him here and there at will and knowing how to be obeyed—when, in a word, a man finds himself treated by God in a manner totally different from any one else he knows or ever heard of, it is plain that he must agonize for the possession of a divine sanction to which he can appeal in common with all men, and which must therefore exist in the external order. He longs, above all things, to test his secret in the light of day.

The problem that Isaac Hecker had to solve, as he described it himself, was whether his life was real—using the word "life" to denote its truest meaning, the interior life. We have been careful to make the reader aware of how deep and continuous were the inner touches of the Holy Spirit which led him on. Before applying for admission to the Church, there was no truth that he could believe more firmly than that he was the temple of the Holy Ghost. Of that he had the certitude which is called personal and the teaching of God which is most direct. Yet something was lacking, and therein lay his agony, for he knew that his fellow-men were entitled to all that he had of truth and virtue. The more distinct the Voice which spoke within, the more perplexing it became to hear no echo from without. He felt sure that what was true and holy for him must be so for all, and yet he could not so much as make himself understood if he told his secret to others. To the born Catholic there is no such difficulty. He is so fully accustomed to the verification of the inner action of God, enlightening his mind and stinging his conscience, by God's external action in the Church, that he often confounds the two. He knows the Voice better by its echo than by its own tones. There are many good Catholics, but few enlightened mystics. This is not for lack of guidance, so far as doctrine is concerned, for accredited authors on such subjects are numerous and their teaching is uniform and explicit, besides being of the most intense interest to those for whose instruction it is adapted. These masters of spiritual doctrine not only dwell upon the interior life itself, but also on the external order of God in His Church which brings His interior teaching into proper relation with the exterior. The interior life thus made integral is alone worthy of the term *real;* is alone worthy of the description of St. Paul when he calls it " the witness of the Spirit." Now, as a witness who cannot be brought into open court to give his testimony might as well be dumb, and is as good as no witness, so the inner life, lacking the true external order of God, is cramped and helpless ; and cramped and helpless Isaac Hecker was. Whatever he did, therefore, toward investigating religious evidences was done primarily as a search for the external criterion which should guarantee the validity of the inspirations of

God within him, and at the same time provide a medium of union with his fellow-men.

Those whose advertence is not particularly aroused to the facts of their interior life, have for their main task either the study of the Church as a visible society, claiming continuity with one established by Christ; or, preceding that, the question whether such a society was ever founded by God. Now, although such questions must be settled by all, they are not the main task of men like Isaac Hecker. In their case the problem transcending all others is where to find that divine external order demanded for the completion of their inner experience. Such men must say: If there is no external order of God in this world, then my whole interior life is fatally awry.

The captain whose voyage is on the track of the trade winds nevertheless needs more than dead reckoning for his course; he needs to take the sun at noon, to study the heavens at night, and to con his chart. To follow one's interior drift only is to sail the ocean without chart or compass. The sail that is wafted by the impulses of the divine Spirit in the interior life must have, besides, the guarantee of divine veracity in the external order to justify him. This he needs, in order to safeguard him in the interior life itself, and to provide a common court of appeal between himself and his fellows, or otherwise he is in danger of fanaticism, and is certain of the mistrust of his fellow-men. No man, unsupported by external miracles, can claim to teach what is vouched for only by his own testimony; and this especially applies to purely subjective experiences. Isaac Hecker was a born teacher of men, and to be shut off from them by an isolated experience was to be robbed of his vocation. A soul like his, led to the truth along the path of social reform, will hail with delight a religion which organizes all humanity on a basis of equality, and at the same time verifies and explains the facts of each one's particular experience. Such a religion is to be longed for, not only because of its universal brotherhood, but also because it can decide between the inspirations of the Holy Spirit and the criminal conceits of passion or the dreams of an imaginative temperament.

Many years afterwards Father Hecker thus stated the harmony between the inner and outer action of God in the soul's life:

"In case of obscurity or doubt concerning what is the divinely revealed truth, or whether what prompts the soul is or is not an inspiration of the Holy Spirit, recourse must be had to the divine teacher or criterion—the authority of the Church. For it must be borne in mind that to the Church, as represented in the first instance by St. Peter and subsequently by his successors, was made the promise of her divine Founder that 'the gates of hell should never prevail against her.' No such promise was ever made by Christ to each individual believer. 'The Church of the living God is the pillar and ground of truth.' The test, therefore, of a truly enlightened and sincere Christian will be, in case of uncertainty, the promptitude of his obedience to the voice of the Church.

"From the above plain truths the following practical rule of conduct may be drawn : The Holy Spirit is the immediate guide of the soul in the way of salvation and sanctification; and the criterion or test, that the soul is guided by the Holy Spirit, is its ready obedience to the authority of the Church. This rule removes all danger whatever, and with it the soul can walk, run, or fly, if it chooses, in the greatest safety and with perfect liberty, in the ways of sanctity."—*The Church and the Age*, p. 35.

In transcribing the above we are reminded that St. Ignatius, who was the divine instrument in establishing and perfecting God's authority in the external order, yet left on record that so clearly had the Holy Spirit shown him by secret teaching the truths of religion, that, if all the Scriptures had been destroyed, his private revelations at Manresa would have sufficed him in their stead.

All that we have just been saying helps to answer the question why Orestes Brownson and Isaac Hecker did not set up systems of their own, and become Carlyles and Emersons or, especially in Father Hecker's case, Emanuel Swedenborgs or Edward Irvings. We find the following among the memoranda of conversations :

"*June* 30, 1886.—Why didn't I switch off from Christianity as Carlyle did ? Because I hope that I was truer to natural reason ; but chiefly because God had given me such an amount of infused lights and graces that I was forced to seek a guide or go off into extravagant fanaticism. They were ready to encourage

me in the latter.　George Ripley said to me, 'Hecker, what have
you got to tell?　Tell us what it is and we will accept it.'"

The impression a perfectly "independent thinker" made on
him, as typified in Emerson, is told in an entry in his diary,
dated April 24, 1844:

"I have had a few words with Emerson.　He stands on the
extreme ground where he did several years ago.　He and his followers seem to me to live almost a purely intellectual existence.
His wife I have understood to be a very religious woman.　They
are heathens in thought, and profess to be so.　They have no conception of the Church: out of Protestantism they are almost
perfectly ignorant.　They are the narrowest of men, yet they think
they are extremely 'many-sided'; and, forsooth, do not comprehend Christendom, and reject it.　The Catholic accepts all the
good they offer him and finds it comparatively little compared to
that which he has."

That he recognized that the test of the character of his inner
experiences, for good or ill, was to be finally found in what they
led him to, is shown by the following passage, already quoted,
from the diary: "What I do I must do, for it is not I that
do it; it is the Spirit.　What that Spirit may be is a question I cannot answer.　What it leads me to do will be the only
evidence of its character.　I feel as impersonal as a stranger
to it."

The aid which fidelity to the light of reason and the cherish-
ing and obeying the inspirations of the Holy Spirit lends to the
discovery of the fulness of truth is shown by the following
extract from an article by Father Hecker in *The Catholic World*
of October, 1887:

"The man who establishes the historical identity of the Church
of to-day with the Apostolic college says the doctrines now
taught must be true; the man who perceives the identity of the
Church's doctrines with his own highest aspirations also proves
them true.　The man who has become responsive to the primitive
action of his reason says that the Church, which is its only authoritative exponent, must be a divinely appointed teacher.　The
infallible authority of the Church in her past, present, and future

teaching is established by the necessity of the truths which she teaches for the welfare of the human race, by thus completing the outlines of natural truth drawn by the divine hand in human consciousness."

By this we see that, if the divine inner life had need of the divine outer life for its integrity, it is equally certain that in his case, and also in that of Dr. Brownson, the intimate action of God within was a pointer to the true Church of the Divine Word incarnate in the actual world of humanity: for Dr. Brownson chiefly in the intellectual order, for Isaac Hecker in both the intellectual and mystical. We have no fear of wearying the reader with the length of an extract of such value as the following:

" The one who reaches Catholicity by the philosophical road, as Brownson did, by no means pretends that the problem of human destiny can be solved by mere force of reason : Catholicity is not rationalism. Nor does he pretend that the product of reason's action, the knowledge of human immortality and liberty and of the being of God, place man apart from or above the universal action of God upon all souls by means of a visible society and external ordinances : Catholicity is well named ; it is universal. But he knows that when a man is persuaded of a truth philosophically he is not called upon by his intelligence or his conscience to base it upon historical evidence ; it is enough that he has one source of certitude in its favor. It may be a truth first known by revelation, but if the human intelligence is capable of receiving it in revelation it must have some element of kinship to the truths of pure reason. As in the order of nature men are like unto God, so is there a likeness between the truth of God naturally known and that known only by revelation.

" As there is an appetite in the human heart which not all the treasures, honors, joys of nature can satisfy, so there is a void in the mind which all the truth within reach of the unaided natural faculties leaves unfilled. When a man without guile is brought face to face with truth he spontaneously desires union with it. Appetite proves the existence of food, and the food affirms itself by satisfying the appetite.

" Where there is question of a principle there is a class of minds which must study the part a principle has played in history, and is mainly influenced for or against it from its effect on former generations of men. This class follows the historical road. Another class is so profoundly moved by the truths of revelation as soon as known, assimilates them so readily and perfectly, becomes so absorbed and lost in them, that the history of revelation is not of primary importance; it is only necessary in order to establish necessary facts, such as the divine institution of an external society, and of other external aids. But with this philosophical class of minds the truth stands sponsor for itself and is its own best witness. The impression produced by revelation here and now upon the soul without guile is one of the best probable proofs to that soul of the historical claims of the society to which God entrusted it. 'The Church Accredits Itself' was the title of one of the most powerful articles Dr. Brownson ever wrote for this magazine.

"Both the historical and the philosophical processes are necessary, but each is more so to one class of minds than to another. To the philosophical mind, once scepticism is gone and life is real, the supreme fact of life is the need of more truth than unaided reason can know. The more this need is felt, and the more clearly the deficiencies of natural reason are known, the better capable one is to appreciate the truths of revelation which can alone supply these deficiencies. In such a state of mind you are in a condition to establish revealed truth in a certain sense *a priori*, and the method *a posteriori* is then outranked. The philosopher outranks the historian. In minds of a speculative turn the historian is never considered of primary importance. The principles which its facts illustrate are furnished him by human reason in philosophy, and by the divine reason in revelation. The historical mind has never been considered in the world of thought as sovereign. The philosopher is broad enough to study all ways leading to the full truth and joy of life, whether logical or traditional; but he knows that the study of principles is higher than that of facts. . . . No man can intelligently become a Catholic without examining and deciding the historical question. But back of this is the consideration that the truths the Church teaches are necessarily in harmony with my reason—nay, that they alone solve the problems of reason satisfactorily and answer fully to the wants of the heart. To some minds the truths standing alone compel assent; that is to say, the truths standing alone, and considered in themselves, demand the submission of my reason. Among these truths, thus imperative, not the least is the need of the very Church herself, viewed in her action on men and nations—viewed quite apart from the historical and Scriptural proof of her establishment by Christ. Once the mind is lifted above subjectivism and is face-to-face with the truth, union with the Church is only a question of time and of fidelity to conscience." — *Catholic World, November,* 1887, " *Dr. Brownson and Catholicity.*"

CHAPTER XIII.

HIS SEARCH AMONG THE SECTS.

HAD Protestantism possessed anything capable of attracting Isaac Hecker he would certainly have found it, for he made due and diligent search. He was, in a manner, bound to do so, for the atmosphere in which he had been born and nurtured had not yet cleared so fully that he could say to himself with positive assurance that there was no safe midway between no-belief and Catholicity.

All the natural influences of his surroundings were such as to draw him to one or other of the Protestant denominations. The power of example and precept in his mother tended that way. The power of public opinion, in so far as it had any religious bearing, was Protestant. The most intelligent and high-minded people he had enjoyed intimate acquaintance with were Protestant by birth and training. True, most of these had fallen away from both the fellowship and the doctrines of orthodoxy; but while they had not the heart to point him to what had been their Egypt, still they had no Promised Land to lead him into, and were confessedly in the Desert. Yet their influence was indirectly favorable to Protestantism as opposed to Catholicity, although no one but the ministers whom he consulted thought of urging him to identify himself with any variety of it until he showed signs of becoming a Catholic.

To this rule Brownson may appear as a partial exception, but until the summer of 1844 he was so in appearance only. It is true that Isaac Hecker had learned from him the claims of most of the great forms of Protestantism, and got his personal testimony as to the emptiness of them all. Brownson was a competent witness, for he had been an accepted disciple of every school, from sterile Presbyterianism to rank Transcendentalism. Although of a certain testiness of temper, he bore malice to no man and to no body of men. His testimony was in the presence of patent facts, and his condemnation of all forms of orthodox Protestantism in the end was unreserved. But, up to the date given above he still made a possible exception in favor of Anglicanism. In the middle of April, 1843, he wrote Isaac a letter, motioning him toward this sect, at the same time affirming that he could not quite accept it for himself. Such counsel was no better than motioning him away from it,

and was but a symbol of Brownson's own devious progress, sway-
ing now to one side and again to the other, but always going
forward to Rome. But young Hecker would learn for himself.
Of an abnormally inquiring mind by nature, he never accepted a
witness other than himself about any matter if he could help it.

In the early part of 1844 the question of religious affiliation
began to press for settlement with increasing urgency, casting
him at times into an agony of mind. It was not merely that
he was impelled by conscience towards the fulness of truth, but
that truth in its simplest elements seemed sometimes to be lacking to him. He was heard to say in after years that, had he not
found Catholicity true, he would have been thrown back into a
scepticism so painful as to suggest suicide as a relief. Yet those
who have trodden any of the paths which lead from inherited
heresy to true doctrine, will appreciate the force of the influences,
both personal and social, which induced him to reconsider, and
make for himself the grand rounds of Protestant orthodoxy before
turning his back upon it for ever.

We find him, therefore, going diligently to all who claimed to
be watchmen on the walls of Sion, to seek from each one personally that countersign which would tally with the divine word
nature and grace were uttering in his own soul. He interviewed
ministers repeatedly. "Not having had," he wrote in this magazine for November, 1887, "personal and experimental knowledge of the Protestant denominations, I investigated them all,
going from one of them to another—Episcopal, Congregational,
Baptist, Methodist, and all—conferring with their ministers and
reading their books. It was a dreary business, but I did it. I
knew Transcendentalism well and had been a radical socialist.
All was found to be as stated above. Brownson's ripe experience
and my own thoroughly earnest investigation tallied perfectly.
Indeed, the more you examine the Protestant sects in the light
of first principles the more they are found to weaken human
certitude, interfere with reason's native knowledge of God and
His attributes, and perplex the free working of the laws of
human thought. Protestantism is no religion for a philosopher,
unless he is a pessimist—if you can call such a being a philosopher—and adopts Calvinism."

Why Calvinism, with its dread consistency of aversion for
human nature, did not attract him in these early inquiries was
expressed by Father Hecker in after years by the saying,

" Heresy always involves a mutilation of man's natural reason."
The typical Calvinist foams against man's natural capacity for the
true and the good, and one of its representatives, a Presbyterian
minister, had the consistency to say to our young disciple of
nature, " Unless you believe that you are totally depraved you
will certainly suffer eternal damnation." These words were spoken
to one who felt some sort of apostleship growing into act within his bosom : to preach the Gospel to those who are totally
depraved he perceived to be both vain and suicidal. Furthermore, the consciousness of his own upright character, his experience and observation of human virtue in others, made abstract
arguments needless to prove that Calvinism is an outrage on
human kind and a blasphemy against the Creator.

Anglicanism, too—uncleansed, as it notoriously is, of a Calvinistic taint, broken up by absolute license of dissent, maintaining
a mere outward conformity to an extremely lax discipline—
affronted Isaac Hecker's ideal of the communion of man and
God ; man seeking and God giving the one only revelation of
divine truth, unifying and organizing the Christian community :
and this in spite of an attraction for the beauty of the Episcopal service which he often confesses in his diary.

In the same scrupulous spirit he tried the Baptists, though he
must have known that they were, almost without exception,
Calvinists. He had a conference with one of their ministers
which, from the account he gives of it, must have degenerated
into something like a wrangle. " If," said young Hecker, " you
admit that baptism is not a saving ordinance, why, then, do you
separate yourselves from the rest of Christendom on a mere
question of ceremonial observance ? " There could be no satisfactory answer to this question.

As to the Methodists, they made fifty years ago much less
pretension to an intellectual footing in the religious world than at
the present day. One thing, Father Hecker tells us, drew his sympathetic regards their way—their doctrine of perfection. He went to
one of their ministers, a Dr. Crawford. " I have read in the Bible,"
said he, " ' If thou wouldst be perfect, go and sell all thou hast ' ;
now, that is the kind of Christian I want to be." The answer was :
" Well, young man, you must not carry things too far ; you are too
enthusiastic. Christ does not require that of us in the nineteenth
century." After conversing with him for some time, the minister
told him to give up such ideas and study for the ministry.

A singular episode in his search was his meeting with two enthusiastic Mormon apostles, and a long and careful examination, under their guidance, of the then newly-delivered revelations and prophecies of Joseph Smith. He describes his Mormon acquaintances as men of some intelligence, but given over, totally and blindly, to Smith's imposture.

But what cut under the claims of every form of Protestantism was the error, common to them all, concerning the rule of faith : the private and independent judgment of the teaching of Scripture made by each man for himself. As the real owner of a homestead has most reason to dread a dealer in false titles, so the truly free man has most reason to dread false liberty. Isaac Hecker was the type of rational individual liberty, hence the very man to abhor most the caricature of that prerogative in the typical Protestant.

Five years before his death, in an article in *The Catholic World* entitled " Luther and the Diet of Worms," Father Hecker put the case thus : "It is a misapprehension common among Protestants to suppose that Catholics, in refusing the appeal of Martin Luther at the Diet of Worms, condemn the use of reason or individual judgment, or whatever one pleases to call the personal act which involves the exercise of man's intellect and free will. The truth is, personal judgment flows from what constitutes man a rational being, and there is no power under heaven that can alienate personal judgment from man, nor can man, if he would, disappropriate it. The cause of all the trouble at the Diet of Worms was not personal judgment, for neither party put that in question. The point in dispute was the right application of personal judgment. Catholics maintained, and always have and always will maintain, that a divine revelation necessitates a divine interpreter. Catholics resisted, and always will resist, on the ground of its incompetency, a human authority applied to the interpretation of the contents of a divinely-revealed religion. They consider such an authority, whether of the individual or the state, in religious matters an intrusion. Catholics insist, without swerving, upon believing in religion none but God. . . . To investigate and make one's self certain that God has made a revelation is of obligation, and consistent with Christianity. But as a divine revelation springs from a source above the sphere of reason, it necessitates a divinely authorized and divinely assisted *interpreter* and teacher. This is one of the essential functions of the Church."

That the use of the Scriptures is not, and cannot be made the ordinary means for making all men Christians, was plain to Isaac Hecker for other reasons than the essential one thus clearly stated. For, if such were the case, God would bestow on all men the gift to read at sight, or cause all to learn how to read, or would have recorded in the Book itself the words, " Unless a man reads the Bible, and believes what he reads, he cannot enter into the kingdom of God," or their plain equivalent; whereas the Bible, as we have it now, did not exist in the apostolic days, the most glorious era of the Christian Church. Such is Father Hecker's argument in a powerful article in *The Catholic World* for October, 1883. He continues :

" But suppose that everybody knew how to read, or all men were gifted to read at first sight; suppose that everybody had a copy of the Bible within his reach, a genuine Bible, and knew with certitude what it means ; suppose that Christ himself had laid it down as a rule that the Bible, without note or comment, and as interpreted by each one for himself, is the ordinary way of receiving the grace of salvation—which is the vital principle of Protestantism ; suppose all these evident assumptions as true. Would the Bible even in that case suffice to make any one man, woman, or child a Christian ? Evidently not. And why ? For that is a personal work, and the personal work of Christ; for Christ alone can make men Christians. And no account of Christ is Christ. . . . The contents of a book, whatever these may be, are powerless to place its readers in direct contact and vital relations with its author. No man is so visionary as to imagine that the mental operation of reading the *Iliad*, or the *Phædo*, or the *Divine Comedy*, suffices to put him in communication with the personality of Homer, or Plato, or Dante. All effort is in vain to slake the thirst of a soul famishing for the *Fountain* of living waters from a brook, or to stop the cravings of a soul for the living Saviour with a printed book. . . . His words are 'Come unto ME all that are weary and heavy laden, and I will refresh you.' It was the attempt to make men Christians by reading the Bible that broke Christendom into fragments, multiplied jarring Christian sects, produced swarms of doubters, filled the world with sceptics and scoffers at all religion, frustrated combined Christian action, and put back the Christian conquest of the world for centuries. Three centuries of experience have made it evident enough that, if Christianity is to be maintained as a principle of life among men, it must be on another footing than the suicidal hypothesis invented in the sixteenth century after the birth of its divine Founder."

His farewell interviews with exponents of the Protestant claims were mainly, if not wholly, with representatives of Anglicanism. This did not arise from any grounded hope of getting all he wanted there, but from an insensible drift of his mind upon those currents of thought set in motion by the great power of Newman. The air was full of promise of non-Roman Catholicity, and the voices which called the English-speaking world to listen were the most eloquent since Shakespeare. It needed but a dim hope pointing along any road to induce the delicate conscience of Isaac Hecker to try if it might not be a thoroughfare. But neither in his copious entries in the diary at this period, nor in his articles in this magazine for the year 1887 on Dr. Brownson's difficulties—and these were much like his own—do we find any trace of his discovering in Anglicanism a germ of Catholicity unfolding from the chrysalis of genuine Protestantism and casting it off. This was readily perceived in Isaac Hecker's bearing and conversation by acute Episcopalians themselves, as in the case of Dr. Seabury, who, as Father Hecker relates in the articles above referred to, prophesied Brownson's conversion to Catholicity, and did so for reasons which Seabury must have known would apply to young Hecker also.

Many at this time were being drawn by poetical sentiment to the beautiful and religious forms of Episcopalian worship; drawn and held rather by imagination and feeling than by any adhesion of their minds to distinctive Anglican doctrines. Father Hecker was, indeed, more poetical in temperament than at first acquaintance he seemed to be, but his mind was so constituted that he must have the main reasons of things, whether religious or not, firmly settled before he could enjoy their use. Nor could he be content with fragments of revealed truth, such as are found in all denominations of non-Catholics. "There is a large floating body of Catholic truth in the world," says Newman; "it comes down by tradition from age to age. . . . Men [outside the church] take up and profess these scattered truths, merely because they fall in with them." Not so Father Hecker: no flotsam and jetsam of doctrine for him, unless some fragment would reveal to him the name of the ship from which it had been torn, and the port from which she had sailed, and so lead him to the discovery of the ship herself, crew, cargo, port, and owner.

Yet he lingered long over the claim of Anglicanism to be the Catholic religion. Of Mr. Haight and of his interviews with him we have already spoken. Through him he came across a published letter of a Mr. Norris, Episcopal minister in Carlisle, Pa., which so pleased him for its Catholic tendency that he wrote to him, asking to be allowed to go to Carlisle and live there as the writer's pupil. The answer, though a refusal of this request, was kind, and contained a cordial invitation to visit Mr. Norris after Easter. On his way to Concord, in the following spring, Isaac made a long detour to the little town in southern Pennsylvania, interviewed Mr. Norris, and came away no wiser than before.

The following words of the diary, under date of March 30, 1844, refer to an Episcopal dignitary of higher grade:

"Mr. Haight gave me a note of introduction to Dr. Seabury. I called to see him two evenings ago and had a very pleasant conversation with him. His sociableness and perfect openness of expression I was quite delighted with. He frankly acknowledged that he thought that error had been committed on both sides in the controversy of the Reformation between the Pope and the Anglican Church. He recommended me to examine those points which kept me from joining the Anglican or Roman Church before I should do anything further, as there was the charge of schism against the Anglican Church and neglect of discipline among the members of her communion. I told him that though the Church of Rome may commit errors in practice, she had not committed any in principle, and that it was easier to prune a luxuriant tree than to revivify a tree almost exhausted of life. I left him with an earnest invitation to call again."

This half-confession of schism and frank avowal of lack of discipline on the part of a perfectly representative official of the Anglican Church was something singularly Providential, for it came within a fortnight after Isaac Hecker's first interview with Bishop Hughes, described in the diary under date of March 22. That powerful man and great prelate was a type of the best form of Catholicism at that day. He was of the Church militant in more senses than one; and the military qualities which have inspired the public action of Catholic champions for the past three centuries were strongly developed in him. That it was for the good of religion that it should have such characters as John Hughes to care for its public welfare there is no room to doubt. Since then the temper of Protestant Americans has undergone a change which is almost radical. It has grown infinitely more just and kindly towards Catholics. The decay of the Protestant bond of cohesion from lapse of time and from the unsettlement of belief in its chief doctrines ; the fighting of two wars, one of them the great Rebellion, which fused the populations of States and acquainted men better with their neighbors; the coming in of millions of Catholic foreigners whose every breath was an aspiration for liberty ; the rise, culmination, and collapse of the anti-Catholic movement termed Know-nothingism ; the polemical warfare of Bishop Hughes himself, and of his contemporaries—these and other causes have made it possible, nay necessary, to treat non-Catholics in a different spirit from what wisdom dictated fifty years ago.

If Dr. Seabury owned to schism and lack of discipline in Anglicanism, Bishop John Hughes brought out to Isaac Hecker the very contrary as the attractive qualities of Catholicity. He was questioned by the young inquirer about the latter's chances for studying for the priesthood should he decide on entering the Church, and he answered according to rigid notions of the place of authority in religion.

"He said," are the words of the diary, ending a summary of the interview, "that their Church was one of discipline. I thanked him for the information that he gave, and told him that it was for just such instruction that I sought him. He seemed to think that I had some loose notions of the Church. So far, this settles my present intention of uniting myself with the Roman Catholic Church. Though I feel not in the least disinclined to be governed by the most rigid discipline of any church, yet I am not prepared to enter the Roman Catholic Church at present. It is not national with us, hence it does not meet our wants, nor does it fully understand and sympathize with the experience and dispositions of our people. It is principally made up of adopted and foreign individuals."

To us this is exceedingly instructive, for it tells us how *not* to meet the earnest seeker after Catholic truth. Even a goodnatured dog does not show his teeth when caressed, nor is an artillery salute the only show of amity between even warlike powers. Yet the repellant attitude of the great controversialist was that of very many representative Catholics of his time, especially those holding his high office. For although he really did know the American people, and although their country was fully his own, and was by him deeply and intelligently loved, yet he did not understand or sympathize with the religious movements of which his strange young visitor was the truest type. He afterwards knew him better and loved him.

The toss thus given Isaac Hecker by Bishop Hughes's catapult of "discipline" had the good effect of throwing him again upon a full and perfect and final investigation of Protestantism. With what immediate result is shown by the Seabury interview already related, and with what honesty of purpose is shown by the following words written the same day:

"If a low passion usurps the place of pure love, if a blind prejudice usurps the place of Catholic truth, he who informs me of it, though he had been my enemy (if enemies it is possible for me to have), I will receive him as an angel from heaven, as an instrument of God. My honor, my consistency, my character consists in faithfulness to God's love, God's truth, and nothing else. Let me be but true to Him—how then can I be false to either man or the world? It is Him who knows our secret thoughts that we should fear (if fear we must) and obey."

Thus it was Anglicanism that engaged Isaac Hecker's last efforts to adjust a Protestant outside to his inward experience with the Holy Spirit; and this for a reason quite evident. That body pretended, then as now, to be the Catholic Christian Church, assisting men to union with God by a divinely-founded external organism, but not demanding the sacrifice of human liberty. To an inexperienced observer such as he, it seemed possible that Anglicanism might be the union of historical Christianity with manly freedom. Closer observation proved to him not only the compatibility of Catholicity and liberty, but that Anglicanism, though assuming some of the forms of Catholic unity, is kept alive by the principle of individual separatism common to all Protestant sects. For a time, or in a place, it may have much or little of Catholicity; but in no place can it live for a day without the Protestant principle of a right of final appeal to the individual judgment to decide upon the verity of doctrine.

CHAPTER XIV.

HIS LIFE AT CONCORD.

" I HAVE been groping in darkness, seeking where Thou wast not, and I found Thee not. But, O Lord my God, *Thou hast found me*—leave me not."

These words are part of a long prayer written by Isaac Hecker in his diary April 23, 1844, after his arrival at Concord, Mass. He appears to have gone directly there from Carlisle, Pa., where he had spent some days with the Rev. William Herbert Norris, whose published letter to "A Sincere Enquirer" had excited in the young man a hope that he might find in him a teacher whose deep inward experiences would be complemented by the adequate external guaranty that he was seeking. We have already noted that he was disappointed. He states the reason very suggestively in a letter written at the time:

" Alas, that men should speak of those things they are most ignorant of! What hopes did he not awaken in my bosom as I read his letter to a Sincere Enquirer, and how were they blasted when I met him and found that it was not he, but Hooker, Newman, Paul, etc.! It is a sad fact that many believe, but very few give themselves up to what they believe so that they may have the substance of their belief."

Isaac Hecker's business in Concord had, as usual, two sides. Externally it meant going on with Greek and Latin, under the guidance of the lately deceased George P. Bradford, a scholar of rare acquirements, whose acquaintance he had made at Brook Farm the previous year. The end he sought in this study was to fit himself for "working in the field of the church." But as the question of which church was not even yet fully settled in his mind, his search for the true religion still remained his deepest and most inmost purpose. Nevertheless, he was enjoying at this time one of his periods of profound interior and exterior peace. " I feel," he writes, " that I am growing in God's grace. To Him I look for support. Will He not impart wisdom as well as love ? "

His surroundings at Concord are so vividly described in the

letters he wrote to his family that we cannot omit quotations
from them. The first of these is dated at Brook Farm, and describes his efforts to find a room after reaching the village. He
seems to have gone at once to Mr. Bradford's house on his arrival.

"*April* 22, '44.—   . . .   After supper we sallied forth
again. We saw a room, and what do you imagine they charged
for it? Seventy-five dollars a year!! This was out of the
question. We went further and found a room, good size, very
good people, furnished, and to be kept in order for eight dollars
a quarter. This seemed reasonable to me, and also to Mr. Bradford. I felt safe in telling the lady that I thought I should take
it. I requested Mr. Bradford to keep a look-out for me while I
was gone, and if we could not find a better place before I returned I would accept this. This morning I left Concord to
come and see Charles Dana concerning the books I shall require,
and to see some of my friends. I got into Boston at ten o'clock,
and walked out here by dinner-time. All of the old set that are
here were delighted to see me. I have conversed with a few of
them, and find them more open to consider the claims of the
Church than I had anticipated."

"*Concord, April* 24, '44.—Dear Friends : This evening I can
say that I am settled, comfortably settled in every particular. All
that is needed for my comfort is here : a good straw bed, a large
table, carpet, washstand, book-case, stove, chairs, looking-glass—
all, all that is needful. And this for seventy-five cents a week,
including lights; wood is extra pay. This is the inanimate about
me. The lady of the house, Mrs. Thoreau, *is a woman.* The
only fear I have about her is that she is too much like dear
mother—she will take too much care of me. She has told me
how she used to sit up nights, waiting for a young man whom
she had taken to board, to come home. He was a stranger to
her, but still she insists that she must treat all as she would her
own, and even with greater care. If you were to see her,
mother, you would be perfectly satisfied that I have fallen into
good hands, and met a second mother, if that is possible."

"*April* 25, 1.30 *P.M.*—I have just finished my dinner; it
was *ein herrliches Essen.* Unleavened bread (from home), maple-

sugar, and apples which I purchased this morning. Previous to taking dinner I said my first lesson to Mr. Bradford in Greek and Latin.

" I am extremely well situated, and feel contented in myself, and deeply grateful to you all for your goodness in helping me to pursue the real purpose of my being. All we can do is to be faithful to God and to the work He has given us to do, and, whatever end He may lead us to, to have that central faith that 'all is for the best.' There is only one life, and that is life in God; and only one death, and that is separation from Him. And this life is not and cannot be measured by the external eye. We must be fixed in God before we can do anything rightly—study, labor, social, political or of any kind. . . .

" I have written this letter full of nothingness; I will be more settled the next time and do better. Send *all* your love to me —think more of heaven and we shall grow happier. If once celestial love has touched us, we cannot rest until it dwells and abides in our hearts. To you all I send my warmest and purest love.—ISAAC."

" *Concord, May* 2, 1844.—Dear Friends: It was my intention not to write home until I had received a letter from you; but as none has yet come, and I am in want of a few things, I will write you immediately.

" You can scarcely imagine how different my life is now from what it was at home. It is like living in another world. It is possible that you might not be suited with the conditions here, but to me they are the very ones which are congenial to my present state of being. I am alone from early dawn to late at night; no one to intrude upon my quiet except Mr. Bradford, who occupies the hour between twelve and one to hear my recitations, and Mrs. Thoreau a few minutes in making my bed in the mornings. The rest of my time is devoted to study, communion, and, a little of it, to reading. How unlike the life at home!

" The thought just occurs to me that if such a life seems desirable to you, how easily you could obtain it. What is it that costs so much labor of mind and body? Is it not that which we consume on and in our bodies? Then, if we reduce the consumption there will be less need of production. Most of our labor is labor for the body. We are treasuring up corruption for the day of death; is this not so? As we rise in spirit above the body we shall bring all its appetites into subjection to the moral law. . . .

"This is what I should like you to do for me. All the food that I brought with me is gone, and as I would like to have my razor sent on, and as the articles you can give me would be better than any I can get here, you will be so kind as to send with it the following list, if you think best: 1. Put in some hard bread. 2. A few unleavened wheat biscuits, such as I used to make. 3. Some unleavened Graham biscuits. 4. A five-cent or ten-cent loaf of bread, if you think it will keep good until it gets here. 5. Get me a linen summer frock-coat such as are worn—those loose ones. Dunster has my measure and he can cut it for you. Let it be made. I have only a summer jacket with me, and that is John's. 6. Do not forget the razor. You can put in any other simple, solid food, if you wish to send any. Do I ask too much from you? If so, you must be kind enough to tell me. Your labor is already too great, and I am burdening you with more. . . .

"How much my heart loves you all! How unkindly I have spoken to you at times! You will forgive me and love me none the less, will you not? May we live together more and more in the unity of love."

"*May*, 1844.— . . . My studies are pursued with the same spirit in which they were commenced, and there seems to me no reason to fear but that they will be continued in the same for some time to come. However, I would affirm what has been affirmed by me for these two years back, the only consistency that I can promise is submission to the Spirit that is guiding me, whatever may be the external appearance or superficial consequences to others. . . .

"How our astonishment should be excited to perceive that we have been in such a long sleep, and that even now we see but dimly. Let us each ask ourselves in whose business we are employed. Is it our Father's, or is it not? If not, let us immediately turn to the business of our Father, the only object of our life. Let us submit wholly to the guidance of Love."

"To Mrs. Catherine J. Hecker. *Concord, May* 31, 1844.—You speak of my situation as pleasant, and so it is to me. Though the house is situated on the street of a village, the street is beautifully arched with trees for some distance, and my room is very pleasant. One window is wholly shaded by sweet honeysuckle, which is now in blossom, filling the room with its mild fragrance. The little humming-birds visit its flowers frequently without being disturbed by my presence."

The diary, which runs side by side with these letters, was, as usual, the recipient of more intimate self-communings than could be shared with any friend. It shows that although he was now well-nigh convinced of the truth of Catholicity, yet that he still felt a lingering indecision, produced, perhaps, by a haunting memory of the stern front of "discipline" he had encountered in Bishop Hughes. This seemed like a phantom of terror to the young social reformer, whose love of liberty, though rational, was then and ever afterwards one of the passions of his soul. Yet we rarely find now in these pages any statement of specific reasons for and against Catholicity such as were plentiful during the period preceding his acquaintance with Mr. Haight, Dr. Seabury, and Mr. Norris. He seems to shudder as he stands on the bank and looks upon the flowing and cleansing stream ; but his hesitancy is caused not so much by any unanswered difficulties of his reason as by his sensibilities, by vague feelings of alarm for the integrity of his manhood. He feared lest the waters might cleanse him by skinning him alive. Catholicity, as typified in Bishop Hughes, her Celtic-American champion, seemed to him "a fortified city, and a pillar of iron, and a wall of brass against the whole land."

Now, Isaac Hecker was built for a missionary, and the extreme view of the primary value of highly-wrought discipline which he encountered everywhere among Catholics, though not enough to blind him to the essential liberty of the Church, was enough to delay him in his progress to her. There can be little doubt that multitudes of men and women of less discernment and feebler will than his, have been and still are kept entirely out of the Church by the same cause.

Only at long intervals, as we near the last pages of the large and closely-written book containing the first volume of his diary, do we meet with those agonizing complaints of dryness, the distress of doubt, the weary burden of insoluble difficulties, so common heretofore. He seems, indeed, no longer battling ; the victory is won ; but it remains to know what are the spoils and where they are to be gathered. Of course there are interludes of his irrepressible philosophizing on moral questions. And at the very end, under date of May 23, 1844, we find the following:

"This afternoon brings me to the close of this book. How different are the emotions with which I close it from those with which I opened it at Brook Farm, now little more (a month) than a year ago! How fruitful has this year been to me! How strangely mysterious and beautiful! And now my soul foreshadows more the next year than ever it presaged before. My life is beyond my grasp, and bears me on will-lessly to its destined haven. Like a rich fountain it overflows on every side; from within flows unceasingly the noiseless tide. The many changes and unlooked-for results and circumstances, within and without, of the coming year I would no more venture to anticipate than to count the stars. It is to me now as if I had just been born, and I live in the Sabbath of creation. Every thing that I see I feel called on to give a name; it has a new meaning to me. Should this life grow—what? It is a singular fact that, although conscious of a more interior and potent force at work within, I am now more quiet and will-less than I was when it at first affected me. I feel like a child, full of joy and pliability; and all ambition of every character seems to have left me. I see where I was heretofore, and the degree of externality which was mixed with the influences that I co-operated with, an externality from which I now feel that I have been freed. It does seem to me that all worldly prospect that ever was before me is gone, and as if I were weak, very weak, in the sight of the world; so I really am. I feel no more potency than a babe. Yet I have a will-less power of love which will conquer through me, and which, O gracious Lord, I never dreamt of before."

In the middle of the above entry he thus notes an interruption, and records a lesson taught by the late New England spring: "George and Burrill Curtis came in, and I have just returned from a walk in the woods with them. May the buds within blossom, and may their fruit ripen in my prayers to God."

He was now, indeed, very near his goal, though even yet he did not clearly see it. And once more all his active powers

deserted him. Study became impossible. His mind was drawn
so strongly in upon itself that neither work nor play, neither
books nor the renewed intercourse which at this period he sought
with his old friends in Boston and at Brook Farm, could any
longer fasten his attention. He opens his new diary with a record
of the trial he has just made in order to discover "whether in
mixing with the world I should not be somewhat influenced by
their life and brought into new relations with my studies. But
it was to no purpose that I went. . . . There was no inducement that I could imagine strong enough to keep me from
returning. Ole Bull, whom I very much wished to hear again,
was to play the next evening; and Parley Pratt, a friend whom
I had not met for a great length of time, and whom I did
wish to see, was to be in town the next day. There were many
other things to keep me, but none of them had the least effect.
I could no more keep myself there than a man could sink himself in the Dead Sea, and so I had to come home.

"I feel a strong inclination to doze and slumber, and more
and more in these slumbers the dim shadows that appear in my
waking state become clearer, and my conversation is more real
and pleasant to me. I feel a double consciousness in this state,
and think, 'Now, is not this real? I will recollect it all, what
I saw and what I said'; but it flies and is lost when I awake.
. . I call this sleeping, but sleep it is not; for in this
state I am more awake than at any other time."

A few days later, on June 5, he notes that

"Although my meals are made of unleavened bread and figs,
and my drink is water, and I eat no more than supports my
body, yet do I feel sinfully self-indulgent."

He resolves, moreover, to trouble himself no more about the
fact that he cannot continue his studies. On this subject, and on
the passivity to which he was now compelled, he had written as
explicitly as he could to his friend Brownson, and on June 7 he
received a response which had such an immediate result upon his
future that we transcribe it entire :

"*Mt. Bellingham, June* 6, 1844.—My dear Isaac : I thank
you for your letter, and the frankness with which you speak of
your present interior state. You ask for my advice, but I hardly

know what advice to give. There is much in your present state to approve, also much which is dangerous. The dreamy luxury of indulging one's thoughts and ranging at ease through the whole spirit-world is so captivating, and when frequently indulged in acquires such power over us, that we cease to be free men. The power to control your thoughts and feelings and to fix them on what object you choose is of the last necessity, as it is the highest aim of spiritual culture. Be careful that you do not mistake a mental habit into which you have fallen for the guidance of the All-wise. Is it not the very sacrifice you are appointed to make, to overcome this spiritual luxury and to become able to do that which is disagreeable ? Where is the sacrifice in following what the natural tendencies and fixed habits of our mind dispose us to do ? What victory have you acquired, what power to conquer in the struggle for sanctity do you possess, when you cannot so far control your thoughts and feelings as to be able to apply yourself to studies which you feel are necessary ? Here is your warfare. You have not won the victory till you have become as able to drudge at Latin or Greek as to give up worldly wealth, pleasures, honors, or distinctions.

"But, my dear Isaac, you cannot gain this victory alone, nor by mere private meditation and prayer. You can obtain it only through the grace of God, and the grace of God only through its appointed channels. You are wrong. You do not begin right. Do you really believe the Gospel ? Do you really believe the Holy Catholic Church ? If so, you must put yourself under the direction of the Church. I have commenced my preparations for uniting myself with the Catholic Church. I do not as yet belong to the family of Christ. I feel it. I can be an alien no longer, and without the Church I know, by my own past experience, that I cannot attain to purity and sanctity of life. I need the counsels, the aids, the chastisements, and the consolations of the Church. It is the appointed medium of salvation, and how can we hope for any good except through it ? Our first business is to submit to it, that we may receive a maternal blessing. Then we may start fair.

"You doubtless feel a repugnance to joining the Church. But we ought not to be ashamed of Christ ; and the Church opens a sphere for you, and you especially. You are not to dream your life away. Your devotion must be regulated and directed by the discipline of the Church. You know that there is a large Roman Catholic population in our country, especially in Wisconsin. The bishop of that Territory is a German. Now, here is your work—to serve this German population. And you can do it without feeling yourself among foreigners. Here is the cross you are to take up. Your cross is to resist this tendency to mysticism, to sentimental luxury, which is really enfeebling your soul and preventing you from attaining to true spiritual blessedness.

"I think you would better give up Greek, but command yourself sufficiently to master the Latin; that you need, and cannot do without. Get the Latin, and with that and the English, French, and German which you already know, you can get along very well. But don't be discouraged.

"I want you to come and see our good bishop. He is an excellent man—learned, polite, easy, affable, affectionate, and exceedingly warm-hearted. I spent two hours with him immediately after parting with you in Washington Street, and a couple of hours yesterday. I like him very much.

"I have made up my mind, and I shall enter the Church if she will receive me. There is no use in resisting. You cannot be an Anglican, you must be a Catholic or a mystic. If you enter the Church at all, it must be the Catholic. There is nothing else. So let me beg you, my dear Isaac, to begin by owning the Church and receiving her blessing.

"My health is very good, the family are all very well; I hope you are well. Let me hear from you often. Forgive me if I have said anything harsh or unkind in this letter, for all is meant in kindness, and be assured of my sincere and earnest affection. Yours truly,

"O. A. BROWNSON."

CHAPTER XV.

THE first effect of Brownson's letter was to throw its recipient into a state of great though brief perplexity. That final struggle, strange and painful, in which the soul for the last time contends against its happiness; in which it is drawn by an invincible attraction, knowing that it will yield yet striving still to resist; is one that must remain but half-comprehended by most of those to whom Catholic truth is an inheritance. And yet there is an explanation which Father Hecker himself would possibly have given. "Do you know what God is?" he said to the present writer in 1882, in that abrupt fashion with which he often put the deepest questions. "That is not what I mean," he went on, after getting a conventional reply: "I'll tell you what God is. *He is the Eternal Lover of the soul.*" That shudder of blind aversion which is a part of the experience of so many converts, is an instinctive testimony that the call to the truth is more than natural, while the overpowering attraction which attends it witnesses that nature must needs obey or perish. The Church, too, is not heard by the soul merely as the collective voice of many men and ages of men agreed upon the truth, but as a mystic personality which makes her the imperative ambassadress of Christ. For she is the Spouse of the Lamb, and in her the Incarnate Word obtains a voice which is no less single in its personality than multitudinous in its tones.

Much as Isaac Hecker had considered the matter, studying, reading, praying, assuring himself from time to time that if any church were true this was the one, and that to enter it was probably his duty, now that Brownson's weight was likewise thrown into the scale and it went down with a warning thud, he thrilled through with apprehension. "I feel like throwing all up," he wrote in the diary on the day the letter reached him. "Some cannot rest. *How much better would it have been could I have remained in quietness at my daily pursuits, and not been led to where I now find myself.*"

Then he questions himself: "What have I against the Catholic Church? At this moment I cannot say that I have anything that is essential. And she meets my wants on every side.

"Oh, this is the deepest event of my life! I would have

united myself to any one of the Protestant sects if I had found any that would have answered the demands of my nature. Why should I now hesitate when I find the Catholic Church will do so? Is not this the self-will which revolts against the involuntary will of the Spirit?

"The fundamental question is, Am I willing to submit my will to the guidance and direction of the Church? If she is the body of Christ; if she is the channel of the Holy Ghost; if she is the inspired body illumined by Christ's Spirit; in a word, if she *is* the Catholic Church; if I would serve God and humanity; if I would secure the favor of God, and heaven hereafter; why should I *not* submit to her?"

But however painful this final indecision may have been, it was of short duration. Brownson's letter reached Concord on Friday morning, and on Saturday Isaac Hecker went into Boston to see Bishop Fenwick and put himself under instruction. That done, his peace not merely returned, but he felt that it rested on more solid grounds than heretofore. Yet, curiously enough, it is at this point we come upon almost the first trace of his stopping seriously to consider the adverse sentiments of others with regard to any proposed action on his part. Now that he means to range himself, he turns to look back at the disorderly host which he is quitting, not so much, or at least not primarily, for the sake of the order and regularity and solidity of that to which it is opposed, but because a true instinct has taught him that unity is the external mark of truth, as equilibrium is the test of a just balance. In his diary of June 11, 1844, after recording that he has just returned from Boston, where he has seen the bishop and his coadjutor, Bishop John Bernard Fitzpatrick, and received from the latter a note of introduction to the president of Holy Cross College, at Worcester, Mass., he adds:

"I intend to stay there as long as it seems pleasant to me, and then go on to New York and there unite myself with the Church.

"I sigh, and feel that this step is the most important of my life. My highest convictions, my deepest wants, lead me to it; and should I not obey them? There is no room to harbor a doubt about it. My friends will look upon it with astonishment, and probably use the common epithets, delusion, fanaticism, and blindness. But so I wish to appear to minds like theirs; otherwise this would be unsatisfactory to me. Men call that superstition which they have not the feeling to appreciate, and that fanaticism which they have not the spiritual perception to perceive. The Protestant world admires, extols, and flatters him who will write and speak high-sounding and heroic words; who will assert that he will follow truth wherever it leads, at all sacrifices and hazards; but no sooner does he do so than it slanders and persecutes him for being what he professed to be. Verily it *has* separated faith from works.

"This is a heavy task; it is a great undertaking, a serious, sacred, sincere, and solemn step; it is the most vital and eternal act, and as such do I feel it in all its importance, weight, and power. O God! Thou who hast led me by Thy heavenly messengers, by Thy divine grace, to make this new, unforeseen, and religious act of duty, support me in the day of trial. Support me, O Lord, in my confessions; give me strength and purity to speak freely the whole truth without any equivocation or attempt at justification. O Lord, help Thy servant when he is feeble and would fall.

"One thing that gives me much peace and joy is that all worldly inducements, all temptations toward self-gratification whatever, are in favor of the Anglican Church and in opposition to the Catholic Church. And on this account my conscience feels free from any unworthy motive in joining it. The Roman Catholic Church is the most despised, the poorest, and, according to the world, the least respectable of any; this on account of the class of foreigners of which it is chiefly composed in this country. In this respect it presents to me no difficulty of any sort, nor demands the least sacrifice. But the new relations in which it will place me, and the new duties which will be required of me, *are* strange to me, and hence I shall feel all their weight at once."

His premonitions were speedily fulfilled, though probably not in the extreme form which he anticipated. The spirit of courtesy which prevailed throughout his family doubtless prevented any but the mildest criticism on his action. But even that had hitherto been spared him. There had been anxiety and much questioning about his final course, but that it would end in *this* way does not seem to have been seriously apprehended. On the same day on which he made the entry just quoted he wrote the following letter to them:

"*June* 11, 1844.—On Saturday last I went into Boston and

did not return until this morning (Tuesday). . . . My purpose in going was to see Bishop Fenwick of the Roman Catholic Church, to learn what are the preliminaries necessary for
one who wishes to be united to the Church. I saw the bishop
and his coadjutor, men of remarkable goodness, candor, and
frankness. I was chiefly interested with his coadjutor, and spent
some hours with him on Monday. And this is the result to
which I have come: That soon, probably next week, I shall go
from here to Worcester, where there is a Catholic college, and
stay there for a few days, perhaps a fortnight, to see the place,
become acquainted with their practical religious life and their
system of intellectual instruction. From there I shall go on
home to New York, and, after having gone through the requisite
preliminaries, be united to the Roman Catholic Church in our
city. . . . Before I make any unalterable step, I wish to see
you all and commune with you concerning this movement on
my part. . . .

"Whatever theories and speculations may be indulged in and
cherished by those opposed to the Roman Catholic Church, their
influence, however important they may seem, is not sufficiently
vital to prevent me from being united to it. It satisfies and
meets my deepest wants; and on this ground, setting aside any
other for the moment, I feel like affirming, in the spirit of the
man whom Christ made to see,* I know not whether this Church
be or be not what certain men call it, but this I know: it has
the life my heart is thirsting for, and of which my spirit is in
great need.

"A case in point: The sermon of Dr. Seabury on the lamented death of Arthur Carey is as far from satisfying my heartfelt longings as Platonism would be to the Christian. Read the
doctrine of the Catholic Church on the Communion of Saints in
the Catechism of the Council of Trent attentively and devoutly,
and you will see and feel the wide difference in doctrine and life
between it and that held even by the high-church Anglican.
It may be said in excuse for Dr. Seabury, that he has to be
prudent and cautious on account of the state of mind of those
whom he has to speak to. Well enough; but why should one
go to a weak and almost dried-up spring when there is one
equally near, fresh, always flowing and full of life?   .

* John ix. 24: We know this man is a sinner. He said therefore to them; If he be a
sinner, I know not; one thing I know, that whereas I was blind, now I see.

There may be those, and I do not question there are many such good persons, who do not feel the deep demands of the spiritual nature as profoundly as others do, and that the Anglican Church fully satisfies all *their* needs. But even in her bosom there are many who think that if the Oxford tendencies are Anglican, she is very idolatrous and exceedingly superstitious, because they feel no need for so much discipline and ceremony, and such faith in the invisible. . . . All reasons that can tempt one in my position are in favor of the Anglican Church, and it is a source of much joy that there is no conceivable inducement of a worldly or mixed nature for me to join the Roman Catholic Church. If there were I should distrust myself. . . It seems to me that the difference between my embracing the Roman Catholic Church and any other is the same as the difference between remaining as I am, and selling all that I have and following Christ."

His deference for his friends' opinions, though he made their views no condition of his action, is beautifully shown by the following words: "John, and all who feel like giving me advice, you will not hesitate in giving it freely and frankly. There are many reasons for my present course; it is impossible for me to put them all on paper. But when I return home and meet you all again, we will in love speak of this in common communion : until then I will not take any decisive step. I suppose you feel as little inclined to speak to others of the decision I have come to as I do to have it prematurely known."

To the brother whose heart was most his own he devotes the concluding words of the letter:

"What is brother George's mind respecting the need of receiving this diviner life in order to bring us into a closer communion with God and make us inhabitants of heaven ? George, shall we go arm-in-arm in our heavenly journey as we have done in our earthly one ?"

While awaiting an answer to this letter he began another, in which he summarizes more explicitly such of his reasons for becoming a Catholic as might appeal on ordinary grounds of controversy to his mother and his brother John, the latter of whom had recently become an Episcopalian. Our extracts, however,

will be made from the passages more strictly personal and characteristic :

" *Concord, June* 14, •1844.—Until I hear from you I cannot
say how you may view my resolution or feel regarding the decision I have come to, and therefore I am at a loss what to say
to you respecting it.   One thing must strike you as inexplicable :
that I relinquish my studies here so suddenly.   This arises from
the fact that I have not kept you perfectly informed concerning
the change my mind has for some time been undergoing with
regard to the object and end of study, its office and its benefits.
I kept silent, thinking that my views might be but temporary,
and that it was unnecessary to trouble you with them.   My
simple faith is, in a few words, that we must first seek the
kingdom of God, and then all necessary things will be given us.
And this kingdom is not found through nature, philosophy,
science, art, or by any other method than that of the Gospel :
the perfect surrender of the *whole* heart to God."

We stop here to remark that such expressions as these are
neither to be taken as evidences of a passing disgust for the
drudgery of text-book tasks, nor as signs of an indolent disposition.   They are the assertion of a principle which Father Hecker
maintained throughout his life.   He never felt the least interest
in studies not undertaken as a result of some supernatural impulse,
or pursued in view of some supernatural aim.   He looked with
the coldest unconcern upon such investigations of science as promise nothing toward solving the problems which perplex humanity on the moral side, or which do not contribute to the natural
well-being of men.   With the pursuit of any science which does
promise such results he was in the fullest sympathy, and was
himself an unwearied student.   It was anything but intellectual
indolence which caused him to put away his books.   He was
naturally of a busy temperament : if men who knew him but
slightly might think him visionary, no man could know him at
all and consider him a sluggard.   We shall see in the sequel
how, under extremely critical circumstances, the assertion of this
principle was wrung from him by the constraining force of his
interior guide.   Much of what follows illustrates this trait of
character.
   The letter last quoted from had not yet been sent when the

answer to his announcement of June 11 reached him, and he added a postscript. The only point in it to which he alludes or makes any direct reply is the gentle expression of his mother's disapprobation of his purpose :

"Your letter and draft, brother George, came this morning. You say mother would prefer my joining the Anglican Church. The reasons why she prefers this are such as would doubtless govern me if I did not feel still deeper and stronger reasons to overcome them. . . . My present convictions are deeper far than any I have ever experienced, and are not hastily decided upon."

Turning now to the diary, the entries made at this time seem especially characteristic :

"*June* 13, 1844.—I feel very cheerful and at ease since I have consented to join the Catholic Church. Never have I felt the quietness, the immovableness, and the permanent rest that I do now. It is inexpressible. I feel that essential and interior permanence which nothing exterior can disturb, and no act which it calls on me to perform will move in the least. It is with a perfect ease and gracefulness that I never dreamed of, that I shall unite with the Church. It will not change but fix my life. No external relations, events, or objects can disturb this un-reachable quietness or break the deep repose in which I am.

"The exoteric eye is double ; the esoteric eye is single.

"The external world is divisional; the internal world is unity.

"The esoteric includes the exoteric, but the exoteric excludes the esoteric.

"The man can move all faculties, organs, limbs ; but they cannot move the man.

"The Creator moves the creature, and the creature moves the created.

"We know God by looking towards Him with the single eye.

"To-morrow I go with R. W. Emerson to Harvard to see Lane and Alcott, and shall stay until Sunday. We shall not meet each other, for I can meet him on no other grounds than those of love. We may talk intellectually together, and remark, and reply, and remark again."

We give the reader from the diary the following estimate of a transcendentalist, mainly to serve as a background for the picture which Isaac Hecker drew of his own mind in the succeeding pages:

"*June* 14.—A transcendentalist is one who has keen sight but little warmth of heart; who has fine conceits but is destitute of the rich glow of love. He is *en rapport* with the spiritual world, unconscious of the celestial one. He is all nerve and no blood—colorless. He talks of self-reliance, but fears to trust himself to love. He never abandons himself to love, but is always on the lookout for some new fact. His nerves are always tight-stretched, like the string of a bow; his life is all effort. In a short period he loses his tone. Behold him sitting on a chair; he is not sitting, but braced upon its angles, as if his bones were of iron and his nerves steel; every nerve is drawn, his hands are closed like a miser's—it is his lips and head that speak, not his tongue and heart. He prefers talking about love to possessing it, as he prefers Socrates to Jesus. Nature is his church, and he is his own god. He is a dissecting critic—heartless, cold. What would excite love and sympathy in another, excites in him curiosity and interest. He would have written an essay on the power of the soul at the foot of the Cross. . . .

"That the shaping of events is not wholly in our own hands my present unanticipated movement has clearly demonstrated to me. . . . I know of no act that I could make which would have more influence to shape my destiny than my union with the Catholic Church. . . . It is very certain to me that my life is now as it never has been. It seems that I live, feel, and act from my heart. That reads, talks, hears, sees, smells, and all. All is unity with me, all love. Instead of exciting thoughts and ideas, as all things have done heretofore, they now excite love, cheerful emotion, and gladness of heart.

"To the Spirit within I address myself: So long as I struggled against Thee I had pain, sorrow, anguish, doubt, weeping, and distress of soul. Again and again have I submitted to Thee, though ever reluctantly; yet was it always in the end for my good. Oh! how full of love and goodness art Thou to suffer in us and for us, that we may be benefited and made happy. It is from Thy own pure love for us, for Thy happiness cannot be increased or diminished, that Thou takest upon Thee all the suffering of the children.

"Lord, if I would or could give myself wholly up to Thee, nothing but pure joy, complete happiness, and exquisite pleasure would fill all my spirit, soul, and body. The Lord desires our whole happiness; it is we who hinder Him from causing it by our struggles against His love-working Spirit.

"Who is the Lord? Is He not our nearest friend? Is any closer to us than He when we are good? Is any further from us when we are wicked? His simple presence is blessedness. Our marriage with the Lord should be so complete that nothing could attract our attention from Him.

"We shall speak best to men when we do not reflect on whom we are talking to. Speak always as if in the presence of God, where you must be if you would speak to benefit your neighbor.

"If we are pure before God the eyes of men will never make us ashamed.

"We must be blind to all things and have our single eye turned toward God when we would act in any manner upon earth—when we would heavenize it."

Here ends the contemporary record of his life in Concord. The next letters are dated at Worcester; the next entry in the diary at New York. There remain, however, some interesting allusions to it in the articles in this magazine of 1887 concerning Dr. Brownson, and some conversations, still more graphic, in the pages of the memoranda.

CHAPTER XVI.

THE first Bishop of Boston, John Louis de Cheverus, who left that diocese to become successively the Bishop of Montauban and the Cardinal-Archbishop of Bordeaux, was, in the strictest sense, a missionary during his American episcopate. Thoroughly French in blood, in training, in manners, and in zeal, his penetrating intelligence not less than his saintly life and his tireless charity recommended him to men of all creeds and of none. His departure from Boston was regarded by all its citizens as a public misfortune, and by himself as cause for profound personal sorrow. He had learned there a lesson of liberty which he found it hard to forget when he went away. One of his biographers records that Charles X., whose offer to make him Minister of Ecclesiastical Affairs Cheverus had declined, once questioned him concerning the liberty enjoyed by the Church in the United States. "There," said the archbishop in reply, "I could have established missions in every church, founded seminaries in every quarter, and confided them to the care of Jesuits without any one thinking or saying aught against my proceedings; all opposition to them would have been regarded as an act of despotism and a violation of right." "That people understand liberty, at least," returned the king; "when will it be understood among us?"

We have spoken of Bishop Cheverus because, at the time of Isaac Hecker's acquaintance with his successors, his influence was still felt in Boston.

His immediate successor was Benedict Joseph Fenwick, a Marylander, descended in direct line from one of the original English Catholic pilgrims who founded that colony under Lord Baltimore. During his episcopate the diocese grew amazingly. When he went to it, in 1826, although it comprised the whole of New England, it contained but two churches fit for divine service, and only two priests besides himself. When he died, in 1846, he left behind him two bishoprics where there had been but one; while in that of Boston alone there were then fifty churches, served by as many priests. Although conversions had not been rare, the increase was mainly due to immigration, which the great famine in Ireland was speedily to increase. The

efforts of Bishop Fenwick and those of his coadjutor and successor were, in the nature of things, conservative rather than aggressive.

Bishop Fitzpatrick, also, was American by birth and training.
A native of Boston, he was reared in its public grammar and
Latin schools until the age of seventeen, when he began his
studies for the priesthood, which he finished in France. Both of
these prelates continued the tradition of Cheverus so far as their
own persons were concerned. But while they easily won and retained the respect of their more intelligent Protestant fellow-citizens, the confidence they inspired as men was not ample enough
to protect the Church over which they ruled when once it began to show signs of solid prosperity. Cheverus was not wrong
in counting with assurance upon American love for and understanding of true liberty, but he doubtless owed more than he
thought at the time to the insignificance and scanty numbers of
his flock. There came a period, even in the career of his immediate successor, when liberty itself seemed but a feeble sap-
ling which a strong wind of stupid bigotry might avail to root
out and cast away; while the chronicle of Bishop Fitzpatrick's
episcopate contains the record of convents invaded under forms
of law, and of both convents and churches sacked and burned
by " Native American " mobs, who were secure of their immunity
from punishment. Such outrages, witnessed by the second and
third Bishops of Boston, and the incessant conflict to which they
were compelled with the bigotry which caused them and which
protected their perpetrators, predisposed both them and their
clergy to a distrustful attitude toward converts like Brownson and
Hecker, in whom American traits of character were very conspicuous. Dr. Brownson has recorded in *The Convert*, p. 374,
the fact that his entrance into the Church was delayed for
months by his fear of explaining to Bishop Fitzpatrick the
precise road by which he had approached it. He says:

"I really thought that I had made some philosophical discoveries which would be of value even to Catholic theologians
in convincing and converting unbelievers, and I dreaded to
have them rejected by the Catholic bishop. But I perceived
almost instantly that he either was ignorant of my doctrine
of life or placed no confidence in it; and I felt that he was
far more likely, bred as he had been in a different philosophical school from myself, to oppose than to accept. I had,

indeed, however highly I esteemed the doctrine, no special attachment to it for its own sake, and could, so far as it was concerned, give it up at a word without a single regret; but, if I rejected or waived it, what reason had I for regarding the Church as authoritative for natural reason, or for recognizing any authority in the bishop himself to teach me? Here was the difficulty. . . . My trouble was great, and the bishop could not relieve me, for I dared not disclose to him its source."

The reader will understand that we do not compare the course of Bishop Fitzpatrick in Brownson's case with that taken by him toward Isaac Hecker. The latter was a young man, unknown to the bishop save by what he may have said of his own antecedents, while Brownson was a well-known publicist, concerning whom some reserve was natural and prudent.

With Bishop Fenwick, who was already in failing health, the new candidate for admission to the fold seems to have had very little intercourse. As we have seen, the journal makes only a passing reference to him, but is more explicit with regard to his coadjutor. Certain points in their interview which remained ever fresh in his memory were, at the time, cast into the shade by his deep preoccupation with what may, perhaps, be called the spiritual as distinguished from the intellectual side of the Church. That in her which makes her the tender and bountiful mother of the simple was what chiefly attracted him, just as others are mainly drawn to her as the adequate teacher and guide of the intellect. If he found the door at which he was knocking something hard in turning on its hinges; if the vestibule into which he was ushered seemed a trifle narrower than he had expected at the entrance of a temple so world-wide; his satisfaction at having determined upon entrance made all other considerations for the moment dwindle. But that the impressions he received were permanent, in their suggestiveness at least, is witnessed by an article in this magazine for April, 1887, entitled " Dr. Brownson and Bishop Fitzpatrick," as well as by the several references to this period which occur in the memoranda.

In the article just named Father Hecker threw into a paragraph or two, which we subjoin, the substance of his first, and perhaps at this time his only, interview with Bishop Fitzpatrick :

" It was always difficult to detect how much of conviction

and how much of banter there was in his treatment of men
engaged in the actual intellectual movement of our times. I
found such to be the case in my own intercourse with him. He
always attacked me in a bantering way, but, I thought, half in
earnest too. Hence I never found it advisable to enter into
argument with him. How can you argue with a man, a brilliant
wit and an accomplished theologian, who continually flashes back
and forth between first principles and witticisms? When I would
undertake to grapple with him on first principles he would throw
me off with a joke, and while I was parrying the joke he was
back again upon first principles.

" An illustration of his way of treating men and questions
was his reception of me when I presented myself to him, some
months before Dr. Brownson did, for reception into the Church.
' What truths were the stepping-stones that led you here?' he
would have asked if he had had the temperament of the apostle.
But instead of searching for truth in me he began to search for
error. I had lived with the Brook Farm Community and with the
Fruitlands Community, and before that had been a member of a
Workingman's party in New York City, in all which organizations
the right of private ownership of property had been a prime
question. . . . But, as for my part, at the time Bishop
Fitzpatrick wanted me to purge myself of communism, I had
settled the question in my own mind, and on principles which
I afterwards found to be Catholic. The study and settlement of
the question of ownership was one of the things that led me
into the Church, and I am not a little surprised that what was
a door to lead me into the Church seems at this day to be a
door to lead some others out. But when the bishop attacked me
about it, it was no longer with me an actual question. I had
settled the question of private ownership in harmony with Catholic principles, or I should not have dared to present myself as
a convert. But I mention this because it illustrates Bishop
Fitzpatrick's character.

" His was, indeed, a first-class mind both in natural gifts and
acquired cultivation, but his habitual bearing was that of suspicion of error; as man and prelate he had a joyful readiness
to search it out and correct it from his own point of view. He
was a type of mind common then and not uncommon now—the
embodiment of a purpose to refute error, and to refute it by
condemnation direct, authoritative even if argumentative : the

other type of mind would seek for truth amidst the error, establish its existence, applaud it, and endeavor to make it a basis for further truth and a fulcrum for the overthrow of the error connected with it.

"It will be seen, then, what kind of man Dr. Brownson first met as the official exponent of Catholicity, one hardly capable of properly understanding and dealing with a mind like his; for he was one who had come into the possession of the full truth not so much from hatred of error as from love of truth. Brownson's soul was intensely faithful to its personal convictions, faithful unto heroism—for that is the temper of men who seek the whole truth free from cowardice, or narrowness, or bias. He has admitted that the effect of his intercourse with the bishop was not fortunate. He confesses that he forced him to adopt a line of public controversy foreign to his genius, and one which had not brought him into the Church, and perhaps could not have done so."

The memoranda contain a more familiar account of this interview :

"I presented myself for instruction and reception into the Church at the episcopal residence, and was received by the old bishop, Fenwick. He questioned me on the essential doctrines and found me as I was; that is, firm as a rock and perfectly clear in my belief. Then he said, 'You had better see Bishop John.' I did so. He tried to get me started on questions of modern theology such as he suspected I might be (as he would doubtless think, knowing my antecedents) unsound on; for example, rights of property, etc. I refused to speak my sentiments on them. I said I had no difficulties about anything to submit to him. I knew the Catholic faith and wished to be received into the Church at once. I had come seeking the means to save my soul, and I wanted nothing from him but to be prepared for baptism."

More interesting than either of these narrations is the following conversation, recorded on July 4, 1884. Besides furnishing a very explicit answer to a question which may occur to some minds, as to why a man who always took such a hopeful view of human nature as Isaac Hecker did, should not have been repelled from Catholicity by the doctrine of original sin, it adds some further particulars to the meagre array of facts in our possession :

"Suppose," he was asked, "that the deliverances of the Council of Trent on original sin, and the theories of Bellarmine on that doctrine, had been offered you during your transition period : what would you have thought of them?"

"I would have received them readily enough. Why, the book I took to Concord to study was the Catechism of the Council of Trent, which has the strongest kind of statement of that doctrine. Bellarmine's formula of *nudus* and *nudatus* would have opened my eyes amazingly to a solution of the whole difficulty." *

The Catechism of the Council of Trent, to which Father Hecker so often refers, was the very best book he could have had for learning just what Catholicity is in doctrine and practice. It is unique in Catholic literature, being the only authoritative expression of the Church, in extended form, on matters of pastoral theology. Outside the dogmatic circle of doctrinal definition it enjoys the fullest and most distinct authorization. The express command of the council caused it to be prepared by a special congregation of prelates and divines, and it was promulgated to the episcopate to be translated into the language of the people and expounded to them by all pastors. It may be said of it that it is the only book which has the Catholic Church for its author. It is a book which never can grow old ; and in witness of that perennial quality, it may be mentioned that Cardinal Newman said that he never preached without using it in preparation. It is an exponent of Catholic truth absolutely free from the danger of private, or national, or racial, or traditional bias— the very book Isaac Hecker was in need of. Its plentiful use of Scripture ; its confident appeal to antiquity ; its perfect clearness; its completeness ; its tone of conviction no less than its attitude of authority ; make it to such minds as his the very all-sufficient organ of truth. Furthermore, the entire system of doc-

---

* Reference is here made to a very famous saying of Bellarmine's in explanation of a prevalent teaching on original sin. According to that teaching, if Adam had been originally constituted in a state of pure nature, devoid of supernatural gifts and graces, his spiritual condition might be described as naked—*nudus*. On the other hand, man as now born is *nudatus*, stripped of those gifts and graces, suffering the penal privation of them on account of Adam's sin.

"The corruption of nature," says Bellarmine, "does not come from the want of any natural gift, or from the accession of any evil quality, but simply from the loss of a supernatural gift on account of Adam's sin."

trine and morals known to revealed religion finds here its adequate exposition. We are glad of an occasion to say these
words, not merely to chronicle the usefulness of the book to
Father Hecker, but also to recommend its restoration to its
proper place, which both by merit and by authority is the first
in the moral and pastoral literature of the Church.

"The truth is," continue the memoranda, "that original sin
as taught by the Church would never have been a great difficulty to me : of course the Calvinistic doctrine is quite a different affair.

"I was led, after I got to work at the Catechism of the
Council of Trent, in a way quite positive. For example, one
thing I wanted was a satisfaction of that feeling and sentiment
which has made so many persons Spiritualists. I found that in
the Church there was no impassable barrier dividing the living from the departed. That was an intense delight to me.*
The doctrine of penance, and the forgiveness of sins in the
Sacrament of Penance, had a wonderful beauty as soon as
I found them. To be taught that God had somehow given
men power to dispense His graces and mercies made me say,
Oh, how delightful a doctrine that is, if I only could believe
it ! The doctrine of the Communion of Saints and that of
the Sacrament of Penance were very pleasing to me. Hence,
I soon saw that what I already had of truth and light ; what
my best nature and conscience and my clearest natural knowledge told me was truth ; was but elevated and lifted up beyond all conception by these and other doctrines of the Church.
From this I was soon in a position to appreciate the Church's
claim to authoritative teaching. If she, and she alone, had
taught such things, she must possess God's teaching authority.

"When, therefore, I went into Boston and saw Bishop Fitzpatrick (who is now, I hope, in the kingdom of heaven), he
had little to do with me in the way of instruction. The Trinity
and other fundamental doctrines I accepted readily on the authority
of the Church. He was very anxious to argue with me about
socialistic theories, on account of my having been at Brook
Farm and Fruitlands. But I told him I had no such difficulties
as he supposed ; that I had only gone to these places in search
of truth, not because I had formed any such theories as they

* Reference is here made to the Catholic doctrine of the Communion of Saints.

generally held. He then asked me whether I would not prefer to be received into the Church in New York, where my friends were. I said I did not care; if he would give me a letter I would present it. He gave me one to Bishop McCloskey, who was then coadjutor in this city."

The reader may be interested in the terms in which the Catechism of the Council of Trent expresses the doctrine of the Communion of Saints. So far as that doctrine concerns the spiritual side of man it is expounded in these words:

"For the unity of the Spirit, by which the Church is governed, establishes among all her members a community of spiritual blessings, whereas the fruit of all the sacraments is common to all the faithful, and these sacraments, particularly baptism, the door, as it were, by which we are admitted into the Church, are so many connecting links which bind and unite them to Jesus Christ."

That it extends to the mystical and miraculous gifts so dear to Father Hecker, was thus explained to him:

"But the gifts which justify and endear us to God are not alone common: 'graces gratuitously granted,' such as knowledge, prophecy, the gifts of tongues and of miracles, and others of the same sort, are common also, and are granted even to the wicked; not, however, for their own, but for the general good; for the building up of the Church of God."

That the doctrine is the foundation of a real though not a legal community of material goods, was evident to our young social reformer from the following:

"In fine, every true Christian possesses nothing which he should not consider common to all others with himself, and should therefore be prepared promptly to relieve an indigent fellow-creature; for he that is blessed with worldly goods, and sees his brother in want, and will not assist him, is at once convicted of not having the love of God within him."

Besides giving him a letter to Bishop McCloskey, Bishop Fitzpatrick also furnished the young catechumen with one to the president of Holy Cross College, an institution which had been established at Worcester, Mass., in 1843 by Bishop Fenwick, and presented by him to the Society of Jesus, of which he had been a member. The following letter was written by Isaac to his family after he had arrived there; his stay was not long:

"*Worcester, Mass., June,* '44.—Respecting the purpose which leads me to New York I have scarcely a word to say. Quietly, without excitement, I come with an immovable determination to be joined to the Roman Catholic Church. There is a conviction which lies deeper than all thought or speech, which moves me with an irresistible influence to take this step, which arguments cannot reach, nor any visible power make to falter. Words are powerless against it and inexpressive of it; to attempt to explain, or give to the intellectual mind the reasons why and wherefore, would be as impossible as to paint the heavens or to utter the eternal Word, the centre of all existence. It would be like asking, 'Wherefore is that which is?' the finite questioning the infinite; an impossibility. . . .

"No man by his own wisdom can find out God; and it is only by the grace of Heaven that we come to, and by the heart perceive, the true Church of Jesus Christ. Grace teaches us to feel and know that which before was unfelt, unknown, invisible. Perfect submission to His love breaks open all seals, unlocks all mysteries, and unfolds all difficulties. . . .

"No external event of any kind or character induces me to take this step. If what does is delusion, what to name my former life I am at a loss to know. . . .

"The heads of the college here appear to be men of good character, devoted to the Church, innocent of the Protestant world of literature, philosophy, etc. The president is a very social, frank, warm-hearted man, of more extensive acquaintance in the world of letters."

CHAPTER XVII

ACROSS THE THRESHOLD.

FROM Worcester Isaac went on to New York, stopping on the way to make a brief visit to the Fourierite community in New Jersey, known as the North American Phalanx. He probably had some personal acquaintances there whom he hoped to inoculate with his newly-found certitude. He reached home June 20, 1844, and five days later presented his letter to Bishop McCloskey. Concerning the acquaintance then begun, which, on the bishop's part, soon took the form of a discerning and wise direction, and eventually deepened into a life-long friendship, we shall have more to say hereafter. The diary chronicles their first meeting and gives the reason of the brief delay which ensued before Isaac was admitted to conditional baptism. The bulk of the entries made between this date and that of his formal reception into the Church, the first of August, contains spiritual doctrine of a kind so eminently characteristic of Father Hecker throughout his life that we continue to make extracts from it :

"*New York, June* 25, 1844.—This morning I went to see Bishop McCloskey. I found him a man of fine character, mild disposition, and of a broader education than any of the Catholics I have had the pleasure of meeting. He was acquainted with Brownson's writings and Emerson's, and personally knew Mr. Channing, whom he had met at Rome. He loaned me some books on matters pertaining to the Church. He is to be gone for a fortnight from New York, and I am to wait until he comes back before I take any further steps toward being united with the Church."

"*July* 5, 1844.—It is the duty of every man to do that which expresses the divine life which stirs within him, and to do nothing which is inconformable to it. So far as he falls short of this, so far he falls short of his duty, his perfection, and divine beauty. I think we may say with very great certainty that this is the only way to obtain happiness in this world and eternal felicity in the world to come. It is to this God calls us, but we—no, not truly we, but the Man of Sin -flatter ourselves, as he did Eve, that if we follow him we shall not die but become as gods. We, to-day, have the same temptation to overcome that Eve had.

"Oh, how much greater God would have us be than we are, and we will not! We must cast out the Man of Sin and submit to the Paradisiacal Man. This we are enabled to do, blessed be Heaven, by the grace of God through Jesus Christ.

"What are the temptations which hold men back from following God and leading a divine life? In one word, the World. Pride, love of praise, riches, self-indulgence, all that refers and looks to time instead of eternity, heaven, God.

"We should encourage all that gives us an impulse heavenward, and deny all that tends to draw us down more into the body, sense, time. Man, alas! is weak, powerless, and unable to perform any good deed which will raise him to God without the free gift, the blessed grace of God the Holy Spirit. We all fail to act up to the divine grace which is given us. O Lord! forgive my manifold transgressions, and empower me to be more and more obedient to thy Holy Spirit. My inward man desires to follow Thy Spirit, but the appetites of my members ever war against and often subdue him. Strengthen him, O Lord! and enable him to govern my whole three-sphered nature. Send down Thy celestial love into my heart and quicken all my heavenly powers.

"It is very true that no man can serve two masters. Between God and Mammon there is no compromise, no mediator. Lord, make me fully sensible of this, and strengthen my resolution to follow Thee. I do look to the Church of Christ for help. Oh, may I find in it that which the Apostles found in Jesus!"

We cannot refrain from reminding the reader of the immature age, and almost total lack of education—in the ordinary meaning of the term—of the man who wrote these lofty and inspiring sentences. He was ignorant of everything but the most rudimentary truths of Catholicity; had never read an ascetic work; had never spoken on ascetical subjects with Catholics; had never read the life of a saint; and had no experience to draw from except his own. Yet mark the absolute certainty of his propositions and their uniform correctness. It should also be made known that these doctrines and sentiments, though written with the most evident haste, follow each other, page after page, without an

erasure or a correction. The truths which had dropped upon
his mind were, indeed, rudimentary, but so well adapted was the
soil to receive the seed that the fruit was instant and mature.
Seldom has spontaneity so well approved itself by its utterances.

"*July* 6.—The immediate effect of Christianity upon humanity has been to increase man's sensibility to the objects of
the spiritual world. Poetry, music, the fine arts, are ennobling
and spiritualizing only so far as they appeal to the nature of man
divinized by the influence of the Divinity. Previous to the
coming of Christ the tendency of the arts was, on the whole,
rather to encourage licentiousness and sin than to elevate and
refine human nature. The tendency of Christianity was to restore
man to his primitive gracefulness, excellence, and beauty. Hence
the expression of man in art—or, rather, of the divinity in man—
became purer and more beautiful in its character. . . .

"In affirming Jesus to be the basis and life of modern civilization, nothing is detracted from the great and good men who
preceded Him; nor" [is it denied] "that they have left traces
of their genius upon modern society.

"When we speak of Jesus as God, we affirm Him to be the
Source of all inspiration, from whom all, ancient and modern,
have derived their life, genius, goodness, and divine beauty.

"Jesus quickened the spiritual powers of the soul which
were deadened by the fall, and man again saw heaven, and
angels descending and ascending to the throne of ineffable Love.

"All the promises of Jesus refer to gifts of spiritual power
over inanimate matter, the animal creation, and the Man of Sin.

"Jesus came to give a spiritual life which would generate all
knowledge and physical well-being. He came, not to teach a
system of philosophy, however useful that might be; not to
direct man how to procure food for his physical existence with
the least possible exercise of physical strength, however necessary
this might seem. But He came to give man a new nature
which shall more than do all this; which will not only secure
his well-being here, but his eternal felicity hereafter.

"As we rise above our *time* nature, and are united with our
eternal nature, we feel more and more our indebtedness to
Christ. It was to this He called us in all His words, and now
calls us in the Spirit. . . .

"So long as low appetites are cherished, and selfish passions harbored, and vanity allowed a seat in our bosoms, so long will men be slaves to their stomachs, backs, and business. Every quickening of our sensibility toward love, heaven, equity, will lead us to change our circumstances so as to make them conformable to our new inward life.

"It is for us to be true to God, however unlike the world we may seem. It is in silence, in private, alone, that deeds can be done which shall outstrip those of the Alexanders and Napoleons in their eternal effects."

"*July* 7.—All that we contend for is that man should obey God, and co-operate in His work *with his will* and *not against it*. Interior submission to the Love Spirit is the answer to all questions concerning man's welfare, here and hereafter. Whatever a man is led to do in obedience to it is well done and godlike, though it lead him to offer up his only dear son.

"We do say, with great emphasis, that nothing under heaven should prevent a man from following God. Unless a man can give up all and follow Christ, he is none of His."

"Every *true* man is a genius.

"All genius is religious.

"The objective forms of genius are the expressions of the beautiful, the good, and the true; in one word—God.

"He is a genius in whom the beautiful, the good, and the true permanently inhabit. . . .

"The genius in every work of art is religious, whatever the subject may be.

"We repeat that every man is called to give expression to the highest, best, divinest in him; and to this, and to this only is he called.

"We add that the Catholic Church is the medium of this divine life, and that she has nurtured and encouraged men of genius in her bosom as a fond mother.

"We do not mean to say that the Church has converted men of ordinary stamp into geniuses, but that she has given the highest inspiration to the inborn capacity of genius, and so, to men thus gifted, has been the means by which they have become more than they could have been without her: so, also, with the most ordinary men.

"We affirm that the influence of Protestantism upon the

business world has been to make it much more unchristian than it was in the middle ages under the influence of Catholicism."

At this period, when Isaac Hecker's search had ceased, but when he had not yet entered into complete and formal posses-sion of the truth, we find him looking back at his past almost as if it were a thing in which his interest was but curious and imper-sonal. The thought of writing a history of it occurred to him, and he jotted down some brief notes, and made a partial col-lection of such letters and other memoranda, apart from the diary, as he found to have been preserved by his family. But this scheme was merely one of the occupations with which he be-guiled the necessary delay imposed on him by Bishop McClos-key's absence. One can easily believe that the plan he proposed to himself has deeply interested the present writer, who, though regretting that it was not followed out by Isaac Hecker himself, has yet been enabled by the diary and the letters to measurably fulfil its purpose. He divided it into five periods, and, with a reminiscence of *Wilhelm Meister*, called it his *Wanderjahr :*

"The first should be named Youth, and give the ideal and the actual in youth.

"The second should be the struggle between the ideal and the actual.

"The third should be the mastery and supremacy of the ideal over the actual and material.

"The fourth should give the absolute union of the ideal and the eternal-absolute in their unconditioned existence.

"The fifth should give the eventual one-ness of the ideal-absolute with humanity and nature.

"Under these five heads I have in mind materials sufficient to make a volume, but lack the close application necessary to connect them. I do not say it would be readable when done. It would be the esoteric and exoteric history of my own life for ten years.   .   .   .

"I would open the first chapter thus : Let men say what they will, God above us, the human soul, and all surrounding nature, are great realities, eternal, solemn, joyous facts of human expe-rience."

In the fine passage that follows we have an anticipation of the prominent modern conception of Christianity, as a developing force in the history of man—closing an epoch and introducing a new species; or, as Father Hecker would have said in later years, raising man from his natural position as a creature of God to true sonship with Him through affiliation with Jesus Christ. The thought, as it stands in the diary, is eminently characteristic of Isaac Hecker, who always felt, in a measure beyond what is ordinary, his solidarity with all his kind, and a longing to keep in step with them on the line of their direct advance:

"*July* 12.—We make no question that God gave to all nations, previous to the birth of Jesus Christ, His beloved and only *Son*, dispensations of light and love in their great men, and led them from time to time to the stage of civilization to which they arrived. The Christian affirms that God is the Parent of humanity, the Father of every human being.* It would be in direct contradiction to his faith to deny this. But Jesus Christ came to introduce a new life, whose light and love should so surpass all that had been before Him as to make it appear as darkness by contrast. This life makes no war against the good and true that already existed in men, but it embraces, includes, and fulfils it all, and then adds more than men had dared to dream before His coming. That Christianity is of this high character, not only did its Author show by the example of His life and death, but it has shown itself to be so wherever it has come in contact with any of the older forms of religious faith and doctrine. It has exhibited a power that is superior to, and which overcomes, all that arrays itself against it. We do not deny that Zoroaster, Pythagoras, Plato, Socrates, Zeno, Cato, etc., were good, great, and religious men, above the age in which they lived, and inspired by a life not only superior to that of their time but above that of a great part of Christendom, so-called. But we say that Christ gave to the world a life infinitely above theirs, and that, had they been His contemporaries, or ours, they would have been as far superior to their actual selves as the inspiration of Christianity is superior to that under which they lived."

Although there is authority for saying that the business partnership between Isaac Hecker and his brothers was not formally dissolved until he went away to Belgium in 1845, he seems never to have resumed any active share in it after his return from Concord. Now and again the old scruples about this apparent inactivity returned upon him, and we find him contracting his personal needs within a compass so narrow that his support shall be felt as the least possible burden. Thus he writes, on July 13, that his present state of suspension from all outward engagements cannot and should not be of long continuance. He adds:

"It is a clear and bounden duty that every one should in some way or other compensate the world for that which he consumes from its store. But I do not see how I can do this consistently with the present state of my mind. To be sure I have contracted my wants as respects eating as far as seems possible to me ; somewhat in dress, but not as far as I should and can do. As for pleasures and many other causes of expenditure, I trust I am not immoderate. In this part of the world I do not see any prepared, congenial conditions. If I were in Europe, I should find in the Catholic Church institutions which I could enter for a time, until this period of my life would either fix itself permanently, or give place to another in which I could see my way more clearly. But here I am, and not in Europe. Some thoughts have arisen in my mind, and I will state them, as to what may come at some future time within the range of the possible :

"If I am joined to the Catholic Church, and there is such an institution in Europe, may I not go there and live for a time? Ah! is this possible?

"If we owned a spot of ground, I would be willing to go on it and engage as much of my time as possible in cultivating and improving it.

"Lastly, I do not know what effect the advice and influence of the Catholic Church may have upon my mind, and do have a slight hope that I may find the exact remedy that I need in my union with her.

"I feel the assurance that if I follow the Spirit of God, and place all my confidence in it, it will do for me what I dare not hope to do for myself."

A day or two later he jots down, casually as it were, one of those profound observations which are like pointers to his whole

* "As some also of your own poets said: For we are also His offspring. Being, therefore, the offspring of God, we must not suppose the Divinity to be like unto gold or silver or stone, the graving of art and the device of man." (Acts xvii. 28, 29.)

career. Occurring at this early period, when, as the reader
may see hereafter, the germs of all his later thought and work
were beginning to unfold, they are like rifts in the darkness which
seemed to himself to lie about his future, and show plainly to
the student of his life how straight and secure his path was amidst
it all. He had been counselling himself to patience and entire
reliance upon God's providence while waiting the opportunity.
" to create or procure the circumstances " necessary to the expression of his own individuality. He felt that this was the especial
task to which all men were called. To use his own words :

" It is for this we are created ; that we may give a new and individual expression of the absolute in our own peculiar character.
As soon as the new is but the re-expression of the old, God
ceases to live. Ever the mystery is revealed in each new birth.
So must it be to eternity. The Eternal-Absolute is ever creating
new forms of expressing itself."

In the next chapter we shall have occasion to give Father
Hecker's choice of an epitaph for Dr. Brownson. We think that the
sentences just quoted are worthy to be his own.

In the middle of July Bishop McCloskey returned to New
York, and Isaac waited upon him without delay. Their first long
conversation made it plain to the bishop that the young man had
very little need of further preliminary instruction, and it was
settled that conditional baptism should be administered to him
within a fortnight. That the nature of Isaac Hecker's vocation
also revealed itself to this prudent adviser is also evident from
this entry, made in the diary as soon as the visit was ended:

" He said that my life would lead me to contemplation, and
that in this country the Church was so situated as to require them
all to be active. I did not speak further on this subject with
him. He asked whether I felt like devoting myself to the order
of the priesthood, and undergoing their discipline, self-denial, etc.,
and becoming a missionary. I answered that all I could say was
that I wished to live the life given me, and felt like sacrificing all
things to this ; but could not say that the priesthood would be
the proper place for me.

" I feel that if, for a certain length of time, and under the
discipline of the Church, I could have the conditions for leading the

life of contemplation, it would be what the Spirit now demands. Whether I shall not be compelled back to this if I attempt to follow some other way, I am not perfectly sure. The bishop intimated that in Europe there were brotherhoods congenial to the state of mind that I am in. If so, and I could remain there for a certain length of time, why should I not go? I will inquire further about it when next I speak with the bishop.

"There is a college at Fordham where there is to be a commencement to-morrow, which the bishop invited me to go and see. Perhaps I shall find this place to be suitable, and may be led to examine and try it. The Lord knows all; into His hands I resign myself."

His impressions of the Catholic college at Fordham he does not record. The next entry in the diary is, as usual, taken up with the large topics which for the most part excluded particular incidents from mention. What his strict abstinence from permitted pleasures, and the rigorous self-discipline which he had so long practised, meant to himself, may be partly gathered from the extract we are about to give. He says he does not call such denial,

"in strict language, the denial of our true, God-created, immortal self, but the denial of that which is *not* myself, but which has usurped the place of my true, eternal, heavenly, Adamic being. It is the restoration of that defaced image of God to its primitive divine beauty, grace, and sweetness. We must feel and possess the love and light from above before we have the disposition and power to deny the body and the wisdom of this world. If we have the Christ-spirit, we will fulfil the Christ-commands.

"Thus was it with man prior to his spiritual death, his fall. He lived in and enjoyed God, and was in communion and society with angels, not knowing good and evil. His life was spontaneous; his wisdom intuitive; he was unconscious of it, even as we would be of light were there no darkness. We should see it and be recipients of all its blessings without knowing its existence. But darkness came, and man knew. Alas! in knowing he lost all that he possessed before.

"Jesus came to restore man to that eternal day from which Adam fell."

About this time he mentions having spent a day in the woods with some friends, at Fort Lee; it is the only allusion we find to any sort of recreation or companionship with others. He sat alone for an hour, he says, in a pleasant spot which overlooked the Hudson and the high Palisade rocks, and "seemed to be in communion with the infinite invisible all around in all the deep avenues of the soul."

Four days before his baptism comes this anticipation of it:

"*New York, July* 27, '44.—I have commenced acting. My union with the Catholic Church is my first real, true act. And it is no doubt the forerunner of many more—of an active life. Heretofore I did not see or feel in me the grounds upon which I could act with permanence and security. I now do; and on this basis my future life will be built. What my actions may be, I care not. It was this deep eternal certainty within I did wish to feel, and I am now conscious that the lack of it was the reason for my inactivity.

"With this guide I ask no other, nor do I feel the need of the support of friends, or kindred, or the world. Alone it is sufficient for me, though it contradicts the advice of my friends and all my former life. It certainly seems to me absolute: if any error arises it will be from my disobedience."

"*July* 30.—The inward voice becomes more and more audible. It says: ' I am—obey ! '

"The new clothes itself in new dress.

"What proof does a man give that *he is* if he does only what has been done ?

"Can a man repeat the past with genius ?

"One true act opens the passage to ten more.

"Man is left to his own destiny; religion but sanctifies it."

When the day comes at last, the Sacrament itself gets only the briefest chronicle. The door seems but a door. Passing through it, he finds himself at home, and apparently without one quickening of the pulse, or any cessation of his desire to penetrate all its secret chambers. The explanation of this is to be looked for in the presumption that his baptism in infancy had been valid. It was conferred by a Lutheran minister who must have been trained in Germany, and whose methodical adherence to the proper form might be counted on. In the sight of God, doubtless, he had never since been outside the Church. He was like a child stolen from the cradle, but in whom racial and family traits had been superior to an uncongenial environment.

"*Friday, August* 1, 1844, 1 *P.M.*—This morning we were baptized by Bishop McCloskey. To-morrow we attend the tribunal of confession."

Then he mentions a curious fact which recalls a similar experience of St. Catherine of Genoa: "We know not why it is we feel an internal necessity of using the plural pronoun instead of the singular."

But if conditional baptism left him silent, the Sacrament he certainly received the following day opened the flood-gates of his speech:

"*August* 2.—Penance! joy! unbounded love! Sweet Jesus, Thy love is infinite! Blessed faith! sweet love! I possess an internal glory, a glowing flame of love! Let my whole life be one act of penance! O dear Jesus, the life-giver! Oh, what a sweet thing it is to be in the way of loveful grace! Jesus, keep me near Thee! Oh, how great a condescension, Jesus is my Friend! Oh! who has the conception of Jesus being his *Friend?* O ancient faith, how dear, how good is God in giving us sinners thee! Blessed is the grace of God that leadeth sinners to thee! Oh, how thou hast comforted the soul! It would turn from thee, but thou strengthenest it. The cup was bitter, but infinitely more sweet is the joy thou givest. My soul is clothed in brightness; its youth is restored. O blessed, ever-blessed, unfathomable, divine faith! O faith of apostles, martyrs, confessors, and saints! Holy Mother of Jesus, thou art my mother. I feel in my heart thy tender love. O holy Mother, thou hast beheld me! Bless me, Virgin Mother of Jesus!"

CHAPTER XVIII

BISHOP McCLOSKEY, afterwards the first American Cardinal, was coadjutor to Bishop Hughes from 1844 to 1847. He was living at the old Cathedral when Isaac Hecker first called upon him. He was still a young man, less than ten years separating him from the youthful catechumen. In temperament they were very different. The bishop, a man of routine in method and of no original views of principles, was so, nevertheless, by mental predisposition rather than by positive choice. He was a man of finished education; a dignified speaker, whose words read as impressively as they sounded. Although the two men were so unlike, the bishop could, at least after brief hesitation, fully appreciate Isaac Hecker; nay, could love him, could further his plans, and stand by him in his difficulties. Before we are done with this Life, the reader will see this more in detail.

Nor was Bishop McCloskey without light as a judge in spiritual matters. By nature calm and self-poised, and readily obedient to reason, the grace of his high office, his wide knowledge of men, his extensive reading, were doubtless supplemented by a special infusion of heavenly wisdom, due to his upright purpose and his spotless life. Though not timid, he was not conspicuous for courage; his refuge in difficulty was a high order of prudence, never cowardice; nor did he err either by precipitancy, by cruelty, or by rigidity of adherence to abstract rules of law. Father Hecker knew him thoroughly well, and admired him; more, he profited by his guidance, and that not only at this earliest period of their intercourse. It was by him that Isaac Hecker's vocation was, though not revealed, yet most wisely directed. Brownson told the young man that he ought to devote himself to the Germans in this country; Bishop Hughes advised him to go to St. Sulpice and study for the secular priesthood; Bishop McCloskey told him to become a religious.

Hitherto Isaac Hecker's environment had been entirely non-Catholic; the ebbing and flowing of a sea of doubt and inquiry upon which floated small boats and rafts which had been cast off from the good ship of Christ. Now that he was on board the ship itself, he found its crew and passengers sailing straight on toward their destined haven, paying small regard, as a rule, to the small craft and the shipwrecked sailors tossing on the wild waves around them, and only surprised when one or another hailed their vessel and asked to be taken on board. Nor did the attitude of non-Catholics, taking them generally, invite anything else. Isaac Hecker, passing into the Church, not only came into contact with its members, but was to be for some years exclusively in their company. But, though carried beyond the Ripleys, the Alcotts, the Lanes, the Emersons, and beyond the theories they in some sort stand for and represent, he had learned them and their lesson, and never lost his aptitude for returning to their company with a Catholic message. His farewell to that class did not involve loss of affectionate interest, for in mind he continually reverted to them. He knew that their peculiar traits were significant of the most imperative invitation of Providence to missionary work. He thought it was to that class, or, rather, to the multitude to whom they were prophets, that the exponent of Catholicity should first address himself. They possessed the highest activity of the natural faculties; they were all but the only class of Americans who loved truth for its own sake, that trait which is the peculiarity of the Catholic mind, and the first requisite for real conversion.

It may have been the latent strength of this conviction that, within a year after his reception into the Church, permanently affected the influence which Brownson had so long exerted over him. It ceased now to be in any sense controlling, and at no future time regained force enough to be directive. They found the Church together, went together into its vestibule, and were received nearly at the same time. And then the wide liberties of a universal religion gave ample scope and large suggestion for the accentuation and development of their native differences. Brownson was a publicist and remained so; Isaac Hecker was a mystic and remained so. To the mysticism of the latter was added an external apostolate; the public activity of the former was, indeed, apostolic, but upon a field not only different from any he would himself have spontaneously chosen, but quite unlike. Our reader already knows how grievous a loss to the public exposition of the Church in America this deflection of Brownson's genius from its true direction seemed to Father Hecker. He never ceased to deplore it as a needless calamity, overruled in great measure, indeed, by the good Providence of God, but not wholly repaired.

Father Hecker's affection for Dr. Brownson never wavered, and his gratitude towards him was only deepened and made more efficacious with the lapse of time and the growth of his own spiritual experience. If they did not always agree, either in principles or in questions of policy, they always loved each other. The memoranda furnish an interesting proof of this abiding affection on the part of Father Hecker. He was asked:

"Don't you think we might have a memorial tablet to Dr. Brownson in our church?"

"Yes! Of all the men I ever knew, he had most influence over me."

"When you were in early life?"

"Yes, of course. Oh! in after life no man has had influence with me, but only God."

This meant, of course, the influence of master upon disciple, and not that of lawful authority or of fraternal love, to both of which Father Hecker was ever very sensitive.

Speaking at another time of Brownson, he quoted this sentence from *The Convert* as so perfect an epitome of the man that it should be put on his monument:

"I had one principle, and only one, to which, since throwing up Universalism, I had been faithful; a principle to which I had, perhaps, made some sacrifices—that of following my own honest convictions whithersoever they should lead me."

And just here is found one of those points of essential difference which it is interesting to note between these two men, so closely drawn together by Divine Providence at one period, and in such a relation that to the elder the function of guidance seemed to have been appointed. In unswerving fidelity to conviction they were on a par, but in native clearness of vision and instinctive aversion from error they were far less closely matched. Brownson in early life had tried, accepted, and preached various forms of aberration from true doctrine. One might say of him, that, having found himself outside the highway at his start, he gathered accretions from hedge and ditch as he struggled toward the true road, and went through an after process of sloughing them one by one. Perhaps that process ended in making him over-timid. It was otherwise with Isaac Hecker. He, too, had stopped to consider many doctrines which purported to be true; more than that, he had recognized in each the modicum of truth which it possessed. But the falsity with which this was over-loaded was powerful enough to repel him, in spite of the truth he knew to be contained in it. He carried in himself the touchstone to which all that was akin to it beyond him responded of neces-sity. The Light which lights every man who comes into the world had not only never been darkened in him by sinful courses, but it seemed to burn with a crystal clearness which threw up into hideous and repellant proportions all that was offensive to it. Many voices had called him from without, but he had refused obedience unto any. He never submitted until his submission was full and not to be withdrawn. So, once in the Church, and enjoying her divine guarantee of external authority, he had few if any disquieting recollections of error to breed dis-trust of the light that shone within him. His soul was of that order to which truth speaks authoritatively and at first hand; of that soil from which institutions which are to stand spring by a true process of development, because it is the soil which first re-ceived their germs. Always it is the soul of man which is in-spired, the mind of man that is enlightened. Then the teaching comes as record of the fact and the doctrine; then the institu-tion solidifies about them, a perpetual witness that to many men and ages of men the same message has been handed down by its first recipients and has produced in them its proper results. The race of such souls has not died out in the Christian Church. The one truth, spoken once for all by the Incarnate Word, takes on for them new aspects and new tones. They are the pioneers of great movements. Nurtured in the Church, their ardor burns away mere conventionalities; born outside the Church, the light she carries is a beacon, and the voice she utters is felt as that of the true Mother. To adapt once more a pregnant sentence from young Hecker, of the truth of which he was himself an example: "It is God in them which believes in God."

But to return to Brownson. An entry in the journal, made nearly a year later, sums up the total impression which Brown-son had made upon his young disciple:

"*June* 22, 1845.—O. A. B. is here. He arrived this morn-ing. Though he is a friend to me, and the most critical periods of my experience have been known to him, and he has frequently given me advice and sympathy, yet he never moves my heart. He has been of inestimable use to me in my intellectual development. He is, too, a man of heart. But he is so strong, and so intellectually active, that all his energy is consumed in thought. He is an intellectual athlete. He thinks for a dozen men. He does not take time to realize in heart for himself. No man reads or thinks more than he. But he is greater as a writer than as a person. There are men who never wrote a line, but whose influence is deeper and more extensive than that of others who have written heavy tomes.

"It is too late for Brownson to give himself to contemplation and interior recollection. He is a controversialist; a doctor. The last he will be before long. Some have wondered why I should have contracted such a friendship for one whom they imagine to be so harsh and dictatorial. I have not felt this. His presence does not change me; nor do I find myself where I was not after having met him. He has not the temperament of a genius, but that of a rhetorician and declaimer. He arrives at his truths by a regular and consecutive system of logic. His mind is of a historical more than of a poetical mould.

"As a man, I have never known one so conscientious and self-sacrificing. This is natural to him. His love of right is supreme, and the thing he detests most is bad logic. It makes him peevish and often riles his temper. He defeats, but will never convince an opponent. This is bad. No one loves to break a lance with him, because he cuts such ungentlemanly gashes. He is strong, and he knows it. There is more of the Indian chief than of the Christian knight in his composition. But he has something of both, though nothing of the modern scholar, so called. His art is logic, but he never aims at art. By nature he is a most genuine and true man; none so much so. By no means E——" [Emerson?] "who ever prates about this thing. If he attempts embellishment, you see at once it is borrowed; it is not in his nature. There is a pure and genuine vein of poetry running through him, but it is not sufficient to tincture the whole flow of his life. He is a man of the thirteenth or fourteenth century rather than of the nineteenth. He is an anomaly among its scholars, writers, and divines. He is not thorough on any one subject though at home on all. What a finished collegiate education would have done for him I am baffled to conjecture. He is genuine, and I love him for that;

it is the crown of all virtues. But I must stop. I only intended to mention that he is here."

The reader may well suppose that Father Hecker fully appreciated Brownson's literary genius. The English language in his grasp was a weapon to slay and a talisman to raise to life. Never was argumentation made more delightful reading; never did a master instruct more exclusively by the aid of his disciple's highest faculties than did Brownson. Habituated his whole life long to the ardent study of the greatest topics of the human understanding, he was able to teach all, as he had taught young Hecker, how to think, discern, judge, penetrate, decide about them with matchless power; and he clothes his conclusions in language as adequate to express them as human language well can be. Clearness, precision, force, purity, vividness, loftiness are terms applicable to Dr. Brownson's literary style. It may be that the general reading public will not study his works merely for the sake of his literary merits; the pleasures of the imagination and of narrative are not to be found in Dr. Brownson. But he certainly will win his way to the suffrages of the higher class of students of fine writing. And let one have any shadow of interest in the great questions he treats, and every page displays a style which is the rarest of literary gifts. The very fact that his writing is untinted by those lesser beauties which catch the eye but to impede its deepest glances, is in itself an excellence all the greater in proportion to the gravity of his topics. Absolutely free from the least obscurity, his diction is a magnetic medium uniting the master's personality, the disciple's understanding, and the essence of the subject under consideration. Cardinal Newman, some may believe, possessed this supreme rhetoric in perhaps even a higher degree than Brownson, but so much can be said of few other writers of English prose. George Ripley, whom Father Hecker deemed the best judge of literature in our country or elsewhere, assured him that there were passages in Dr. Brownson which could not be surpassed in the whole range of English literature.

CHAPTER XIX

"COULD I but give up all my time to contemplation, study, reading, and reflection!"

Upon this aspiration as a background the whole matter of Isaac Hecker's vocation must be considered. In substance we have met with it very frequently already; in the shape just given it confronts us on the first page of the new diary begun a few days before his baptism. And as our reader accompanies us through the records he made during the year that still elapsed before he entered the Redemptorist Order, nothing, we think, will become more evident than that he was called to something beyond adhesion to the Church, the worthy reception of the sacraments, or even the ordinary sacerdotal state.

To make this still plainer at the start, it may be useful to describe briefly the special grounds whereon Isaac Hecker fought his life-long battles. These were, first: The validity of those natural aspirations which are called religious, and which embrace the veracity of reason in its essential affirmations. Second: Whether man be by nature guileless or totally depraved: Third, Whether religion be or be not intrinsically and primarily an elevating influence whose end is to raise men to real union with God.

To many inquirers after the true religion such preliminary doubts have been already settled, either by natural bent of mind or docility to previous training; and they pass on to consider apostolical succession, the primacy of Peter, the nature and number of the sacraments, and other matters wherein heresy errs by denial or by defect. But to Isaac Hecker all such points as these were, in a sense, subsidiary. He had asked admission into the Church because he found it to be the only teaching society on earth whose doctrines gave complete and adequate satisfaction to that fundamental craving of his nature which prompted his questions. She accredited herself to him as fully by that fact as she must have done to many a philosophic pagan among those who were the first disciples to the new faith preached by St. John or St. Paul. All else he accepted with an implicit, child-like confidence not different from that which moves the loyal descendant of ages of Catholic ancestors. It was clear to him that these accompanying doctrines and institutions must have been enfolded within the original germ, and must be received on the same authority, not by an analytic process and on their merits, one by one.

What he wanted was, in the first place, sustenance for what he invariably calls "the life" given him; and next, light to see in what way he was to put to use the strength so gained. The first effect of the sacraments was what one might call the natural one of making more visible the shadows which enveloped his path, as well as stimulating his instinctive efforts to pierce through them. After the rapturous joy which succeeded confession and absolution, a period of desolation and dryness heavier than he had ever known at once set in. Perhaps he had expected the very reverse of this. At all events, it was not many days before it drew from him the complaint that in leaving Concord he had also left behind him the great interior sweetness which had buoyed him up. On August 11 he writes:

"How hard it has been for me to go through with all these solemn mysteries and ceremonies without experiencing any of those great delights which I have [before] felt. Why is this? Is it to try my faith? O Lord! how long shall I be tried in this season of desolation? Are these [delights] never to return? Have I acted unworthily? What shall I do to receive these blessings again?"

Then he resolves to make a novena, fasting the while on bread and water, to entreat their renewal. But at once a better mood sets in and he adds:

"The highest state of perfection is to be content to be nothing. Lord, give me strength not to ask of Thee anything that is pleasant to me. I renounce what I have just asked for, and will try to do all without the hope of recompense. If Thou triest my soul, let it not go until it has paid the uttermost farthing."

"*August* 15, 1844.—To-day is the holyday of the Assumption of the dear, Blessed Mary, Mother of our Lord and Saviour Jesus. Oh! may I be found worthy of her regard and love."

"He that has not learned the bitterness of the drops of woe

has not learned to live. One hour of deep agony teaches man more love and wisdom than a whole long life of happiness. . .

"In many faces I see passing through the crowded streets there seems a veiled beauty, an angel quickening me with purer life as I go by them in anxious haste. Do we not see the hidden worth, glory, and beauty of others as our own becomes revealed to us? Would the Son of God have been needed to ransom man if he were not of incomparable value?"

One of the dreams that at this time occupied Isaac's mind was that of undertaking a pilgrimage to Rome. He wrote to Henry Thoreau, proposing that they should go in company, and felt regret when his invitation was not accepted. His notion was to "work, beg, and travel on foot, so far as land goes, to Rome. I know of no pleasanter, better way, both for soul and body, than to make such a pilgrimage in the old, middle-age fashion ; to suffer hunger, storm, cold, heat—all that can affect the body of flesh. If we receive hard usage, so much the better will it be for us. Why thump one's own flesh here ? Let it be done for us by others, our soul, meanwhile, looking at higher objects. . . . I feel that I have the stuff to do it in me. I would love to work and beg my way to Rome if it cost me ten or fifteen years of my life."

Thoreau replied to this proposal that such a tour had been one of his own early dreams, but that he had outlived it. He had now "retired from all external activity in disgust, and his life was more Brahminical, Artesian-well, Inner-Temple like." So the scheme, which had secured Bishop McCloskey's approbation, although he had forcibly represented to young Hecker that to go absolutely destitute of money, and dependent for all things upon alms, would be impossible, was presently shelved. It was but one of the diversions with which certain souls, not yet enlightened as to their true course, nor arrived at the abandonment of themselves to Divine Providence, are amused. Their inactivity seems idleness to them, and they mistake the restless impulse which bids them be up and doing for the voice of conscience or the inspiration of heavenly wisdom ; but it is neither. Sometimes it is a superfluity of natural energy seeking an outlet ; sometimes it is the result of the strain placed upon nature by a very powerful influx of grace. The infusion of power from above is often greatly in excess of the light necessary for guidance in its use.

This last rarely comes entirely from the inner touch of the Holy Spirit. In the lives of the Fathers of the Desert we read of a certain young brother, Ptolemy, who went astray from sound spirituality. When admonished he asserted that he need learn the spiritual life from none save the Holy Ghost, of whose inspirations any man of good will could be certain. He was told by the old monks that the inspiration of the Holy Ghost and the understanding of the same are two distinct things, and that this understanding is disclosed only to him whose will has been purified by the practice of obedience and humility. In truth, it is rarely that the inner voice of God does not call for an external interpreter, which, if it does no more than furnish a divinely authorized test and criterion, is none the less necessary. Moreover, the inner voice seldom provides ways and means for its own purposes. Father Hecker was ever a strenuous defender of this inner and outer unity of the Divine guidance, and his vocation was an illustration of it. However masterful the inner voice of God which called him away from the world, he was helpless till he heard its tones harmonized by the counsel of Bishop McCloskey. When he found that even with this backing secured, the external obstacles to his plan proved invincible, he was once more nonplussed. " If not this, what ? " he asks himself.

" I feel deeply and strongly that the circle of family happiness is not sufficient for my nature, but what I can profitably do outside of this I have not the ability to say.

" That our real wishes are presentiments of our capabilities is a very true proverb, no doubt; but are we not most ignorant of what these are ? It seems as though we are all unconsciously educated for unknown ends and purposes.

" I look upon myself as belonging to that class of decidedly unfortunate beings who have no marked talent for any particular pursuit. The words talent, genius, have for me no application whatever. I stand on the confines of both worlds, not feeling the necessity nor having the true valor to decide for either sphere.

" O heaven ! why was this deep, ever-burning life given me, unless it be that I might be slowly and painfully consumed by it ? All greatness is in the actor, not in the act. He whom God has blessed with an end in life, can earnestly labor to accomplish that end. But alas for that poor mortal whose existence only serves to fill up space in the world! How excruciating to him to be conscious of this! O Prometheus!

"Simply to be what God would have us, is to be greater than to have the applause of the whole world otherwise. All such statements as this are necessarily one-sided. Because there are always good and virtuous men in the world whose approbation is that of God.

"There is an instinct in man which draws him to danger, as in battle-fields; as there is also in the fly, drawing it to the flame of light. It is the desire of the spirit within, seeking for release.'

"*August* 20, 1844.—Scarce do I know what to say of myself. If I accuse myself by the light given me, it would lead me to leave all around me. My conscience thus accuses me. And in partaking of worldly things and going into the company around me, my interior self has no pleasure, and I feel afterwards that the labor and time have been misspent. How to live a life which shall be conformable to the life within and not separate from the persons and circumstances around me, I cannot conceive. I am now like one who tastes a little of this and then a little of that dish, while his time is wasted and his mind distracted from that pure enjoyment which is a foretaste of the bliss of the angels. I feel my primitive instincts and unvitiated tastes daily becoming more sensible to inspirations from above, from the invisible. The ideal world, the soul world, the kingdom of heaven within, I feel as if I were more a friend and citizen of. O Lord! my heart would break forth in praise of the riches of the life given within! It seems that in this that we enjoy all, know all, and possess all. If we have Thee, O Lord! if Thou hast taken up Thy dwelling in us, we enjoy heaven within and paradise without!"

"*August* 21, 1844.—The object of education should be to place each individual mind in vital union with the One Universal Educator. . . .
"The only pleasure for man is his union with *à priori* principles."

"*August* 23, 1844.—If the animal passions are indulged, of course you must pay the cost. If you get a large family of children about you, and please your animal appetites with all sorts of luxury, and indulge your pride in all the foolish fashions of show, do not wonder that it cost all your time to uphold such an expensive life. This is necessary, unless you cheat some one else out of the hard-earned value of his labor. I cannot conceive how a Christian, under the present arrangements, can become wealthy without violating repeatedly the precepts of his religion. . . ."

"Where shall we find God? Within.

"How shall we hear the voices of angels? Listen with the inward ear.

"When are we with God? When we are no more with ourselves.

"When do we hear the music of heaven? When we are entirely silent.

"What is the effect of sin? Confusion.

"Where does God dwell? In silence.

"Who loves God? He who knows nothing and loves nothing of himself.

"What is prayer? The breath of silence.

"What is love? The motion of the pure will.

"What is light? The shadow of love.

"What is force? The power of love.

"Where does God dwell? Where there is peace.

"Who is most like God? He who knows he is the least like Him.

"What is the innermost of all? Stillness.

"Who is the purest? He who is most beyond temptation.

"What is the personality of man? The absolute negation of God.

"What is God? The absolute affirmation in man.

"What is it to know? It is to be ignorant.

"What should we desire? Not to desire.

"What is the most positive answer? Silence.

"What is the truest? That which cannot be proven."

"*August* 25, 1844.—In silence, suffering without murmuring. An eternal thirst, enduring without being quenched. Infinite longings without being met. Heart ever burning, never refreshed. Void within and mystery all around. Ever escaping

that which we would reach. Tortured incessantly without relief.
Alone—bereft of God, angels, men—all. Hopes gone, fears vanished, and love dead within. These, and more than these, must
man suffer."

"*August* 28, 1844.—Is it not because I have been too much
engaged in reading and paid too little attention to the centre
that I have lost myself, as it were? My position here distracts
my attention and I lose the delight, intimate knowledge, and
sweet consciousness of my interior life. How can this be remedied? I am constantly called off to matters in which I have no
relish; and if I retreat for a short time, they rest on me like a
load, so that I cannot call myself free at any moment. I see
the case as it stands, and feel I am losing my interior life from
the false position in which I am placed.

"The human ties and the material conditions in which I am
should unquestionably be sacrificed to the divine interior relation to the One, the Love-Spirit, which, alas! I *have* so sensibly
felt. Can a man live in the world and follow Christ? I know
not; but, as for me, I find it impossible. I feel more and more
the necessity of leaving the society and the distracting cares of a
city business for a silent and peaceful retreat, to the end that I
may restore the life I fear I am losing. Our natural interests should be subject to our human ties; our human ties
to our spiritual relations; and who is he who brings all these
into divine harmony?

"How shall I make the sacrifice which shall accomplish the
sole end I have, and should have, in view? Thrice have I left
home for this purpose, and each time have returned unavoidably
—so, at least, it seems to me. Once more, I trust, will prove a
permanent and immovable trial."

To some, a most striking incidental proof of his inaptitude
for the ordinary layman's life, is found in the subjoined extract
from the memoranda. Speaking of this period, Father Hecker
said:

"Some time after my reception into the Church, I went to
Bishop McCloskey and told him I had scruples against renting a seat in the Cathedral in Mott Street. 'If I do,' I said,
'I shall feel sore at the thought that I have set apart for me in
the house of God a seat which a poor man cannot use.' I told

him that for this reason I had knelt down near the doorway, among the crowd of transient poor people. Oh, how he eased my spirit by sympathizing with my sentiment, and satisfied me by declaring that the renting of pews was only from necessity, and he wished we could get along without it."

His relations with some of his former friends at Brook Farm still continued, though in a somewhat attenuated condition. From a long and appreciative letter sent him by Burrill Curtis, we make an extract, followed by Isaac's comments on it:

"*October* 13, 1844.—Your preparedness for any fate has been one of the chief attractions of your character to me, for I believe it is deeper than a mere state of mind. But, for all that, your restlessness is uppermost just now; not as a contradictory element, for it is not; but as a discovering power."

Isaac's journal, just at this time, was chiefly devoted to what he calls "the many smaller, venial sins which beset my path and keep me down to earth. Also to prescribe such remedies as may seem to me best for these thorns in the flesh." On October 26 he notes that he has received the letter just quoted, and remarks:

"It showed more regard for me than I thought he had. The truth is, I do not feel myself worthy to be the friend of any one, and would pass my life in being a friend to all, without recognizing their friendship towards me.

"To-day I have felt more humanly tender than ever. The past has come up before me with much emotion. —————— has been much in my thoughts.

"I have experienced those unnatural feelings which I have felt heretofore. I feel that the spirit world is near and glimmering all around me. The nervous shocks I have been subject to, but which I have not experienced for some time back, recurred this evening. I am known to spirits, or else I apprehend them."

He had taken up Latin and Greek again, and seems to have entered a class of young men under the tutorship of a Mr. Owen. The entry just quoted from goes on as follows:

"I do not devote as much time to study as I should, or as

I might. I fear I shall never make anything of my studies. I do not endeavor with all my might. This study has thrown me into another sphere. I like it not. I feel apprehensive of something, of somewhat. Ten years from now will fix my destiny, if I have any."

Much good as he continued to receive from the sacrament of penance, he found a not altogether usual difficulty in preparing for it. Perhaps it was in the counsel he received there that he got courage to gird himself for his renewed attack upon the languages, for his delinquencies in this respect have the air of being the most tangible of the matters on his conscience.

"I must prepare for confession this week," he writes on November 5, 1844. "Oh! would that I could accuse myself as I should. Man is not what he should be so long as he is not an angel. Oh, dear God! give me Thy aid, and help me in my weaknesses. What sins can I accuse myself of now? First—oh, Love! give me light to accuse myself—to see my sins. *This is my greatest sin; that I cannot accuse myself and am so wicked.*
"Each day I omit a hundred duties that I should not. Lord, give me Thy Spirit, that I may be humble, meek, and sweet in all my walk and conversation. Fill my heart with Thy love."

In a little while he found himself able to study more diligently, and though he continually regrets the inroad this makes upon his interior life, he seems not only to have persevered, but to have taken considerable interest and an active part in the debates got up at regular intervals by the class he had joined. He notes that he has serious doubts whether it will be wise for him to express his full mind on some of the subjects brought up. His fellow-pupils were all Protestants, and some of them well-informed and talented young men. His views would be new to them, and so would many of his authorities for his statements of fact, and he thought it not unlikely that a commotion might sometimes be raised which would not at all commend itself to the teacher of the institution. He concluded, however, to throw prudence to the winds, and on controverted points to express his sentiments freely and frankly. There were some animated discussions, no doubt.

He was endeavoring at this time to retrench his hours of sleep to the narrowest dimensions compatible with health, and found it, we may note, the most difficult of his austerities. In other respects they remained severe, as this entry may witness:

"*November* 27, 1844.—I am sorely perplexed what to eat. Nuts, apples, and bread seem not a diet wholly suitable, and what to add I know not. Potatoes are not good; I think they were the cause of my illness last week. I do not wish to partake of anything that comes even remotely from an animal. Cooking, also, I wish, as far as possible, to dispense with. *I would I could dispense with the whole digestive apparatus!* Cheese, butter, eggs, milk, are for many reasons not a part of my diet."

The balance of this fourth volume of his diary, begun September 9, 1844, and ended January 2, 1845, is mainly occupied with addresses to his guardian angel. He was, as those who knew him will remember, always extremely devout to the angelic choirs. On his birthday this year he writes as follows:

"*December* 18, 1844.—Let me look back for a few moments and see where I stood last year this time (an incomprehensible length), and where I now stand. Then my path was dim, unfixed, unsettled. Then I was not so disentangled from the body and its desires as, I hope in God, I now am. In all I feel a consciousness that since then I have spiritually grown—been transformed. For my present I cannot speak. For my future, it seems I dare not speak. .

"Dreams of the future! Exalted visions! Beautiful, unspeakable hopes! Deep, inarticulate longings that fill the conscious soul! Ah! so sweet, so harmonious, so delightful, like an angel, like the bride of the pure and bright soul adorned for the nuptials, do I see the future beckoning me with a clear, transparent smile onward to her presence. 'Ah!' my soul would say, 'we will meet, for I am in thy presence, and faithful in God may heaven grant me to be.' The beauty, the grace, the love, the sweetness that attract me, are beyond all comparison. Ah! thou eternal, ever-blooming virgin, the Future, shall I ever embrace thee? Shall I ever see thee nearer to my heart? I look at myself and I am bowed down low in grief; but when I cast my eyes up to thee, in seeing thee I am lost. The grace and beauty I see in thee passes into my soul, and I am all that thou art. I am then wedded to thee, and I would that it were an eternal union. But ah! my eyes, when turned upon myself, lose all sight of thee, and meet nothing but my own spots and blemishes. How canst thou love me? I say; and for thy pure love I am melted into thee as one."

He continues:

"Lord, let me speak of my many and grievous sins; but oh! when I would do so, my mouth speaks nothing forth but Thy praises.

"I would offer my whole soul afresh to *all* that is, for the sake of the love of God. . . . Lord, I am Thine, for Thou dost teach me this by Thy unutterable, ever-present love."

"*January* 3.—Last Saturday my confessor was not at home when I called. I have waited until this morning, the Saturday following. It is sad to me to wait to partake of the Blessed Sacrament. How much joy, love, and sweetness it is to the soul! I feel my soul to glow again with renewed love when I have partaken of the blessed communion of Christ. This is my spiritual food. It is the goodness, mercy, and love of God which keeps me from sadness."

CHAPTER XX.

ISAAC HECKER'S zeal for social reform lent force to his strictly personal cravings for a more religious life; he longed for wider scope than individual effort could possibly bestow, and also for a supernatural point of vantage. "If we would do humanity any good," he writes in his diary while considering his vocation, "we must act from grounds higher than humanity; our standpoint must be above the race, otherwise how can we act *upon* humanity?" He also speaks of the fundamental necessity of "an impulse of divine love" actuating the reformer of social evils. He addresses himself thus: "If thou wouldst move the race to greater good and higher virtue, lose thyself in the Universal. Be so great as to give thyself to something nobler than thyself if thou wouldst be ennobled, immortalized." In many pages of the last two volumes of his diary these notes of sympathetic love for his fellow-men are mingled with yearnings for solitude. "This book," he writes on the last page of one of them, "has answered some little purpose; for when I wanted to speak to some one and yet was alone, it cost me no labor to scribble in it. It would give me great pleasure if I had a friend who would exchange such thoughts with me." He was soon to enter into that spiritual heritage which among its other treasures bestows the beatitude of the sage, "Blessed is the man who hath found a true friend."

Little by little a distinctly penitential mood came over him, and it occupies nearly the whole of the last volume of the diary with the most unreserved expressions of grief for sin, or, rather, for a state of sinfulness, since the specific mention of sins is nearly altogether wanting. We meet with page after page of self-accusation in general terms: "I am in want of greater love for those around me; I perform my spiritual duties too negligently; too little of my time is devoted to spiritual exercises. I feel all over sick with sin! Here is my difficulty, O Lord, and do Thou direct me: I am always in doubt, when I do not think of Thee alone, that I am sinning and that my time is misspent."

His protestations of sorrow are extremely fervent and very numerous; and as the Lent of 1845 approached he records his purpose of restricting himself to one meal a day. As he never ate meat, nor any "product of animal life," and drank only water, his "nuts, bread, and apples" once a day must have been his diet all through the penitential season. The reader will remember *ein herrliches Essen* at Concord: "bread, maple-sugar, and apples."

In the middle of February he opened his mind more fully to Bishop McCloskey, whom he continually calls his spiritual director. He had now to reveal the discoveries of holy penance, and to add to his other motives for leaving the world the dread of falling into mortal sin. He had, he tells us, misgivings as to whether he was ambitious or not. One of his spiritual states he thus alludes to:

"I will ask my confessor how it is—if it is so with others, that they feel no sense of things, no joy, no reality, no emotion, no impulse, nothing positive within or around," but only the consciousness of the need of a terrible atonement. This is accompanied by frantic prayers to God, invocations of the Blessed Virgin, St. Francis of Assisi and other saints. And he says that he has been told that he is scrupulous, and complains that at confession he can only accuse himself in general terms.

Complete abandonment to the divine will seems to have been the outcome of a season of much distress of soul, and bodily mortification. On April 2 he writes: "The last time I saw my director he spoke to me concerning the sacred ministry, and this is a subject I feel an unspeakable difficulty about. I told him that I desired to place myself wholly in his hands and should do whatever he directed. I do not wish to be any more than nothing. I give myself up. So far the Lord seems to be with me, and I hope that He will not forsake me in the future."

As might have been anticipated, Bishop McCloskey's advice was wise. Plainly, his own hope was that young Hecker should enter the secular priesthood, but there is no evidence in the numerous references to the matter in the diary, that this caused him to do more than make his young friend fully acquainted with that state of life. He had him call at the newly-opened diocesan seminary at Fordham and become acquainted with the professors. Bishop Hughes, whom he also consulted, urged him to go to St. Sulpice in Paris, and to the Propaganda in Rome, and make his studies for the secular priesthood. But they failed to win him to their opinion, and were too enlightened to seek to influence him except by argument. Father Hecker ever held the very highest views on the dignity of the priesthood, considering its vocation second to none. But while he was irresistibly inclined to a state of retirement quite incompatible with the duties of the secular priesthood in America, he also felt the most urgent need of constant advice and companionship for guidance in his interior life. These seemingly contradictory requirements he hoped to find united in a religious community, and Bishop McCloskey emphatically assured him that his anticipations would not be disappointed. In addition to this, Isaac Hecker had at least some premonitions of an apostolic vocation calling for a wider range of activity than can be usually compassed by the diocesan clergy. But we have often heard him say that the immediate impulse which induced his application to be made a Redemptorist was need of "intimate and careful spiritual guidance."

His director therefore became satisfied that he should become a religious, and turned his attention to the Society of Jesus, giving him the lives of St. Ignatius and St. Francis Xavier to read, and, doubtless, answered his inquiries about that order. " But," he said in after years, "I had no vocation to teach young boys and felt unfitted for a student's life"; added to this was the certainty of the postponement of any public activity on his part for many years if he became a Jesuit.

After mentioning that he had read the life of St. Francis Xavier, he says that an acquaintance had written him that a German priest, living in Third Street, wanted to see him. This was one of the Redemptorist Fathers who were newly established in the city. This priest, whose name is not given, undertook to assume direction of Isaac, and was very urgent with him to make a spiritual retreat with a view to deciding his vocation. " He is a very zealous person—too much so it seems to me," is the comment in the diary, and the answer was a refusal. But what he saw in the community pleased and attracted Isaac, for everything was poor and plain, and there was an air of solitude. However, he would by no means change his spiritual adviser, writing, " I strive to follow my spiritual director or else I should be fearful of my state. All my difficulties, sins, and temptations I make him acquainted with. . . . Though the world has no particular hold upon me, I give it up once and for all. It gives me pain to feel my perfect want of faith in myself as being in any way useful."

Meantime, on Trinity Sunday, he had been confirmed with his brother George, whose entrance into the Church is here first indicated; no other member of the family became a Catholic. Isaac took the additional name of Thomas on receiving this sacrament, in honor of St. Thomas Aquinas.

Again he writes:

"I have tried to study to-day, but I cannot. Is it not the business of man to save his own soul, and this before all things? Does the study of Greek and Latin help a soul towards its salvation? Is it not quite a different thing from grace? Sometimes I feel strongly inclined to set aside all study, all reading, as superficial and not so important as contemplation and silence."

The time was coming when the Holy Spirit would do this in spite of him and in a way the reverse of pleasant. Meantime he worked away at his books and attended his classes at Cornelius Institute, which was the name of the private school he had been attending, till July 16, the commencement day. In recording his impressions of the school and the acquaintances there made, he says that with one possible exception the young men were of little interest to him, lacking earnestness of character. He does not name the teachers or give the location of the school. Yet he says his experience there had been useful "and chastened my hopes. I have seen by means of it much more clearly into the workings of Protestantism, its want of deep spirituality, its superficiality, and its inevitable tendency to no-religion."

As may be supposed, his visits to Third Street became frequent, and his acquaintance with the Fathers better established. This was especially true with regard to Father Rumpler, who was rector of the house, a learned and able man and one of mature spirituality. He was a German born and bred, with the hard ideas of discipline peculiar to a class of his countrymen though foreign to the genuine German character. He impressed young Hecker as a sedate man, wise and firm. The friendship then begun was maintained until Father Rumpler was deprived of his reason by an attack of acute mania several years later. But more than the friendship of Rumpler, as far as immediate results were concerned, was the providential circumstance of two other young Americans having applied to join the Redemptorists. To Isaac this was a stimulant of no ordinary power. Like himself, they were converts and very fervent ones; but, unlike him, they had come into the Church from Episcopalianism. Clarence A. Walworth, son of the Chancellor of the State of New York, was a graduate of Union College. He studied law in Albany and practised his profession for a short time, but finally undertook the ministry. After three years in the Episcopal seminary he became a Catholic. Those who know him now can see the tall and graceful youth, pleasing and kindly, with the face and voice and soul of an orator ; for the force and charm of youth have not been weakened in receiving the dignity of old age.

James A. McMaster was of Pennsylvania Scotch-Irish parentage. His name is familiar to our readers as editor of the *Freeman's Journal*. Those qualities of aggressive zeal which made McMaster so well known to Catholics of our day were not wholly undeveloped in the tall, angular youth, still a catechumen, and intoxicated with the new wine of Catholic fervor. Young Mr. Walworth had been made a Catholic but a short time before, and McMaster was received into the Church by the Redemptorists in Third Street, his two young friends being present. While he was kneeling at the altar, candle in hand, piously reading his profession of faith to Father Rumpler, he accidentally set fire to Father Tschenhens' hair, one of the fathers assisting at the ceremony. Walking together afterwards in the little garden of the convent, Father Rumpler said to him : " Mr. McMaster, you begin well—setting fire to a priest." " Oh," answered he, " if I don't set fire to something more than that it will be a pity." These new friends of Isaac had applied to enter the Redemptorist novitiate and they had been accepted. This meant a voyage to Europe, for the congregation had not yet established a novitiate in America.

One Friday, then, during the last days of July—the exact date we have not been able to discover—Isaac Hecker was informed by Father Rumpler that Walworth and McMaster would sail for Belgium the evening of the next day. " I decided to join them," he said when relating the circumstances afterwards. " Father Rumpler was favorable, but puzzled. And I must first present myself to the Provincial, Father de Held, who was in Baltimore. I arrived in Baltimore at four o'clock

in the morning on Saturday, travelling all night. Father de
Held looked at me, as I presented myself, and said that he
must take time to consider. I explained about the departure of
the others that day. He ordered Brother Michael to get me
a bowl of coffee from the kitchen, and me to hear his Mass. I
heard the Mass and after that he examined me a little—asked
me to read out of the *Following of Christ* in Latin, which I
did. He gave me my acceptance, and I rushed back to New
York by the half past eight o'clock morning train. George had
packed my trunk, and I sailed that day with the others."

The picturesqueness of the group was certainly not lessened
by the accession of Isaac Hecker, whose leap to and from
Baltimore, though hardly to be expected from a contemplative,
was in accord with the sudden energy of his nature. One who
saw him at the time says that " he had the general make-up of
a transcendalist, not excepting his long hair flowing down on his
neck."

The ship was an American one named the *Argo*, and she
was bound for London. The voyage was every way pleasant,
lasting but twenty-five days from land to land, with bright skies,
quiet sea, and fair winds. Their berths were in the waist of the
ship, in the second cabin, all the places in the first cabin having been taken ; this pleased them well, for they loved the poor
man's lot. Isaac's passage money was paid by his brothers, and
he was supplied by them and his mother with all sorts of conveniences; and these, of course, he made to conduce to the
comfort of the entire party. The lower and larger berth of their
little state-room was occupied by Walworth and McMaster, and
Isaac took the upper and smaller one. None of them suffered
from sea sickness.

The young pilgrims were overflowing with happiness, as if
they were going to the enjoyment of a rich heritage, as, indeed,
in a spiritual sense they were. It was a first voyage to the Old
World for all of them and they found everything interesting.
They made friends with the crew, who were nearly all Yankee
sailors, and who struck them as exactly like themselves, except
that they were not religious; and they sought entertainment with
such of the passengers as were congenial, though in this Isaac
Hecker was more ready than his companions. Father Walworth
tells an incident characteristic of both himself and his transcendental
companion. He was admonishing young Hecker to be more reti-

cent among the crew and was asked why. "You wouldn't like
to kneel down and kiss the deck before all those sailors," said
Walworth. "Why not?" was the reply. "Then do it."
And down dropped Hecker to the deck and kissed it in all
simplicity.

They had many topics of interest to occupy their time; Isaac
favored such as were philosophical and social, his companions
were absorbed by the Tractarian movement, its phases of thought
and variety of persons, and all must have had much to tell of
friends and relatives whom they hoped soon to see members of
the Church. One night the harmony with their fellow-passen-
gers was threatened with rupture. They were much annoyed by
a violent dispute about the Trinity carried on in the adjoining
cabin far into the night. McMaster finally lost patience, sprang
out of bed, rushed among the disputants, and smote the table
with a tremendous blow and shouted "*Silence!*" His remedy
was efficacious; the theologians scattered and went to bed.

There was a marked difference between Isaac and his companions in controversial views. All three used their reason with
the utmost activity, but he had travelled into the Church by
the road of philosophy and they by that of history and Scripture.
Their conversation must have been the exchange of intellectual
commodities of very different kinds and for that reason expediting
a busy commerce. They could profit by his bold and original
views of principle and he was in need of their idea of the external integrity of organized religion. Then, too, they had much to
say of the future, chiefly by way of conjecture, for no member of
the order accompanied them. No one was superior and no superior was needed. As to devotional exercises each suited himself, kneeling down and saying his prayers night and morning
and at other times, in his own way and words.

There was also difference in matters of devotion, for Isaac
. Hecker had little or no religious training, and as to the traditional forms of religious practice he was very backward. The
others had long since familiarized themselves with all Catholic
usages. Young Walworth taught young Hecker how to say the
rosary and initiated him, doubtless, into other common practices,
which he assumed with the simplicity and docility of the child
of guileless nature that he was.

The ship, as we have said, was bound to London, but our
party were too impatient to wait till the end of the voyage and

left her at Portsmouth in the pilot's boat; the sea was running high, but so were their spirits, and although the boat was tossed about in a way to scare a landsman, they gladly went ashore and took the cars to London. We have before us a letter from Isaac Hecker to his brothers, dated the 29th of August, saying that they had been in London three days after a pleasant voyage, and expressing deep joy at nearing the place of retirement and prayer for which he had been longing. He asks them to write to Brownson and especially to assure his mother of his happiness

McMaster insisted on visiting Newman at Littlemore, and afterwards gave a glowing account of his visit. He had been received by the great man, who did not enter the Church till a few months later, with the utmost kindness. He found him standing in his library, reading a book. He asked many questions about the tendency of men's minds in America, and was especially interested in Arthur Carey, with whose influence among American Episcopalians and early death the reader has been made acquainted. They lodged at a decent little inn over a pastry cook's shop and did not go sight-seeing to any extent. McMaster's companions did not wait for his return from Oxford, but when the packet sailed for Antwerp, which was Sunday, the 30th of August, they went down to Folkestone and took passage. They arrived the following morning, and, armed with a letter from Father Rumpler to a Madame Marchand, a warm friend of the congregation, they went straight to the nearest Church to inquire the way to her house. It happened to be the Jesuit church, and one of the fathers kindly guided them to the lady's house. She was delighted to serve them; gave them an excellent dinner, and, after they had visited Rubens' great picture, the Descent from the Cross, set them forth on their journey; but the " yea, yea and nay, nay " of Scripture, or rather *jah, jah, nein, nein,* was their only conversation with the good lady, for although young Walworth could speak French and Isaac German, she knew nothing but Flemish. Distances are not great in little Belgium, and so before night they were at St. Trond, a little city about thirty-five miles southeast of Antwerp and twenty miles from Liège. Here they were soon joined by Mr. McMaster, and their novitiate began. Isaac Hecker was now twenty-five years and nine months old.

CHAPTER XXI.

BROTHER HECKER.

THE Redemptorist novitiate at St. Trond, as well as the house of studies at Wittem, Holland, had been established by the immediate disciples of St. Clement Hofbauer. That great servant of God had introduced the Congregation of the Most Holy Redeemer into Austria and other parts of Germany several years before the time of which we write. A saint himself, and of wonderful missionary gifts, he was worthy of the title of second founder of the order of St. Alphonsus Liguori. St. Clement was the son of a Moravian peasant, and in early life had been a baker by trade. St. Alphonsus was still alive when Clement, while on a pilgrimage to Rome, was enrolled there in the Redemptorist novitiate. This event was auspicious of the future of the entire community, since his apostolate was the means of propagating the order among the northern nations, and giving to it some of its present dominant characteristics of Teutonic discipline; whereas in the land of its origin it has never fully recovered from the disasters which befell it during the lifetime of its founder. In Germany and the Low Countries, on the other hand, the children of St. Alphonsus and St. Clement were, at the time when the three Americans joined them, the most powerful preachers in the Church. Their vocation called them to give missions—spiritual exercises lasting from a week to a month —to the faithful in every part of Catholic Europe, not excepting France. Their fame was established as the foremost preachers of penance and of the Redeemer's love for sinners.

St. Trond was the novitiate of the Belgian Province, which embraced Belgium and Holland as well as the newly established convents in England and America. The Provincial was Father de Held, whom we saw in Baltimore while he was there on a tour of inspection of the American houses. He was an Austrian German, a man of noble presence, matured spirituality and an accomplished missionary. Father Hecker knew him well in after years, and always counted him as one who understood his spirit and approved his aspirations.

The convent in St. Trond was in a narrow street of the quaint little city; so narrow, indeed, that one almost fancied that he could touch both walls by stretching out his arms. It was a solid old structure, built in the first half of the fifteenth century by St. Colette for her Poor Clares, an ample guarantee of its conformity to the ideas of religious poverty. It was not architecturally fine, but was a curious and interesting building. Isaac in one of his letters home says that the house was very roomy, with long corridors having cells on each side. It abutted on a church which was open to the public and served by the fathers; a window in the convent chapel looked into the sanctuary. Attached to the house was a garden of three or four acres.

The country around the town is a typical Flemish landscape, flat, fertile, thickly dotted with farm buildings, and highly cultivated. The people are wholly Catholic. The town is an old one, and in its time has had some military importance. Our young novices often walked upon the ramparts which encircled it. In the neighborhood are structures which were built before the Christian era; quite near by was one of Cæsar's round towers, as well as the deserted ruins of an ancient city named Leo. Curious old churches and monasteries might often be seen by the novices on their long walks into the country. All this antiquity was the more pleasing to the American novices because in their own land the forests, the rivers, and the everlasting hills are all that represent the distant past.

Besides twenty novices there were ten or twelve fathers at St. Trond, who either served the church or went about on missions; and there were also a number of lay brothers. By nationality the greater portion of the novices were Belgians and Hollanders, the others being mostly Germans. The language of the house was French, though Latin was sometimes used. Of course this was an added difficulty to *Brother* Hecker, as he was now called, for he knew practically nothing of that language, though he had studied it a little. But he attacked it resolutely, and, as one of his companions said, learned it heels over head. He never feared to make mistakes, nor dreaded a smile at his expense, and as a consequence was soon able to talk to any one. But his French was always curious, and when he took his turn at reading during meals he gave the community some hearty laughs.

All the new-comers were invested with the Redemptorist habit about three weeks after their arrival, in September, 1845. "You can scarce imagine the happiness I felt on my arrival here," he writes to his mother in his first letter home. "For three days my heart was filled with joy and gladness. I was like one who had been transported to a lovelier, a purer, and a better world." He tells her that he had waited for a fortnight before writing, to learn the place, and then, after expressing his satisfaction with everything in such sentences as the above, he fills the rest of the letter with arguments in favor of the Catholic Church and exhortations to join it. Such was the burden of all of his letters home from both St. Trond and Wittem. We have ten written from the novitiate. An exception must be made as to one which describes in detail the daily order of life in the novitiate. It is addressed to his mother.

He tells her that the first bell rings at half-past four in the morning and the last at half-past nine at night. The time is divided between various common and private devotional exercises, including Mass, meditations, recitation of the office in common, study of the rule of the order, spiritual conferences, spiritual reading, and the like. Silence is broken only for an hour after dinner and another hour after supper. About an hour of out-door exercise is taken every day, and a long walk once a week and on feast-days. All of Thursday in each week and the more important feasts of the year are days of recreation, when silence need not be observed during the greater part of the day, and much relaxation is otherwise allowed. All Fridays are days of total silence and special devotion. The letter fails to mention the discipline, or flagellation, which was taken twice a week.

He ends thus: "The time of the novitiate is one year, and its object is to prove our vocation, and form the religious character—the heart. The exercises may seem too many to you, but to us they are quite otherwise. Their frequent changes prevent them from being monotonous, and their variety makes them agreeable. Our time passes without our taking count of it, and our joy is that of a pure conscience, and our happiness that of a clean heart."

It might seem a matter of peculiar difficulty for a free nature like Isaac Hecker's to conform to the stiff rules of such a system. But this was not the case, and a closer look into the matter shows that such a regimen is of much use to an earnest man, however free his character, at the outset of his spiritual career. Experience proves that one test of the genuineness of the

interior disposition to serve God perfectly is readiness to surrender exterior peculiarities. There is nothing in the special
graces of God which should hinder a placid acceptance of the
routine of a novitiate. The merging of individual conduct into
the common custom is the contribution which community life
must exact from every member. If a man is to be a hermit he
may act from individual impulses alone, though, even so, rarely
without counsel. But if one would live and work with others,
special graces and individual traits of character must not be allowed to interfere with a certain degree of uniformity. On the
other hand, that uniformity should not be allowed to cripple the
spontaneous action of natural independence, and the inspiration
of graces which are personal.

It must be granted that with many souls a novitiate will tend
to a routine use of religious aids. Yet it cannot be denied that
its discipline forcibly concentrates the scattered purposes of life
into one powerful stream. It contributes to symmetry of character. It furnishes efficacious tests of sincerity. It drills disorderly natures into regularity. It acquaints the beginner with
the literature of his holy profession, and herein it is of priceless
worth. And finally, it provides advisers of approved wisdom
during the period of the spiritual life when counsel is most needed,
as well as most gratefully accepted. But if it fails in each of
these particulars, as no doubt it sometimes does, the novitiate
may be said never to fail in detecting an inaptitude for the
common life, if such exists ; that is to say, a serious lack of
the qualities which fit one to get along in peace with the
brethren.

Into the novitiates of the religious orders, and into the seminaries which hold their place for the secular priesthood, the
noblest men of our race have entered joyfully ; some to be
wedded to the Divine Spouse in the quiet seclusion of holy contemplation, and others, of the more militant orders, to be trained
to follow worthily the standards of the apostolic warfare against
vice and error.

The novice-master was puzzled by his three Americans,
though Brother McMaster was easily comprehended—an over-
frank temperament, impulsive, and demonstrative. Not only
were his banners always hanging on the outward wall, but his
plan of campaign also. The other two were a study, and Brother
Hecker was a curiosity. Yet both were cheerful, obedient, ear-

nest, courageous. The novice-master was annoyed at the Americans' incessant demand for the reason why of all things permitted, and the reason why not of all things prohibited; until at last Brother Walworth was named Brother Pourquoi. As to Brother Hecker, besides showing the same stand-and-deliver propensity, he occupied much of the time of conversation in philosophizing, plunging into the obscurest depths of metaphysical and ethical problems, using terms which were often quite unfamiliar to strictly orthodox ears, and exhibiting a fearless independence of thought generally conceded among Catholics only to practised theologians. Yet the novice-master was well pleased with both, though we shall see that his journey with Brother Hecker was for some time in the dark.

When the Fourth of July came around he learned that it was the great American holiday, and he called the three Americans to him and asked, " How do you celebrate your national holiday at home ? " " By shooting off fire-crackers," they answered with a twinkle. This being out of the question, and the grand military parade which was next suggested also impracticable, Brothers Walworth and Hecker both exclaimed, " Ginger-bread ! " " Take all you want," was the answer, " and go off on a long walk, and spend the day by yourselves." And off they went to wander among the ruins of the outposts of the old Roman republic, and make Fourth of July speeches in honor of the great new Republic beyond the sea. Those who have been novices themselves will not be surprised at the boyishness of these three manly characters under the circumstances.

Isaac Hecker's spirit was not anywise cramped by the routine exercises of the novitiate ; he made them easily and well. He always seemed to his companions what he actually was, and what he described himself to be in his letters to New York, a cheerful and contented novice. But, as one of them since expressed it, he was not a " dude " novice, not the very pink of external perfection, and had a long period of interior trial. He did not exhibit at any time the least hesitancy about his vocation, for his mind was made up. Yet once, when he took a walk with Brother Walworth to visit a house of Recollects, Franciscans of the strict observance, both he and his companion were greatly struck by that charming poverty which the poor man of Assisi has bequeathed to his children; they did ask each other whether they had not made a mistake. This question, however, was but the expression of a shadowy doubt, vanishing as suddenly as it had come.

The novice-master was Father Othmann, and he was by universal testimony entirely competent for his place. He was himself the novitiate. Its austerities, and they were not trifling, its long and frequent prayer, its total seclusion from the world, all were refined and adjusted to each one by passing through his soul and being dispensed by his wisdom. Father Hecker regarded him as a very remarkable man. He was a student of character, and wise and sagacious in varying the application of religious influences according to temperament and spiritual gifts. Under him the danger of formalism, which occurs to one's mind immediately as the incessant round of exercises is mentioned, was rendered remote; for he gave his instructions, and especially used the chapter of faults, in a way to infuse into the souls of the novices the ever-recurring freshness of individual initiative. His model (after St. Alphonsus) was St. Francis de Sales. He followed him constantly in his doctrine and methods, and often spoke of him and quoted him. Of other methods and their advocates he spoke respectfully, but, however much they were in vogue, he did not follow them. Brother Hecker was a faithful student in his school and learned much from Father Othmann. The latter especially insisted on the principle of accepting Providence as the chief dispenser of mortifications. He had no objection to self-imposed spiritual exercises, but he did not positively favor them. He taught his young men that the traditional practices of devout souls as embraced in the routine of the novitiate, were good mainly to break the resistance of corrupt nature and render their souls pliant subjects of the Divine guidance in the interior life, as well as submissive to the order of God in the events of His external Providence.

The assistant novice-master, who took Father Othmann's place during his absence, was a Walloon. His name we have been unable to discover, but he was a holy priest, held up to the novices as their model and esteemed by them as the saint of the novitiate. He was a very pleasant man withal, and no doubt added in every way to the fruits of the long year of spiritual trial.

When Isaac Hecker presented himself as a novice he took his place among the youths learning the A, B, C of the spiritual life, while he himself had experienced for many months the most rare dealings of the Holy Ghost with the soul. This could not fail to come to the knowledge of Father Othmann, and, taken with the other peculiarities of his subject, to elicit his most skilful treatment. "Père Othmann, my novice-master," said Father Hecker, in after years, "had a right to be puzzled by me, and so he watched me more than he did the others." He watched and studied him and gradually applied the two sovereign tests of genuine spirituality, obedience and humiliation. These were all the more efficacious in this case, because Brother Hecker was a man of great native independence of character and naturally of an extremely sensitive disposition.

Such was the common austerity of the life that it took some ingenuity to inflict on a novice a mortification which had not grown stale by use in the case of one or more of the others. But in searching the interior of the soul the director could find tender places into which his weapon would be plunged to the bone. But it is more than probable that he misunderstood Brother Hecker, and that for a time he even suspected him of being under delusions. For several months, at any rate, he treated him at his weekly confession with the utmost rigor, producing indescribable mental agony. Many years afterwards, and when near his death, Father Hecker once said to the writer: "While I was kneeling among the novices, outside Père Othmann's room, waiting to go to confession, I often begged of God that it might be His will that I should die before my turn came, so dreadful an ordeal had confession become on account of the severity of the novice-master." Yet, as recorded in the memoranda, the victim was eager for the sacrifice when the knife was not actually lifted over him. "I begged the novice-master," he said on another occasion, "to watch me carefully, and when he saw me bent on anything to thwart me. I did not know any other way of overcoming my nature. He took me at my word, too. For example, once a week only we had a walk, a good long one, and we enjoyed it, and it was necessary for us. I enjoyed it very much indeed. So, sometimes when we were starting out, my thoughts bounding with the anticipated pleasure, he would stop me midway on the stairs: 'Frère Hecker,' he would say, 'please remain at home, and instead of the walk wash and clean the stair-way.' It would nearly kill me to obey, such was my disappointment, grief, humiliation."

In conjunction with these trials from without came a recurrence of resistless interior impulses. "During my novitiate," he is recorded as saying in 1885, "I found myself under impulses of grace which it seemed to me impossible to resist. One was to conquer the tendency to sleep. I slept on boards or on the floor. After a while I was able to do with five hours sleep, and often with only three, in the twenty-four. Père Othmann was not unwilling for me to follow these impulses as soon as he became convinced of their imperative strength. Yet I now see that such practices were in a certain sense mistaken. They necessarily consumed in mortification vitality that I could now use, if I had it, in a more useful way. Still, how could I help it?"

The end of this period of his humiliations, which was not far from the end of his noviceship, is thus described: "One day after Communion I was making my half-hour thanksgiving in my room, when Père Othmann came in and examined me about my form of prayer. Oh! it was just then that I had reached the passive state of prayer: *I* did nothing, *Another* did everything in my prayer. From that time, having put me down in the gutter, the novice-master raised me up to the pinnacle, whereas I should have been in neither place." On another occasion he told how the change of prayer had happened: "I was on my knees one day after Communion, making a regular thanksgiving, when suddenly God stopped me, and I was told not to pray that way any more. *Question:* How were you told—what words were spoken to you? *Answer:* Cease your activity. I have no need of your words when I possess your will. 'Tis I, not you, who should act. My action in you is more important than your thanks. I cease to act when you begin, and begin to act when you cease. Be still—tranquil—listen—suffer me to act. Abandon yourself to me, and I will take care of you."

When in Rome, in the winter of 1857-8, he was compelled by circumstances, which will be told in their place, to make a written summary of his spiritual experience. In it he says: "My novitiate was one of sore trials, for the master of novices seemed not to understand me, and the manifestation of my interior to him was a source of the greatest pain. After about nine or ten months he appeared to recognize the hand of God in my direction in a special manner, conceived a great esteem (for me), and placed unusual confidence in me, and allowed me without asking it, though greatly desired, daily Communion.

During my whole novitiate no amount of austerity could appease my desire for mortification, and several gifts in the way of prayer were bestowed on me."

On March 6, 1886, while in a state of almost utter physical prostration, he communicated to the writer the following : " Forty years ago, in my novitiate, God told me that I was to suffer in every fibre of my being." " Perhaps," was remarked, "you have not suffered all yet." *Answer :* " Perhaps not, but God has kept His promise in every limb, member, and function of my body." It may become necessary to refer again to these interior experiences. We leave them with the remark that his novitiate was characterized by a continuance of Divine interferences similar to those which had occurred at intervals from the time he was driven from home and business to seek the fulfilment of his aspirations.

The following is the record of a brave soul's failure to become a Redemptorist. It is given in a letter dated September 14, 1846 : " Brother McMaster, who returns to the U. S., gives me the opportunity of writing a few lines to you," etc. It was a profound disappointment for Mr. McMaster to be obliged to return home a layman, and it shocked his companions. It is a little singular that Father Othmann told him that his vocation was not to be a religious, but an editor. He carried with him Brother Hecker's messages of affection to his friends and relatives, and rosaries of Isaac's own making for his mother and his brother George.

Writing to the latter, on August 26, 1846, after some tender and affectionate words, he says : " I have now nearly eight weeks until the time of taking the vows. Oh that it were but eight minutes, nay, eight seconds, when I shall be permitted, with the favor and grace of God, to consecrate my whole being and life to His sole service ! Millions of worlds put on top of one another could not purchase from me my vocation. We make fifteen days' retreat before we take the vows. You must recommend me very particularly to the Rt. Rev. Bishop McCloskey ; tell him the time of my taking the vows (Feast of St. Teresa, October 15), and give him my humble request to remember me at that time in his prayers."

On the feast of St. Teresa, October 15, 1846, therefore, the two American novices took their vows, and became members of the Congregation of the Most Holy Redeemer. On the very morning of that event, at half-past eight, Brother Hecker wrote a letter to his mother, in which he goes over all of his trials and experiences in following the Divine guidance since he first quitted business. He breathes intense affection in every word, and writes in a solemn mood. We would give the letter to the reader entire, but that he has already learned what it narrates. It ends thus : " Dear mother, in half an hour I go to the chapel to consecrate my whole being for ever to God and His service. What peace, what happiness this gives me ! To live alone for His love, and to love all for His love, in His love, and with His love ! "

After the ceremony was over he wrote as follows to his brother John :

" DEAR BROTHER JOHN : This day, with the special grace of God, I have taken the holy vows of the Catholic religion, which are obedience, poverty, chastity, and final perseverance. These vows bind me to the Congregation of the Most Holy Redeemer for my natural life, and the Congregation in the same manner to me. Thanks to God for His kind Providence. My vocation is once for all, for ever settled, firmly fixed. During the year and more of my novitiate I have not had any temptation against my vocation, nor any desire on my part to return to the world.

" As you were not certain whether I would return after the novitiate or not, I suppose you left my name in connection with yours and brother George's in the firm. But now that this (separation) is certain, would it not be best for you to destroy that agreement we made with each other some time ago, that no future difficulty can or may arise ? All this I leave to your judgments ; and as for me, dear brothers John and George, in respect to the business, you may regard me as though I had never been connected with it, nor had any title or claim upon it whatever. I am simply your dear brother Isaac, who loves you from the depth of his heart. This love, be assured, will never be diminished by any event ; whatever happens will only give me new motives to love you the more. My conduct is under your inspection, yours especially, dear John, as being the eldest of us three, and I trust your sincere love for me will not let any word or action of mine pass unnoticed which may be the least unpleasant to you.

" My love, my gratitude, and my prayers to and for you all. Remember me to all my friends.

                    " Your brother,   ISAAC.

" *St. Trond, October* 15, 1846.

"I have forgotten to say that if you have not already made use of the things that I left, such as clothing, you should do so.   I."

In bidding adieu to the novitiate we think Father Hecker's last meeting with his old novice-master, as we find it recorded in the memoranda, will be of interest : " Père Othmann was one of my best friends. Shortly before he died I happened to be in France (this was after leaving the Redemptorists), and I heard that he was extremely ill at the Redemptorist house at Nancy. I wrote to him that if he wished I would call and see him. He answered me at once, begging me to come immediately, as he desired above all things to see me before he died. So I made a journey to Nancy, and we had some hours of pleasant conference together, and I bade him farewell."

CHAPTER XXII.

HOW BROTHER HECKER MADE HIS STUDIES AND WAS ORDAINED PRIEST.

THE day after the taking of the vows, Brothers Hecker and Walworth started by stage-coach for the house of studies, at Wittem in Dutch Limburg. The route lay nearly east through a country pleasant on account of the fertility of its soil and the industry of its inhabitants, and interesting from its churches, monasteries, and curious old villages. The travellers crossed the Meuse at Maestricht and reached their destination before nightfall. Wittem is a small town, thirty miles east of St. Trond and about ten west of Aix-la-Chapelle. This part of Holland is entirely Catholic, and its people possess a fervor which has sent missionaries to the ends of the earth. Everywhere shrines were to be seen by the roadsides. The country is not so level as that west of the Meuse, and the Redemptorist students often made excursions among the hills, our young Americans admiring the shepherds guarding their flocks, with their crooks and their dogs.

The house of studies was an old Capuchin monastery, large and plain and very interesting. The friars had buried their dead under the ground floor, which enabled the students to dig up an abundant supply of skulls as *memento moris* till the rector forbade it. The students were more numerous at Wittem than the novices had been at St. Trond. They were mostly Dutchmen, with a sprinkling of Belgians and a few Germans; but the language of the house was French or Latin. We have not been able to make quite sure of the name of the Rector; possibly it was Father Heilig, who certainly was there at this time, either in charge of the house or as one of the professors. The Master of Studies was Father L'hoir, who soon became one of Brother Hecker's dearest friends.

The two Americans found their fellow-students men of fine character and every way lovable, being earnest and devoted religious. They admired their thorough proficiency in all classical and literary studies, the result of old-world method and application. Mentally and physically they were splendid men. The whole race of Flemings and Dutch was found by our young recruits to be a grave and powerful people, although exceptional cases of mercurial temperament were not rare. Some curious individuals were to be found among them, as is more the case in European nationalities in general than in our own. Both Americans were much liked and respected by all their new-found brethren, though Brother Hecker, for reasons soon to be told, was sometimes ridiculed in a way that distressed him. Brother Walworth, having studied much before entering the order, was placed at once in the theological department and Brother Hecker in the philosophical. The former was even dispensed from one year of his theology, taking but two years of the three which formed the full course. The difference of studies separated the two companions almost wholly from each other, members of the two departments not being allowed even to speak together except on extraordinary occasions.

All went smoothly with Brother Walworth. Not so with Brother Hecker, who was expected to make two years of philosophy and meantime to increase his stock of Latin. But his faculties had been subjected to spiritual experiences of so absorbing a nature that he found study impossible. And when Brother Walworth was in due course ordained priest, in August, 1848, his companion was stuck fast where he had begun. It need not be said that so earnest a soul made every effort to study, but all was in vain. In the statement made in Rome ten years later, and referred to before, we find the following:

"My wish was to make a thorough course (of studies) and begin with philosophy. This the superior granted. My intellect in all scientific (scholastic) matters seemed stupid, it was with great difficulty that its attention could be kept on them for a few moments, and my memory retained of these things nothing. At the close of the first year (at Wittem) all ability to pursue my studies had altogether departed. This state of things perplexed my superiors, and on being asked what they could do with me, my answer was, 'One of three things: make me a lay brother; send me to a contemplative order which does not require scientific (scholastic) studies; or allow me to pursue, at my free moments, my studies by myself.' Instead of either of these they gave me charge of the sick, which was my sole (regular) occupation for the whole year following. During this year my stupidity augmented and reduced me to a state next to folly, and it was my delight to be treated as a fool. One day, when my fellow-students were treating me as such, and throwing earth at me, an ancient father, venerated for his gifts and virtues, suddenly turned around to them and with emotion exclaimed, ' You treat him as a fool and despise him ; the day will come when you will think it an honor to kiss his hand.' At the expiration of the second year (at Wittem) the question came up again, what was to be done with me. My superior put this question to me, and demanded of me under obedience to tell him in writing how, in my belief, God intended to employ me in the future. Though the answer to this question was no secret to me, yet to express it while in a condition of such utter helplessness required me to make an act of great mortification. There was no escape, and my reply was as follows : It seemed to me in looking back at my career before becoming a Catholic that Divine Providence had led me, as it were by the hand, through the different ways of error and made me personally acquainted with the different classes of persons and their wants, of which the people of the United States is composed, in order that after having made known to me the truth, He might employ me the better to point out to them the way to His Church. That, therefore, my vocation was to labor for the conversion of my non-Catholic fellow-countrymen. This work, it seemed to me at first, was to be accomplished by means of acquired science, but now it had been made plain that God would have it done principally by the aid of His grace, and if (I were) left to study at such moments as my mind was free, it would not take a long time for me to acquire sufficient knowledge to be ordained a priest. This plan was adopted."

A more explicit statement of the supernatural influences by means of which God informed him of his mission was made in after years to various persons, singly and in common. It was to the effect that the Holy Spirit gave him a distinct and unmistakable intimation that he was set apart to undertake, in some leading and conspicuous way, the conversion of this country. That this intimation came to him while he was at Wittem is also certain ; but it is equally so that he had premonitions of it during the novitiate. It was the incongruity of such a persuasion being united to a helpless inactivity of mind in matters of study that made Isaac Hecker a puzzle to his very self, to say nothing of those who had to decide his place in the order. Father

Othmann, in bidding him farewell at St. Trond, had told him to become "*un saint fou*," a holy fool; a direction based upon his excessive abstraction of mind towards mystical things, and his consequent incapacity for mental effort in ordinary affairs. Once, at least, during those two eventful years at Wittem, Father Othmann visited the place, and when he saw Brother Hecker he embraced him and exclaimed, "O here is the spouse of the Canticles!" His farewell injunction on parting at St. Trond had been perforce complied with.

It must have taken more than ordinary penetration to perceive anything but a kind of grandiose folly in Brother Hecker. The impulse to talk about the conversion of America, to plan it and advocate it, to proclaim it possible and prove it so, and to philosophize on the profoundest questions of the human reason, was irrepressible. This he did with an air of matured conviction and with the impact of conscious moral authority, but in terms as strikingly eccentric as the thoughts were lofty and inspiring, and in execrable French, the declaimer being known as *minus habens* in his studies and utterly incapable. All this was the very make-up of folly; and Brother Hecker was no doubt thought a fool. But how holy a fool he was his superiors soon discovered. We find the following among the memoranda:

"Père L'hoir was my superior in the studentate. He was a holy man and a good friend, but he was surprised at my state of prayer. He asked me how it could happen that I, a convert of only a few years, should have a state of prayer he had not attained though in the Church all his life and striving for perfection. I told him that it was God's will to set apart some men for a certain work and specially prepare them for it, and cause them, as He had me, to be brought under the influence of special Divine graces from boyhood. L'hoir then began to send anybody with difficulties to me, and God gave me grace to settle them. Then murmurs arose that he was too much under my influence, and he was removed from his position over the studies. But afterwards they replaced him; he was very efficient in his place."

The confidence of his superiors in Brother Hecker was shown by their causing him to receive tonsure and minor orders at the end of his first year at Wittem, though he had made no progress whatever in his studies.

The following notes are found in the memoranda:

" The time in my whole life when I felt I had gained the greatest victory by self-exertion was when, after weeks of labor, I was able to recite the *Pater Noster* in Latin.

" My memory finally failed me in my studies to that degree that at last I took all my books up-stairs to the library and told the prefect of studies I could do no more to acquire knowledge by study.

" *Question.* How long were you unable to study? *Answer.* Two years in Holland and one year in England. I never went to class those years. I was a kind of a scandal, of course, in the house. When I got a lucid interval of memory I studied, though much of the time I hadn't a book in my room. Yet, when they came to ordain me, I knew enough and was sent at once to the work of the ministry."

That his stupidity was not blameworthy is shown by the sympathy of Isaac's superiors; that it was not natural is known to our readers by their acquaintance with his native ability exhibited in his journals and letters. The difficulty was confined almost wholly to study; to fix his attention on the matter in the text-books, or to grasp it and hold it in memory, was beyond his power. Meantime his letters to his friends in New York and elsewhere were full of life. He kept a copy of a carefully written one, addressed to an old-time friend of the Brook Farm community. It is a model of brief statement of great truths, and proves that the social difficulty can only be fully remedied by the Catholic Church, which has an elevating force incomparably more powerful than any other known to humanity. The method used and the choice of arguments are peculiarly Isaac Hecker's own, and the tone, though affectionate, is one of authority, as that of an exponent of evident truth. His letters to his mother and his brothers are full of controversy, abounding in appeals to Scripture, to the voice of conscience, to the dictates of reason; and although the tone is one of deep affection, the attacks on Protestantism are keen, and the use of facts and persons as illustrations full of intelligence. Most of the letters which we have found were addressed to his mother, for whose conversion he had an ardent longing. With one of them he sends her a little manuscript treatise on true Bible Christianity which he had himself prepared. We give the reader extracts from two letters, the first from one to his brother John and the second from one to his mother :

" Your lamentation, dear John, on my separation from you, excites in me a great astonishment. To justify this separation it seems to me that you have only to open a page of the Gospels of Christ, and to read it with a sincere belief in the words and a generous love of the Saviour. As for me, I regret nothing so much as that I have not a thousand lives to sacrifice to His service and love. Yes, I love you all more than I ever did, and I would count nothing as a cost for your present and eternal good. Yet, by the grace of God, I love my Saviour infinitely, infinitely, infinitely more. Alas! when will those who profess to be Christians learn the significance of Christ's Gospels and His blessed example. I am not ignorant nor insensible of the love we owe to our parents and relatives—no, I am not insensible of this love ; but in me it is all in Christ, as I would wish yours were. . . . I embrace you, dear brother, in the love of our crucified Lord."

" DEAR MOTHER : There have been times when, considering the wickedness of the world, sensible of its miseries and my own, and at the same time beholding obscurely and as it were tasting the things of heaven, I have longed and wished to be separated from the body. But when coming back to myself, and thinking that with the aid of grace I can still increase in God's love and hence love Him still more in consequence for all eternity, I feel willing to love and suffer until the last day, if by this I should acquire but one drop more of Divine love in my heart. And so it is, as St. Paul declares, that we should count the trials here as nothing compared with the glory that awaits us. Now, all these considerations, dear mother, join together to increase my desire to see you in the communion of the Holy Catholic Church, to which God has singularly given so many means of growing in grace," etc., etc.

Notwithstanding these marks of active intelligence, Brother Hecker could not study, except by fits and starts. Often he could not get through the common prayers, and in ordinary conversation his tongue would sometimes be tangled among the words of a sentence before he was half through with it. The reader has already learned that the penalties of utter stupidity were not unknown to the unwritten law of the Wittem student-ate, notwithstanding that the young men were devout religious; and hence Brother Hecker must have had many hours of anguish. But we cannot suppose that his native cheerfulness was quite suppressed. His dulness of mind was accompanied, or rather was the result of, the close embraces of Divine love. It was the bitter part of that intimate communion with God which is granted to chosen souls. No doubt he was profoundly humiliated by the disgrace involved in his failure to study, but he was willing to suffer that external degradation which was the complement of, and the means of emphasizing, the teaching of the Holy Spirit in his interior, as well as the means of purify-ing his soul more and more perfectly. In after years he related an instance of his lightness of heart, a natural quality which he shared with his companion, Brother Walworth. The bishop of some neighboring diocese, Aix-la-Chapelle, if we remember rightly, happening to visit the house at Wittem, was told of the two American students. He conversed with them in the recrea-tion, the language being French. Then he said: "I know how to read English, but I have never heard it spoken; can you not speak a little piece for me?" "Certainly," was the answer. After a moment's consultation the two young men in all serious-ness recited together "Peter Piper picked a peck of pickled peppers," etc. No wonder that the prelate was astonished at the peculiar sound of English. Then he asked them for a song. "Oh, of course," was the answer, and they sang in unison "The Carrion Crow," with full chorus and imitations.

Besides taking care of the sick, for which he was admirably fitted by nature, Brother Hecker made himself generally useful about the house. He spent much time working among the brothers in the kitchen, and the writer has heard him say that for nearly the whole of his stay in Wittem he baked the bread of the entire community. He also carried in the fuel for the house, using a crate or hod hoisted on his back.

In August, 1848, Brother Walworth was ordained priest, and it was decided that he and Brother Hecker, together with two young Belgian priests, Fathers Teunis and Lefevre, should pro-ceed to England, the Redemptorists having been recently in-troduced there. As the cassock is not worn in the streets in England they were sent from Wittem to Liège and there equipped with clerical suits, the tailor being cautioned not to be too ecclesiastical in the cut of the garments. He produced a ridiculous compromise between a fashionable frock-coat and a cassock, the waist being high and tight and the tails full and flowing, and flopping about the young clerics' heels. As they journeyed from Liège to Amsterdam, and thence to London, people stopped and stared at them in their stylish array, and some laughed at them. In this instance Brother Hecker's chagrin was not overcome by his sense of the ludicrous, for he was naturally very sensitive of personal unbecomingness, and although not precisely a martinet for clerical exactness, he had strict notions of propriety.

The new Redemptorist foundation was at Clapham, three miles south of London Bridge. The house was a large, old-fashioned mansion and had been owned by Lord Teignmouth, a notorious anti-Catholic bigot. Some of the larger rooms had been thrown together into one, and this was used temporarily as a public chapel. Just as the young Redemptorists arrived, Father Petcherine was preaching to the congregation. He was a Russian convert, and the new-comers were astonished at his good English and his eloquence. He was one of the many extraordinary men who adorned the order at that time. He was master not only of his native tongue, but of English, German, Italian, French, and modern Greek, and could preach well in all of these languages. Clapham was reached on September 23, 1848, and shortly afterwards Father Walworth was sent to do missionary as well as parish work in Worcestershire, and remained there the greater part of the two years which were spent by our Americans in England.

From Clapham Brother Hecker wrote, on September 27, 1848:

" I am at present, dear mother, in a newly-established house in the city of London, having come here by order of my superiors to continue and finish my studies. Bodily I am nearer to you than I was, and naturally speaking I am much more at home here than I was on the Continent. But this is of little or no moment, for a good religious should find his home where he can best execute the will of his Divine Master. And would you not, dear mother, rather see me in China than in the United States if, by being there, I should be more agreeable to our Blessed Saviour, who left the house of His Father to save us poor abandoned sinners upon the earth? Our house here is situated somewhat out of the dense and busy part of the city, at Clapham; a fine garden is attached to it, and even in a worldly view I could not desire it to be more agreeable. And did not our Lord promise to give those who would leave all to follow Him, 'a hundred fold more in this world and life everlasting in the world to come'? Alas! how many profess to believe in the Bible and have no faith in the words which our Lord spoke," etc., etc.

The difficulties of Wittem were not abated at Clapham; rather they were aggravated by Brother Hecker having to deal with new superiors. "I remember seeing Hecker at Clapham, looking hopelessly into his moral theology," said Father Walworth to the writer. Father Frederick de Held, whom we left in Baltimore, had returned to Europe, being Provincial of the Belgian Province, which at that time included the English as well as the American missions. It must have seemed strange to him that Brother Hecker had been sent to England; he had no house of studies to put him into and could give him no regular course of instruction. We cannot even surmise what word was sent to Father de Held about this curious young man, whom early one summer's morning three years before he had seen flitting into Baltimore and out of it, taking with him the Provincial's leave to enter the novitiate. Perhaps the case had been sent to him because it was too perplexing for any authority less than his to settle. At any rate, it placed him in an awkward position, to decide the case of this lone applicant for orders, who had made no studies and could make none, and yet who was of so marked a character, so full of life, so zealous, working willingly about the church, eagerly working in the kitchen, talking deep philosophy and forming plans for the conversion of nations. His case was peculiar. The difficulty was not confined to the question of divinity studies. Brother Hecker's general education was scant, and his English was still faulty. And yet he was silently asking ordination in a preaching order, for which a thorough education is a prerequisite. Father de Held, therefore, is not to be condemned for his harshness as wanting in sympathy or in judgment of character. Gold is tried by fire, and fire is an active agent and a painful one. But Brother

Hecker soon found both solace and assistance in a new friend.

We quote from the memoranda:

"Father de Held was superior at Clapham and for a year he treated me as Henry Suso says a dog treats a rag—he took me in his teeth and shook me. At last I went to him and begged him to settle my case one way or the other: ordain me, or make a lay brother of me, or take off my habit and dismiss me to another order; though I told him that would be like taking off my skin. Father de Buggenoms then went my surety. He had been my confessor at Clapham and was then absent. But he wrote to De Held that he would guarantee my conduct if ordained. De Held then changed and became my fast and constant friend."

This is the first mention we find of Father de Buggenoms. Father Hecker ever venerated him and cherished his memory as that of a saintly friend and benefactor.

On another occasion we find a fuller account of the same events:

"Only for Father de Buggenoms I should not have been ordained at all."

"Who was De Buggenoms?"

"A Belgian, and my confessor while I was at Clapham. I was there, not ordained, nor yet making my studies. I had been forced to give them up; I could not go on with them. De Held did not know what to make of me, and he treated me harshly and cruelly. Finally I went to him and told him my thoughts; I said I was absolutely certain I had a religious vocation; that he might compel me to take off the habit, but it would be like taking off my skin; and so on. After that interview De Held changed toward me and was ever after my warm friend. He was a very prominent member of the Congregation. You know he came within a few votes of being Rector-major. He was very warm in his sympathy with us during our trouble in Rome. Well, Heilig, a German, was about coming over to England as superior. He had been my director for two years. Before he came he wrote me a letter that gave me indescribable pain. He wrote that I must change—that I was all wrong, and so on. I answered that it was too late to change; that he had been my director for two years, knew me well, and had been cognizant of my state If he wanted me changed he must do it for me, for I did not see how to do it for myself. When he came, De Buggenoms told him to have me ordained, set me to work at anything, and he (De Buggenoms) would be responsible for me in every respect. Heilig complied. I asked him afterwards why he wrote that letter. 'Because,' said he, 'I thought you needed to be tried some more.' 'Why,' said I, 'I have had nothing but trial ever since I came.'"

From this it would seem that the case was finally settled by Father Heilig after Father de Held's departure for the Continent, which took place, as well as we can discover, some time in the summer of 1849. Father Heilig's letter, written from Liège, is before us; it is dated the 24th of March, 1849. It is a complete arraignment of Isaac Hecker's spiritual condition. It is gentle, considerate, choice of terms, but condenses all that could be said to show that his young friend had been deluded by a visionary temperament, applying to himself what he had read in mystical treatises and the lives of the saints. The letter was indeed a deadly blow. Father Heilig had been Brother Hecker's confessor for two years at Wittem, and had at least tacitly approved his spirit; and now came his condemnation. No wonder that Isaac was profoundly distressed by it. Yet his conviction of the validity of his inner life was not shaken for an instant. Nor was the trial of long duration. We have found a letter from Father Heilig dated two months later than the one we have been considering, and it is full of messages of reassurance and encouragement. The intervention of De Buggenoms completed the work. It is possible that Father Heilig had not simply a desire to test Brother Hecker's humility, but, by studying the effect of the trial imposed, to remove doubts still lingering in his own mind. Some words in both the letters referred to lead us to this inference.

Father L'hoir had not forgotten his young friend, who received a letter from him a couple of months after leaving Wittem, which breathes in every word the tenderest utterance of friendship; and a year after, another one similarly affectionate, congratulating him on his ordination. This Father L'hoir must have been a noble soul to write so lovingly; we wish that space permitted us to give his letters to the reader.

Amongst the papers left by Father Hecker we found one carefully preserved, bearing date at St. Mary's, Clapham, the feast of St. Raphael (Oct. 24) 1848, a month after his arrival there. It is a manuscript of thirty-nine closely-written pages of letter-paper. It is an account of conscience made, no doubt, to Father de Held, though its preparation may have occupied some of his time before leaving Wittem. We will make some extracts. It begins thus:

" Before commencing what is to follow, I cannot resist making the confession of my feebleness and incapacity to express even conveniently those things which I feel it my duty to relate, that I may walk with greater security and quicker step in the way of God. It would not surprise me if one who has not taken the pains to investigate this matter sufficiently should doubt indeed whether such singular graces, seeing the faults I daily commit and my many imperfections, had really been given to such an individual. A similar remark to this was made by my last director. But this is a cause of much joy and consolation to me; (that is to say) that my interior life is hid and unknown to others except those who direct me. All that I can adduce in behalf of its truth and credibility are these words of sacred Scripture: Spiritus ubi vult spirat (the Spirit breatheth where He will); and, ubi autem abundavit delictum, superabundavit gratia (but where sin abounded there did grace more abound.)

. . . .

" At that time (towards the end of the novitiate) I felt a special attraction and devotion toward Our Blessed Lord in the Holy Sacrament and an almost irresistible desire of receiving the blessed Communion of Divine love. This desire so far from having abated has greatly increased, so that I have a constant hunger and thirst for Our Lord in the sacrament of His body and blood. If it were possible I would desire to receive no other food than this, for it is the only nourishment that I have a real appetite for. I cannot consider it other than the source and substance of my whole spiritual and interior life. The day on which I have been deprived of it I have experienced a debility and want of both material and spiritual life like one who is nearly famished. The doctrine of the real presence of our Lord seems to be with me a matter of conviction arising more from actual experience than from faith. At times, when I would make my visit, I am seized with such a violent love towards the Blessed Sacrament that I am forced to break off immediately, being unable to support the attraction of the Spouse, the Beloved, the Only One of my soul. For some time back, wherever I may be, or on whatever side I turn, I seem to feel the presence of Our Lord in the Sacrament in the tabernacle. It seems as though I were in the same sphere as our Lord in the sacrament, where there appears no time nor space, yet both are.

"At times, especially during the great retreat before making the vows, I was as it were inebriated with love, so that I scarcely knew what I said or did.

"This was the stage of my interior life on entering the house of studies at Wittem, October, 1846. Here the principal acts in all my spiritual exercises were those of resignation and conformity to the will of God, an entire fidelity to the inspirations and attractions of the Holy Spirit, and a total abandonment of myself to the conduct of Divine Providence. God seemed always engaged in my soul by means of His grace in repressing my own activity. The end of my proper activity, I said to myself, is its destruction. God commands a total and entire abandonment of the soul to Him in order that He may with his grace destroy and annihilate all that He finds in it against His designs and will. God at times seemed to demand of me a frightful and heroic abandonment of my soul to His good pleasure. God alone knows how to exercise the soul in virtue, and the Holy Spirit is its only true master in the spiritual life. Not only did the spirit of God excite and elicit in me voluntary acts of self-abandonment, but often my soul was as if stripped of all support, and placed, as it were, over a dark and unfathomable abyss, and thus I was made to see that my only hope was to give myself up wholly to Him. The words of Job well express this purgation of the soul when he says: 'The arrows of the Lord are in me, the rage whereof drinketh up my spirit, and the terrors of the Lord war against me.' [Here follow other quotations from the book of Job.] Sometimes these pains penetrate into the remotest and most secret chambers of the soul. The faculties are in such an intensive purgation that from the excessive pain which this subtile and purifying fire causes they are suspended from their ordinary activity, and the soul, incapable of receiving any relief or escaping from its suffering, has nothing left but to resign itself to the will and good pleasure of God. Though enveloped with an unseen but no less real fire, suffering in every part, limb, and fibre from indescribable pains, fixed like one who should be forced to look the sun constantly in the face at midday, she is nevertheless content, for she has a secret consciousness that God is the cause of all her sufferings, and not only content—she would suffer still more for His love."

[Here follows an account of the mortifications to which this interior pressure drove him, shortening of sleep, wearing hair-shirts, severe discipline, abstinence and fasting, and the like.]

. . . . .

"There were no penances that I have read of that seemed to me impossible. The vilest habits and other things that I was allowed to wear and to use gave me the greatest pleasure. The thought of not having wherewith to cover my nakedness, to be contemned, ridiculed, and spit upon, gave me an extreme joy. My delight consisted in wanting that which is considered necessary. . . . All this I did not only do without reluctance, difficulty, and pain, but with great pleasure, ease, and joy. They seemed as nothing, and I was as though I had scarcely need of a body in order to live, or, in other words, it seemed that I lived for the most part independent of the body.

"It was about this period that God gave me the grace which I had long desired and sighed after : to be able to act and suffer without the idea of any recompense. I call it a gift, for although I had so long wished and demanded of God the power to act and to love Him disinterestedly, still I was unable to do so. I felt myself a slave and hireling in the service of God, and this mortified me and made me much ashamed of myself. But when this grace was given, which happened unexpectedly, I could not forbear going immediately to my director to express my joy of the favor I had received, and the freedom and magnanimity of soul which it inspired me with. I do not mean to say that the soul has no idea of any recompense, for she has it tacitly, but this is not her formal intention in her actions ; for she is to such a degree animated to act for the good pleasure and sole glory of God, that she quasi forgets all else. .

"Sometimes I have felt singularly present and in intimate communion with certain of the saints, such as St. Francis of Assisi, St. Bonaventure, St. Thomas, St. Peter of Alcantara, our holy father Alphonsus, etc. During this time—and sometimes it is for many days—the life, the virtues, the spirit with which the saint acted occupies almost exclusively my mind. I seem to feel their presence much more intimately and really than that of those who are around me. I understand and comprehend them better, and experience a more salutary influence from them than perhaps I would have done had I lived and been with them in their time. . . . Twice I remember having experienced in this manner the presence of Our Blessed Lord. While this lasted I felt myself altogether another person. His heroic virtues, His greatness, tenderness, and love seemed to inspire me with such a desire to follow Him and imitate His example that I lost sight of all things else. His presence excited in me a greater love and esteem for the Christian virtues than I could have acquired otherwise in years and years. . . .

"About the commencement of the second year of studies, during some weeks my faculties were drawn and concentrated to such a degree towards the centre of my soul that I was as one bereft of his exterior senses and activity. Before the vacation I had desired to pass that time in solitude and retreat, but it was not allowed."

We have omitted much of this singular document, including detailed accounts of supernatural occurrences, and also quotations from the works of Görres, St. Teresa, St. John of the Cross, St. Bonaventure, Father Rigoleu, Richard of St. Victor, Scaramelli's *Directorium Mysticum*, and other mystical writings. These references he had collected to certify to the reality of his experience.

Throughout all these three years of trial he had employed what he calls his "lucid intervals" of mental power in studying in his own way, God aiding him in *His* own way to the destined end, as He had hindered him from choosing any other way. These intervals seemed so slight in his memory that the reader has seen his statement that he had not studied at all. When he had been a year at Clapham he was found, on examination, to be well enough prepared, as he had promised he would be. Having been ordained sub-deacon and deacon at Old Hall

College, by Bishop Wiseman, he was ordained priest by the same prelate in his private chapel in London. The event took place on the 23d of October, 1849, the feast of the Most Holy Redeemer. Father Hecker said his first Mass the following day at Clapham, that being the feast of St. Raphael the Archangel: one year from the date of his account of conscience written out and given to his superiors.

The following is from a letter to his mother announcing his ordination:

"DEAR MOTHER: You have been doubly blessed by Almighty God within the past few weeks. Your youngest son has been ordained priest in God's one, holy, Catholic Church, and prays for you daily when he offers up to God the precious body and blood of His beloved Son, our Lord; and besides you have received, by the marriage of another of your sons [George], a new daughter, who, being also a child of the Holy Church, must be kind, dutiful, pious, fearing God, and loving above all things our Lord and Saviour, Jesus Christ. Are not these, dear mother, blessings? Do they not convey to your heart joy and consolation? They ought and surely do. Your latter days dear mother, will be your happiest."

The remainder of the letter is filled with exhortations to enter the Church, and arguments drawn from Scripture.

We may mention a letter written to Father Hecker by Father Heilig on the eve of the former's departure for America; a message full of affectionate good wishes and claims of friendship and union in prayer with the singular young pilgrim from the Western World.

The following extracts from the memoranda may be of interest as embodying Father Hecker's views of how to study divinity, resulting from his own experience in preparing for the priesthood:

"*March*, 1884.—I told Father Hecker, in course of conversation, about my reading the life of the Curé of Ars. He said: 'A saintly man indeed, and one gifted with a supernatural character to an extraordinary degree. But it seems to me that his biographer misunderstood him somewhat. He seems to admit that the Curé of Ars had a naturally stupid mind, because he had so much difficulty in getting through his studies for the priesthood. The truth, probably, was that just at that time the supernatural action of the Holy Spirit came upon him and incapacitated him for his studies. But everything about his after life shows that, though a rustic man, he had a good mind, a keen native wit, quick and clear perception. I had something the same difficulty myself.

"During my novitiate and studies one of my great troubles was the relation between infused knowledge and acquired knowledge; how much one's education should be by prayer and how much by study; the relation between the Holy Ghost and professors.

"In the novitiate they were all too much on the passive side —unbroken devotional and ascetic routine. In the studentate, too much on the active side—leaving nothing for infused science and prayer as a part of the method of study. They soon broke me down. I told them so. If I went on studying I would have been driven mad. Let me alone, I said. Let me take my own way and I will warrant that I will know enough to be ordained when the time comes. They said I was a scandal. Then they sent me to England to De Held. I am persuaded that in the study of divinity not enough room is given to prayer and not enough account made of infused science."

CHAPTER XXIII.

A REDEMPTORIST MISSIONARY.

" I WOULD not have become a priest had I lived in Europe, for I never had or could have any strong attrait for sacerdotal functions. But I felt that the Church in America was in need of all the help that could be given by her children for the work of the priesthood." Father Hecker said this when near his end, and a full knowledge of his character bore him out in it. The sacerdotal, the ecclesiastical, were qualities which he had assumed with full consciousness of their sanctity, yet they united with his other characteristics in a way to leave traces of the point of contact. He was certainly an edifying priest, and to hear his Mass was to be spiritually elevated by his joyous fervor. But you would never say of him " he is a thorough ecclesiastic, he is a typical priest." The external aids of religion he imparted with a reverence which displayed his faith in his priestly character as a dispenser of the sacramental mysteries of God. But the other mysteries of God which are hidden in his providential guidance of men, he could expound with the instinctive familiarity of a native gift ; the voice of God in nature, in reason, and in conscience, and its response in revelation, he could elicit with a power and unction rarely met with. He has left the following words on record: " After my ordination the duties of the sacred ministry appeared to me most natural; the hearing of confessions and the direction of souls was as if it had been a thing practised from my childhood, and was a source of great consolation."

The year spent in England after ordination was occupied by Father Hecker mainly in parochial duties at Clapham and some neighboring stations attended by the Redemptorists of that house. Father Walworth enjoyed some missionary experience with Fathers Pecherine and Buggenoms, but Father Hecker had only been at one or two small retreats—one at Scott-Murray's estate in company with Father Ludwig and another at that of Weld-Blundells in Lancashire; but in neither of these had he preached or given any instructions, serving only in the confessional and in hunting up obstinate sinners. He certainly did preach once before leaving England, perhaps only once, and that was at Great Marlowe, near London, in the church built by the Hornihold family.. It was on Easter Sunday, 1850, and was well remembered by Father Hecker and referred to in after years. He thought the sermon a good one as a beginning, but it seems to have given him no encouragement, and we venture to think that if it profited his hearers somewhat it also amused them a little. He needed a teacher, and he found one in Father Bernard, the newly appointed provincial of the American province.

In 1850 Father Bernard Joseph Hafkenscheid * was made Provincial of the Redemptorist houses in America. His patronymic was too formidable for ordinary use, and he was universally known as Father Bernard. He was in the prime of life on taking this office, and although he had spent twenty years on the missions in Holland, his native country, in Belgium and England, he yet showed no signs of these labors; he continued them for fourteen years longer, for the most of the time in the Netherlands, his death resulting from accident in 1865. By common consent he is ranked in the highest order of popular preachers. He had entered the community from the secular priesthood shortly after his ordination; he had made a brilliant course of studies at Rome, which was crowned by the doctorate of the Roman College. He was physically a tall, powerful man, and of majestic bearing. His features were full of intelligence, his glance penetrating, his voice clear, sympathetic, and vibrating, his gestures expressive. If half that is handed down of Father Bernard be true, he was a wonderful preacher of penance and of hope, his high gifts of natural eloquence served by a perfect education and inspired by a most enthusiastic love of the people.

He was a popular preacher in the best sense of the term, calm in demeanor and simple in language as he opened, but when at the point of fervor pouring forth his soul in a fiery torrent of oratory, whose only restraint was the inability of the human voice to express all that the heart contained. In style impassioned, he yet often chose language bordering on the familiar, but was not vulgar. He is an instance of the fallacy of the saying that the preacher must stoop to his auditory if he would be popular. Father Bernard was ever true to himself,

---

* The reader is referred to his life by Canon Claessens (Catholic Publication Society Co.) It is all too brief, yet is a good summary of the career of the great Redemptorist missionary, one of St. Alphonsus' noblest sons.

never appeared less than an educated priest and grave religious, and yet he was a most popular preacher. The great truths of eternal life, are a universal heritage, and the use of plain words is not getting down from good style even in the literary sense, and a familiar manner is a trait of affection. We have stopped the reader for this moment with Father Bernard because he was Father Hecker's teacher of mission preaching and instructing, and was ever beloved by him as an appreciative friend and a wise and indulgent preceptor. He had made his first visit to America with Father de Held in 1845, but remained only a few months to acquire information and gain impressions for a report to the Rector Major. He made a second voyage in January, 1849, acting as superior of the American houses, as Vice Provincial, and remained about eighteen months. The United States now forming a separate province and Father Bernard made Provincial, he demanded Fathers Hecker and Walworth as his subjects, and they were given to him.

A letter from Father Hecker announces his departure for New York as fixed for some time in October, 1850; but delays occurred, and the following is an extract from one to his mother, dated January 17, 1851; it says that the departure is fixed for some day the same month:

"Oh! may Almighty God prosper our voyage, and may His sweet and blessed Mother be our guide and protector on the stormy sea. And may my arrival in America be for the good of many souls who are still wandering out of the one flock and away from the one shepherd! I hope that to no one will it be of more consolation and benefit than to you, my dearest mother."

The ship was named the *Helvetia* and sailed from Havre the 27th of January, the captain being a genuine down-east Yankee, and the crew a mixed assortment of English and American sailors. Father Bernard's party consisted of Fathers Walworth, Hecker, Landtsheer, Kittell, Dold, and Giesen, and the students Hellemans, Müller, and Wirth, the American fathers having come to Havre from London by way of Dover, Calais, and Paris. The weather was unfavorable during nearly the entire voyage, the ship being driven back into the English Channel and forced to anchor in the Downs. They were beaten about for two weeks before they got fairly upon the Atlantic, and while crossing the

Newfoundland banks were in danger from icebergs. Nearly all the party were more or less sea-sick, including Father Hecker. This did not prevent his attempting the conversion of the boatswain, who seemed the only hopeful subject in the ship's company. There were a hundred and thirty steerage passengers, emigrants for the most part from Protestant countries, though a party of Garibaldian refugees and a few equally wild Frenchmen enlivened the monotony of sea-life by some bloody fights. There were but two cabin passengers besides the Redemptorists, and the former being confined to their staterooms by nearly continual sea-sickness, the cabin was turned into a "floating convent," to borrow Father Dold's expression in a long letter descriptive of the voyage, given by Canon Claessens in his *Life of Father Bernard.*

The wintry and stormy voyage had already tested the missionaries' patience for some weeks, when Father Bernard informed the captain that he and his companions were going to make a novena to St Joseph to arrive at New York on or before his feast, March the 19th. "St. Joseph will have to do his very prettiest to get us in," was the answer. And when the ship was still far to the east, being off the banks, and the weather quite unfavorable, and only three days left before the feast, the captain called out: "St. Joseph can't do it—give it up, Father Bernard." But the latter would still persevere; and that night the wind changed. The Yankee ship now flew along at the rate of fourteen miles an hour. When the eve of St. Joseph's Day came they were wrapped in a dense fog, and the captain, dreading the nearness of the coast, hove to. When day dawned the fog lifted, and the ship was found to be off Long Branch, and a wrecked ship was seen on the shore; she had been driven there during the night. The pilot soon came aboard and they sailed through the Narrows and into the harbor of New York, having spent fifty-two days on the ocean. As they approached the city a little tug-boat was seen coming to meet them. It bore George and John Hecker and Mr. McMaster, whose cordial greetings were the first welcome the young Redemptorists heard on their return to the New World. They were soon at their home in the convent in Third Street, and on the sixth of April following the first mission was opened in St. Joseph's Church, Washington Place, New York.

Here is Dr. Brownson's greeting, from his home in Chelsea, Mass., received by Father Hecker soon after his arrival:

"My very dear friend, you cannot imagine what pleasure it gives me to learn of your arrival in New York. . . . I want to see you much, very much. You have much to tell me that it is needful that I should know, and I beg you to come to see me. Tell your superiors from me that your visit to me will be more than an act of charity to me personally, and that it is highly necessary—not merely as a matter of pleasure to us two—that we should meet; and tell them that I earnestly beg to have you come and spend a few days with me. I am sure that they will permit you to do so in furtherance of the work in which I as well as you are engaged, and I have a special reason for wishing to see you now. I would willingly visit you at New York or anywhere in the United States, but there is no place so appropriate as my own house. . . . I am more indebted to you for having become a Catholic than to any other man under heaven, and while you supposed I was leading you to the church, it was you who led me there. I owe you a debt of gratitude I can never repay. . . . Come, if possible, and as soon as possible."

At the Third Street house the new-comers found Father Augustine F. Hewit, a convert from the Episcopal Church, in which he had tarried for a few years on his way from Calvinism to the true religion. He had been a secular priest for a short time previous to entering the order. He was directed to join the newly-formed missionary band, and was destined to be more to Father Hecker than any other man, and to succeed him as superior of the Paulist community.

After more than five years' absence Father Hecker thus finds himself in America, the land of his apostolate, a member of a missionary community whose external vocation is the preaching of penance, and the conversion of sinful Catholics to a good life. A mission is a season of renewal of the religious life among the people of a parish. It is a course of spiritual exercises in which the principles of religion are called forth and placed in more active control of men's conduct, and by means of which their emotional nature is stimulated to grief for sin, love of God, yearning for eternal happiness. The sermons and instructions are given twice, and sometimes oftener, each day, during the early mornings and in the evenings. These exercises are conducted in the parish church, but not by the parish clergy. The people see among them the members of a religious order, men set apart, by the interior touch of the Holy Spirit and the public approval of the church, for this particular work— powerful preachers, confessors as indefatigable as they are patient, priests full of masterful zeal, moving in disciplined accord together against vice. The call they address to the people is the peremptory one : " Do penance, for the kingdom of heaven is at hand." Their words are given forth not from the usual pulpit, but from a platform at the communion railing, and in the presence of a high black cross set up in the sanctuary. They wear no surplice or stole while preaching, the only insignia of their office being a crucifix on their breasts. The bishop usually extends to them greater powers than are commonly given for reconciling sinners who have incurred ecclesiastical censures. The Holy See empowers them to extend the most abundant spiritual favors in its gift in the form of indulgences, and the pastor informs the congregation several Sundays beforehand that he expects the entire Catholic population of his parish to attend the mission and receive the sacraments.

To be absorbed in such labors as above described was not the primary object of Father Hecker's vocation, but he accepted his place joyfully as chosen by the evident will of God. The missionary life was never in his eyes what the reader might surmise it to be—a mere interlude in his career, a period of patient waiting. Such is far from having been the case. The missions are eminent works of Catholic zeal, and there is not any vocation known to the active ministry which may not commute with them on equal terms. Human nature has never felt influences more deeply religious than those set at work by missions, recalling the effects of the preaching of the Apostles themselves. Remorse of conscience, loathing for sin, terror at the divine wrath, confidence in God, sympathy for our crucified Saviour, the ecstatic joy of the new-found divine friendship, utter contempt for the maxims of the world, iron determination to love God to the end—these are the sentiments which, by the preaching of missions, are made to dominate entire parishes in a degree simply marvellous. Nor can it be said that these dispositions are fleeting. Allowing for exceptions, especially in large cities, their permanency is often an evidence of the solidity of the motives which inspired them, as well as of the supernatural graces which gave them life. Every missionary will bear witness, as Father Hecker often did, that he has never assisted at a mission in which he was not profoundly impressed by the tears of hardened sinners. Every parish priest, however much he may regret the backsliding of some, will testify to the valuable results of missions among his people: the quickening of faith and the revival of supernatural motives, drunkards' reformed, restitutions made, lust cleansed away, families united, the church thronged with worshippers, saloons deserted. Father Hecker never thought that all this was too dearly bought by the dreary toil of the confessional, the discomforts of for ever changing residences and living in strange places, nor even by the growing nerve-troubles which the fathers are often subject to, from brains superheated over and over again in the burning fires of mission preaching. Father Hecker did not think the privileges of such a life too dearly bought even by the postponement of his proper apostolate, and was ever glad of his labors as a missionary.

They schooled him in public speaking. In his antecedents there was abundant reason for diffidence, and he knew full well that what was good enough language for an harangue to the Seventh Ward Democracy would be ridiculous in a Catholic pulpit. Nor was he deceived into the notion of his ability to preach because he could influence men in private. Conversation is not public speaking, and the defects of grammar, or any other such defects, if pardoned in an earnest and honest man in private interchange of views, if committed on the public rostrum are unpardonable and are usually fatal. Father Hecker found in the incessant practice of the missionary platform, and in the assistance of his present superior, exactly what he needed by way of preparation. Besides the mission sermon at night—the great sermon, as it was called—there is a short doctrinal instruction at the same service and a moral one on the sacraments or commandments in the morning. These became his share of the mission preaching, and the school in which he acquired that direct, convincing, and popular manner of discourse for which he was afterwards renowned as a lecturer.

We find the following among the memoranda :

" When I came over to America with Fathers Bernard and Walworth, Bernard wanted to know what I could do. Well, by that time I had given up all hopes of any public career. I couldn't preach. My memory and intellectual faculties generally were so influenced by my interior state that theology was out of the question. The lights that God had given me about the future state of religion in this country were still clear as ever, but I thought that I should have to confine myself to imparting them to particular and individual souls whom the providence of God should throw in my way; for I was persuaded that the Redemptorist community was unfitted for the future work I had caught a glimpse of, and I was entirely contented to live and die a Redemptorist, and was quite certain that I should. So, when Bernard asked me what I could do, I told him to get me some place as chaplain of a prison or public institution of charity, as that was about all that I was capable of. But he thought differently.

"My first instructions on the missions were almost word for word given me by Bernard. I didn't seem to have a single thought of my own."

To preach, whether to Catholics or to non-Catholics, one must learn how, and Father Hecker with all his gifts knew that this gift seldom comes from above except by way of reward for steady labor. The opportunity of the missions, and of Father Bernard as a guide, was eagerly accepted in lieu of the prison chaplaincy.

The missions also enabled him to know the Catholic people. The non-Catholics he already knew from vivid recollection of his own former state and from that of his early surroundings; Brook Farm and Fruitlands had completed his knowledge of the outside world; but the Redemptorist novitiate and studentate and his sojourn in England did not give him a similar knowledge of the Catholic people, priesthood, and hierarchy. To the average looker-on Catholicity is what Catholics are, and Catholics in America viewed from a standpoint of morality were then and still are a very mixed population. Why the fruits are worse than the tree is a sore perplexity even to expert controversialists, and Father Hecker had need to equip himself well for meeting that difficulty, a patent one in the rushing tide of stricken immigrants then pouring into America. The missions are an unequalled school for learning men. All men and women in a parish are made known to the missionary, for they walk or stumble through his very soul.

Nor can one fail to see the use of missions as an evidence to the non-Catholic public itself of the supernatural power of Catholicity over men's lives. To practical people like Americans there is no oral or written evidence of the true religion so valid as the spectacle of its power to change bad men into good ones. Such a people will accept arguments from history and from Scripture, but those of a moral kind they demand; they must see the theories at work. A mission is a microcosm of the church as a moral force. It shows a powerful grasp of human nature and an easy supremacy over it. It is an energetic, calm, and clean-sweeping influence for good, bold in its choice of the most sublime truths of supernatural religion as the sole motives of repentance. And it uniformly achieves so complete a victory over the best-entrenched vices that non-Catholic prejudice is invariably shaken at the spectacle. And in America the pioneer work of the apostolate must be to remove prejudice. The character of the men who conduct these exercises, their courage, intelligence, devotedness, discipline, and ready command of the people; the indiscriminate humanity which rushes to hear them, to pray, to confess their sins, to listen with mute attention—long before day-break and in the hours of rest after work —all regardless of social differences or of moral ones, soon become well known to the public and generally excite comment in the press. All this contributes to prepare non-Catholics to hear from the same teachers the invitation which our Lord intended in saying: "Other sheep I have which are not of this fold; them also must I bring, and they shall hear my voice, and there shall be one fold and one shepherd."

Furthermore, it was necessary that Father Hecker should be made personally known to the bishops and priests of the country. The time was coming when he would have a public cause to advance, and their approval is a necessary sign of divine favor. Now, the missionary is closely studied by them and soon is intimately known, for there are too many things in common between priests but that they can readily test each other. Before the Paulist community had been organized, Father Hecker had been the guest of the most prominent clergymen of the entire United States, and of many even in the British Provinces, and was a well-known man throughout the Catholic community. Meantime the humiliations of his study-time had been quickly recovered from, if they had ever been a real hindrance to public effort, and we find no sign of protest on his part or of request to be let off from giving instructions beyond his answer to Father Bernard as above recorded. As he loved his vows as a Redemptorist, so he loved the work of the missions, because they were God's will for him; because they are a work of the highest order of good for souls; because the reputation of Catholicity is always raised in a community by a mission, and a good name is necessary for a controversial standing; because in them he daily learned more of men and of the means to win them; and because the members of the divine order of the episcopate and secular priesthood must be well known by him and he well known to them before any extensive work could be done among non-Catholics; and the missionary becomes a familiar friend everywhere he goes. Hence controversial sermons were sometimes preached during the missions, lectures of the same sort given after them, and during their continuance many converts received into the church. Father Hecker, as we have tried to show the reader, was a very observant nature, always learning lessons from life, and ready to try his 'prentice hand on what material offered in the way of converting Protestants at every opportunity public and private.

Nevertheless, the missions could not be made the ordinary channel of direct influences for turning sceptics and Protestants to the true religion. The attempt to make them so, involving, as it does, a notable interspersion of controversial sermons, has never been tried by the Redemptorist or Paulist Fathers to our knowledge, and when done by others has resulted in not enough of controversy for making solid converts, and too little penitential preaching for the proper reformation of hard sinners among Catholics. Father Hecker fully appreciated this. He threw himself into the mission work just as it was with the utmost ardor, and learning from Father Bernard how to prepare the matter for the morning and evening instructions, his natural gifts, together with hints and suggestions from his brethren, supplied him with the best possible manner of giving them. The writer has often served on missions in parishes where Father Bernard's new-formed band had preached in former years, and the testimony is universal that as a doctrinal and moral instructor Father Hecker was unequalled among missionaries. He was so frank, so clear, so lively, so impressible, and, in a certain way, so humorous, that he carried the people away with him. And he carried them all, high and low, learned and simple. With persons of education his homely words did not break the charm, nor did his simple but extremely well chosen illustrations do so—all taken, as they were, from common life or the lives and writings of the saints. He never preached the great sermons and never aspired to do it. He never sought to arouse terror or to be pathetic. He always reasoned and *instructed.* In truth, he was not competent to deal adequately with such subjects as Death, Judgment, and Hell—that is to say, as they are preached at missions, for the emotions have honest rights on such occasions, and Father Hecker acknowledged his deficiency in emotional oratory. But, to tell you the qualities of true sorrow, or to show you how to make a true confession, to picture the manliness of virtue and the dignity of the Christian state, he was unsurpassed. And the general effect remaining after his instructions was always a bright understanding of just what to do for a good life, with many happy examples to aid the memory, together with a strong personal affection for the holy man who showed religion to be a most happy as well as most reasonable service of God. To his penitents in the confessional he was ever most kind and patient. "No school of perfection," he once said, "can equal the self-denial necessary to hear confessions well." God is now rewarding him, we trust, for the cheerful, often even bantering, words of encouragement he gave to the multitudes of poor sinners who knelt at his feet during the toilsome years he spent on the missions; and for the enlightenment and encouragement of his big-hearted influence, and for his trumpet notes of hope in the early morning instructions. After the hard pounding of the night sermons it is always sought to pick the sinner up out of the dust and to hearten him by the early instructions, as well as to guide him to the precise methods and means of reform and of a good life for the future. As to the sacrament of penance, the saying of St. Alphonsus is a maxim with us all : "Be a lion in the pulpit, but a lamb in the confessional."

The reader must indulge us in thus dwelling so long on the Catholic missions, for we are inclined to say many words of praise of so lovely a life, in which the same men sow and reap a great harvest in the same week, expend their vitality in preaching the word and administering the sacraments and comforting sinners who are wholly broken down with the truest contrition.

In 1851 the American Redemptorists had before them a missionary field almost untouched. Public retreats had been given from time to time in the United States by Jesuits and others, but the mission opened at St. Joseph's Church, New York City, on Passion Sunday, 1851, was the first mission of a regular series carried on systematically by a body of men especially devoted to the vocation. The merit of inaugurating them is chiefly due to Father Bernard, who had no hesitation in getting to work with his three American fathers; though Father Joseph Müller, rector of the Third Street convent, and Rev. Joseph McCarron, the rector of St. Joseph's Church, had something to do in arranging the details and in facilitating the work. Several Redemptorists from Third Street helped in the confessionals.*

We have space for only the following extracts from the brief record of the missions, preserved by the fathers. They illustrate how earnestly Father Hecker worked. In the record of the second mission at Loretto, Pa., we find this:

The instructions and Rosary were generally given by Father Hecker, who received from the people the name of " Father Mary." . . . During the first few days the people did not attend well; but after Father Hecker had gone through the village and among a clique of young men who were indifferent and disaffected to the clergy, and the evil geniuses of the place, and after some fervent exhortations had been made to the people, they flocked to the mission and crowded the church.

At Johnstown, Pa.: After two or three days a man happened to die on the railroad, and all the men at that station, perhaps a hundred in number, accompanied the corpse to the church. Father Hecker seized the opportunity to address them and to give them a mission *ferveroso*. And the next day he went on horseback, accompanied by the pastor, Father Mullen (since Bishop of Erie), to several stations and addressed the men, inviting them to attend the mission. The result was suc-

* Observers of coincidences will be interested to notice the arrival of the missionaries in America on St. Joseph's day, under the Provincial Bernard Joseph Hafkenscheid, to open their first mission at St. Joseph's Church, the pastor being Joseph McCarron, the mission having been negotiated by Joseph Müller, the rector of the Third Street convent. Father Hecker had a special devotion for St. Joseph.

cessful. Procession after procession marched in, filling the church, and numbers of them stayed all day, lying on the grass about the church. . . . Father Hecker called out a noted politician, who had not been to the sacraments for many years until the mission, to receive the scapular as an example, and the good man did not fail to receive a plentiful supply of holy water from the vigorous arm of the said father.

The following entry in the record under date of February, 1852, made after a mission given in St. Peter's Church, Troy, N. Y., will be of interest to missionaries, and to others who are observant of their methods : " At Youngstown, Pa., (the preceding December) the experiment of preaching from a platform had been successfully tried and was repeated here, as at other missions since (Youngstown). On the platform a large black cross, some ten feet or more in height, was erected, from the arms of which a white muslin cloth was suspended. This use of cross and platform has thus been regularly introduced into the missions." Previously it had been the custom to erect a large cross out of doors in front of the church as one of the closing ceremonies of the mission.

Fathers Hecker, Hewit, and Walworth, led by Father Bernard, made a unique band of missionaries, one, we think, hardly equalled since they yielded their place to others. Each was a man of marked individuality, whose distinct personality was by no means obscured by the strict conformity to rule evident in their behavior. Fathers Hewit and Walworth were orators, differing much from each other, both full of power. Father Hecker was a born persuader of men, and could teach as a gift of nature, earnest in mind and manner. His two companions saw him learn by hard work how so to modulate his voice and to manage it and his manner as to exactly suit himself to his duties as the instructor of the band, while they delivered finished discourses at the night services, many of them masterpieces of mission oratory. Their very poise and glance on the platform stilled the church, and their noble rhetoric clothed appeals to the intelligence and to the heart in most attractive garb. In Father Hecker you saw a man who wanted to persuade you because he was right and knew it, and because he was deeply interested in your welfare. He sought no display, and yet held you fast to him by eye and ear. He had no tricks to catch applause, for he had no vanity. He said what he liked, for he was totally devoid of diffidence or awkwardness, and his best aid was his invariable equipment of an earnest purpose. "But I don't believe," said Father Walworth to the writer, "that Demosthenes ever worked through greater difficulties than Father Hecker in making himself a good public speaker."

Father Bernard managed the missions for the first year, and dealt with the pastors as superior of the band, meanwhile devouring more than his share of the work in the confessional. The least experience shows that there can be little of the discipline of the barracks order on the missions, and all the fathers must of necessity consult together, the superior leading in the observance of such community devotional customs as are possible, and setting a good example in stooping to the burdens which all must bear. As to Father Bernard, the Americans could only admire and love him. In his own tongue a renowned orator, he yet never preached in English while with these three men unless on rare occasions, such as when one of them was prevented by sickness. From him they received the manner of giving missions handed down from St. Alphonsus, and they have transmitted the tradition to their spiritual children in all its integrity.

Nearly two years passed of hard missionary campaigning under Father Bernard, when he was recalled to Europe, and Father Alexander Cvitcovicz took his place. His last name was seldom used, for the same evident reason as in his predecessor's case. Father Alexander was a Magyar, past the meridian of life, long accustomed to missions in Europe, learned, devout, kindly, and of a zeal which seemed to aspire at utter self-annihilation in the service of sinners. "It was not unusual for Father Alexander," says Father Hewit in his memoir of Father Baker, "to sit in his confessional for ten days in succession for fifteen or sixteen hours each day. He instructed the little children who were preparing for the sacraments, but never preached any of the great sermons. In his government of the fathers who were under him he was gentleness, consideration, and indulgence itself. In his own life and example he presented a pattern of the most perfect religious virtue, in its most attractive form, without constraint, austerity, or moroseness, and yet without relaxation from the most ascetic principles. He was a most thoroughly accomplished and learned man in many branches of secular and sacred science and in the fine arts; and in the German language, which was as familiar to him as his native language, he was among the best preachers of his order. . . . We went through several long and hard missionary campaigns under his direction, until at last we left him, in the year 1854, in the convent at New Orleans, worn out with labor, to exchange his arduous missionary work for the lighter duties of the parish."

Father Walworth now became superior, and the missions went on in the same spirit and with the same success as before. In the record of the one given at the church of Our Lady, Star of the Sea, Brooklyn, we find the following entry: "Missionaries, Fathers Walworth, Hecker, Hewit, and George Deshon (late lieutenant Ordnance, U. S. A., a convert from the Episcopal Church. This was his first mission)." Father Deshon had been ordained not long before, and soon began to share the instructions with Father Hecker. This was in February, 1856, and in November of the same year, at St. Patrick's Mission, Washington, D. C., they were joined by Father Francis A. Baker, ordained in the preceding September, a distinguished convert from the Episcopal ministry of the city of Baltimore. Much we would say of him, his eloquence and his very amiable traits of character, but all this and more is well said by Father Hewit, in his memoir of Father Baker, published after the latter's death in 1865 (Catholic Publication Society Co.) This increase of members allowed a division of the band for smaller-sized missions.

In our judgment those men were a band of missionaries the like of whom have not served the great cause among the English-speaking races these recent generations. Fathers Walworth, Hewit, and Deshon have survived their companions of those early days, and may they long remain with us, calm and beautiful and devout old veterans of the divine warfare of peace!

Father Hecker gave several retreats to religious communities of men and of women during the six or seven years we are considering, devoting for the purpose portions of the summer months usually unoccupied by missions. Copies of notes of his conferences, taken down by some of his hearers, are in our possession and may aid us further on in giving the reader a view of his spiritual doctrine.

The following extract from the Roman statement summarizes what we have been telling in this chapter, and introduces the reader to Father Hecker's first missionary activity as a writer:

"My superiors sent me back to the United States, and on my return being asked by my immediate superior in what way he could best employ me, my reply was, in taking care of the sick, the poor, and the prisoners. The stupidity which still reigned over my intellectual faculties, and the helplessness of my will, and my sympathy with those classes led me to choose such a sphere of action as most suitable to my then condition. And although the conversion of the non-Catholics of my fellow-countrymen was ever before my mind, yet God left me in ignorance how this was to be accomplished. Such strong and deep impulses, and so vast in their reach, took possession of my soul on my return to the United States in regard to the conversion of the American people, that on manifesting my interior to one of the most spiritually enlightened and experienced fathers of the congregation on the subject to obtain his direction, he bade me not to resist these interior movements, they came from God; and that God would yet employ me in accordance with them. Such were his words. After a few weeks in the United States the work of the missions began. My principal duties on these were to give public instructions and hear confessions, and up to this time (1858) these missionary labors have occupied me almost exclusively.

"The blessings of God upon our missions were most evident and most abundant and my share in them most consoling, as usually the most abandoned sinners fell to my lot. But holy and important as the exercises of the missions among Catholics are, still this work did not correspond to my interior attrait, and though exhausted and frequently made ill from excessive fatigue in these duties, yet my ardent and constant desire to do something for my non-Catholic countrymen led me to take up my pen. That took place as follows: One day alone in my cell the thought suddenly struck me how great were my privileges and my joy since my becoming a Catholic, and how great were my troubles and agony of soul before this event! Alas! how many of my former friends and acquaintances, how many of the great body of the American people were in the same most painful position. Cannot something be done to lead them to the knowledge of the truth? Perhaps if the way that divine Providence had led me to the church was shown to them many of them might in this way be led also to see the truth. This thought, and with it the hope of inducing young men to enter into religious orders, produced in a few months from my pen a book entitled *Questions of the Soul.* The main features of this book are the proofs that the Sacraments of the Catholic Church satisfy fully all the wants of the heart. . . .

"But the head was left to be yet converted; this thought led me to write a second book, called *Aspirations of Nature;* and which has for its aim to show that the truths of the Catholic faith answer completely to the demands of reason. My purpose in these two books was to explain the Catholic religion in such a manner as to reach and attract the minds of the non-Catholics of the American people. These books were regarded in my own secret thoughts as the test whether God had really given to me the grace and vocation to labor in a special manner for the conversion of these people. The first book, with God's grace, has been the means of many and signal conversions in the United States and England, and in a short period passed through three editions. The second has been published since my arrival in Rome. . . .

"On an occasion of a public conference (discourse) given by me before an audience, a great part of which was not Catholic, the matter and manner of which was taken from my second book, my fellow-missionaries were present; and they as well as myself regarded this as a test whether my views and sentiments were adapted to reach and convince the understanding and hearts of this class of people, or were the mere illusions of fancy. Hitherto my fellow missionaries had shown but little sympathy with my thoughts on these points, but at the close of the conference they were of one mind that my vocation was evidently to work in the direction of the conversion of the non-Catholics, and they spoke of such a work with conviction and enthusiasm."

This last event occurred in St. Patrick's Church, Norfolk, Va., in April, 1856, and is thus mentioned by Father Hewit in the record of the mission: "Father Hecker closed with an extremely eloquent and popular lecture on 'Popular Objections to Catholicity.'"

The *Questions of the Soul* was well named, for it undertakes to show how the cravings of man for divine union may be satisfied. It does this by discussing the problem of human destiny, affirming the need of God for the soul's light and for its virtue, proving this by arguments drawn from the instincts, faculties, and achievements of man. The sense of want

in man is the universal argument for his need of more than
human fruition, and in the moral order is the irrefragable proof
of both his own dignity and his incapacity to make himself
worthy of it. Father Hecker urged in this book that man is
born to be more than equal to himself—an evident proof of the
need of a superhuman or supernatural religion. Eleven chapters, making one-third of the volume, are devoted to showing
this, and include the author's own itinerarium from his first consciousness of the supreme question of the soul until its final
answer in the Catholic Church, embracing short accounts of the
Brook Farm and Fruitlands communities, and mention of other
such abortive attempts at solution. Three chapters then affirm
and briefly develop the claim of Christ to be the entire fulfilment of the soul's need for God, with the Catholic Church as
his chosen means and instrument. These are entitled respec-
tively, " The Model Man," " The Model Life," and " The Idea
of the Church." Three more chapters discuss Protestantism,
stating its commonest doctrines and citing its most competent
witnesses in proof of its total and often admitted inadequacy to
lead man to his destiny. Bringing the reader back to the
Church, the fourteen last chapters fully develop her claims, dealing mostly with known facts and public institutions, and citing
largely the testimony of non-Catholic writers.

It is something like the inductive method to infer the existence of a food from that of an admitted appetite, as also to
learn the kind of food from the nature of the organs provided
by nature for its reception and digestion. So the longings of
man's moral nature, Father Hecker felt, when fairly understood, must lead to the knowledge of what he wants for their
satisfaction—the Infinite Good—and that by a process of reasoning something equivalent to the scientific. Such is the statement of his case, embracing with its argument the introductory
chapters. The inquiry then extends to the claimants in the
religious world, not simply as to which is biblically authentic
or historically so, but rather as to which religion claims to
satisfy the entire human want of God and makes the claim
good as an actual fact. It is wonderful how this line of argument simplifies controversy, and no less wonderful to find how
easily the victory is won by the Catholic claim. The reader
will also notice how consistent all this is with Father Hecker's
own experience from the beginning.

The literary faults of the book are not a few ; for if the argument is compact, its details seem to have been hastily snatched up and put together, or perhaps the occupations of the missions prevented revision and consultation. There is a large surplusage of quotations from poets, many of them obscure, and worthy of praise rather as didactic writers than as poets ; yet every word quoted bears on the point under discussion. To one who has labored in preparing sermons, each chapter looks like the cullings of the preacher's commonplace book set in order for memorizing ; and very many sentences are rhetorically faulty. But, in spite of all these defects, the book is a powerful one, and nothing is found to hurt clearness or strength of expression. What we have criticised are only bits of bark left clinging to the close-jointed but rough-hewn frame-work.

The *Questions of the Soul* was got out by the Appletons, and was at the time of its publication a great success, and still remains so. The reason is because the author takes nothing for granted, propounds difficulties common to all non-Catholics, sceptics as well as professing Protestants, and offers solutions verifiable by inspection of every-day Catholicity and by evidences right at hand. Catholicity is the true religion, because it alone unites men to God in the fulness of union, supernatural and integral in inner and outer life—a union demanded by the most resistless cravings of human nature: such is the thesis. There can be little doubt that prior to this book there was nothing like its argument current in English literature ; a short and extremely instructive account by Frederick Lucas of his conversion from Quakerism is the only exception known to us, and that but partially resembles it, is quite brief, and has long since gone out of print.

The *Aspirations of Nature* deals with intellectual difficulties in the same manner as the *Questions of the Soul* does with the moral ones. The greatest possible emphasis is laid upon the two-fold truth that man's intellectual nature is infallible in its rightful domain, and that that domain is too narrow for its own activity. The validity of human reason as far as it goes, and its failure to go far enough for man's intellectual needs, are the two theses of the book. They are well and thoroughly proved ; and no one can deny the urgent need of discussing them : the dignity of human nature and the necessity of revelation. Like

Father Hecker's first book, the *Aspirations of Nature* is good
for all non-Catholics, because in proving the dignity of man's
reason Protestants are brought face to face with their fundamental error of total depravity; enough for their case surely.
If they take refuge in the mitigations of modern Protestant beliefs, they nearly always go to the extreme of asserting the
entire sufficiency of the human intellect, and are here met by
the argument for the necessity of revelation.

An extremely valuable collection of the confessions of heathen
and infidel philosophers as to the insufficiency of reason is found
in this book, as well as a full set of quotations from Protestant
representative authorities on the subject of total depravity. Over
against these the Catholic doctrine of reason and revelation is
brought out clearly. The study of the book would be a valuable preparation for the exposition of the claims of the Catholic
Church to be the religion of humanity, natural and regenerate—
the intellectual religion.

As might be expected from one who had such an aversion
for Calvinism, the view of human nature taken by the author is
what some would call optimistic, and the tone with regard to
the religious honesty of non-Catholic Americans extremely hopeful. Perhaps herein was Dr. Brownson's reason for an adverse,
or almost adverse, criticism on the book in his *Review*. He had
given the *Questions of the Soul* a thoroughly flattering reception, and now says many things in praise of the *Aspirations
of Nature*, praising especially the chapter on individuality.
But yet he dreads that the book will be misunderstood;
he has no such lively hopes as the author; he trusts he is not
running along with the eccentricities of theologians rather than
with their common teaching; fears that he takes the possible
powers of nature and such as are rarely seen in actual life as
the common rule; dreads, again, that Transcendentalists will be
encouraged by it; and more to the same effect. But Father
Hecker, before leaving for Europe in 1857, had submitted the
manuscript to Archbishop Kenrick and received his approval;
nor did Brownson's unfavorable notice ruffle the ancient friendship between them.

The *Aspirations of Nature* was put through the press by
George Ripley, at that time literary editor of the New York
Tribune, Father Hecker having gone to Rome on the mission
which ended in the establishment of his new community. Mr.

McMaster had assisted him similarly with the *Questions of the Soul.* The second book sold well, as the first had done, and has had several editions. It is not so hot and eager in spirit as the *Questions of the Soul*, but it presses its arguments earnestly enough on the reader's attention. It is free from the literary faults named in connection with its predecessor, reads smoothly, and has very many powerful passages and some eloquent ones.

CHAPTER XXIV.

THE events which led to the separation of the band of American missionaries from the Redemptorist community took place in the spring and summer of 1857. A misunderstanding arose about the founding of a new house in Newark, N. J., or in New York City, which should be the headquarters for the English-speaking Fathers and become the centre of attraction for American subjects, and in which English should be the language in common use. Application had been made by Bishop Bayley, and afterwards by Archbishop Hughes, for such a foundation, but superiors, both in the United States and in Rome —the latter dependent on letter-writing for understanding the difficulties which arose—became suspicious of the aims of the American Fathers and of the spirit which actuated them. To establish their loyalty and to explain the necessity for the new foundation, the missionary Fathers believed that one of their number should go to Rome and lay the matter in person before the General or Rector Major of the order. The choice fell on Father Hecker, who sailed on August 5, 1857, arrived in Rome the 26th, and was expelled from the Congregation of the Most Holy Redeemer on Sunday, the 29th of the same month, the General deeming his coming to Rome to be a violation of the vows of obedience and poverty.

The grounds of his expulsion were then examined by the Propaganda, from which the case passed to the Holy Father, who sought the decision of the Congregation of Bishops and Regulars. Pius IX. gave his judgment as a result of the examination made by the last-named Congregation ; but he had made a personal study of all the evidence, and had given private audiences to both the General and Father Hecker. It was decided that all the American Fathers associated in the missionary band should be dispensed from their vows as Redemptorists, including Father Hecker, who was looked upon and treated by the decree as if he were still as much a member of the Congregation as the others, his expulsion being ignored. This conclusion was arrived at only after seven months of deliberation, and was dated the 6th of March, 1858. The decree, which will be given entire in this chapter, contemplates the continued activity of the Fathers as missionaries, subject to the authority of the American bishops; their formation into a separate society was taken for granted. Such is a brief statement of the entire case. If the reader will allow it to stand as a summary, what follows will serve to fill in the outline and complete a more detailed view.

And at the outset let it be fully understood that none of the Fathers desired separation from the order or had the faintest notion of its possibility as the outcome of the misunderstanding. One of the first letters of Father Hecker from Rome utters the passionate cry, " They have driven me out of the home of my heart and love." We have repeatedly heard him affirm that he never had so much as a temptation against his vows as a Redemptorist. But in saying this we do not mean to lay blame on the Redemptorist superiors. In all that we have to say on this subject we must be understood as recognizing their purity of intention. Their motives were love of discipline and obedience, which they considered seriously endangered. They were persuaded that their action, though severe, was necessary for the good of the entire order. And this shows that the difficulty was a misunderstanding, for there is conclusive evidence of the loyalty of the American Fathers—of Father Hecker no less than the others; as also of their fair fame as Redemptorists with both the superiors and brethren of the community up to the date of their disagreement. When Father Hecker left for Rome the Provincial gave him his written word that, although he disapproved of his journey, he bore witness to him as a good Redemptorist, full of zeal for souls; and he added that up to that time his superiors had been entirely satisfied with him; and to the paper containing this testimony the Provincial placed the official seal of the order. On the other side, a repeated and careful examination of Father Hecker's letters and memoranda reveals no accusation by him of moral fault against his Redemptorist superiors, but on the contrary many words of favorable explanation of their conduct. When the Rector Major, in the midst of his council, began, to Father Hecker's utter amazement, to read the sentence of expulsion, he fell on his knees and received the blow with bowed head as a visitation of God. And when, again, after prostrating himself before the Blessed Sacrament and resigning himself to the Divine Will, he returned to the council and begged the General on his knees for a further consideration of his case, and was refused, he reports that the General affirmed that his sense of duty would not allow him to act otherwise than he had done, and that he by no means meant to condemn Father Hecker in the court of conscience, but only to exercise jurisdiction over his external conduct.

In truth the trouble arose mainly from the very great difference between the character of the American Fathers and that of their superiors in the order. It is nothing new or strange, to borrow Father Hewit's thoughts as expressed in his memoir of Father Baker, that men whose characters are cast in a different mould should have different views, and should, with the most conscientious intentions, be unable to coincide in judgment or act in concert:

"There is room in the Catholic Church for every kind of religious organization, suiting all the varieties of mind and character and circumstance. If collisions and misunderstandings often come between those who have the same great end in view, this is the result of human infirmity, and only shows how imperfect and partial are human wisdom and human virtue."

What Father Hewit adds of Father Baker's dispositions applies as well to all the Fathers. In ceasing to be Redemptorists, they did not swerve from their original purpose in becoming religious. None of them had grown discontented with his state or with his superiors. They were all in the full fervor of the devotional spirit of the community, and as missionaries were generously wearing out their lives in the toil and hardship of its peculiar vocation. But both parties became the instruments of a special providence, which made use of the wide diversities of temperament existing among men, and set apart Father Hecker and his companions, after a season of severe trial, for a new apostolate. They did not choose it for themselves. Father Hecker had aspirations, as we know, but he did not dream of realizing them through any separation whatever. But Providence led the Holy See to change what had been a violent wrench into a peaceful division, exercising, in so doing, a divine authority accepted with equal obedience by all concerned.

What Father Hewit further says of Father Baker applies exactly to Father Hecker:

"For the Congregation in which he was trained to the reli-

gious and ecclesiastical state he always retained a sincere esteem
and affection. He did not ask the Pope for a dispensation from
his vows in order to be relieved from a burdensome obligation,
but only on the condition that it seemed best to him to terminate
the difficulty which had arisen that way. When the dispensation
was granted he did not change his life for a more easy one. . .
Let no one, therefore, who is disposed to yield to temptations
against his vocation, and to abandon the religious state from
weariness, tepidity, or any unworthy motive, think to find any
encouragement in his example; for his austere, self-denying, and
arduous life will give him only rebuke, and not encouragement."

After the expulsion the General begged Father Hecker to
make the convent his home till he was suited elsewhere, and
Father Hecker, having thanked him for his kindness and
stayed there that night, took lodgings the following day in a quiet
street near the Propaganda. During the seven months of his stay
in Rome he frequently visited the General and his consultors,
sometimes on business but at other times from courtesy and
good feeling.

He at once presented the testimonials intended for the General to Cardinal Barnabo, Prefect of the Propaganda, who examined them in company with Archbishop Bedini, the Secretary
of that Congregation. As may be imagined, the attitude of these
prelates was at first one of extreme reserve. But every case gets
a hearing in Rome, and that of this expelled religious, and therefore suspended priest, could be no exception. A glance at the
credentials, a short conversation with their bearer, a closer examination of the man and of his claim, produced a favorable impression and led to a determination to sift the matter thoroughly.
The principal letters were from Archbishop Hughes and Bishop
Bayley. The former spoke thus of Father Hecker: "I have
great pleasure in recommending him as a laborious, edifying,
zealous, and truly apostolic priest."

Some of the letters were from prominent laymen of the City
of New York, including one from Mr. McMaster, another from
Dr. Brownson, and another from Dr. Ives; in addition he had
the words of praise of the Provincial in America already referred
to. Finally he showed letters from each of the American Fathers,
one of whom, Father Hewit, was a member of the Provincial
Council, all joining themselves to Father Hecker as sharing the
responsibility of his journey to Rome, and naming him as the
representative of their cause.

It is not our purpose to trace the progress of the investigation through the Roman tribunals. We will but give such facts and such extracts from letters as throw light on Father Hecker's conduct during this great crisis. One might be curious to know something about the friends he made in Rome. The foremost of them was the Cardinal Prefect of the Propaganda.

" The impression that Cardinal Barnabo made upon me," he writes in one of his earliest letters, " was most unexpected ; he was so quick in his perceptions and penetration, so candid and confiding in speaking to me. He was more like a father and friend ; and both the cardinal and the archbishop (Bedini) expressed such warm sympathy in my behalf that it made me feel, . . . in a way I never felt before, the presence of God in those who are chosen as rulers in His Church."

In another letter he says :

" He (the cardinal) has been to me more than a friend ; he is to me a father, a counsellor, a protector. No one enjoys so high a reputation in every regard in Rome as the cardinal. He gives me free access to him and confides in me."

There is much evidence, too much to quote it all, that the cardinal was drawn to Father Hecker on account of his simplicity and openness of character, his frank manner, but especially for his bold, original views of the opportunity of religion among free peoples. Cardinal Barnabo was noted for his sturdy temper and was what is known as a hard hitter, though a generous opponent as well as an earnest friend. He espoused Father Hecker's cause with much heartiness ; official intercourse soon developed into a close personal attachment, which lasted with unabated warmth till the strong old Roman was called to his reward.

Father Hecker speaks in his letters of spending time with him, not only on business but in discussing questions of philosophy and religious controversy, and in talking over the whole American outlook.

The cardinal became the American priest's advocate before the Pope, and also with the Congregation of Bishops and Regulars after the case reached that tribunal. " When I heard him speak in my defence," he said in after times, " I thanked God that he was not against me, for he was a most imperious character when aroused, and there seemed no resisting him."

Archbishop Bedini, the Secretary of the Propaganda, was another hearty friend. Our older readers will remember that he had paid a visit to America a few years before the time we are considering, and that his presence here was made the occasion for some of the more violent outbreaks of the Know-nothing excitement. He knew our country personally, therefore, and was acquainted with very many of our clergy; his assistance to the Roman Court in this case was of special value. He became so demonstrative in his friendship for Father Hecker that the Pope was amused at it, and Father Hecker relates in his letters home how the Holy Father rallied him about the warmth of his advocacy of the American priest's cause, as did various members of the Pontifical court.

At that time and for many years afterwards Doctor Bernard Smith, an Irish Benedictine monk, was Professor of Dogmatic Theology in the College of the Propaganda ; he is now the honored abbot of the great Basilica of St. Paul without-the-walls. How Father Hecker came to know the learned professor we have been unable to discover ; but both he and Monsignor Kirby, of the Irish College, became his firm friends and powerful advocates. Without Doctor Smith's advice, indeed, scarcely a step was taken in the case.

An unexpected ally was found in Bishop Connolly, of St. John's, New Brunswick. He had been robbed on his way between Civita Vecchia and Rome, and that misfortune gave him a special claim to the regard of the Pope, with whom he soon became a favorite. The Holy Father admired in him that energy of character and zeal for religion which distinguished him in after years as Archbishop of Halifax. On hearing of Father Hecker's case he studied it on account of sympathetic interest in the aspects of Catholicity in the United States, part of his diocese being at that time, we believe, in the State of Maine. How ardent his friendship for Father Hecker soon became is shown by his exclamation: "I am ready to die for you, and I am going to tell the Pope so." He even offered to assist Father Hecker in paying his personal expenses while in Rome. In a letter to the American Fathers of December 18 Father Hecker writes :

" Another recent and providential event in our favor has been the friendship of Bishop Connolly, of St. John's, New Brunswick. By his extraordinary exertions and his warm friendship for us he has succeeded in giving us the vantage ground in all quarters where we were not in good favor. I told you in the last note that he had spoken to the Holy Father in favor of our cause, but I had no time to give you the substance of what was said. Bishop Connolly is a full-blooded Irishman, but, fortunately for us, not implicated in any party views in our country, and seeing that the Propaganda regarded our cause as its own and had identified itself with our success, . . . it being friendly to us as missionaries, he exerted all his influence in our favor. His influence was not slight, for the Pope had conceived a great friendship for him, and heaped all sorts of honors on him. Well, he had a regular tussle with his Holiness about us and our cause, and when the Holy Father repeated some things said of me—against me, of course—he replied: 'Your Holiness, I should not be at all surprised if some fine day you yourself would have to canonize one of these Yankee fellows.' In one word, he left nothing unsaid or undone with the Pope in our favor; and the Pope suggested to him obtaining dispensation of our vows and forming a new company. 'They cannot expect me,' he said, ' to take the initiatory step; this would be putting the cart before the horse. Let *them* do this, and present their plan to me, and if I find it good, it shall have my consent.' . . . The bishop has also seen and won over to our favor Monsignor Talbot, who said to him : ' The only way now of settling the difficulties is to give the American Fathers the liberty to form a new company for the American missions.' In addition, the bishop wrote a strong document in favor of our missions and of us, and presented it to Cardinal Barnabo, which will be handed in to the Congregation of Bishops and Regulars, who have our affairs in hand. . . . If this good bishop should come in your way, whether by writing or otherwise, you cannot be too grateful for what he has done for us. After Cardinal Barnabo and Archbishop Bedini we owe more to him than to any one else.

" Wind and tide are now in our favor, and my plan is to keep quiet and stick close to the rudder to see that the ship keeps right."

On his way home from Rome Bishop Connolly wrote the following letter to Father Hecker, dated at Marseilles, January 20, 1858 :

"From the deep interest I feel in your concerns you will pardon my curiosity in wishing to have the earliest intelligence of your fate in the Congregation of Bishops and Regulars. I could wish I were near you all the time, and have nothing else to attend to; but you have got One more powerful than I at your right hand. Fix your hopes in Him and you will not be confounded. After having done everything on your part that unsleeping energy as well as prudence could suggest, you must take the issue, however unpalatable it may be, as the undoubted expression of God's will, and act (as I am sure you will act) accordingly. . . . You must keep steadily in view the glorious principle for which you came to Rome, and which I am convinced is for the greater glory of God and the greater good of religion in America. If you can start as a religious body with the approbation of Rome, this would be the holiest and most auspicious consummation. . . . Be guided at every step by the holy and enlightened men whose sympathies you have won and in whose hands you will be always safe: Cardinal Barnabo *in primis*, and after him Monsignor Bedini and Doctors Kirby and Smith. United with them at every step, failure is impossible—you must and you will succeed. . . . I am sure that you know and feel this as well as I do (for we have been marvellously of the same way of thinking on nearly all points), but as I feel I must write to you, as it may be, perchance, of some consolation to you in your troubles, I thought it better to say it over again. . . . If a letter or anything else from me could be of any service, I need not tell you that I am still on hand and only anxious to be employed. [Here follows his address in Paris and Liverpool.] With all good wishes for your success, and with the hope of hearing the happy tidings from your own hand before I leave Europe, I am, Reverend dear Sir,

"Very faithfully yours in Christ,

"† Thomas L. Connolly,

"*Bishop of St. John's, N. B.*"

From what has been so far communicated to the reader, it will be seen that Father Hecker's case had the strength of friendship to assist it. But he was himself his best advocate. His traits of character were lovable, and the very incongruity of such a man forced to plead against the direst penalty known to a religious, was a singularly strong argument. His cheerful demeanor while fighting for his life; his puzzling questions on social and philosophical points; his mingled mysticism and practical judgment; his utterance of political sentiments which, as he truly said in one of his letters, if spoken by any one but an

American would elicit instant reproof; his total lack of obse-
quiousness united to entire submission to lawful authority, all
helped to make for himself and his cause friends in every direction.

The unanimous adhesion of the American Redemptorist missionaries was a powerful element in his favor, and a priceless
boon for his own consolation. He was continually in receipt of
such words as these: " We all desire you to consider us fully
identified with you and to act in our name." " We have the
utmost confidence in your discretion, and your conservative
views are quite to our mind." His whole heart went out in
response to these greetings. On October 24 he writes to the
Fathers :

" The contents of your note were what I had a right to expect from you : sympathy, confidence, and reliance on Divine
Providence. How much these trials will endear us to each
other ! If we keep together as one man and regard only God,
defeat is impossible. Do not forget to offer up continually
prayers for me. How much I see the hand of Providence in
all our difficulties ! And the end will, I trust, make it evident as the sun."

But where he placed his entire trust is shown by the following, a part of the same letter :

" Our affairs are in the hands of God. I hope no one will
feel discouraged, nor fear for me. All that is needed to bring
the interests of God to a successful issue is grace, grace, grace;
and this is obtained by prayer. And if the American Fathers
will only pray and get others to pray, and not let any one
have the slightest reason to bring a word against them in our
present crisis, God will be with us and help us, and Our Lady
will take good care of us. So far no step taken in our past
need be regretted. If it were to be done again it would have
my consent. The blow given to me I have endeavored to receive with humility and in view of God. It has not produced
any trouble in my soul, nor made me waver in the slightest degree in my confidence in God or my duty towards Him. Let
us not be impatient. God is with us and will lead us if we
confide in Him."

During his stay in Rome he corresponded regularly with his brother George, whose ever-open purse paid all his expenses. We have also found a very long letter of loving friendship--from Doctor Brownson, conveying the profoundest sympathy. This came during the most critical period of the case and gave much consolation. It called forth an answer equally affectionate.

He received exceedingly sympathetic letters from Fathers de Held and de Buggenoms. The former was at the time rector of the house in Liège, and wrote a letter to Cardinal Barnabo, a copy of which has been preserved, which treats most favorably of Father Hecker's character and discusses his case at length, petitioning a decision which should reinstate him in the order.

Late in November he sought an interview with Cardinal Reisach, holding him closely interested for two hours, conversing upon American religious prospects and quite winning his friendship. By means of such interviews, which, at Cardinal Barnabo's suggestion, he sought with the chief prelates in Rome, he became widely known in the city, and the state of religion in America was made a common topic of conversation.

The following introduces a singular phase in the case. It is from a letter written before the end of September, less than a month after his arrival:

"My leisure moments are occupied in writing an article on the 'Present Condition and Future Prospects of the Catholic Faith in the United States,' for the *Civilta Cattolica*. They have promised to translate and publish it."

The *Civilta* is still a leading Catholic journal, the foremost exponent of the views of the Society of Jesus. At that time it was the official organ of Pius IX., who read all its articles in the proofs, and it went everywhere in Catholic circles. The editors became fast friends of Father Hecker, though we are not aware that they took sides in his case. His article was divided in the editing, and appeared in two successive numbers of the magazine. It attracted wide attention, being translated and printed in the chief Catholic periodicals of France, Belgium, and Germany, and published by Mr. McMaster in the *Freeman's Journal*. In Rome it served a good purpose. To some its views were startling, but its tone was fresh and enlivening. It undertook to show that the freest nation in the world was the most inviting field for the Catholic propagandist. We suppose that the author's main purpose in writing was but to invite attention to America, yet he so affected public opinion in Rome as to materially assist the adjustment of the difficulty pending before the high tribunals. Cardinal Barnabo was quite urgent with Father Hecker that he should write more of the same kind, but either his occupations or his expectation of an early return home hindered his doing so. As it was, he had caused himself and the American Fathers to be viewed by men generally through the medium of the great question of the relation of religion to the young Republic of the Western World. That topic was fortunate in having him for its exponent. He was an object-lesson of the aspirations of enlightened Catholic Americans as well as an exalted type of Catholic missionary zeal. Very few men of discernment ever really knew Father Hecker but to admire him and to be ready to be persuaded by him of his life-thesis : that a free man tends to be a good Catholic, and a free nation is the most promising field for apostolic zeal.

Soon after his arrival in Rome he made the acquaintance of George L. Brown, an American artist of some note, and a non-Catholic. He was an earnest man, and Father Hecker attacked him at once on the score of religion, and before December had received him into the Church. This event made quite a stir in Rome. The city was always full of artists and their patrons, and Mr. Brown's conversion, together with the articles in the *Civilta*, influenced in Father Hecker's favor many persons whom he could not directly reach. This was especially the case with the Pope, to whose notice such matters were brought by Archbishop Bedini, his office enabling him to approach the Holy Father at short intervals. He exerted a similar influence on all the high officials of the Roman court.

In spite of all this favor the usual delays attendant upon serious judicial investigations oppressed Father Hecker with the heavy dread of "the law's delay," detaining him in Rome from the first week in September, 1857, when the case was opened in the Propaganda, till it was closed by the decision of the Congregation of Bishops and Regulars early in the following March. Nor was the "insolence of office" quite absent. He was once heard to tell of his having been snubbed in the Pope's antechamber by some one in attendance, and often put aside till he was vexed with many weary hours of waiting and by being compelled to repeatedly return.

"I had to wait for three days," we read in the memoranda, "and then was reproached and scolded by the monsignor in attendance for coming late. I had not come late but had been kept waiting outside, and I told him so. 'You will see those hills of Albano move,' said I, 'before I move from my purpose to see the Holy Father.' When he saw my determination he changed and gave me my desired audience."

When events had taken the question out of the jurisdiction of the Redemptorist order and into the general court of the Catholic Church, its settlement was found to be difficult. The restoration of Father Hecker by a judicial decision would not, it is plain, have left him and his companions in that harmonious relation so essential to their personal happiness and to their success as missionaries. It was then suggested that they should petition for a separate organization under the Rule of St. Alphonsus approved by Benedict XIV., acting directly subject to the Holy See, thus making two Redemptorist bodies in the United States, as is the case with various Franciscan communities. It was also suggested that the Cisalpine, or Neapolitan Redemptorists, at that time an independent congregation, would gladly take the American Fathers under their jurisdiction. The alternative was what afterwards took place—the dispensation of the Fathers from their vows, in view of their forming their own organization under direction of the Bishops and the Holy See. A petition praying the Holy Father to give them either the Rule of Benedict XIV. in the sense above suggested, or their dispensations from the vows, was drawn up and forwarded by the Fathers remaining in America, the dispensation being named as the last resort. Father Hecker's legal case not being decided, he was advised by Cardinal Barnabo to reserve his signature to this document for the present. It will be seen at a glance that the dispensation from the vows and an entirely new departure in community existence was more in accordance with his aspirations. But no aspiration was so strong in him as love of his brethren, and he was fully determined not to be separated from them if he could prevent it.

Much delay was caused by waiting for further testimonials from American bishops confirmatory of the good character of the Fathers and of the value of their labors as missionaries. Father

Hecker, meantime, wrote many letters to his brethren discussing the alternatives in question.

In one of October 24 he tells of a pilgrimage he made to Nocera, to the tomb of St. Alphonsus, bearing his brethren in his heart with him. He also visited the Redemptorist house there and in Naples, and was quite charmed with the fathers, who were entirely willing to receive the Americans into their organization, which, as the reader knows, was separate from that of the General in Rome. Knowing the mind of his brethren, and determined to take no step alone, Father Hecker would have been content with this arrangement had it seemed good to the Holy See. Meantime he tells how greatly he enjoyed his visit to Nocera, how he said Mass over the holy body of the founder, and adds : " Ever since I feel more consoled and supported and confident."

The following is from a joint letter of the American Fathers dated November 17 ; they prefer, in case Father Hecker is not reinstated, being separated from the order and made " immediately dependent on the Holy See, or the Prefect of the Propaganda, rather than anything else ; . . . called, for instance, ' Religious Missionaries of the Propaganda,' if the Holy Father would make us such. With the Rule of St. Alphonsus and the same missionary privileges we now enjoy, and our dear Father Hecker among us again, we should feel happy and safe. . . . But we wait for the words of the Holy See to indicate our course."

His words to them are to the same effect : " Our first effort should be directed to the securing our hopes through the Transalpine Congregation [this means .the regular Redemptorist order to which they then belonged]. . . . If this is not successful, then to endeavor to accomplish our hopes through the Cisalpine [Neapolitan] Fathers, who will be heart and soul with us and grant all our best desires. Or, thirdly, to obtain permission to act as a band of missionaries in our country under the protection, for the present, of some bishop. . . . It is a consolation to me to see that our affairs are so far developed and known, and our views are so identical that you can act on your part, and write, without having to delay for information [from me]. You can easily imagine that it was no pleasant state for me to be in while in suspense about what would be the determination you would come to. Thank God and Our Lady, your recent letter set that all aside! The work now to be done is plain, and the greatest care and prudence is to be exercised not to commit any fault, or make any mistake which may be to us a source of regret afterwards."

In another letter he says that Cardinal Barnabo spoke of the unpleasant relations likely to exist after his restoration to the order, and then continues:

"The cardinal had a long conversation with me, and he suggested whether God might not desire of me a special work. I told him I would not think of this while the dismission was over my head. He said, 'Of course not; for if you are a *mauvais sujet*, as the General thinks, God will surely not use you for any special mission.'" The letter here details more of the exchange of views between the cardinal and Father Hecker, the latter astounded to hear from this direction suggestions so closely tallying with his own interior aspirations about the apostolic outlook in America. "But," continues the letter, "you must well understand that I should not accept such a proposition for myself before having asked the best counsel of men of God and received their unhesitating approval of its being God's will. There are holy men here, and I take counsel with them in every important step; and they are religious, so that they are good judges in such important matters. . . . If God wishes to make use of us in such a design, and I can be assured of this on *competent authority*, whatever it may cost, with His grace I will not shrink from it. I call competent authority the approbation of good and holy men, and one like the cardinal, who knows the country, knows *all* our affairs now, and has every quality of mind and heart to be a competent judge in this important matter. Though you have made me your plenipotentiary, yet this is an individual affair, one we did not contemplate, one of the highest import to our salvation and sanctification, and must depend on God and our individual conscience.

"Even before making this proposition to you I asked advice from my spiritual director, and he approved of it. You may be confident that in every step which I take I endeavor to be actuated by the spirit of God, and take every means to assure myself of it, so that hereafter no scruple may trouble my conscience, and God's blessing be with me and you also."

He writes thus towards the end of September: "The more I think of our difficulties the more I am inclined to believe that they may have been permitted by a good God for the very purpose of a work of this kind. If wise and holy men say so, and we have the approbation of the Holy See, is it not a mission offered to us by Divine Providence, and ought we not cheerfully to embrace it?"

And on October 5: "I hope God has inspired you with some means of coming to my help. Indeed, it is a difficult position, and the best I can do is to throw myself constantly on Divine Providence and be guided by Him. You will remember, and I hope, before this reaches you, will have answered my proposition in my last note, whether or not you would be willing to form an independent band of missionaries to be devoted to the great wants of the country. I have considered and reconsidered, and prayed and prayed, and in spite of my fears this seems to me the direction in which *Divine Providence calls us.* . . . With all the difficulties, dangers, and struggles that another [community] movement presents before me, I feel more and more convinced that it *is this that Divine Providence asks of us.* If we should act in concert its success cannot be doubted—success not only as regards our present kind of labors, but in a variety of other ways which are open to us in our new country. . . . If you are prepared to move in this direction it would be best, and indeed necessary, not only to write to me your assent, but also a memorial to the Propaganda—to Cardinal Barnabo—stating the interests and wants of religion and of the country, and then petition to be permitted to turn your labors in this direction. . . .

"Such a course involves the release of your obligations to the [Redemptorist] Congregation, and this would have to be expressed distinctly in your petition, and motived by good reasons there given."

Further on in the same letter he adds: "Since writing the above I have had time for more reflection, and consulted with my spiritual adviser, and this course appears to be the one Divine Providence points out."

This very important letter ends as follows: "I endeavor to keep close to God, to keep up my confidence in His protection, and in the aid of Our Blessed Lady. I pray for you all; you cannot forget me in your prayers."

Then follow suggestions about obtaining testimonials from the American hierarchy for the information of the Holy See in a final settlement of the entire case. The prelates who wrote, all very favorably, were: Archbishops Hughes of New York, Kenrick of Baltimore, Purcell of Cincinnati, Bishops Bayley of Newark, Spalding of Louisville (both afterwards Archbishops of Baltimore), Lynch of Charleston, Barry of Savannah, and De Goesbriand of Burlington, Vermont.

On October 26, while wondering what would next happen, he writes: "As for my part, I do not see one step ahead, but at the same time I never felt so closely embraced in the arms of Divine Providence." But on the next day: "It seems to me a great and entire change awaits us. . . . We are all of us young, and if we keep close and true to God—and there is nothing but ourselves to prevent this—a great and hopeful future is at our waiting. I know you pray for me; continue to do so, and believe me always your wholly devoted friend and brother in Jesus and Mary."

On November 12: "My present impression is that neither union with the Cisalpine Fathers nor separation as a band of [independent Redemptorist] missionaries in the United States will be approved of here. . . . What appears to me more and more probable is that we shall have to start entirely upon our own basis. This is perhaps the best of all, all things considered. . . . Such a movement has from the beginning seemed to me *the one to which Divine Providence calls us*, but I always felt timid as long as any door was left open for us to act in the Congregation. . . . I feel prepared to take this step with you without hesitation and with great confidence. . . . I should have been glad, as soon as my dismission was given, to have started on in such a movement. But then it was my first duty to see whether this work could not be accomplished by the Congregation [of the Most Holy Redeemer]; and, besides, I was not sure, as I now am, of your views being the same as mine. . . . All indicates the will of Divine Providence in our regard and gives me confidence. . . .

"Father Hewit's letter, confirming your readiness to share your fortunes with me, was most consoling and strengthening. God knows we seek only His interest and glory and are ready to suffer anything rather than offend Him. . . .

"We should take our present missions as the basis of our

unity and activity; at the same time not be exclusively restricted to them, but leave ourselves at liberty to adapt ourselves to the [religious] wants which may present themselves in our country. Were the question presented to me to restrict myself exclusively to missions, in that case I should feel in conscience bound to obtain from holy men a decision on the question whether God had not pointed out another field for me. . . . Taking our missions and our present mode of life as the groundwork, the rest will have to be left to Divine Providence, the character of the country, and our own spirit of faith and good common sense."

In the same letter, that of December 25, he hopes that if the Holy See separates them from old affiliations they will form a society " which would embody in its life what is good in the American people in the natural order and adapt itself to answer the great wants of our people in the spiritual order. I must confess to you frankly that thoughts of this kind do occupy my mind, and day by day they appear to me to come more clearly from heaven. I cannot refuse to entertain them without resisting what appear to me the inspirations of God. You know that these are not new opinions hastily adopted. From the beginning of my Catholic life there seemed always before me, but not distinctly, some such work, and it is indicated both in *Questions of the Soul* and *Aspirations of Nature*. And I cannot resist the thought that my present peculiar position is or may be providential to further some such undertaking. . . . It might be imagined that these views were but a ruse of the devil to thwart our common cause and future prospects. To this I have only to answer that the old rascal has been a long time at work to reach this point. If it be he, I shall head him off, because all that regards my personal vocation I shall submit to wise and holy men and obey what they tell me."

Father Hecker had his first audience with Pius IX., after much delay, on December 22. " I felt," he said, in giving an account of it in after years, " that my trouble in Rome was the great crisis in my life. I had one way of telling that I was not like Martin Luther: in my inmost soul I was ready, entirely ready, to submit to the judgment of the Church. They had made me out a rebel and a radical to the Holy Father, and when I saw him alone, after the usual salutations, and while on my knees, I said: ' Look at me, Holy Father; see, my shoulders are broad. Lay on the stripes. I will bear them. All I want is justice. I want you to judge my case. I will submit.' The Pope's eyes filled with tears at these words, and his manner was very kind." The rest of the interview is given in a letter: "The Pope bade me rise and told me he was informed all about my affairs. Then he asked what was my desire. I replied that he might have the goodness to examine the purpose of my coming to Rome, 'since it regarded the conversion of the American people, a work which the most intelligent and pious Catholics have at heart, among others Dr. Ives, whom you know.' 'Yes,' he said; 'has his wife become a Catholic?' I replied in the affirmative. 'But what can I do?' he said; 'the affair is being examined by Archbishop Bizarri (Secretary of the Congregation of Bishops and Regulars), and nothing can be done until he gives in his report; then I will give my opinion and my decision.' 'Your decision, most Holy Father, is God's decision, and whatever it may be willingly and humbly will I submit to it.' While I was making this remark his Holiness paid the greatest attention, and it seemed to satisfy and please him. 'The American people,' he continued, 'are much engrossed in worldly things and in the pursuit of wealth, and these are not favorable to religion; it is not I who say so, but our Lord in the Gospel.' 'The United States, your Holiness,' I replied, 'is in its youth, and, like a young father of a family occupied in furnishing his house, while this is going on he must be busy; but the American people do not make money to hoard it, nor are they miserly.' 'No, no,' he replied; 'they are willing to give when they possess riches. The bishops tell me they are generous in aiding the building of churches. You see,' he added, 'I know the bright side as well as the dark side of the Americans; but in the United States there exists a too unrestricted freedom, all the refugees and revolutionists gather there and are in full liberty.' 'True, most Holy Father; but this has a good side. Many of them, seeing in the United States that the Church is self-subsisting and not necessarily connected with what they call despotism, begin to regard it as a Divine institution and return to her fold.' 'Yes,' he said, 'the Church is as much at home in a republic as in a monarchy or aristocracy. But then, again, you have the abolitionists and their opponents, who get each other by the hair.' 'There is also the Catholic faith, Holy Father, which if once known would act on these parties like oil upon troubled waters, and our best-informed statesmen are becoming more and more convinced that Catholicity is necessary to sustain our institutions, and enable our young country to realize her great destiny. And allow me to add, most Holy Father, that it would be an enterprise worthy of your glorious pontificate to set on foot the measures necessary for the beginning of the conversion of America.'

" On retiring he gave me his blessing, and repeated in a loud voice as I kneeled, ' Bravo ! Bravo ! ' "

" Pius IX.," said Father Hecker afterwards, " was a man of the largest head, of still larger heart, moved more by his impulses than by his judgment; but his impulses were great, noble, all-embracing."

It will not be out of place here to look more closely into Father Hecker's conscience and study his motives. One might ask why he did not simply submit to the infliction visited upon him by his superior in the order, and humbly withdraw from notice till God should find a way to vindicate him. But his case was not a personal one. He was in Rome representing a body of priests and a public cause, and every principle of duty and honor required an appeal to higher authority. Nor was vindication the chief end in view, but rather freedom to follow the dictates of the Holy Spirit in accordance with Catholic traditions and wholly subject to the laws and usages of the Church. Beyond securing exactly this he had no object whatever. On February 19, 1858, he thus wrote to his brother George :

" But there is no use of keeping back anything. My policy has all along been to have no policy, but to be frank, truthful, and have no fear. For my own part I will try my best to be true to the light and grace given me, even though it reduces me to perfect insignificance. I desire nothing upon earth except to labor for the good of our Religion and our Country, and whatever may be the decision of our affairs here, my aims cannot be defeated. I feel, indeed, quite indifferent about the decision which may be given, so that they allow us freedom."

As illustrating Father Hecker's supernatural motives and rectitude of conscience the following extracts from letters to the Fathers will be of interest. In September, when the arrow was yet in the wound, he wrote :

" I have no feelings of resentment against any one of the

actors [in this matter]. On the contrary I could embrace them all with unfeigned sentiments of love. God has been exceedingly good not to let me be even tempted in this way."

Again, on December 5:

"Your repeated assurances of being united with me in our future fills me with consolation and courage. We may well repeat the American motto, 'United we stand, divided we fall.' Never did I find myself more sustained by the grace of God. How often I have heard repeated by acquaintances I have made here: 'Why, Father Hecker, you are the happiest man in Rome!' Little do they know how many sleepless nights I have passed, how deeply I have suffered within three months. But isn't Almighty God good? It seems I never knew or felt before what it is to be wholly devoted to Him."

On December 9, after a long exposition of the need of a new religious missionary institute for America:

"Considering our past training, and many other advantages which we possess, I cannot but believe that God will use us, provided that we remain faithful to Him, united together as one man, and ready to make any sacrifice for some such holy enterprise; and my daily prayer is that the Holy Father may receive a special grace and inspiration to welcome and bless such a proposition."

With his Christmas greetings he wrote: "From the start I have not suffered myself to repose a moment when there was anything to be done which promised help. Whatever may be the result of our affairs, this consolation will be with me—I did my utmost, and everything just and honorable, to deserve success. No one would believe how much I have gone through at Rome, but I do it cheerfully, and sometimes gaily, because I know it is the will of God."

On February 19, 1858: "The experience I have made here is worth more than my weight in gold. If God intends to employ us in any important work in the future, such an experience was absolutely necessary for us. It is a novitiate on a large scale. I cannot thank God sufficiently for my having made it *thus far* without incurring by my conduct the displeasure or censure of any one."

And a week afterwards: " You should write often, for words of sympathy, hope, encouragement are much to me now in these trials, difficulties, and conflicts. In all my Catholic life I have not experienced oppression and anxiety of mind in such a degree as I have for these ten days past."

March 6: "So far from my devotion to religion being diminished by recent events, it has, thank God, greatly increased; but many other things have been changed in me. On many new points my intelligence has been awakened; experience has dispelled much ignorance, and on the whole I hope that my faith and heart have been more purified. If God spares my life to return, I hope to come back more a man, a better Catholic, and more entirely devoted to the work of God."

The following is from a copy of a letter to Father de Held dated November 2: " One thing my trials have taught me, and this is the one thing important—to love God more. It almost seems that I did not know before what it is to love Him."

When it became evident that the Holy See would decide the case so as to make it necessary for the Fathers to form a new society, Father Hecker did not accept even this as a final indication of Providence that external circumstances had made it possible for him to realize his long-cherished dreams of an American apostolate; for he was at liberty still to refuse. He redoubled his prayers. His pilgrimage to the shrine of St. Alphonsus is already known to the reader; he caused a novena of Masses to be said at the altar of Our Lady of Perpetual Help in the Redemptorist Church in Rome; he said Mass himself at all the great shrines, especially the Confession of St. Peter, the altar of St. Ignatius and that of St. Philip Neri; he earnestly entreated all his friends, old ones at home and new-found ones in Rome, to join with him in his prayers for light.

He furthermore took measures to obtain the counsel of wise and holy men. Every one whom he thought worthy of his confidence was asked for an opinion. Finally he drew up a formal document, known in this biography as the Roman Statement, and already familiar by reference and quotation, and placed it in the hands of the three religious whose names, in addition to those of Cardinal Barnabo and Archbishop Bedini, appear at the end of the extract we make from its original draft. It opens with a summary of his conversion, entrance into religion, and missionary life, and embraces a full enough statement of the trouble with the General of the order—a matter of notoriety at the time in the city of Rome. He then describes his own interior aspirations and vocation to the apostolate in America, backing up the authority of that inner voice with the external testimonials of prelates and priests and laymen, whose letters had been procured by the Propaganda as evidence in the case before the Congregation of Bishops and Regulars.

"If God has called me," he continues, "to such a work, His providence has in a singular way, since my arrival at Rome, opened the door for me to undertake it. The object of my coming to Rome was to induce the General to sustain and favor the extension of our missionary labors in the United States. It was undertaken altogether for the good of the order, in the general interests of religion, and in undoubted good faith. Under false impressions of my purpose, my expulsion from the Congregation was decreed three days after my arrival. This was about three months ago, and it was the source of the deepest affliction to me, and up to within a short time my greatest desire was to re-enter the Congregation. At present it seems to me that these things were permitted by Divine Providence in order to place me in the position to undertake that mission which has never ceased to occupy my thoughts."

After some description of the state of religion in America the statement concludes:

"These [American non-Catholics] require an institution which shall have their conversion to the Catholic faith as its principal aim, which is free to develop itself according to the fresh wants which may spring up, thus opening an attractive future to the religious vocations of the Catholic young men of that country.

"Regarding, therefore, my early and extensive acquaintance among my own people, politically, socially, religiously, with the knowledge of their peculiar wants, with their errors also; and the way in which God has led me and the graces given to me; and my interior convictions and the experience acquired confirming them since my Catholic life, and also my singular position at present—the question, in conclusion, is to know from holy, instructed, and experienced men in such matters whether or not there is sufficient evidence of a special vocation from God for me to undertake now such a work."

What follows is placed at the bottom of the last page of the statement:

" EPIPHANY, 1858, ROME.

" This document I had translated into Italian, and I gave it to Cardinal Barnabo, Archbishop Bedini, Father Francis, Passionist—my director while in Rome—Father Gregorio, definitor, Carmelite, and Father Druelle, of the Congregation of the Holy Cross, and each gave a favorable answer."

Father Hecker often said that he was fully determined to forego the entire matter, go back to the Redemptorists, or drift whithersoever Providence might will, if a single one of the men whom he thus consulted had failed to approve him, or had so much as expressed a doubt. He had inquired who were the most spiritually enlightened men in Rome, and had been guided to the three religious whom he had associated with Cardinal Barnabo and Archbishop Bedini to assist him in coming to a decision.

The end came at last, and is announced in a letter of March 9, 1858:

" The Pope has spoken, and the American Fathers, including myself, are dispensed from their vows. The decree is not in my hands, but Cardinal Barnabo read it to me last evening. The General is not mentioned in it, and no attention whatever is paid to his action in my regard. The other Fathers are dispensed in view of the petition they made, as the demand for separation as Redemptorists would destroy the unity of the Congregation, and in the dispensation I am associated with them. The Cardinal [Barnabo] is wholly content; says that I must ask immediately for an audience to thank the Pope.   . Now let us thank God for our success."

On March 11 : " We are left in entire liberty to act in the future as God and our intelligence shall point the way. Let us be thankful to God, humble towards each other and every one else, and more than ever in earnest to do the work God demands at our hands. . . . The Pope had before him all the documents, yours and mine and the General's, and the letters from the Archbishops and Bishops of the United States. Archbishop Bizarri (Secretary of the Congregation of Bishops and Regulars) gave him a verbal report of their contents and read some of the letters. Subsequently the Pope himself examined them and came to the conclusion to grant us dispensation. But there was *I* in the way, who had not petitioned for a dispensation. And why not? Simply because Cardinal Barnabo would have been offended at me if I had done so. . . . I could not go against the wishes of the cardinal. A few days after he had given me his views, and with such warmth that I could not act against them, he saw the Pope, who informed him of his intention to give us dispensation and to set aside the decree of my expulsion. On seeing the cardinal after this audience he told me that I might communicate this to Archbishop Bizarri. I did so by note, telling him that if the Pope set aside my expulsion and was determined to give the other American Fathers dispensation from their vows, in view of the circumstances which had arisen I would be content to accept my dispensation also. This note of mine was shown to the Pope, and hence he immediately associated me with you in the dispensation.

"The wording of the decree is such as to make it plain that it was given in view of your memorial, and its terms are calculated to give a favorable impression of us. . . . Archbishop Bizarri told me yesterday, when I went to thank him for his part, that in it the Holy See had given us its praise, and he trusted we would show ourselves worthy of it in the future. I rejoined that since the commencement of our Catholic life we had given ourselves soul and body entirely to the increase of God's glory and the interests of His Church, and it was our firm resolve to continue to do so to the end of our lives. He was quite gratified with *our* contentment with the decision, for I spoke, as I always have done, in your name as well as my own.

"But whom do you think I met in his antechamber? The General [of the Redemptorists]. When he came in and got seated I immediately went across the room and reached out my hand to him, and we shook hands and sat down beside each other. . . . In the course of the conversation he inquired what we intended to do in the future. My reply was that we had been guided by God's providence in the past and we looked to Him for guidance in our future. . . . As to my return [home], the cardinal says I must not think of departing till after Easter. Indeed, I see that before I can obtain an audience to thank the Holy Father it will be hard on to Easter. If there be a few days intervening I will go to Our Lady of Loretto to invoke her aid in our behalf, and for her protection over us as a body and over each one in particular. In May, earlier or later in the month, with God's blessing and your prayers, I hope to be with you. . . .

"The decree, which places us, according to the Canons, under the authority of the Bishops, you will, of course, understand, does not in any way make us parish priests. The Pope could not tell us in it to commence another congregation, although this is what he, and Cardinal Barnabo, and Archbishop Bedini, and others, expect from us. He [the Pope] said that for him to tell us so [officially] would be putting the cart before the horse. These are his words."

On March 18: "It is customary here, before giving dispensation of vows to religious, to require them to show their admission into a diocese. As this was not required in our case, we are consequently at liberty now to choose any bishop we please who will receive us. 'Choose your bishop, inform him of your intentions, and if he approves, arrange your conditions with him.' These are the cardinal's words, and both he and Archbishop Bedini suggested New York. . . . My trip to Loretto has come to naught, as I can find no one to accompany me, and then my health, I fear, will not bear so much fatigue. I shall come back with some gray hairs; I thought to pull them all out before my return, but on looking this morning with that intention I found them *too many.* However, that is only on the outside; within all is right—young, fresh, and full of courage, and ready to fight the good fight.' "

The following is a memorandum of his second audience with Pius IX. :

" Yesterday, the 16th of March, the Pope accorded me an audience, and on my entering his room he repeated my name, gave me his blessing, and after I had kissed his ring he told me

to rise, and said : 'At length your affairs are determined. We
have many causes to decide, and each must have its turn;
yours came finally, and now you have our decision.' ' True,'
I replied, ' and your decision gives me great satisfaction, and
it appears to me that it should be satisfactory to all concerned.'
' I found you,' he rejoined, ' like Abraham and Lot, and (making a motion with his hand) I told one to take this, the other
that direction.' ' For my part,' I said, ' I look upon the decision
as providential, as I sought no personal triumph over the General,
but entertain every sentiment of charity towards him, and every
one of my former religious brethren.' This remark appeared to
move the Pope, and I continued : ' I thought of your Holiness'
decision in the holy Mass of this morning, when in the Gospel
our Lord reminds us not to decide according to the appearances
of things, but render a just judgment; and such is the one you
have given, and for our part we trust that you will receive in
the future consolation and joy [from our conduct].' ' As you
petitioned,' he said, ' with the other Fathers as one of the Congregation, in giving you dispensation I considered you a member of the Congregation.' ' So I understood it,' was my reply;
' and as a [private] person I felt no inclination to defend my
character, but as a priest I felt it to be my duty; and in this
regard your Holiness has done all that I have desired.' ' But
you intend to remain,' he inquired, ' together in community?'
' Most assuredly, your Holiness; our intention is to live and
work as we have hitherto done. But there are many [spiritual]
privileges attached to the work of the missions very necessary to
their success, and which we would gladly participate in.' ' Well,
well,' he answered, ' organize, begin your work, and then demand
them, and I will grant them to you. The Americans, however,
are very much engrossed in material pursuits.' ' True, Holy
Father,' I replied, ' but the faith is there. We five missionaries
are Americans, and were like the others, but you see the grace
of God has withdrawn us from these things and moved us to
consecrate ourselves wholly to God and His Church, and we
hope it will do the same for many of our countrymen. And
once our countrymen are Catholics, we hope they will do great
things for God's Church and His glory, for they have enthusiasm' ' Yes, yes,' he rejoined, ' it would be a great consolation
to me.' I asked him if he would grant me a plenary indulgence
for my brethren and my friends in the United States. ' Well,'

he said, 'but I must have a rescript.' 'I have one with me
which perhaps will do,' I answered. Looking over it, he made
some alterations and signed it. I knelt down at his feet and
begged him to give me a large blessing before my departure,
in order that I might become a great missionary in the United
States—which he gave me most cordially, and I retired.

"His manner was very affectionate, and in the course of the
conversation he called me '*caro mio*' and '*figlio mio*' several
times. We could not desire to leave a more favorable impression than exists here in regard to us and our part in the recent
transaction, and we have the sympathy of the Pope and the
Propaganda. Rome will withhold nothing from us if we prove
worthy of its confidence, and will hail our success with true
joy. I look upon this settlement of our difficulties as the work
of Divine Providence, and my prayer is that it may make me
humble, modest, and renew my desire to consecrate myself
wholly to God's designs."

He writes to the Fathers, March 27: "The seven months
passed here in Rome seem to me an age; and have taxed me
to that extent that I look forward to home as a place of rest
and repose. When I think of the fears, anxieties, and labors undergone I say to myself—enough for this time. On the other
hand, when I remember the warm and disinterested friends
God has given us on account of these difficulties, and the happy
issue to which His providence has conducted them, my heart is
full of gratitude and joy. To me the future looks bright, hopeful, full of promise, and I feel confident in God's providence,
and assured of His grace in our regard. I feel like raising up
the cross as our standard and adopting one word as our motto
—CONQUER!

" I have just received the documents for you to give the
Papal benediction at the missions, and will send them. A letter
reached here this week from the Bishop of Burlington, Vt., and
it is strongly in our favor; it concludes by saying that all that
we required to make us a religious Congregation was the special
blessing of the Holy Father."

Again, on April 3: "Monsignor Bedini asked of the Pope the
special benediction that Bishop De Goesbriand suggested, and he
replied: 'Did I not give it to Père Hecker, and through him to
his brethren, when he was here?' 'But,' answered Monsignor

Bedini, 'give them this benediction this time on the request of the bishop.' And he answered: 'It is well; I do.' So there is a special blessing from the Holy Father in view of our forming a religious body. Indeed, that is so well understood here that several have inquired what name we intend to adopt, etc. Of course to all such questions my answer is: 'I can say nothing; the future is in God's hands, and we intend to follow His providence.' . . .

"Good Cardinal Barnabo looks upon us with a paternal regard, and when I expressed in your name how warmly we returned his affection, and what a deep gratitude we owed him, he was deeply moved, and replied that he did not deserve such sentiments, and that he had only done justice. Since the settlement of our affairs I have let no occasion pass to express our gratitude to those who have befriended us; and as for Cardinal Barnabo, Monsignor Bedini, Bishop Connolly, and Doctor Bernard Smith, Benedictine monk, they should be put at the head of the list of our spiritual benefactors and remembered in all our prayers. Now that we are a body, I would advise this to be done at once. The Holy Father stands No. 1; that is understood.

"How much I have to relate to you on my return! Many things I did not venture to write down on paper, and many I can communicate to no one else but you. How great is my desire to see you!—it seems that I have no other.

"I have taken passage for Marseilles on Tuesday after Easter, the 6th of April, and intend to take passage on the *Vanderbilt*, which leaves Havre on the 28th. . . . I saw the General on Tuesday of this week, to take leave of him. After some conversation we left in good feeling, promising to pray *pro invicem*. God bless him!"

Before leaving Paris Father Hecker received extremely affectionate letters of congratulation from his old friends, Fathers de Held and de Buggenoms.

The following is the decree of the Congregation of Bishops and Regulars: *

* Nuper nonnulli ex Presbyteris Congregationis SSmi Redemptoris in provinciis Americæ Septentrionalis fœderatis existentibus SSmum D. N. Pium PP. IX. supplici prece deprecabantur, ut eis ob speciales circumstantias concederet ab auctoritate et jurisdictione Rectoris Majoris subtrahi, ac a proprio Superiore Apostolicæ Sedi immediate subjecto juxta regulam a Benedicto XIV., sanctæ memoriæ, approbatam gubernari. Quod si id eis datum non esset, dispensationem a votis in dicta Congregatione emissis, humillime expostulabant. Re sedulo perpensa, Sanctitas Sua existimavit hujusmodi separationem unitati Congregationis officere,

"Certain priests of the Congregation of the Most Holy Redeemer in the United States of North America recently presented their most humble petition to our Most Holy Lord Pope Pius IX., that in view of certain special reasons he would grant that they might be withdrawn from the authority and jurisdiction of the Rector Major and be governed by a superior of their own, immediately subject to the Apostolic See, and according to the [Redemptorist] Rule approved by Benedict XIV., of holy memory. If, however, this should not be granted to them, they most humbly asked for dispensation from their vows in the said Congregation. After having carefully considered the matter, it appeared to his Holiness that a separation of this kind would be prejudicial to the unity of the Congregation and by no means accord with the Institute of St. Alphonsus, and therefore should not be permitted. Since, however, it was represented to his Holiness that the petitioners spare no labor in the prosecution of the holy missions, in the conversion of souls, and in the dissemination of Christian doctrine, and are for this reason commended by many bishops, it seemed more expedient to his Holiness to withdraw them from the said Congregation, that they might apply themselves to the prosecution of the works of the sacred ministry under the direction of the local bishops. Wherefore his Holiness by the tenor of this decree, and by his Apostolic authority, does dispense from their simple vows and from that of permanence in the Congregation the said priests, viz.: Clarence Walworth, Augustine Hewit, George Deshon, and Francis Baker, together with the priest Isaac Hecker, who has joined himself to their petition in respect to dispensation from the vows, and declares them to be dispensed and entirely released, so that they no longer belong to the said Congregation. And his Holiness confidently trusts that under the direction and jurisdiction of the lo-

et S. Alphonsi instituto minime respondere ideoque haud permittendum esse. Cum autem relatum sit oratores nulli labori parcere in sacris expeditionibus peragendis, et in proximorum conversione, Christianaque institutione curanda, et idcirco a pluribus Antistibus commendentur, visum est SSmo Domino magis expedire eos a præfata Congregatione eximi, ut in sacri ministerii opera promovenda sub directione Antistitum locorum incumbere possint. Quapropter Sanctitas Sua presbyteros Clarentium Walworth, Augustinum Hewit, Georgium Deshon, et Franciscum Baker, una cum presbytero Isaac Hecker, qui eorumdem postulationibus quoad dispensationem a votis adhæsit, a votis simplicibus, etiam permanentiæ in Congregatione SSmi Redemptoris emissis, hujus Decreti tenore, Apostolica auctoritate dispensat, et dispensatos, ac prorsus solutos esse declarat, ita ut ad eamdem Congregationem amplius non pertineant. Confidit vero Sanctitas Sua memoratos Presbyteros, qua opere, qua exemplo, qua sermone, in vinea Domini sub directione et jurisdictione Antistitum locorum, ad præscriptum SS. Canonum adlaboraturos, ut æternam animarum salutem alacriter curent, atque proximorum sanctificationem pro viribus promoveant.

Datum Romæ, ex Secretaria Sacræ Congregationis Episcoporum et Regularium, Die 6 Martii, 1858.

[L. ✠ S.]   G. CARD. DELLA GENGA, *Præf.*

A., ARCHIEPISCOPUS PHILIPPEN, *Sec.*

cal bishops, according to the prescription of the sacred Canons, the above-mentioned priests will labor by work, example, and word in the vineyard of the Lord, and give themselves with alacrity to the eternal salvation of souls, and promote with all their power the sanctification of their neighbor.

> "Given at Rome, in the office of the Sacred Congregation of Bishops and Regulars, the 6th day of March, 1858.

[L. S.]   G. CARDINAL DELLA GENGA, *Prefect.*

" A., ARCHBISHOP OF PHILIPPI, *Secretary.*"

NOTE.—I wish to add to this, that the relations between the Redemptorists and Paulists are, and I trust will continue to be, most amicable.

AUG. F. HEWIT, C.S.P., *Superior.*

CHAPTER XXV

DURING the seven months of Father Hecker's stay in Rome the band of American missionaries were busily occupied. Missions were given in the following order : Newark, N. J.; Poughkeepsie, Cold Spring on the Hudson, and Utica, N. Y.; Brandywine, Del.; Trenton, N. J.; Burlington, Brandon, East and West Rutland, Vt., and Plattsburgh, Saratoga, and Little Falls, N. Y. All these labors were undertaken subject to the authority of the Redemptorist Provincial and in a spirit of entire obedience. The mission at Little Falls closed on Palm Sunday, March 28, and the missionaries, with the exception of Father Baker, who was sent to Annapolis, Md., returned to the Redemptorist house in Third Street, New York. On the Tuesday after Easter, April 6, 1858, the official copy of the Pope's decision reached them, and they bade farewell to their Redemptorist brethren and to the community in which they had spent so many happy years, and witnessed, as Father Hewit has written, "so many edifying examples of high virtue and devoted zeal, to enter upon a new and untried undertaking."

Archbishop Kenrick, as soon as he heard of this, made a determined effort to secure Father Baker for the diocese of Baltimore, but the latter never for a moment faltered in his purpose to cast his lot with his brethren, and the archbishop gave up his claim upon him at the request of Cardinal Barnabo.

Their engagements called for two more missions before the season ended—one at Watertown, N. Y., and the other at St. Bridget's Church, New York City. The first of these opened on the 18th of April, and while waiting for that date the Fathers lived with Mr. George Hecker in Rutger's Place, saying Mass in his private chapel and following their religious rule as far as circumstances allowed, continuing meantime to obey Father Walworth, their former superior of the missions. They journeyed to Watertown, fearful lest the faculties for giving the Papal blessing and the mission indulgences should not arrive there in time. But late on Saturday night, April 17, they were received, much to the joy of the Fathers.

Here occurred a noteworthy coincidence. Watertown was at that time in the diocese of Albany, of which Bishop McCloskey

was then the ordinary. He had received Father Hecker into
the Church and had been his first guide in the spiritual life, and
now he was the first to publicly welcome his brethren at the beginning of their new career. The following is from a letter of
his to Father Walworth in answer to one announcing the recent
changes:

"I am happy to hear that your difficulties have at length received their solution, and in a manner, I presume, as satisfactory
as you could well expect. The future must now in great measure depend upon yourselves. You will, of course, have difficulties
to surmount and prejudices to encounter, but I trust that with
God's blessing your new community when once organized will
continue from day to day to gain increased stability and strength,
and be enabled to carry out successfully all its laudable aims for
the good of our holy religion. The faculties already given you
in this diocese you will not consider as being withdrawn by the
act of your separation from the Redemptorist order, and there is
nothing that I know of to interfere with your proposed mission
in Watertown."

During the mission at St. Bridget's—that is, in the first half
of the month of May—Father Hecker arrived in New York and
measures were at once taken for the practical organization of the
new community. Nothing was done hurriedly; a fair and full
consideration of all questions from every point of view, which lasted
until early in the month of July, enabled each one clearly to understand his new relation in its every aspect. Father Walworth
not being entirely in agreement with the others, withdrew to the
diocese of Albany and took charge of a parish; he returned again
in 1861, remaining with the community till 1865, when his health
becoming quite shattered, he reluctantly decided to withdraw altogether. It need hardly be said that the relations between him
and the community have always been most cordial. Meantime
the others, Fathers Hecker, Hewit, Deshon, and Baker, organized
by electing the first-named the Superior, and drew up and signed
what was termed a Programme of Rule. This was submitted to
Archbishop Hughes and by him approved and signed on July 7,
1858. The Apostle of the Gentiles was chosen as patron, and the
name selected was, The Missionary Priests of St. Paul the Apostle, which has been popularized into Paulists. The habit agreed
upon was in form somewhat like that of the students of the
Propaganda in Rome, black throughout, with a narrow linen

collar and buttoned across the breast, being held at the waist by a cincture.

The Programme of Rule adopts an order of spiritual exercises similar to that observed by the Fathers while Redemptorists. A perpetual voluntary agreement takes the place of the vows as the security of stability, the members affirming that they are fully determined to promote their sanctification by leading a life in all essential respects similar to that led in the religious orders. Besides the chastity imposed upon them by the priesthood the other evangelical counsels of obedience and poverty are adopted and their observance enjoined upon the members, together with the daily and periodical exercises of community life. As to the external vocation, the missions are named as the basis of general apostolic labors, and parish work also, though in a subordinate degree. The entire document looks forward to a complete Rule to be drawn up and submitted to the Holy See at a future day, for which it actually furnished the outlines some twenty years afterwards. The approval of the Programme of a Rule by the Archbishop of New York gave the Fathers the canonical status anticipated by the decree *Nuper nonnulli*. This was confirmed by an official permission of the Holy See to the Archbishop of New York to establish the Paulist Institute in his diocese, with the consent of his suffragans, which was asked for and obtained.

A little more than a fortnight after these events Father Hecker wrote as follows to a friend :

"Before leaving Rome our Holy Father Pius IX. gave us his special blessing for the commencement of our new organization, promised us any privileges we might need to carry on our missionary labors, and held out the hope of his sanction, in proper time, of the rules which we might make. In my last visit to his Eminence Cardinal Barnabo he gave me advice how to organize, what steps were to be taken from time to time, and expressed a most lively interest in our undertaking. The same did Monsignor Bedini. On my return we organized as advised, wrote out an outline of our new institution and submitted it to the ordinary of this diocese, the initiatory step of all such undertakings. He gave it his cordial approbation, and said that he found no word to alter, to add, or improve. Thus we are so far regularly canonically instituted.

"Our aim is to lead a strict religious life in community, starting with the voluntary principle; leaving the question of vows to further experience, counsel, and indications of Divine Providence. Our principal work is the missions, such as we have hitherto given, but we are not excluded from other apostolic labors as the wants of the Church may demand or develop. . . . We begin early this fall our campaign of missions, and we never had before us so fine a list. One thing I may say, and I trust without boasting, we are of one mind and heart, resolved to labor and die for Jesus Christ, for the good of His holy Church, for the advancement of the Catholic faith. We have the encouragement of a number of bishops, and also, we trust, the prayers, sympathy, and assistance of the faithful. We shall have to face obstacles, opposition from friends and foes; but if we are the right kind of men and have the virtues which such a position as ours demands, our trials will only strengthen us and make us the better Christians. Every good work must expect opposition from pious men, and our minds are made up to that."

After St. Bridget's mission the little community found itself homeless, and it remained so till the spring of the year 1859. But during part of this period Mr. George Hecker, taking his family to the country, gave up his whole house to the Fathers, servants and all, making provision for the supply of every want in the most generous manner. For the greater portion of the time, however, especially between missions in the winter and spring of 1858–9, the Fathers depended for temporary shelter upon the hospitality of friends among the clergy and laity, even lodging for a short while in a respectable boarding-house in Thirteenth street, at a convenient distance from several churches and chapels where Mass could be said daily.

But in the spring of 1858 arrangements had been made with Archbishop Hughes for establishing a house and parish in New York. The present site of St. Paul's Church and convent, then in the midst of a suburban wilderness, was chosen, and, by dint of hasty collections from private friends and with the help of a very large gift from Mr. George Hecker, money enough was paid down to obtain the deeds. Sixtieth Street was not quite opened at the time, and this part of Ninth Avenue existed only on paper; but by energetic efforts made by all the Fathers and their friends, and by personal appeals in every direction, especially in the down-town parishes in which they had given missions, sufficient funds were raised to clear the ground and lay the foundations of a building which was to include both convent and church. Early in the summer of 1858 circulars asking assistance had been sent out to the clergy of the United States, and by this means also a considerable amount was secured, the very first answer with a handsome donation coming from Father Early, President of Georgetown College. In the spring of 1859 the Fathers rented a frame house on Sixtieth Street, just west of Broadway, fitted up a little chapel in it, and lived there in community till the new house was finished.

The corner-stone of the new structure was laid by Archbishop Hughes on Trinity Sunday, June 19, 1859, in the presence of an immense concourse of people. During that summer and fall every effort was made to keep the builders at work. The task was no easy one. The times were hard, the country still suffering from the effects of the financial crisis of 1857, the financial depression being aggravated by the ominous outlook in the political world. But the house was finally completed, and was blessed by Father Hecker on the 24th of November, the feast of St. John of the Cross, one of his very special patrons. This was within a few weeks of his fortieth birthday. On the 27th of the same month, the first Sunday of Advent, the chapel was blessed and Solemn Mass was celebrated in it. Thereafter the Fathers had to act as parish priests as well as missionaries. A few weeks before this the first recruit joined the little band in the person of Father Robert Beverly Tillotson, a convert, who, though an American, had been for some time a member of Dr. Newman's Oratory. He was a charming preacher and a noble character, much beloved by all the fathers, and especially by Father Hecker. He died, deeply mourned, in the summer of 1868, having given the community nine years of most valuable service. He came just in time to set free three of the Fathers for missionary duty, the other two remaining in care of the parish. This was at first small enough in numbers, though in territory it reached from Fifty-second Street to very near Manhattanville. The accession of Father Alfred Young, of the diocese of Newark, and the return of Father Walworth considerably relieved the pressure, though the rapid growth of the parish and the widening scope of the community's labors kept every one busy enough.

The newly-founded Paulist community was heartily welcomed by both clergy and people. Missions were given in various parts of the country, applications being often declined for want of time and missionaries. Several prelates, among whom were the Archbishops of Baltimore and Cincinnati, wrote to Father Hecker offering to establish the community in their dioceses; Bishop Bayley, of Newark, also wished to secure the Fathers, and he was especially urgent in his request. One has but to know the intensely conservative spirit of the Catholic hierarchy and clergy to appreciate how stainless must have been the record of the Fathers to elicit such testimonials of good-will just after they had fought a hard battle on the ground of authority and obedience. As to the Catholic laity, the following extract from a letter of the poet George H. Miles, whose early death some years after was so deeply lamented, shows how they regarded the new community. It was written from Baltimore under date of August 13, 1858:

"MY VERY DEAR FATHER HECKER: . . . Since we last parted you have been to me one of those grand, good memories we take to heart and cherish. I have loved you better than you could believe, for I felt that in the extremity of sorrow or temptation you were the man and the priest I would have recourse to, could my own wish be granted. You are not wrong in considering me a friend; that is, if much love may atone for little power to befriend. . . . *Providentially*, it now appears, you men have always had an individual force that detached you completely from your *confrères*. To me and to the multitudes you were never Redemptorists, never Liguorians, but Hecker, Walworth, Hewit, Deshon, Baker. I mean to utter nothing disrespectful to the society which has blessed this nation in training and developing you and your new body of preachers, but I maintain that you stood so completely apart from that society, so absolutely individualized, that, etc."

The three years following Father Hecker's return from Rome were exceedingly active ones. The missions were maintained, money collected for the purchase of the property and the building of the convent at the corner of Fifty-ninth Street and Ninth Avenue, and, after the opening of the new church in November, 1859, the regular duties of a city parish were added.

"I am hard at work," writes Father Hecker to a friend, in

the very midst of these labors, " in soliciting subscriptions for our convent and temporary church. I have worked hard in my life, but this is about the hardest. However, it goes. I had, a couple of weeks ago, a donation of $200 from a Protestant. Yesterday a subscription of $50 from another. *Sursum Corda* and go ahead, is my cry!" And, indeed, he was full of courage and confidence in the future, all his letters breathing a cheerful spirit.

Before giving Father Hecker's principles for community life, which we will do in the next chapter, it may be well to say a few words more about the attitude in which he and his companions had been placed, by the action of the Holy See, toward the Catholic idea of authority.

Just as he was about to sail for America he wrote to his brother George: "I return from Rome with my enthusiasm unchilled and my resolution to labor for the conversion of our people intensified and strengthened. I feel that the knowledge and experience which I have acquired are most necessary for the American Fathers in their present delicate position." And in truth his stay in Rome had prepared him for the new responsibilities in store for him. His sufferings there had purified his motives, his humiliations and his anguish had taught him the need of reliance, total and loving, on Divine Providence. He had studied authority in its chief seat, and he had done so with the depth of impression which a man on trial for his life experiences of the power of the advocates and the dignity of the judges. The result of that trial was of infinite benefit. The test of genuine liberty is its consonance with lawful authority, and in Father Hecker's case the newest liberty had been roughly arraigned before the most venerable authority known among men, tried by fire, and sent forth with Rome's broad seal of approval.

Without doubt the chief endeavor of authority should be to win the allegiance of free and aspiring spirits; but, on the other hand, no one should be so firmly convinced of the rights of the external order of God as the man who is called to minister to the aspirations of human liberty.

No man ought to be so vividly conscious of the prerogatives of authority as he who lays claim to a vocation to extol the worth of liberty. It was, therefore, fitting that Father Hecker should learn his lesson of the prerogatives of the visible Church from that teacher who has no master among men. At the same time Rome sent forth in the person of Father Hecker a living and powerful argument addressed to this Republic, that the Catholic Church is worthy of the heartiest allegiance of our citizens.

This providential aspect of the case should not be forgotten. When Father Hecker had been expelled from the Redemptorists it might have been thought that he was done for, and that if he had ever had a mission it had suffered total shipwreck, whether deserved or not. But in reality the very reverse was the truth. The disgrace of expulsion, the sudden horror of being thus cast out, a calamity which set him forth to all Catholics as a ruined priest, had but served to bring him into the notice of the supreme authority of the Church. And when in this God had wrought all His work His servant was purified within and mightily strengthened without. In his inmost soul he was conscious of his divine mission with a deeper certitude than ever before; and as he began his apostolate he bore on his arm the buckler of Rome, against which all the darts of enemies, if any should arise, would strike harmless and fall to the ground.

It was fitting that the Paulist community, appealing to the men and women of to-day with the credentials as well of their own individual independence as of the good will of the Pope and the Bishops, should be launched into existence from the very deck of Peter's bark, and furnished with all the testimonials of ecclesiastical authority short of canonical sanction. This was the more proper because, in a few years after the beginning of the community, European revolutionists were to be scourged with the Syllabus, whose every word agonized the souls of unworthy advocates of liberty. That Pontifical document has created a literature of its own in comment and explanation, some tying more knots in every lash and others mitigating its severity or palliating the errors it smote with such pitiless rigor. But the best interpretation of the Syllabus is the Paulist community. It is a body of free men whose origin was the joint result of the personal workings of the Holy Spirit in the soul of a man who loved civil and political freedom with a mighty love, and the decision of the highest court of Catholicity declaring him worthy of trust as an exponent of the Christian faith. If the Syllabus shows what the Church thinks of those who in the guise of freemen are conspirators against religion and public order, the approval of the Paulist community shows the Church's attitude towards men worthy to be free.

Nor was Rome's course chosen without weighing the consequences, without a full estimate of the public significance of the act. Father Hecker's adversaries fixed upon him every stigma of radicalism and rebellion possible in a good but deluded priest. For seven long months they poured into ears which instinctively feared revolt in the name of liberty, every accusation his doings and sayings could be made to give color to, in order to prove that he and the American Fathers were tainted with false liberalism. And he seemed to lend himself to their purpose. His guileless tongue spoke to the cardinals, prelates, and professors of Rome about nothing so much as freedom, and its kinship with Catholicity. He seemed to have no refuge but the disclosure of the very secrets of his soul. During those months of incessant accusation and defence Father Hecker talked Rome's high dignitaries into full knowledge of himself, until they saw the cause mirrored in the man and gave approval to both. Some, like Barnabo, were actuated by the quick sympathy of free natures; others, like Pius IX., arrived at a decision by the slower processes of the removal of prejudice from an honest mind, and the careful comparing of Father Hecker's principles with the fundamental truths of religion.

CHAPTER XXVI.

FATHER HECKER'S IDEA OF A RELIGIOUS COMMUNITY.

THE beginnings of the Paulist community having been sketched, it is now in order to state the principles with which Father Hecker, guided no less by supernatural intuition than by enlightened reason, intended it should be inspired; and this shall be done as nearly as possible in his own words. The following sentences, found in one of his diaries and quoted some chapters back, embody what may be deemed his ultimate principle:

"It is for this we are created: that we may give a new and individual expression of the absolute in our own peculiar character. As soon as the new is but the re-expression of the old, God ceases to live. Ever the mystery is revealed in each new birth; so must it be to eternity. The Eternal-Absolute is ever creating new forms of expressing itself."

What the new order of things was to be in the spiritual life could be learned, Father Hecker held, by observing men's strivings after natural good. The tendencies which shape men's efforts to secure happiness in this world, in so far as they are innocent, indicated to him what choice of means should be made to propagate the knowledge and love of God. According to this, the most successful worker for a people's sanctification will be kindred to them by conviction and by sympathy in all that concerns their political and social life. Men's aspirations in the natural order point out the highway of God's representatives. As these aspirations change from era to era, so do the main lines of religious effort change, the highways of one age becoming the byways of another. It is true that no method for the elevation of human nature to divine union, which the Church has sanctioned, ever becomes quite obsolete, but the merest glance at the differences between the spiritual characteristics of the martyrs, the hermits, the monks, the friars, shows that one form of the Christian virtues succeeds another in general possession of men's souls. The new spirit, without crowding the old one off its beaten track, follows men to the new ways whither the providence of God in the natural order has led them. "First the natural man," says St. Paul, "and then the spiritual." Different types of spirituality are brought forward by Almighty God to

290

sanctify men in new conditions of life. Among the foremost of these are religious communities of men and women. Hence their duty to adjust themselves, as far as faith and discipline permit, to the circumstances of the times. The power of a religious community for good will be measured by its ability to elevate the natural to the supernatural without shocking it or thwarting it.

Now, every one knows that this age differs materially from past ones. It differs by a wider spread of education and an uncontrollable longing after liberty, civil, political, and personal. Father Hecker was penetrated with the belief that the intelligence and liberty, whose well-ordered enjoyment he had witnessed in America, and which he loved so deeply himself, were divine invitations to the apostolate of the Holy Spirit. He was profoundly impressed with the certainty of the development, the extension, and the permanence of these political and social changes; and he knew that they demanded of men a personal independence of character far in advance of previous generations. And he knew, also, that for the sanctification of such men the aids of religion, though not changed in themselves, must be applied in a different spirit. Discipline and uniformity, though never to be dispensed with, must yield the first places to more interior virtues. The dominant influence must be docility to the guidance of the Holy Spirit dwelling within every regenerate soul. Applying this, towards the end of his life, to religious communities, Father Hecker wrote: "The controlling thought of my mind for many years has been that a body of free men who love God with all their might, and yet know how to cling together, could conquer this modern world of ours." The sentence may be taken as a brief description of the Paulist community as he would have it. And it is easily seen why free men loving God with all their hearts are suited to conquer this modern world; because men are determined to be free.

The following extracts from notes, letters, and diaries more fully develop this idea:

"A new religious order is an evidence and expression of an uncommon or special grace given to a certain number of souls, so that they may be sanctified by the practice of particular virtues to meet the special needs of their epoch, and in this way to renew the spiritual life of the members of the Church and to extend her fold. A new community is this, or it has no reason for its existence. The means to accomplish its special work are both new and old. It should lay stress on the new, and not despise but also make use of the old. 'The wise householder bringeth forth from his treasury *new* things and old.'"

"The true Paulist is a religious man entirely dependent on God for his spiritual life; he lives in community for the greater security of his own salvation and perfection, and to meet more efficiently the pressing needs of the Church and of humanity in his day."

"The Church always finds in her wonderful fecundity wherewith to supply the new wants which arise in every distinct epoch of society."

"A new religious community, unless its activity is directed chiefly to supplying the special needs of its time, wears itself out at the expense of its true mission and will decline and fail."

"We must realize the necessity of more explicitly bringing out our ideal if we would give a sufficient motive for our students and members, keep them in the community, bring about unity of action, and accomplish the good which the Holy Spirit demands at our hands. A Paulist, as a distinct species of a religious man, is one who is alive to the pressing needs of the Church at the present time, and feels called to labor specially with the means fitted to supply them. And what a member of another religious community might do from that divine guidance which is external, the Paulist does from the promptings of the indwelling Holy Spirit."

"A Paulist is a Christian man who aims at a Christian perfection consistent with his natural characteristics and the type of civilization of his country."

"So far as it is compatible with faith and piety, I am for accepting the American civilization with its usages and customs; leaving aside other reasons, it is the only way by which Catholicity can become the religion of our people. The character and spirit of our people, and their institutions, must find themselves at home in our Church in the way those of other nations have done; and it is on this basis alone that the Catholic religion can make progress in our country."

"What we need to-day is men whose spirit is that of the early martyrs. We shall get them in proportion as Catholics cultivate a spirit of independence and personal conviction. The highest development of religion in the soul is when it is assisted by free contemplation of the ultimate causes of things. Intelligence and liberty are the human environments most favorable to the deepening of personal conviction of religious truth, and obedience to the interior movements of an enlightened conscience. To a well-ordered mind the question of the hour is how the soul which aspires to the supernatural life shall utilize the advantages of liberty and intelligence."

" The form of government of the United States is preferable to Catholics above other forms. It is more favorable than others to the practice of those virtues which are the necessary conditions of the development of the religious life of man. This government leaves men a larger margin for liberty of action, and hence for co-operation with the guidance of the Holy Spirit, than any other government under the sun. With these popular institutions men enjoy greater liberty in working out their true destiny. The Catholic Church will, therefore, flourish all the more in this republican country in proportion as her representatives keep, in their civil life, to the lines of their republicanism."

" The two poles of the Paulist character are : first, personal perfection. He must respond to the principles of perfection as laid down by spiritual writers. The backbone of a religious community is the desire for personal perfection actuating its members. The desire for personal perfection is the foundation stone of a religious community ; when this fails, it crumbles to pieces; when this ceases to be the dominant desire, the community is tottering. Missionary works, parochial work, etc., are and must be made subordinate to personal perfection. These works must be done in view of personal perfection. The main purpose of each Paulist must be the attainment of personal perfection by the practice of those virtues without which it cannot be secured—mortification, self-denial, detachment, and the like. By the use of these means the grace of God makes the soul perfect. The perfect soul is one which is guided instinctively by the indwelling Holy Spirit. To attain to this is the end always to be aimed at in the practice of the virtues just named. Second, zeal for souls ; to labor for the conversion of the country to the Catholic faith by apostolic work. Parish work is a part, an integral part, of Paulist work, but not its principal or chief work and parish work should be done so as to form a part of the main aim, the conversion of the non-Catholic people of the country. In this manner we can labor to raise the standard of Catholic life here and throughout the world as a means of the general triumph of the Catholic faith."

"I do not think that the principal characteristic of our Fathers and of our life should be poverty or obedience or any other special and secondary virtue, or even a cardinal virtue, but zeal for apostolic works. Our vocation is apostolic—conversion of souls to the faith, of sinners to repentance, giving missions, defence of the Christian religion by conferences, lectures, sermons, the pen, the press, and the like works; and in the interior, to propagate among men a higher and more spiritual life. To supply the special element the age and each country demands, this is the peculiar work of religious communities: this their field. It is a fatal mistake when religious attempt to do the ordinary work of the Church. Let religious practise prayer and study; there will always be enough of the work to which they are called."

"Are the Paulists Religious? Yes, and no. Yes, of their age. No, of the past; the words in neither case being taken in an exclusive meaning."

"As regards the growth of the Paulist, he must develop in an apostolic vocation—that is, in apostolic works, Catholic, universal; not in works which confine his life's energies to a locality. He must do the work of the Church. The work of the Church, as Church, is to render her note of universality more and more conspicuous—to render it sensible, palpable. This is the spirit of the Church in our country."

The following refers to the second trait of the character above given: "A Paulist is to emphasize individuality; that is, to make individual liberty an essential element in every judgment that touches the life and welfare of the community and that of its members. Those who emphasize the community element are inclined to look upon this as a dangerous and impracticable experiment."

"*Individuality is an integral and conspicuous element in the life of the Paulist.* This must be felt. One of the natural signs of the true Paulist is that he would prefer to suffer from the excesses of liberty rather than from the arbitrary actions of tyranny."

"The individuality of a man cannot be too strong or his liberty too great when he is guided by the Spirit of God. But when one is easily influenced from below rather than from above, it is an evidence of the spirit of pride and that of the flesh, and not 'the liberty of the glory of the children of God.' "

What follows touches the relation between the personal and common life :

"Many other communities lay the main stress on community life as the chief element, giving it control as far as is consistent with fundamental individual right; the Paulists, on the contrary, give the element of individuality the first place and put it in control as far as is consistent with the common life."

"The spirit of the age has a tendency to run into extreme individuality, into eccentricity, license, revolution. But the typical life shows how individuality is consistent with community life. This is the aim of the United States in the political order, an aim and tendency which we have to guide, and not to check or sacrifice."

"The element of individuality is taken into account in the Paulist *essentially*, integrally, practically. But when it comes into conflict with the common right, the individual must yield to the community : the common life outranks the individual life in case of conflict. But the individual life should be regarded as sacred and never be effaced. How this is to operate in particular cases belongs, where it is not a matter of rule, to the virtue of prudence to decide."

"When the personality of the individual comes into conflict with the life of the community, the personal side must not be sacrificed, but made to yield to the common. In case of conflict, as before said, common life and interests outrank personal life and interests. It may be asked how, in the ordinary regulation and government of a community of this kind, the individual and common elements are to be made to harmonize ? The answer is, that the one at the head of affairs must be a true Paulist—that is to say, keenly sensitive of personal rights as well as appreciative of such as are common : where the question is not a point of rule, its decision is dependent on the practical sagacity and prudence of the superior more than on any minute regulations which can be given. He who interprets the acts of legitimate authority as an attack on his personal liberty, is as far out of the way as he who looks upon the exercise of reason as an attack on authority."

"How about persons of dull minds or of little spiritual ambition coming into the use of this freedom? First, no such person should be allowed to enter into the community: such persons should be excluded. Second, a full-fledged Paulist should have passed a long enough novitiate to have acquired the special virtues which are necessary for his vocation. Absence of supernatural light is the cause why a man is not fit to be a Paulist, for he cannot understand rightly or appreciate the value of the liberties he enjoys. He either is or he becomes a turbulent element in the community."

"A Paulist, seeing that he has so much individuality, should have a strong, nay, a very strong attrait for community life; he should be fond of the Fathers' company, prefer them and their society when seeking proper recreation, feel the house to be his *home* and the community and its surroundings very dear to him; in the routine of the day all the community exercises and labors are, in his judgment, of paramount obligation and importance.

"The civil and political state of things of our age, particularly in the United States, fosters the individual life. But it should do so without weakening the community life: this is true individualism. The problem is to make the synthesis. The joint product is the Paulist."

"A Paulist should cultivate personal freedom without detriment to the community spirit; and, *vice versa*, the community spirit should not be allowed to be detrimental to personal freedom. But when the individual life runs into eccentricity, license, and revolution, that is a violation and sacrifice of the community life."

"The duty of the Paulist Superior is to elicit the spontaneous zeal of the Fathers and to further it with his authority. For lack of one's own initiative that of another may be used, and herein the Superior offers a constant help. But the centre of action is individual, is in the soul moved by the Holy Ghost; not in the Superior of the community or in the authorities of the Church. And if he be moved by the Holy Spirit, he will be most obedient to his superior; and he will not only be submissive to the authority of the Church, but careful to follow out her spirit."

In explaining the routine of daily life Father Hecker said: "The member of a community who does not make the common exercises [of religion] his first care is derelict of his duty. A common exercise should be preferred to all other devotional prac-

tices or occupations whatever; as far as possible all other exercises ought to be made subordinate to common ones, which
should never be omitted without permission of the superior."

Father Hecker was once asked : " Which would you prefer : to
have a rule and manner of life adapted to a large number of men,
embracing many of a uniform type, men good enough for average
work, intended to include and seeking to retain persons of medi-
ocre spirit, and having a dim understanding of our peculiar institute ? or would you prefer the rule to be made only for a select
body, composed of such men as ——— and ———, and the like ? ' "
[Answer :] "I should prefer the rule to be made for the smaller
and more select body of men. Religious vocations are not common, but special. It is a fatal mistake for religious to take the
place of secular priests."

No one can be misled by what he has read in the foregoing
pages into the notion that Father Hecker had any other aim than
the entire consecration of liberty and intelligence to the influence
of the Holy Spirit. To know Father Hecker well was to be more
deeply impressed with his longing for the reign of the Spirit of God
in men's souls than even with his love of human liberty. In his
esteem the worth of the latter was altogether in proportion to its
aptitude for the former. His love of liberty was that of a means
to an end—the perfect oblation of the inner man to God. He
aimed at individuality because of his belief in the action of the
Holy Ghost in the individual soul. Such action, he was quick to
maintain, is given to every Christian, but it is to be looked for in
a high degree in those who are called by a special vocation to
assist independent characters to find the spirit of God within
them ; or, if already known, to obey His direction implicitly.
Paulists after Father Hecker's heart would be men whom experience and study had rendered fit instruments for disseminating the
knowledge of the ways of God the Holy Ghost in men's hearts ;
for instructing the faithful how to distinguish the voice of God
in the soul from the vagaries of the imagination or the emotions
of passion, and able to stimulate a ready and generous response
to every call of God from within.

It is because of this indwelling of the Holy Spirit in every
regenerate soul that Father Hecker so vigorously maintained that
the freedom of the individual is a golden opportunity for the
Catholic apostolate, according to the text " Where the Spirit of

the Lord is, there is liberty." Freedom, he affirmed, was in absolute consonance with Catholic doctrine. But he furthermore
insisted that it has become the world-wide aspiration of men by
interposition of Divine Providence and with a view to their higher
sanctification ; and however grossly abused, it is yet a direct
suggestion to an apostolate whose prospects are in the highest
degree promising. And this is the answer to the question
which reasonable persons may well ask, namely: Why should
the new institution differ so radically from the old ones, which
were certainly works of God ? Because the change of men's
lives in the entire secular and natural order is in the direction
of personal liberty and independence, and this change is a radical one. "The Eternal-Absolute is ever creating new forms of
expressing itself." If, indeed, men's aspirations for liberty and
intelligence be all from the powers of darkness, then let every
longing for freedom be repressed and condemned, crushed by
authority in the state, anathematized by the Church. But if
men are yearning to be free, however blindly, because God
by their freedom would make them holier, then let us hail the
new order as a blessing ; and let those who love freedom and
are worthy of it use its privileges to advance themselves and
their brethren nearer to immediate union with the Holy Spirit.

It has been seen that the important question whether the
end of the new community would be better attained with the
usual religious vows or without them was decided in the negative. They were not definitely rejected in the beginning ; but
starting without them, the Fathers were willing to allow experience to show whether or not they should be resumed. The
lapse of time but confirmed the view that the voluntary agreement
and the bond of fraternal charity were, under the circumstances,
preferable as securities for stability and incentives to holiness.

There can be little doubt that Father Hecker's ideas on
this feature of the religious state had been greatly modified between the writing of the *Questions of the Soul* and the end of
the struggle in Rome. Much is said in that book of community life in the Catholic Church, and generally as rendered stable
and its spirit of sacrifice made complete by the vows; and in
the statement given in Rome to his five chosen advisers, he
says that one reason for writing the volume named was to induce young men to enter the religious orders as the only means
of perfection—meaning orders under vows. But when he was

released from his own obligations and was confronted with the choice of means for following his vocation, the horizon broadened away until he could see beyond the institutions and traditions in which he had lived since entering the novitiate at St. Trond. His ideas of perfection in its relation to states of life underwent a change. Therefore he said, Let us wait for the unmistakable will of God before we bind ourselves with vows amidst a free people. He never depreciated the evident value of these obligations; indeed, he seldom was heard to speak of them. But he knew from close observation the truth of the words of the Jesuit Avancinus :

"The net (St. Matthew xiii. 44) is the Catholic Church, or, to take a narrower view, it means the station in which you are placed. As in a net all kinds of fish are to be found, so in your position, as in all others, there are good and bad Christians. . . . Should yours be a sacred calling, you are not, on that account, either the better or the more secure ; your sanctity and your salvation depend on yourself, not on your calling." (*Meditations*, Fourteenth Friday after Pentecost.)

It never entered into the minds of the Fathers to question the doctrine and practice of the Church concerning vows. But personal experience proves the lesson of history, that what religion needs is not so much holy states of life as holy men and women.

Looking back into the past, Father Hecker saw St. Philip Neri, to whom he had a great devotion and for whose spiritual doctrine he had a high admiration. The following is from an exponent of that doctrine, and is much in point:

"Although our Fathers and lay brothers [Oratorians] make no vow of obedience, as do religious, they are, nevertheless, no way inferior in the perfection of this virtue to those who profess it in the cloister with solemn vows. They supply the want of vows with love, with voluntary promptitude, and perfection in obeying every wish of the superior. And it is a thing for which we must indeed thank God, that without the obligation of obeying under pain of sin, without fear of restraint or other punishment (except that of expulsion in case of contumacy), all the subjects are prompt in this obedience, even in things most humiliating and severe, according to the terms of the rule. All take pleasure in meeting the wishes of the superior, etc." (*The Excellences of the Oratory of St. Philip Neri*, p. 136. London: Burns & Oates.)

Father Hecker did not dream that by relinquishing the vows
he and his companions in the Paulist community had cast away
a single incentive to virtue capable of moving such men as they,
or had even failed to secure any of the insignia adorning the
great host of men and women in the Catholic Church whose
entire being has been given up to the divine service. "The true
Paulist," said he once, "should be fit and ready to take the
solemn vows at any moment." He felt strongly the truth of the
following words of the Jesuit Lallemant:

> "A desire and hunger after our perfection, a determined will
> to be constantly tending towards it with all our strength—let this
> be always our chief object and our greatest care. Let us bear in
> mind that this care is more of the essence of religion [*i.e.*, of a
> religious order] than vows themselves; for it is on this that our
> whole spiritual progress depends. Herein consists the difference
> between true religious and those who are so only in appearance
> and in the sight of men. Without this care to advance in per-
> fection the religious state does not secure our salvation; but
> nothing is more common than to deceive ourselves on this point."
> (*The Spiritual Doctrine of Father Louis Lallemant, S.J.*, p. 111.
> New York: Sadlier & Co.)

With regard to stability, men of stable character need no
vow to guarantee adherence to a divine vocation, and men of
feeble character may indeed vow themselves into an outward
stability, but it is of little fruit to themselves personally, and
their irremovability is often of infinite distress to their superiors and brethren. The episcopate is the one religious order
founded by Our Lord, and its members are in the highest state
of evangelical perfection; yet they are neither required nor advised
to take the oaths or vows of religious orders.

Neither Father Hecker nor any of his associates had the least
aversion to the vows. On the contrary, they had lived con-
tentedly under them for many of their most active years, and it
will be remembered of Father Hecker that he never found them
irksome, had never known a temptation against them.

The question which arose was a choice between two kinds
of community, the one fast bound by external obligations to the
Church in the form of vows, placing the members in a relation of
peculiar strictness to the Canon Law; or another kind, in which
the members trusted wholly to the strength of Divine grace, and
their own conscious purpose never to give up the fight for per-

fection ; which of these states would better facilitate the action of the Holy Spirit in the present Providence of God; and which of them would tend to produce a type of character fitted to evangelize a nation of independent and self-reliant men and women ? The free community was chosen.

No doubt this involved some risk of criticism, particularly in the beginning, for it was a wonder to many that men should organize for a life-long endeavor after perfection and not swear to it, especially as none of the free communities existing in Europe had houses in America, for the Sulpitians belong to the secular clergy. And there was also danger of unworthy subjects creeping in under favor of a freedom they were unfit to enjoy. For it may be reproached against us that we are apt to be victimized by men ruled by caprice, indulging in extravagant schemes or deluded by wandering fancies ; and also by superiors who would let everybody do as he pleased. No doubt such dangers are to be guarded against. But vowed communities do not claim to be free from difficulties. No state of life and no organization claims to be so perfect as totally to prevent abuse of power on the part of superiors or caprice and sloth on the part of members.

Both kinds of organized religious life have their difficulties : the one, the martinet superior and the routine subject ; the other, the capricious subject and the lax superior. In one kind the bond of union as well as the stimulus of endeavor is mainly obedience, fraternal charity assisting ; in the other it is mainly fraternal charity, obedience assisting ; each has to overcome obstacles peculiar to itself.

What has been said in this chapter, besides serving to exhibit Father Hecker's principles as a founder, will be, we trust, a sufficient answer to the silly delusion which the Paulists have encountered in some quarters, that their society tolerates a soft life and supposes in its members no high vocation to perfection ; or that the voluntary principle allows them a personal choice in regard to the devotional exercises, permitting them to attend or not attend this or that meditation or devotion laid down in the rule, as " the spirit moves them " This is as plain an error as another one which had much currency for years and which is not yet everywhere corrected : that the Paulist community was open to converts alone and received none others.

CHAPTER XXVII.

FATHER HECKER'S SPIRITUAL DOCTRINE.

HAVING given in the preceding chapter Father Hecker's principles of the religious life in community, a more general view of his spiritual doctrine, as well as of his method of the direction of souls, naturally follows. And here we are embarrassed by the amount of matter to choose from ; for as he was always talking about spiritual doctrine to whomsoever he could get to listen, so in his published writings, in his letters to intimate friends, and in his notes and memoranda, we have found enough falling under the heading of this chapter to fill a volume. Let us hope for its publication some day.

It need hardly be said that Father Hecker did not claim to have any new doctrine ; there can be none, and he knew it well. Every generation since Christ has had His entire revelation. Development is the word which touches the outer margin of all possible adaptation of Christian principles to the changing conditions of humanity. But in the transmission of these principles from master to disciple, in practically assisting in their use by public instruction, or by private advice, or by choice of devotional and ascetical exercises, there is as great a variety of method as of temperament among races, and even among individuals ; and there are broadly marked differences which are conterminous with providential eras of history. This was a truth which Father Hecker, in common with all discerning minds, took carefully into account.

His fundamental principle of Christian perfection may be termed a view of the Catholic doctrine of divine grace suited to the aspirations of our times. By divine grace the love of God is diffused in our hearts ; the Holy Spirit takes up his abode there and makes us children of the Heavenly Father, and brethren of Jesus Christ the Divine Son. The state of grace is thus an immediate union of the soul with the Holy Trinity, its Creator, . Mediator, and Sanctifier. To secure this union and render it more and more conscious was Father Hecker's ceaseless endeavor through life, both for himself and for those who fell under his influence, whether in cleansing the soul of all hindrances of sin and imperfection, or advancing it deeper and deeper into the divine life by prayer and the sacraments.

His doctrine of Christian perfection might be formulated as a profession of faith: I believe in God the *Father* Almighty; I believe in Jesus Christ the Only Begotten *Son* of the Father; I believe in the Holy Ghost the *Life Giver*, the spirit of adoption by whom I am enabled to say to the Father, *My Father*, and to the Son, *My Brother*.

He wished that men generally should be made aware of the immediate nature of this union of the soul with God, and that they should become more and more personally conscious of it. He would bring this about without the intervention of other persons or other methods than the divinely constituted ones accessible to all in the priesthood and sacraments. It was the development of the supernatural, heavenly, divine life of the regenerate man, born again of the Holy Ghost, that Father Hecker made the end of all he said and all he did in leading souls; and he maintained that to partake of this life which is " the light of men," many souls needed little interference on the part of others, and that in every case the utmost care should be taken lest the soul should mingle human influences, even the holiest, in undue proportion with those which were strictly divine.

" Go to God," he wrote to one asking advice, "go entirely to God, go integrally to God; behold, that is sincerity, complete, perfect sincerity. Do that, and make it a complete, continuous act, and you need no help from me or any creature. I wish to provoke you to do it. That is my whole aim and desire. Just in proportion as we harbor pride, vanity, self-love—in a word, self-hood—just so far we fail in integrally resigning ourselves to God. Were we wholly resigned to God He would change all in us that is in discord with Him, and prepare our souls for union with Him, making us one with Himself. God longs for our souls greatly more than our souls can long for Him. Such is God's thirst for love that He made all creatures to love Him, and to have no rest until they love Him supremely. If my words are not to your soul God's words and voice, pay no heed to them. If they are, hesitate not a moment to obey. If they humble you to the dust, what a blessing! He that is humbled shall be exalted."

" Peace is gained by a wise inaction, and strength by integral resignation to God, who will do all, and more than we, with the boldest imagination, can fancy or desire."

"May you see God in all, through all, and above all. May the Divine transcendence and the Divine immanence be the two poles of your life."

The natural faculties of the understanding and will, whose integrity Father Hecker so much valued, were to be established in a new life infinitely above their native reach, glorified with divine life, their activity directed to the knowledge of things not even dreamed of before, and endowed with a divine gift of loving. In this state the Holy Spirit communicates to the human faculties force to accomplish intellectual and moral feats which naturally can be accomplished by God alone. This is called by theologians supernatural infused virtue, and is rooted in Faith, Hope, and Love, is made efficacious by spiritual gifts of wisdom and understanding, and knowledge and counsel, and other gifts and forces, the conscious and daily possession of which the Christian is entitled to hope for and strive after, and finally to obtain and enjoy in this life.

That this union is a personal relation, and that it should be a distinctly conscious one on the soul's part, all will admit who think but a moment of the infinite, loving activity of the Spirit of God, and the natural and supernatural receptivity of the spirit of man. Although not even the smallest germ of the supernatural life is found in nature, yet the soul of man ceaselessly, if blindly, yearns after its possession. Once possessed, the life of God blends into our own, mingles with it and is one with it, impregnating it as magnetism does the iron of the lodestone, till the divine qualities, without suppressing nature, entirely possess it, and assert for it and over it the Divine individuality. "Now I live, yet not I, but Christ liveth in me." An author much admired by Father Hecker thus describes the effects produced in the soul by supernatural faith, and hope, and love :

"These virtues are called and in reality are *Divine* virtues. They are called thus not because they are related to God in general, but because *they unite us in a divine manner with God*, have Him for their immediate motive, and can be produced in us only by a communication of the Divine nature. . . . For the life that the children of God lead here upon earth must be of the same kind as the life that awaits them in heaven." (Scheeben's *Glories of Divine Grace*, p. 222 ; Benziger Bros.)

To partake thus of the inner life of God was Father Hecker's one spiritual ambition, and to help others to it his one motive for dealing with men. He was ever insisting upon the closeness of the divine union, and that it is our life brought into actual touch with God, whose supreme and essential activity must, by a law of its own existence, make itself felt, dominate as far as permitted the entire activity of the soul, and win more and more upon its life till all is won. Then are fulfilled the Apostle's words: " But we all beholding the glory of the Lord *with open face* are transformed into the same image from glory to glory, as by the Spirit of the Lord " (II. Cor. iii. 18).

Here are some of Father Hecker's words, printed but a year or two before his death, which treat not only of the interior life in general, but in particular of its relation to the outer action of God on the soul through the divine organism of the Church :

"St. Thomas Aquinas attributes the absence of spiritual joy mainly to neglect of consciousness of the inner life. ' During this life,' he says (*Opuscula de Beatitudine*, cap. iii.), 'we should continually rejoice in God, as something perfectly fitting, in all our actions and for all our actions, in all our gifts and for all our gifts. It is, as Isaias declares, that we may particularly enjoy him that the Son of God has been given to us. What blindness and what gross stupidity for many who are always seeking God, always sighing for Him, frequently desiring Him, daily knocking and clamoring at the door for God by prayer, while they themselves are all the time, as the apostle says, temples of the living God, and God truly dwelling within them; while all the time their souls are the abiding-place of God, wherein He continually reposes! Who but a fool would look for something out of doors which he knows he has within? What is the good of anything which is always to be sought and never found, and who can be strengthened with food ever craved but never tasted? Thus passes away the life of many a good man, always searching and never finding God, and it is for this reason that his actions are imperfect.'

"A man with such a doctrine must cultivate mainly the interior life. His answer to the question, What is the relation between the inner and the outer action of God upon my soul? is that God uses the outer for the sake of the inner life.

"There seems to be little danger nowadays of our losing sight of the Divine authority and the Divine action in the government of the Church, and in the aids of religion conveyed through the external order of the sacraments. Yet it is only after fully appreciating the life of God within us that we learn to prize fittingly the action of God in His external Providence. Such is the plain teaching of St. Thomas in the extract above given.

"By fully assimilating this doctrine one comes to aim steadily at securing a more and more direct communion with God. Thus he does not seek merely for an external life in an external society, or become totally absorbed in external observances; but he seeks the invisible God *through* the visible Church, for she is the body of Christ the Son of God.

"Once a man's hand is safe on the altar his eye and voice are lifted to God.

"It is not to keep up a strained outlook for times and moments of the interior visitations, but to wait calmly for the actual movements of the Divine Spirit; to rely mainly upon it and not solely upon what leads to it, or communicates it, or guarantees its genuine presence by necessary external tests and symbols.

"Not an anxious search, least of all a craving for extraordinary lights; but a constant readiness to perceive the Divine guidance in the secret ways of the soul, and then to act with decision and a noble and generous courage—this is true wisdom.

"The Holy Spirit is thus the inspiration of the inner life of the regenerate man, and in that life is his Superior and Director. That His guidance may become more and more immediate in an interior life, and the soul's obedience more and more instinctive, is the object of the whole external order of the Church, including the sacramental system.

"Says Father Lallemant (*Spiritual Doctrine*, 3d principle, chap. i. art. 1): 'All creatures that are in the world, the whole order of nature as well as that of grace, and all the leadings of Providence, have been so disposed as to remove from our souls whatever is contrary to God.'"

What follows has been culled from notes and memoranda:

"When authority and liberty are intelligently understood, when both aim at the same end, then the universal reign of

God's authority in the Church will be near and the kingdom of God be established universally."

"The whoie future of the human race depends on bringing the individual soul more completely and perfectly under the sway of the Holy Spirit."

"What society most needs to-day is the baptism of the Holy Spirit."

"That soul is perfect which is guided habitually by the instinct of the Holy Spirit."

"The aim of Christian perfection is the guidance of the soul by the indwelling Holy Spirit. This is attained, ordinarily, first by bringing whatever is inordinate in our animal propensities under the control of the dictates of reason by the practice of mortification and self-denial; for it is a self-evident principle that a rational being ought to be master of his animal appetites. And second, by bringing the dictates of reason under the control and inspiration of the Holy Spirit by recollection, and by fidelity and docility to its movements."

"To attain to the spiritual estate of the conscious guidance of the indwelling Holy Spirit, the practice of asceticism and of the natural and Christian moral virtues are the preparatory means."

"To rise before the light appears, is vain; to hinder the soul from rising when it does appear, is oppression. In the first place, the soul is exposed to delusions; in the second, it is subjected to arbitrary human authority. The former opens the door to all sorts of extravagances and heresies; the latter breeds a spirit of servility and bondage."

"To reach that stage of the spiritual life which is the consciousness of the indwelling and guidance of the Holy Spirit some souls need the practice of asceticism more than others, these latter being more advanced by the practice of the Christian virtues. Others, again, need the strenuous practice of both of these means of advancement until the close of their lives. And there is another class which reaches this degree of spiritual growth sooner and with less difficulty than the generality of souls."

"Whenever the guidance of the Holy Spirit is sufficiently recognized, then the practice of the virtues immediately related to this action and proper to increase it in the soul are to be recommended, such as recollection, purity of heart, docility and fidelity to the inner voice, and the like."

"It should ever be kept in view that the practice of the virtues is not only for their own sake and to obtain merit, but mainly in order to remove all obstacles in the way of the guidance of the Holy Spirit, and to assist the soul in following His operations with docility."

"Obedience in its spiritual aspect divests one of self-will and makes him prompt to submit to the will of God alone. Viewed as an act of justice, obedience is the payment of due service to one's superior, who holds his office by appointment of God."

"The essential mistake of the transcendentalists is the taking for their guide the instincts of the soul instead of the inspirations of the Holy Spirit. They are moved by the natural instincts of human beings instead of the instinct of the Holy Ghost. But true spiritual direction consists in discovering the obstacles in the way of the Divine guidance, in aiding and encouraging the penitent to remove them, and in teaching how the interior movements of the Holy Spirit may be recognized, as well as in stimulating the soul to fidelity and docility to His movements."

"The director is not to take the place of the Holy Ghost in the soul, but to assist His growth in the soul as its primary and supreme guide."

"The primary worker of the soul's sanctification is the Holy Spirit acting interiorly; the work of the director is secondary and subordinate. To overlook this fundamental truth in the spiritual life is a great mistake, whether it be on the part of the director or the one under direction."

The great obstacle to the prevalent use of this privilege of divine interior direction is lack of practical realization of its existence by good Christians. And this want of faith is met with almost as much among teachers as among learners, resulting in too great a mingling of the human element in the guidance of souls. What is known as over direction is to be attributed, as Father Hecker was persuaded, to confessors leading souls by self-chosen ways, or laboriously working them along the road to perfection by artificial processes, souls whom the Holy Spirit has not made ready for more than the beginning of the spiritual life. This is like pressing wine out of unripe grapes. Another practice which Father Hecker often deprecated was the binding of free and generous souls with all sorts of obligations in the way of devotional exercises. This is forcing athletes to go on crutches. The excuse for it all is that it really does stagger human belief to accept as a literal matter of fact that God the Holy Ghost personally comes to us with divine grace and gives Himself to us; that He actually and essentially dwells in our souls by grace, and in an unspeakably intimate manner takes charge of our entire being, soul and body, and all our faculties and senses.

"By sanctifying grace," says St. Thomas (p. 1, q. xxxiii. art. 2), "the rational creature is thus perfected, that it may not only use with liberty the created good, but that it may also enjoy the uncreated good; and therefore the invisible sending of the Holy Ghost takes place in the gift of sanctifying grace and the Divine Person Himself is given to us."

It is the soul's higher self, thus in entire union with the Spirit of God, that Father Hecker spent his life in cultivating, both in his own interior and in that of others. He insisted that in the normal condition of things the mainspring of virtue, both natural and supernatural, should be for the regenerate man the instinctive obedience of the individual soul to the voice of the indwelling Holy Spirit.

To what an extent this inner divine guidance has been obscured by more external methods is witnessed by Monsignor Gaume, who places upon the title-page of his learned work on the Holy Spirit the motto "Ignoto Deo"—to the Unknown God!

Objections to this doctrine are made from the point of view of caution. There is danger of exaggeration, it is said; for if in its terms it is plainly Catholic, it may sound Protestant to some ears. And in fact to those whose glances have been ever turned outward for guidance it seems like the delusions of certain classes of Protestants about "change of heart" and "inner light."

"But," says Lallemant (and the reader will thank us for a detailed reply to this difficulty from so venerable an authority), "it is of faith that without the grace of an interior inspiration, in which the guidance of the Holy Spirit consists, we cannot do any good work. The Calvinists would determine everything by their inward spirit, subjecting thereto the Church herself and her decisions. . . . But the guidance which we receive from the Holy Ghost by means of His gifts presupposes the faith and authority of the Church, acknowledges them as its rule, admits nothing which is contrary to them, and aims only at perfecting the exercise of faith and the other virtues. The second objection is, that it seems as if this interior guidance of the Holy Spirit were destructive of the obedience due to superiors. We reply: 1. That as the interior inspiration of grace does not set aside the assent which we give to the articles of faith as they are externally proposed to us, but on the contrary gently disposes the mind to believe; in like manner the guidance which we receive from the gifts of the Holy Spirit, far from interfering with obedience, aids and facilitates the practice of it. 2. That all this interior guidance, and even [private] divine revelations, must always be subordinate to obedience; and in speaking of them this tacit condition is ever implied, that obedience enjoins nothing contrary thereto. . . .

"The third objection is that this interior direction of the Holy Spirit seems to render all deliberation and all counsel useless. For why ask advice of men when the Holy Spirit is Himself our director? We reply that the Holy Spirit teaches us to consult enlightened persons and to follow the advice of others, as He referred St. Paul to Ananias. The fourth objection is made by some who complain that they are not themselves thus led by the Holy Spirit, and that they know nothing of it. To them we reply: 1. That the lights and inspirations of the Holy Spirit, which are necessary in order to do good and avoid evil, are never wanting to them, particularly if they are in a state of grace. 2. That being altogether exterior as they are, and scarcely ever entering into themselves, examining their consciences only very superficially, and looking only to the outward man and the faults which are manifest in the eyes of the world, . . . it is no wonder that they have nothing of the guidance of the Holy Spirit, which is wholly interior. But, first, let them be faithful in following the light which is given them; it will go on always increasing. Secondly, let them clear away the sins and imperfections which, like so many clouds, hide the light from their eyes: they will see more distinctly every day. Thirdly, let them not suffer their exterior senses to rove at will, and be soiled by indulgence; God will then open to them their interior senses. Fourthly, let them never quit their own interior, if it be possible, or let them return as soon as may be; let them give attention to what passes therein, and they will observe the workings of the different spirits by which we are actuated. Fifthly, let them lay bare the whole ground of their heart to their superior or to their spiritual father. A soul which acts with this openness and simplicity can hardly fail of being favored with the direction of the Holy Spirit" (*Spiritual Doctrine*, 4th principle, ch. i. art. 3).

Father Hecker had himself suffered, and that in the earliest

days of his religious life, from want of explicit instruction
about this doctrine. Father Othmann, whom our readers remember as the novice-master at St. Trond, was too spiritual a man to
have been ignorant of its principles. Yet he seemed to think
that either no one would choose it in preference to the method
in more common use, or that he would not find his novices ready
for it. But to Father Hecker it was all-essential. "When I
was not far from being through with my noviceship," he was
heard to say, "I was one day looking over the books in the
library and I came across Lallemant's *Spiritual Doctrine.* Getting
leave to read it, I was overjoyed to find it a full statement of
the principles by which I had been interiorly guided. I said to
Père Othmann : 'Why did you not give me this book when I
first came ? It settles all my difficulties.' But he answered that
it had never once occurred to his mind to do so." Besides the
Scriptures, Lallemant, Surin, Scaramelli's *Directorium Mysticum,*
the ascetical and mystical writings of the contemplatives, such as
Rusbruck, Henry Suso (whose life he carried for years in his
pocket, reading it daily), Tauler, Father Augustine Baker's *Holy
Wisdom* (Sancta Sophia), Blosius, the works of St. Teresa, and
those of St. John of the Cross—these and other such works
formed the literature which aided Father Hecker in the understanding and enjoyment of the guidance of the Holy Spirit.
Lallemant he returned to ever and again, and St. John of the
Cross he never let go at all. It was always with him, always
read with renewed joy, and its wonderful lessons of divine wisdom, expressed as they are with the scientific accuracy of a
trained theologian and the unction of a saint, were to Father
Hecker a pledge of security for his own state of soul and a
source of inspiration in dealing with others.

To the ordinary observer a knowledge of the men and
women of to-day does not give rise to much hope of the widespread use of this spirituality. But Father Hecker thought otherwise. He ever insisted that it must come into general preference among the leading minds of Christendom ; for independence
of character calls for such a spirituality, and that independence is
by God's providence the characteristic trait of the best men and
women of our times. God must mean to sanctify us in the way
He has placed us in the natural order. He believed that the
Holy Spirit would soon be poured out in an abundant dispensation of His heavenly gifts, and that such a renewal of men's

souls was the only salvation of society. Some may think that he was over-sanguine; many will not interest themselves in such "high" matters at all. But some of the wisest men in the Church are of his mind, notably Cardinal Manning. And the signs of the times, if interrogated with regard to the problem of man's eternal destiny, give no other answer than the promise of a new era in which the Holy Ghost shall reign in men's souls and in their lives with a supremacy peculiar to this age.

The following extract from *The Church and the Age*, a compilation of Father Hecker's later essays, shows his estimate of the form of spirituality we have been discussing, as bearing upon the regeneration of society in general:

"The whole aim of the science of Christian perfection is to instruct men how to remove the hindrances in the way of the action of the Holy Spirit, and how to cultivate those virtues which are most favorable to His solicitations and inspirations. Thus the sum of spiritual life consists in observing and yielding to the movements of the Spirit of God in our soul, employing for this purpose all the exercises of prayer, spiritual reading, the practice of virtues, and good works.

"That divine action which is the immediate and principal cause of the salvation and perfection of the soul, claims by right the soul's direct and main attention. From this source within the soul there will gradually come to birth the consciousness of the indwelling presence of the Holy Spirit, out of which will spring a force surpassing all human strength, a courage higher than all human heroism, a sense of dignity excelling all human greatness. The light the age requires for its renewal can come only from the same source. The renewal of the age depends on the renewal of religion. The renewal of religion depends on a greater effusion of the creative and renewing power of the Holy Spirit. The greater effusion of the Holy Spirit depends on the giving of increased attention to His movements and inspirations in the soul. The radical and adequate remedy for all the evils of our age, and the source of all true progress, consist in increased attention and fidelity to the action of the Holy Spirit in the soul. 'Thou shalt send forth Thy spirit and they shall be created: and Thou shalt renew the face of the earth.'"

Lallemant's answer to the difficulty of excess of personal

liberty in this method has been already given. Father Hecker's own is as follows:

" The enlargement of the [interior] field of action for the soul, without a true knowledge of the end and scope of the external authority of the Church, would only open the door to delusions, errors, and heresies of every description, and would be in effect only another form of Protestantism. But, on the other hand, the exclusive view of the external authority of the Church, without a proper understanding of the nature and work of the Holy Spirit in the soul, would render the practice of religion formal, obedience servile, and the Church sterile.

" The solution of the difficulty is as follows: The action of the Holy Spirit embodied visibly in the authority of the Church, and the action of the Holy Spirit dwelling invisibly in the soul form one inseparable synthesis; and he who has not a clear conception of this two-fold action of the Holy Spirit is in danger of running into one or the other, and sometimes into both, of these extremes, either of which is destructive of the end of the Church. The Holy Spirit, in the external authority of the Church, acts as the infallible interpreter and criterion of divine revelation. The Holy Spirit in the soul acts as the divine Life-giver and Sanctifier. It is of the highest importance that these two distinct offices of the Holy Spirit should not be confounded.

" The increased action of the Holy Spirit, with a more vigorous co-operation on the part of the faithful, which is in process of realization, will elevate the human personality to an intensity of force and grandeur productive of a new era to the Church and to society—an era difficult for the imagination to grasp, and still more difficult to describe in words, unless we have recourse to the prophetic language of the inspired Scriptures."

" The way out of our present difficulties," said Father Hecker, speaking of the conflicts of religion in Europe, " is to revert to a spirituality which is freer than that which Providence assigned as the counteraction of Protestantism in the sixteenth century—to a spirituality which is, and ever has been, the normal one of the Christian inner life. That era accentuated obedience, this accentuates no particular moral virtue, but rather presses the soul back upon Faith and Hope and Love as the springs of life, and makes the distinctive virtue fidelity to the guidance of the

Holy Spirit, impelling the Christian to that one of the moral virtues which is most suitable to his nature and to the requirements of his state of life, and other environments."

But from what has been said it must not be inferred that Father Hecker thought it safe to be without spiritual counsel, above all when the soul seemed led in extraordinary ways. He firmly believed in the necessity of direction, and that in the sense intended by spiritual writers generally. In practice he himself always consulted men of experience and piety. We have seen how he sought advice, and was aided by it at every crisis of his life. But he did not accept all that is said by some writers about the surrender of the soul to one's father confessor. He thought that confession was often too closely allied with direction, and he was convinced that many souls could profit by less introspection in search of sin, and more in search of natural and supernatural movements to virtue. He condemned over-direction, and thought that there was a good deal of it. He thought that there were cases in which spontaneity of effort was too high a price to pay for even the merit of obedience. His sentiment is well expressed by St. John of the Cross in the ninth chapter of *The Ascent of Mount Carmel :*

"Spiritual directors are not the chief workers, but rather the Holy Ghost; they are mere instruments, only to guide souls by the rule of faith and the law of God according to the spirit which God gives to each. Their object, therefore, should be not to guide souls by a way of their own, suitable to themselves; but to ascertain, if they can, the way which God Himself is guiding them."

Leave much to God's secret ways, was one of Father Hecker's principles. "When hearing some confessions on the missions," he once said, "and when about to give absolution, I used to say, in my heart, to the penitent, Well, no doubt God means to save you, you poor fellow, or He wouldn't give you the grace to make this mission. But just how He will do it, considering your bad habits, I can't see ; but that's none of my business."

Leave much to natural or acquired inclinations, was one of his maxims. He was not deeply interested in souls who by temperament or training needed very minute guidance in the spiritual life ; to him they seemed so overloaded with harness as to have no great strength left for pulling the chariot. But he would not interfere with them; he knew that it was of little avail to try to change such methods once they had become habitual; and he recognized that there were many who could never get along without them. At any rate he was tolerant by nature, and slow to condemn in general or particular anything useful to well-meaning souls.

"It is vain to rise before the light," was another motto. "Make no haste in the time of clouds." These two texts of Scripture he was fond of repeating. "When God shows the way," he once said, "you will see; no amount of peering in the dark will bring the sun over the hills. Pray for light, but don't move an inch before you get it. When it comes, go ahead with all your might." Self-imposed penances, self-assumed devotional practices he mistrusted. He was convinced that the only way sure to succeed, and to succeed perfectly, was either that shown by an interior attraction too powerful and too peaceful to be other than divine, or one pointed out by the lawful external authority in the Church.

When asked for advice on matters of conscience his decisions were generally quick and always simple. Yet he often refused to decide without time for prayer and thought, saying, " I have no lights on this matter; you must give me time." And not seldom he refused to decide altogether for the same reason. One thing annoyed him much, and that was the blank silence and stupid wonder with which some instructed Catholics listened to him as he spoke of the guidance of the Holy Spirit as the way of Christian perfection, treating it as beyond the reach of ordinary mortals, intricate in its rules, " mystical," and visionary; whereas Father Hecker knew it to be the one only simple method, with a minimum of rules, useful for all, readily understood. What follows is a brief outline of the entire doctrine in its practical use in the progress of the soul from a sinful life onwards ; we have found it among his memoranda :

"What must one do in order to favor the reception of the Holy Spirit, and secure fidelity to His guidance when received ? First receive the Sacraments, the divinely instituted channels of grace : one will scarcely persevere in living in the state of grace, to say nothing of securing a close union with God, who receives Holy Communion only once or twice a year. Second,

practise prayer, above all that highest form of prayer, assisting
at Holy Mass; then mental and vocal prayer, the public offices
of the Church, and particular devotions according to one's
attrait. Third, read spiritual books daily—the Bible, Lives of the
Saints, *Following of Christ, Spiritual Combat,* etc. But in all
this bear ever in mind, that the steady impelling force by which
one does each of these outward things is *the inner and secret
prompting of the Holy Ghost, and that perseverance in the mis
secured by no other aid except the same hidden inspiration.*
Cherish that above all, therefore, and in every stage of the
spiritual life; be most obedient to it, seeking meantime for good
counsel wherever it is likely to be had."

Father Hecker was of opinion that a larger number of persons can be led to perfection than is generally supposed, and
he would sound the call in the ears of Christians generally
far more than is commonly done. He was also persuaded
that there are many souls whose whole lives have been entirely,
or almost entirely, free from the taint of mortal sin, and these
he considered should be the most active spirits among Christians. He thought that more room should be made for them
in our discourses, and that everybody should not be lumped
together in one mass as hardened sinners or as penitents.

To these innocent men and women the mediatorship of Christ
should be made as distinct as possible, the elevation of the soul
to divine union through the Incarnation brought out fully, and
the redemption of man from sin and hell be included in it, and
be absorbed by it. Too many souls who have never sinned
mortally fail to struggle for perfection, Father Hecker often
said, because they never have heard any invitation but the call to
repentance. The positive side of Christianity is the Incarnation,
which lifts all men of good will, repentant and innocent alike, into
participation with the Deity. Father Hecker would talk by the
hour of the need of bringing that view of our Lord's mission
most prominently forward, the idea of redemption applying to
innocent souls only on account of original sin, and by sympathy with their brethren infected by actual sin. And he would
show that even hard sinners could often be brought to a good
life more surely, and be enabled more certainly to persevere, by
forcibly emphasizing the Incarnation and its benefits than by
any other method. Their blindness and selfishness hinder hard

sinners from easily appreciating our Lord's sufferings as borne
on their account. Father Hecker regretted that the idea of
redemption was so often presented in a way to give the impression that atonement was the whole office of Christ. There
are many souls for whom access to Christ as Mediator was
more in consonance with the truth than access to Him as Redeemer, Mediator in that case including Redeemer, rather than
the Redeemer absorbing the idea of Mediator. Redemption from
original sin is, of course, necessary to the mediatorship of a fallen
race. But our Lord became Redeemer that he might be Mediator;
he cleansed us from sin that he might lift us up to the God-
head; and in many souls Father Hecker knew that the process of cleansing began and ended with original sin and venial
sins. Such souls often go their lives long with no compelling
stimulus to perfection, because they cannot apply to themselves
the accusations of sin commonly put into the directions for be-
ginners.

Much has been already said of the aids to perfection which
Father Hecker perceived in a right use of the liberty and intelligence of our times. He also insisted that the commercial
and industrial features of our civilization were no obstacles to a
high state of Christian perfection.

In a remarkable sermon, entitled "The Saint of Our Day,"
published in the third volume of the Paulist series, Father
Hecker, after making a powerful exposition of the advantages
of liberty and intelligence as helps to the interior life, insists
that the opportunities and responsibilities peculiar to our civilization are capable of being sanctified to the highest degree. The
model he proposes in this sermon is St. Joseph. He was no
martyr, yet showed a martyr's fidelity by his trust in God.

"Called by the voice of God to leave his friends, home, and
country, he obeys instantly and without a murmur. To find
God and to be one with God, a solitary life in the desert was
not necessary to St. Joseph. He was in the world and found
God where he was. He sanctified his work by carrying God
with him into the workshop. St. Joseph was no flower of the
desert or plant of the cloister; he found the means of perfection in the world, and consecrated it to God by making its cares
and duties subservient to divine purposes.

"The house of St. Joseph was his cloister, and in the bosom

of his family he practised the sublimest virtues. While occupied with the common daily duties of life his mind was fixed on the contemplation of divine truths, thus breathing into all his actions a heavenly influence. He attained in society and in human relationships a degree of perfection not surpassed, if equalled, by the martyr's death, the contemplative of the solitude, the cloistered monk, or the missionary hero.

" Our age is not an age of martyrdom, nor an age of hermits, nor a monastic age. Although it has its martyrs, its recluses, and its monastic communities, these are not, and are not likely to be, its prevailing types of Christian perfection. Our age lives in its busy marts, in counting-rooms, in workshops, in homes, and in the varied relations that form human society, and it is into these that sanctity is to be introduced. St. Joseph stands forth as an excellent and unsurpassed model of this type of perfection. These duties and these opportunities must be made instrumental in sanctifying the soul. For it is the difficulties and the hindrances that men find in their age which give the form to their character and habits, and when mastered become the means of divine grace and their titles to glory. . Indicate these, and you portray that type of sanctity in which the life of the Church will find its actual and living expression.

"This, then, is the field of conquest for the heroic Christian of our day. Out of the cares, toils, duties, afflictions, and responsibilities of daily life are to be built the pillars of sanctity of the Stylites of our age. This is the coming form of the triumph of Christian virtue."

With all, moreover, Father Hecker insisted on the practice of the natural virtues, honesty, temperance, truthfulness, kindliness, courage, and manliness generally, as preceding any practical move towards the higher life. He first explored the character and life of his penitent in search of what natural power he had, and then demanded its full exertion. He began with the natural man, and made every supernatural force in the sacraments and prayer aid in establishing and increasing natural virtue as a necessary preliminary and ever-present accompaniment of supernatural progress. Perhaps Father Hecker's antipathy to Calvinism sharpened his zeal for the natural virtues, and strengthened his advocacy of human innocence. The craving for the supernatural, he was convinced, would be strong in proportion to the enlightenment of the natural reason ; the need of the grace of God is, of course, most urgent in a sinful state, but it would be more quickly perceived in proportion to the possession of natural virtue. As the exercise of reason is necessary to faith and precedes its acts, so the integrity of natural virtue is the best preparation for the grace of God. Many pages of *The Aspirations of Nature,* from which the following brief quotations are made, are devoted to the dignity of humanity and the need of placing the excellence of human nature in the foreground when considering how man may attain to a high supernatural state :

"Every faculty of the soul, rightly exercised, leads to truth ; every instinct of our nature has an eternal destiny attached to it. Catholicity finds its support in these and employs them in all her developments."

"The Catholic religion is wonderfully calculated and adapted to call forth, sustain, and perfect the tastes, propensities, and peculiarities of human nature. And let no one venture to say that these characteristics which are everywhere found among men are to be repressed rather than encouraged. This is to despise human nature, this is to mar the work of God. For are not these peculiarities inborn ? Are they not implanted in us by the hand of our Creator ? Are they not what go to constitute our very individuality ? "

Humanity is a word of vague meaning to most ears, but to Father Hecker its meaning was a living thing of value second only to Christianity. Here is his summary of the relation of Catholicity to human nature, taken from the same source as the foregoing :

"Catholicity is that religion which links itself to all the faculties of the mind, appropriates all the instincts of human nature, and by thus concurring with the work of the Creator affirms its own Divine origin."

We give the following extracts from letters of spiritual advice, to show Father Hecker's views of mortification :

"Exterior mortifications are aids to interior life. What we take from the body we give to the spirit. If we will look at it closely, two-thirds of our time is taken up with what we shall eat, and how we shall sleep, and wherewithal we shall be clothed. Two-thirds of our life and more is animal—including sleep. I do not despise the animal in man, but I go in for fair play for the soul. The better part should have the greater share. The right order of things has been reversed : *con*-version is necessary. Read the lives of the old Fathers of the Desert. They determined on leading a rational and divine life. How little are they known or appreciated in our day! Their lives are more interesting than a novel and stranger than a romance."

" Self-love, self-activity, self-hood, is something not easily destroyed. It is like a cancer which has its roots extending to the most delicate fibres of our mental and moral nature. Divine grace can draw them all out. But how slowly! And how exquisitely painful is the process—the more subtle the self-love the more painful the cure."

" Never practise any mortification of a considerable character without counsel. The devil, when he can no longer keep us back, aims at driving us too far and too fast."

" How can the intellect be brought under direction of divine grace except by reducing it to its nothingness ?—and how can this be done except by placing it in utter darkness ? How can the heart be filled with the spirit of divine love while it contains any other ? How can it be purified of all other inordinate love except by dryness and bitterness ? God wishes to fill our intelligence and our hearts with divine light and love, and thus to deify our whole nature—to make us one with what we represent—God. And how can He do this otherwise than by removing from our soul and its faculties all that is contrary to the divine order ? "

" All your difficulties are favors from God ; you see them on the wrong side, and speak as the block of marble would while being chiselled by the sculptor. When God purifies the soul, it cries out just like little children do when their faces are washed. The soul's attention must be withdrawn from external, created things and turned inward towards God exclusively before its union with Him ; and this transformation is a great, painful, and wonderful work, and so much the more difficult and painful as the soul's attention has been attracted and attached to transitory things—to creatures."

He was often heard repeating the following verse from *The Imitation* (book iii. chap. xxxi.), as summarizing the necessary conditions of the active life: " Unless a man be elevated in spirit, and set at liberty from all creatures, and wholly united to God, whatever he knows and whatever he has is of no great weight." He wrote to a friend that he had studied that verse for thirty years and still found that he did not know all it meant.

We give what follows as characteristic of Father Hecker's manner as a director:

" At first, in all your deliberate actions, calm your mind, place yourself in the attitude of a receiver or listener, and then decide. Imperceptibly and insensibly grace will guide you."

" Don't care what people say ; keep your own counsel. Use your own sense and abound in it ; as the apostle says : ' Let every one abound in his own sense.' Don't try to get anybody to agree with you. No two noses are alike, much less souls. God never repeats."

" Nobody nowadays wants God. Every one has the whole world on his shoulders, and unless his own petty ideas and schemes are adopted and succeed, he prophesies the end of the world. You are on the right road—push on ! Our maxim is : Be sure you are right and then go ahead ! "

" How much that is good and noble in the soul is smothered by unwise restraint ! The whole object of restraint is to reject that which is false and to correct the preference given to a lower good instead of to a higher one. As for the rest—*freedom !*"

" I know a man who thinks he don't know anything—who every day knows that he knows less ; and who hopes to know nothing before he dies. O blessed emptiness which fills us with all ! O happy poverty which possesses all ! O beatified nothingness which can exclaim, *Deus meus et omnia !* "

It will have been seen by this time that Father Hecker's first and fundamental rule of direction was to have as little of it as possible. His method started out with the purpose to do away with method at the earliest moment it could safely be done. To be Father Hecker's penitent meant the privilege of sooner or later being nobody's penitent but the Holy Ghost's. The following rules of direction he printed in 1887 :

" The work of the priesthood is to help to guide the Christian people, understanding that God is always guiding them interiorly.

"An innocent soul we must guide, fully understanding that God is dwelling within him; not as a substitute for God.

"A repentant sinner we must guide, understanding that we are but restoring him to God's guidance.

"The best that we can do for any Christian is to quicken his sense of fidelity to God speaking to him in an enlightened conscience.

"Now, God's guidance is of two kinds: one is that of His external providence in the circumstances of life; the other is interior, and is the direct action of the Holy Spirit on the human soul. There is great danger in separating these two.

"The key to many spiritual problems is found in this truth: The direct action of God upon the soul, which is interior, is in harmony with his external providence. Sanctity consists in making them identical as motives for every thought, word, and deed of our lives. The external and the internal (and the same must be said of the natural and supernatural) are one in God, and the consciousness of them both is to be made one divine whole in man. To do this requires an heroic life-sanctity.

"All the sacraments of the Church, her authority, prayer both mental and vocal, spiritual reading, exercises of mortification and of devotion, have for their end and purpose to lead the soul to the guidance of the Holy Spirit. St. Alphonsus says in his letters that the first director of the soul is the Holy Ghost Himself.

"It is never to be forgotten that one man can never be a guide to another except as leading him to his only Divine Guide.

"The guide of the soul is the Holy Spirit Himself, and the criterion or test of possessing that guide is the Divine authority of the Church."

What follows was published by Father Hecker in *The Catholic World* in 1887. It throws new light on the questions we have been considering, abounding in practical rules of direction, and therefore, though somewhat long, we venture to close the chapter with it:

"'If any one shall say that without the previous inspiration of the Holy Spirit and His aid, a man can believe, hope, love, or repent as he should, so that the grace of justification may be conferred upon him, let him be anathema.'

"These are the words of the holy Council of Trent, in which the Catholic Church infallibly teaches that without an interior movement of the indwelling Holy Spirit no act of the soul can be meritorious of heaven. This doctrine, embodying the plain sense of Holy Scripture and the unbroken teaching of the Church in all ages, bases human justification on an interior impulse of the Third Person of the Divine Trinity. This impulse precedes the soul's acts of faith, hope, and love, and of sorrow for sin: the first stage in the supernatural career, then, is the entering of the Holy Spirit into the inner life of the soul. The process of justification begins by the divine life of the indwelling Spirit taking up into itself the human life of the soul.

"Nor is this to the detriment of man's liberty, but rather to its increase. The infinite independence of God and his divine liberty are shared by man exactly in proportion as he partakes of God's life in the communication of the Holy Spirit.

"If it be asked how the Holy Spirit is received, the answer is, Sacramentally. ' Unless a man be born again of water and the Holy Ghost, he cannot enter into the kingdom of God.' As man by nature is a being of both outer and inner life, so, when made a new man by the Spirit of God and elevated into a supernatural state, God deals with him by both outer and inner methods. The Holy Spirit is received by the sacramental grace of baptism and renewed by the other sacraments; also in prayer, vocal or mental, hearing sermons, reading the Scriptures or devout books, and on occasions, extraordinary or ordinary, in the course of daily life ; and when once received every act of the soul that merits heaven is done by the inspiration of that Divine Guide dwelling within us. Even though unperceived, though indistinguishable from impulses of natural virtue, though imperceptibly multiplied as often as the instants are, yet each movement of heaven-winning virtue, and especially love, hope, faith, and repentance, is made because the Holy Spirit has acted upon the soul in an efficacious manner.

"It is not to induce a strained outlook for the particular cases of ·the action of the Spirit of God on us, or the signs of it, that these words are written. The sacraments, prayer and holy reading, and hearing sermons and instructions, are the plain, external instruments and accompaniments of the visitations of God, and are sufficient landmarks for the journey of the soul, unless it be led in a way altogether extraordinary. And apart from these external marks, no matter how you watch for God, his visitations are best known by their effects; it is after the cause has been placed, perhaps some considerable time after, that the faith, hope, love, or sorrow becomes perceptibly increased—always excepting extraordinary cases. Not to 'resist the Spirit' is the first duty. Fidelity to the divine guidance, yielding one's self up lovingly to the impulses of virtue as they gently claim control of our thoughts —this is the simple duty.

"Having laid down in broad terms the fundamental doctrine of the supernatural life, it is proper to say a word of the natural virtues and of their relation to the supernatural. It has been already intimated that the goodness of nature is often indistinguishable from the holiness of the supernatural life; and, indeed, as a rule, impulses of the Holy Spirit first pour their floods into the channels of natural virtue, thus rendering them supernatural. These are mainly the cardinal virtues: Prudence, Justice, Fortitude, and Temperance. Practised in a state of nature, these place us in our true relations with our nature and with God's providence in all created nature around us; these are the virtues which choice souls among the heathen practised. They are not enough. When they have done their utmost they leave a void in the heart that still yearns for more. It is the purpose of the Spirit of God to raise our virtue to a grade far above nature. The practice of the virtues of faith, hope, and love, which bring the soul into direct communication with God, and which, when practised under the guidance of the Holy Spirit, are supernatural, following upon the practice of the cardinal virtues under the same guidance, place the soul in its true and perfect relation with God—a state which is more than natural.

"Let us, if we would see things clearly, keep in sight the difference between the natural and supernatural. In the natural order a certain union with God was possessed by man in all ages in common with every creature. The union of the creature with the divine creative power is something which man can neither escape from nor be robbed of. But in the case of rational creatures this union is, even in a state of nature, made far closer and its enjoyment increased by a virtuous life—one in which reason is superior to appetite; a life only to be led by one assisted, if not by the indwelling Holy Spirit peculiar to the grace of Christ, yet by the helps necessary to natural virtue and called medicinal graces. The practice of the four cardinal virtues—Prudence, Justice, Fortitude, and Temperance—in the ordinary natural state gave to guileless men and women in every age a natural union with their Creator. Although we maintain that such natural union with God is not enough for man, yet we insist that the part the natural virtues play in man's sanctification be recognized. In considering a holy life natural virtues are too often passed over, either because the men who practised them in heathen times were perhaps few in number, or because of the Calvinistic error that nature and man are totally corrupt.

"And we further insist on the natural virtues because they tend to place man in true relations with himself and with nature, thus bringing him into more perfect relation or union with God than he was by means of the creative act—a proper preliminary to his supernatural relation. Who will deny that there were men not a few among the heathen in whom Prudence, Justice, Fortitude, and Temperance were highly exemplified? They knew well enough what right reason demanded. Such men as Socrates, Plato, Epictetus, and Marcus Aurelius had by the natural light of reason a knowledge of what their nature required of them. They had faults, great ones if you please; at the same time they knew them to be faults, and they had the natural virtues in greater or less degrees. Thus the union between God and the soul, due to the creative act, though not sufficient, never was interrupted. The Creator and the Mediator are one."

CHAPTER XXVIII.

THE PAULIST PARISH AND MISSIONS.

IN serving the parish, the Paulists, led by Father Hecker, endeavored to utilize the individual qualities of each member, as well as the advantages of a community, so as to bring them to bear as distinct forces upon the people. What George Miles had said of them as missionaries, as quoted in a previous chapter, applied to them as parish priests, and told accordingly in results. Their personal excellences found free room for activity, without any lack of oneness of spirit and without interfering with harmony of action.

The missionary makes an efficient parish priest. Accustomed to severe labor as well as to very moderate recreation, he pours the energy of apostolic zeal into parochial channels. A high order of preaching is often the result, combined with tireless application to visiting the sick, hunting up sinners, and hearing confessions. On the other hand, the experience of regular parish duty is of assistance to the missionary when he returns to his "apostolic expeditions," as Pius IX. called them ; he is all the better fitted to plan and execute his proper enterprises from having obtained a fuller knowledge of the ordinary state of things in a parish.

It will not be expected that a detailed account of the parish work of St. Paul's will here be given, or more than a brief summary of that of the missions. These latter were kept up with vigorous energy from 1858 till the close of the war in the spring of 1865. On April 4 of that year Father Baker died, and the missions, which had been a grievous burden to the little band, now became an impossibility. They were suspended till 1872, excepting an occasional one, given not so much as part of the current labor of the community, as to retain their sweet savor in the memory and as an earnest of their future resumption. But up to Father Baker's death this small body of men had preached almost everywhere throughout the country, getting away from the South just before the war blocked the road. Eighty-one missions had been given, hundreds of converts had been received into the Church and many scores of thousands of confessions heard. Numerous applications for missions were refused for want of men to preach them. Scarcely a city of any size in the United States and Canada but knew the Paulists and thanked God for their missions.

The Fathers conducted them in the same spirit as when they were Redemptorists, and followed, as the community still continues to do, substantially the same method. It is not easy to improve on St. Alphonsus. But they did not fail to bring out the qualities and call for the peculiar virtues demanded by Divine Providence in these times. Their preaching was distinguished by appeals to manliness and intelligence, as well as to the virtues distinctly supernatural. The people were not only edified by their zeal and religious discipline, but the more observant were attracted by the Paulists' freedom of spirit, and by their constant insistence on the use of the reasoning faculties to guide the emotions aroused by the sermons. The missionaries were men of native independence, and their religious influence was productive of the same quality. Great attention was paid to the doctrinal instructions. As to special devotions, the Paulists have never had any to propagate, though competent and willing to assist the pastor in his own choice of such subsidiary religious aids. Non Catholics of all classes were drawn to hear the convert missionaries, and the exercises usually received flattering notices from the secular press. An unrelenting warfare was carried on against the dangerous occasions of sin peculiar to our country and people, and the Fathers were from the beginning, and their community is yet well known for particular hostility to drunkenness, and to the most fruitful source of that detestable and widespread vice, the saloon. Their antagonism to drunkenness showed their appreciation of its evil supremacy among the masses, and the condemnation of the saloon was a necessary result.

This attitude of the missionaries was often a bitter-sweet morsel to the pastors, nearly all of whom at that time had been trained in the Old World. They were glad of the good done, yet sorry to see their liquor-dealers put to public shame. One pastor is recorded as saying: "The only people that have looked sad at this mission are the first men in my parish, the rum-sellers." The following is a piece of evidence worth publishing, though it is but one of very many which could be produced. It is found in the Mission Record in Father Baker's handwriting:

"A Catholic one evening, on his way to the mission, stopped

in a grog-shop and took a glass with the proprietor. 'Won't you go with me to hear the Fathers?' said the guest. 'No,' said the other, 'these men are too hard on us. They want all of us liquor-dealers to shut up our shops. If we were rich we could do it; but we an't—we are poor. These men are too high and independent; Father —— wouldn't dare to speak as they do. But after all,' continued he, 'they are good fellows; see the effect of their labors.' Then, taking out of his pocket a crumpled letter which he had received through the post-office, and which was badly spelled and badly written, he read as follows: 'SIR: I send you three dollars which I received by mistake three years ago from your clerk. And now I hope that you will stop *selling damnation*, and that God may give you grace to stop it. Yours: A Sinner.'"

Whatever may have been the misgivings of some, the opposition of the Paulists to the liquor-traffic was approved by the most enlightened and influential prelates and priests of the country, as is shown by the number of cathedrals and other prominent churches in which the missions were preached. It should be added that this antagonism to drunkenness, to convivial drinking, and to saloon-keeping, not only received the unanimous applause of the Catholic laity, but edified the non-Catholic public, and brought out many commendations from the secular press as well as from the police authorities of our crowded cities. A mission is a terror to obstinate evil-doers of all kinds, but to habitual drunkards and saloon-keepers it is especially so. The attitude of the Church in America on this entire subject, as officially expressed by the decrees of the Third Plenary Council and by its pastoral letter, fully justifies the action of Father Hecker and his companions.

As soon as the church in Fifty-ninth Street was opened the community exerted itself to make the surroundings attractive. The building occupied but a small part of the property, the rest of which was laid out in grass-plats and gravel walks; many shade-trees and some fruit-trees were set out, and a flower and vegetable garden planted. It was Father Hecker's delight to superintend this work, and to participate actively in it when his duties allowed. The grounds soon became an attractive spot, to which in a few years church-goers from all parts of the city began to make Sunday pilgrimages. They came in considerable numbers every Sunday to assist at Mass or Vespers in St. Paul's quiet, country-like church. Meantime the residents of the parish, not very numerous and nearly all of the laboring class, formed deep attachments for their pastors, and an almost ideal state of unity and affection bound priests and people together.

Nearly the entire region was covered with market gardens, varied with huge masses of rock, and groups of shanties. Very many of the parishioners of that early period lived in these nondescript dwellings, of which they were themselves both the architects and builders, a fact which added not a little to their quaint and picturesque appearance. The sites upon which these " squatters' " homes were placed, and over which roamed and sported their mingled goats, dogs, and children, are now occupied in great part by blocks of stately residences and apartment houses; but we know not whether the grace of God abounds more plentifully now than it did then. At any rate, whoever heard Father Hecker in those primitive days call his parish " Shantyopolis," could see no sign of regret on his part that he had a poor and simple people as the bulk of his parishioners.

Much attention was given to the preparation and preaching of sermons, with the result of a full attendance at High Mass on Sundays. Beginning with 1861, a volume of these discourses was published under Father Hecker's direction each year, till a series of seven volumes had been completed. These were very well received by the Catholic public, and were bought in considerable numbers by non-Catholic clergymen. They had an extensive sale, though when their publication was first proposed it was feared that they would not succeed. They are almost wholly of a strictly parochial character, brief, direct in style, abounding in examples from every-day life, and plentifully illustrated with Scripture quotations. Although Father Hecker preached regularly in his turn, only a few of his sermons were contributed to these volumes, but his suggestions and encouragement greatly assisted the other Fathers in preparing theirs, as indeed in all their duties, parochial and missionary. Some years after the series was ended two volumes of Five-Minute Sermons were published, providing short instructions for Low Masses on Sundays.

The Paulist Church also became well known for the attention paid to the public offices of religion, as well as for rubrical exactness in ceremonies, the greater feasts of the year being celebrated with all the splendor which a simple church-building and limited pecuniary means allowed.

Father Hecker was from first to last strongly in favor of congregational singing, and assisted to the best of his power in introducing it. It began in our church in modest fashion back in those early days, and was fostered zealously at the Lenten devotions and society meetings. It never failed of some good results, and has finally attained a flourishing state of success in this parish. His attention to the children was constant. No matter who had charge of the Sunday-school, as long as his health permitted Father Hecker was there every Sunday that he was at home, asking questions, talking to the teachers and children, enlivening all by his encouragement and cheerfulness.

He was a martinet on one question, and that was cleanliness, and its kindred virtue, orderliness. He was never above working with mop, broom and duster indoors, and shovel and rake in the garden; and this trait added much to the appearance of things as well as to the comfort of all concerned in the use of the convent and the church.

Though assiduous in every parish duty, his favorite task was the relief of the poor. They multiplied in number in undue proportion to the increase of the parish, drifting out this way from the overcrowded quarters down town. Father Hecker enlisted the best men and women in the congregation in the work of caring for them, organizing a conference of the St. Vincent de Paul Society, in whose labors he joyfully and energetically participated.

The death of Father Baker was, humanly speaking, a loss to the community beyond all calculation, and was the great event of the first period of the Paulist community. Father Hecker had the very highest estimate of his holiness, and mourned him with the mingled sorrow and joy with which saints are mourned. The reader should get Father Hewit's Memoir of Father Baker if he would know his virtues. Father Hecker was often heard to say that few men understood his ideas so clearly as did Father Baker and had so much sympathy with them. And his death was the signal for an impulse whose power plainly indicated its supernatural origin. Up to that time there had been but two priests added to the community, and those who had offered themselves as novices and been rejected were, as a rule, little calculated to inspire hope. But from 1865 onwards good subjects, mostly converts, applied in sufficient numbers, and in a few years the missions were resumed. But what was of even more importance, the apostolate of the press, started in the publication of THE CATHOLIC WORLD the month in which Father Baker's death occurred, assumed a national prominence, and together with the Catholic Tracts and the Catholic Publication Society set the Paulists at work in their primary vocation, the conversion of non-Catholics to the true religion. To this, and to Father Hecker's lectures, we now turn. Of course we might dwell longer on the parish and the missions, about which there are many things of interest left untold, but only the lapse of time can sufficiently dissociate them from living persons to allow of their being made public.

CHAPTER XXIX.

FATHER HECKER'S LECTURES.

THE suspension of the missions, if it was the result of neces-sity, was yet an aid to Father Hecker in devoting himself to public speaking in the interests of the Catholic faith. Between missions, it is true, he seized every favorable opportunity to address audiences on controversial topics, often doing so in public halls, as well as in churches. Meantime he could still further mature his plans, and, testing his methods by experiment, secure for future occasions a course of lectures fully suited to the end he had in view. More than ever did he study to fit himself for his apostolate. How, he asked himself, shall the living word be framed anew for our new people ? How shall religious teaching be suited to the special needs of this age without detracting from the integrity and the venerable antiquity of the truth ? He sought to answer these questions by recalling his own early difficul-ties, and by opening his soul to the voices of struggling hu-manity uttered everywhere around him. What men outside the Church were yearning for in matters social and religious was his incessant study. He read every book, he read every periodical which promised to guide him ever so little to know by what road Divine Providence was moving men's minds towards the truth. His eyes were ever strained to read the signs of God's provi-dence in men's lives. And his conclusion was always the same : proclaim it on the house-tops that no man can be consistent with his natural aspirations till he has become a Catholic ; preach it on the street-corners that the Catholic religion elevates man far above his highest natural force into union with the Deity—intimate, conscious, and perpetual.

As to systematic preparation for discourses to non-Catholics, Father Hecker had his own peculiar equipment. As the reader will remember, God had led him in no way more singularly than in his studies, and had led him straight. The doctrines of the Church were familiar to him, for they had quenched his soul's thirst. And he had preached them on the missions, the instructions on the Creed and the Sacraments falling to his share. He had given these waters of life to other souls, and knew their value. He was a close student of the dogmatic side of religion. He had, it is true, little taste for the refinements of theologians, unless they touched the questions of human dignity and the scope of the grace of Christ, which were vital ones to himself. He viewed religion with wide-sweeping glances, trying to discover every hill of vision or stream of sanctity. He had plain truths to teach, and he needed none other. He knew the organism of the Church in clergy and in people, for he had seen it both from without and within. He had felt the grip of authority fixed in his soul. He had agonized under the brand of punishment as it burnt into his flesh, and he had seen it changed into the badge of approval. Within and without he knew Catholicity, loved it daily more and more, and was daily more and more anxious to proclaim it to the world.

It was not from labored preparation of his lectures that success came to Father Hecker. Even those which seemed the most elaborately prepared he did not write out word for word. His verbal memory was not trustworthy, and he had to confide in his extemporizing faculty, which was very good, and which became in course of time quite reliable, giving out sentences clear, grammatical, and fit to print. " I have to *produce* a sermon for next Sunday," he once wrote to a friend. " For me a sermon is always a spontaneous production ; I cannot *get one up*. The idea must arise and grow up in my own mind. It is usually hard labor for me to produce it outwardly and give it suitable expression." But the effort did not appear in the delivery, for his style, although emphatic, was easy and familiar; his delivery, if not altogether according to the rules of elocution, nevertheless gained his point completely. No word of his was dead-born. His voice was not always clear, as he often suffered from bronchial troubles, but it was not unpleasant, and had a penetrating quality, being of that middle pitch which carries to the ends of a large auditorium without provoking the echoes. His appearance was very dignified, his tall frame, his broad face and large features showing with striking effect. His action was simple and not ungraceful, though frequently exceedingly energetic. As he never sought emotional effects his power may be known by his unfailing success in holding his audience perfectly attentive throughout long argumentative discourses. Energy of conviction was one of the strongest forces he possessed, and it took the shape of a gentle constraint with which his positive utterances of Catholic principles compelled assent. Sincerity of belief and liberty of soul were admirably blended in his manner. He never appeared in public without attracting many representatives of the mottled sectarianism of our population; and this pleased him much, for he loved them, felt at home with them, and was full of joy at the opportunity of addressing them.

He was chagrined at the apathy he sometimes met with among Catholics concerning the American apostolate. He found priests who would devote much labor to collecting money for the propagation of the faith among distant heathen races, but very few who would make a serious effort for the conversion of their American fellow-citizens. Are Americans of less worth in God's eyes than pagans and Buddhists? he would ask. He thought no differently of the people of the United States than St. Paul did of the Corinthians and Macedonians, groaning and travailing with them to bring them forth members of Christ; or than St. Francis Xavier did of the Japanese.

If asked how he was going to convert people, he would answer: "I am a Catholic, and I know that I am right. I can prove that I am right. What more do I want than this, and honest men and women who will listen to me?" The confidence he had in the strength of the Catholic argument was absolute, and this he showed by his zeal. His sole study was how to transmute this force into missionary form. Of all the wonders of the intellectual world he felt that the greatest is the faith of Catholics, and he knew by the lesson of his early life that it is but slightly appreciated by the non-Catholic mind. That Catholics permit this ignorance to continue was a puzzle to him. And it was all the more annoying because any single one of them can multiply his influence indefinitely by his union with the most perfect organism ever known—the Catholic Church. The quiescence of a body of men, sincere and intelligent, infallibly certain of the means of obtaining eternal happiness, living in daily contact with other men ignorant and *inquiring* about this unspeakable privilege, and yet not taking instant measures to impart their knowledge, was to Father Hecker almost as great a wonder as the divine gift of faith itself, especially as Catholics are well furnished with leaders and are organized to spread the truth as one of their most sacred duties.

Mr. Wilfrid Ward, a Catholic philosophical writer of distinction, has explained in a brilliant little volume the influence upon controversy of what he styles *The Clothes of Religion*—race, political traditions, education, physical temperament. He puts into his instructive pages the sense of the great scholastic maxim, *Quidquid recipitur secundum modum recipientis recipitur—*

Whatever is received, is received according to the mode (or character) of the recipient. The national character, the tendencies, the antecedents of the people addressed, the relative power of thought and of emotion in their mental activity ; all these are not, indeed, the souls of men but the clothing of them, their armor and their weapons ; and Father Hecker felt that such things must be taken into account in dealing with people, and that with the utmost discretion. His view about controversy with non-Catholics was indeed aggressive—that we had reached the point in the battle at which the legion, having cast its javelins, rushes on with drawn swords to closer conflict. But the combatants should be well trained, the captains should know the ground to be traversed, should understand thoroughly the weakness and strength of the enemy. It was not a new thing to bring Protestantism into court at the suit of human liberty. But it was a novelty to attack Protestantism as the very torture-chamber of free and innocent souls, and to do it in such a way as to draw thousands of the best Protestants in the land to listen. Such sentences in the morning papers as " An overflowing house greeted Father Hecker," " The immense hall has seldom been so completely filled," " Representative men of all creeds and of none were scattered through the large audience," had a tremendous meaning when the lecturer was known to be the most fearless assailant of Protestantism who had appeared for many a day.

Father Hecker well knew that the non-Catholic American aspires to deal with God through the aid of as few exterior appliances as possible. To come near God by his own spiritual activity without halting at forms of human contrivance is his spiritual ambition. His religious joy is in a spiritual life which deals with God directly, His inspired Word, His Holy Spirit. Father Hecker longed to tell his fellow-countrymen that the Catholic Church gives them a flight to God a thousand times more direct than they ever dreamed of. They think that the authority of the Church will cramp their limbs ; he was eager to explain to them that it sets them free, clears the mind of doubt, intensifies conviction into instinctive certitude, quickens the intellectual faculties into an activity whose force is unknown outside the Church.

It was not with the truths of revelation alone that Father Hecker dealt in his lectures. The first principles of natural religion were the background of all his pictures of true Christianity: that God is good, that men will be punished only for their personal misdeeds, that men are born for union with God and in their best moments long for Him, that they are equal, being all made in the Divine image, endowed with free will and called to the one eternal happiness—such were the great truths with which he would impress his audience first of all, using them afterwards as terms of comparison with Protestant doctrine. This plan he followed rather than institute a comparison of historical claims or of Biblical credentials, the well-trodden but weary road of ordinary controversy. To him Protestantism was more an offence against the integrity of human nature than even against the truths of Christian revelation. And he would place Catholicity in a new light, that of reason and liberty.

The revolt of Protestantism was not more against God's external authority among men than it was against the equal brotherhood of the human race. Well done, Luther, Father Hecker would say, well and consistently done; when you have proclaimed man totally depraved you have properly made his religion a Cain-like flight from the face of his Maker and his kindred by your doctrine of predestination. Father Hecker deemed it plainly unwise to forego the advantages of attacking such vulnerable points as the Protestant errors of total depravity and predestination for the sake of dwelling on the Biblical and historical credentials of Church authority. He knew, indeed, that extravagant individualism is to this day a fundamental Protestant error, but the waning power of its doctrinal assertion has deprived it of aggressive vigor. There is less danger of its assault upon the Church, Father Hecker thought, than of its sceptical tendency upon its own adherents. To emphasize the obligation of organic unity, in such a condition of things, was not good tactics; it was to revive the spirit of resistance without arresting the evils of doubt. Authority in religion has high and undoubted claims; but it is nevertheless true that the normal development of man is in freedom. Man is fitted for his destiny in proportion to his ability to use his liberty with wisdom, and Father Hecker endeavored to set non-Catholics themselves to work removing the obstacles to true spiritual liberty which Protestantism had planted in the way.

An appeal from Luther and Calvin to the standards of rational nature, to human virtue, to human equality, rather than to exclusively Catholic standards, was certain of success in a large class of minds. And this but led to the consideration of the Church's claims to elevate rational nature and natural virtue to that divine order which is above nature, and which is organic in the Catholic Church. Moral rectitude is a simpler test of truth than texts from a dead book, whose original tongues and whose perplexed exegesis are quite unknown to the vast mass of mankind. And Father Hecker recognized that the elementary truths of reason and the aspirations of humanity for better things are not unknown to any man or woman; these are everybody's personal means of testing truth. To pass them by in order to apply the remoter test of revelation is either to admit that Protestantism is not against the dictates of reason and man's aspirations, or to commence the argument against it at the wrong end.

In a letter to Cardinal Barnabo written in July, 1863, Father Hecker gives an account of how he went to work to secure and interest a non-Catholic audience :

" For several years past it has seemed to me that some more effectual means should be taken to reach the Protestant community. This last winter I ventured with this view upon an experiment. In three different cities I gave, in a large public hall, a course of conferences on religion, one every evening from Sunday to Sunday inclusive. The expense of the hall was paid by the priest of the place, the lectures were all free, and addressed exclusively to Protestants. The halls were crowded at each place, and that my audiences might be such as I desired to address, I begged Catholics to stay away. At the close of one of my lectures there were present twenty-five hundred persons, chiefly Protestants.

" My method was as follows : In treating any doctrine of our holy faith with a view to convincing my audience, I considered first what want in our nature it was related to, and to which it addressed itself. This want being discovered, I developed and illustrated it until my hearers were fully convinced of its existence and importance. Then the question came up, Which religion recognizes this element or want of our nature, and meets all its legitimate demands ? Does Protestantism ? Its answers were given, and found either hostile or incomplete. Then the Catholic Church was interrogated, and she was found to recognize this want, and her answers adequate and satisfactory. These answers were then shown to be supported by the authority of Holy Scriptures.

"The interest shown by my audience was remarkable, and the effect of this method was equal to my hopes. My experience convinces me that, if this work were continued, it would prepare the way for a great change of religion in this country, more particularly at the present time, when the public mind is favorably disposed to consider the claims of the Catholic Church."

The "want in our nature" appealed to was often in the political order, such as the love of liberty or man's capacity for self-government. This he dwelt upon at considerable length in the opening part of his lecture, viewing it as a philosopher would, and extending its application, as far as possible, to men generally. He thus chose his criterion for comparison of the two claimants in the religious world. His triumph was, therefore, often in an arena only semi-religious, or rather in that of natural religion. The effect was wonderfully good, though doubtless due in great measure to the manner in which his plan, so simply sketched in the letter above quoted, was developed before the audience. The entire doubting body of intelligent men was enlisted in varying degrees in favor of the Catholic teaching of man's relation to God and to his fellow-men, and against Protestantism. Americans could not help feeling disgust for doctrines which were condemned by the maxims of the Declaration of Independence.

Although there was nothing positively new in the method—something like it had been used by Archbishop Hughes against the Presbyterian champion, Breckenridge—yet the public was taken by surprise. The style of controversy universally in vogue was that of setting up texts of Scripture and bowling them down with other texts. But here comes an American Catholic and arraigns Protestant doctrine at the tribunal of American liberty. The thick-and-thin Protestant was thrown into a rage, and became abusive and often incoherent in his reply. The easy-going Protestant claimed that the doctrines assailed were obsolete, as his church had, at least implicitly, changed them. "Then change your church," said Father Hecker; "if you have come back to the right doctrine, why not come back to the true Church?" As to the average intelligent inquirer, he was uniformly influenced by these lectures against the Reformation and its entire teaching, with its dreadful effects of doubt and division among Christians.

Father Hecker had an intuitive perception of the peculiar difficulties of the American people, and ever showed the utmost readiness and skill in meeting them. He had a matchless power of laying bare the wants of the human heart, and an equal facility of pointing out the light and strength of Catholicity for their supply. His immense sympathy for an aspiring and guileless soul deprived of the truth, was most evident; he always looked it and spoke it and acted it before his audience. To do so was no effort on his part. He told of the promised land not as a native of it, but as a messenger sent into it, and now returned with such tidings as should hasten the steps of his brethren still wandering in the desert; and this sympathetic interest embraced the civil as well as the religious side of human nature. He claimed everything really American for the Catholic faith, and this was joy and gladness to many a weary heart drawn to the Church by her charities, or her beautiful symbolism, yet hindered by the phantom of absolute authority and the dread of losing the integrity of free citizenship. Incivism—will Catholic apologists never learn it?—is the heaviest stone flung at the Church in all free lands to-day. Father Hecker's blood fairly boiled that the Church of Christ, the very home of Christian freedom, and the nursing-mother of all civil well-being, should be thus assailed, while Calvin's and Luther's degrading doctrines should be paraded as alone worthy of a free people.

To say that Father Hecker "Americanized" in the narrow sense would be to do him injustice. The American ideas to which he appealed he knew to be God's will for all civilized peoples of our time. If fundamentally American they were not for that reason exclusively American. His Americanism is so broad that by a change of place it can be made Spanish, or German; and a slight change of terms makes it religious and Catholic. Nor had form of government essentially to do with it; human equality cannot be monopolized by republics; it can be rightly understood in a monarchy, though in such a case it does not assume the conspicuous place which it does in a republic. It was this broadness of Father Hecker's Americanism that made him acceptable to the extremely conservative circles of Rome, in his struggle there in the winter of 1858–9. Many men in the monarchies of the Old World may doubt the advent of republicanism there, but what sensible man anywhere doubts the aspiration of all races towards liberty and intelligence?

Father Hecker's repertory covered the entire ground between scepticism and Catholicism. In refutation of Protestantism the principal lectures were: *The Church and the Republic; Luther and the Reformation; How and Why I became a Catholic, or A Search after Rational Christianity;* and *The State of Religion in the United States.* On the positive side his chief topics were: *The Church as a Society, Why we Invoke the Saints,* and the Sacraments of Penance and Holy Communion. Others he had against materialism, spiritualism, etc.

As may naturally be supposed, some of his lectures succeeded better than others. One of those he personally preferred was *The Church and the Republic.* He opened by affirming, as the fundamental principle of the American nation, that man is naturally virtuous enough to be capable of self-government. He developed this in various ways till his audience felt that it was to be the touchstone of the question between the churches. He then exhibited the Protestant teaching on human virtue and human depravity, quoting extensively from Luther and from Calvin, as well as from the creeds of the principal Protestant sects, until the contrast between their teaching and the fundamental American principle was painfully vivid. There was no escape; doctrinal Protestantism is un-American. He then gave the Catholic doctrine of free will, of merit, of human dignity, and of the equality of men and human brotherhood. The impression was profound. Great mountains of prejudice were lifted up and cast into the sea. The elevating influences of the Church's faith fixed men's eyes and won their hearts. To have it demonstrated that Catholicity was not a gigantic effort to combine all available human forces to maintain a central religious despotism in the hands of a hierarchy, was a surprise to multitudes of Protestants. To not a few intelligent Catholics the style of argument was a great novelty. Father Hecker's success proved that the claim of authority on the part of the Church could be established without much difficulty in men's minds, if it were not associated with the enslavement of reason and conscience, and if shown to be consistent with rational liberty. He insisted upon the positive view of the subject. He proclaimed the purpose of Catholic discipline to be essentially conservative of human rights, a divinely-appointed safeguard to the liberty and enlightenment of the soul of man. He further proclaimed

that the infliction of penalties by Church authority was an accidental exercise of power provoked by disobedience to lawful
authority.

Luther and the Reformation excited widespread remark, and yet
to one accustomed to old-time controversy it seemed but a fragment of an argument. The lecture proved that Luther was not
an honest reformer, because, having started to reform inside the
Church and as a Catholic, he finished by leaving the Church and
therefore the real work of reform. At the outset Father Hecker
proved that Luther was but one, and by no means the most important one, of the great body of Catholic reformers of his time.
These set to work to remedy abuses which had grown to such
an extent as to have become intolerable. The genuine reformers,
led by the Popes, went right on and did reform the Church most
thoroughly, ending by the decrees of the Council of Trent. All
this the lecturer proved by citations from numerous high authorities, all of them Protestants. Why did Luther leave the company
of the true reformers? or, as Father Hecker puts it, "Why did
Luther change his base?" Whatever reason he had for leaving
Catholicity, it was not, as a matter of fact, on account of zeal for
reform. The lecture concluded by emphatically and, in different
terms, repeatedly denying to Luther the name of Reformer and to
his work the name of Reformation. Such was the line of argument
in a lecture which entertained the general public and enraged
bigoted Protestants more, perhaps, than any of the others. The
secret of its success was that it overturned the great Protestant
idol.

With humanitarians, rationalists, indifferentists, and sceptics
Father Hecker's lectures were popular, and such were his
favorite audience. If he so much as aroused their curiosity
about the Church, he deemed that he had gained a victory;
this and more than this he always succeeded in doing. Regular "church members" he did not hope much from,
though they came to hear him and he sometimes made converts even among them. The lecture system, then far more
in vogue than at present, gave him hearers from all classes
of minds, and especially those most intellectually restless and
inquiring. He took his turn in the list which contained the
names of Wendell Phillips, Beecher, Emerson, and Sumner, and
found his golden opportunity before such audiences as had
been gathered to listen to them. Thus into the drifts of

thought and into the intellectual movements around him, into
the daily and periodical press, into the social and political and
scientific groupings of men and women, his lectures enabled
him to breathe the peremptory call of the true religion, sure
to provoke inquiry in all active minds, and in some to find
good soil and bear the harvest of conversion. He searched
for earnest souls; and his confidence that they were everywhere to be found was rewarded not only in many particular
instances, but also by the removal of much prejudice throughout the entire country.

The writer of these pages saw Father Hecker for the first
time on the lecture platform. He was then in the full tide
of success, conscious of his opportunity and of his power to
profit by it. We never can forget how distinctly American
was the impression of his personality. We had heard the
nation's greatest men then living, and their type was too
familiar to be successfully counterfeited. Father Hecker was
so plainly a great man of that type, so evidently an out-
growth of our institutions, that he stamped American on every
Catholic argument he proposed. Nor was the force of this
peculiar impression lessened by the whispered grumblings of a
few petty minds among Catholics themselves, to whom this
apostolic trait was cause for suspicion. Never was a man
more Catholic than Father Hecker, simply, calmly, joyfully,
entirely Catholic. What better proof of this than the rage
into which his lectures and writings threw the outright enemies
of the Church? Grave ministers lost their balance and foamed
at him as a trickster and a hypocrite, all the worse because
double-dyed with pretence of love of country.

For the Protestant pulpits felt the shock and stormed in unison against this new exposition of Catholicity and against its
representative. In some cases, not content with one onslaught,
they returned to the charge Sunday after Sunday. All this
was not unexpected. The secular press, however, were very
generally favorable in their notices, excepting some of the
Boston dailies. As a rule, the lectures were very fully re-
ported and sometimes appeared word for word.

To reply to one's assailants after one has left the field of
battle is no easy matter, and for the most part Father
Hecker trusted for this to local champions of Catholicity;
and not in vain. But it happened on one occasion that after

he had lectured in a large town in Michigan, and had journeyed on to fulfil engagements farther West, he was attacked in a public hall by a minister of the place. On his return East Father Hecker stopped over and gave another lecture in the town, and not only refuted the minister but covered him with ridicule. In fact there was no great need of defence of Father Hecker's arguments, they were so simply true and so readily understood, Not one of his antagonists compared well with him for frankness, good humor, courtesy; and they almost invariably shirked the issue and confined themselves to stale calumnies against the Church.

At Ann Arbor, Michigan, Father Hecker lectured in the Methodist meeting-house, then the largest hall in the town. The Michigan State University, at this town, had at the time about seven hundred students, nearly all of whom came to the lecture. The subject chosen was *Luther and the Reformation.* As it was announced, the audience loudly applauded Luther's name, and some one called for three cheers for him, which were given vociferously, especially by the students. Father Hecker smiled, waited till the noise was over, then bade them give him a fair hearing; which, of course, they did. Before he had concluded, his audience seemed won to his view of the question in hand, and showed it by the names and the sentiments applauded. At the end some one called out "Three cheers for Father Hecker!" and they were given most heartily.

There seems nothing like a new discovery, as we have already said, in Father Hecker's controversial matter, or even in the method of its treatment. But joined with its exponent, blended into his personality, as it was, by the sincerity of his conviction, it was a discovery; flavored and tinctured by him, this wayside fountain had a new life-giving power to both Catholics and non-Catholics. Bishops, priests, and Catholic men and women in the world heard him with mute attention. Some Catholics, it is true, were stunned by·his bold handling of those traditional touch-me-nots of conservatism—reason and liberty; and such drew off suspicious. But multitudes of Catholics felt that he opened up to full view the dim vistas of truth towards which they had long been groping; these could agree with him ·without an effort. A few had reached his stand-point before they knew him, and hailed with rapture the leader who, unlike themselves, was not kept back by either dread of novel-sounding terms or by the impotency of private station. But here and there he met Catholics as dead-set against him as the Judaizing converts had been against his patron, St. Paul. Their only love was for antiquity, and that they loved passionately and in all its forms, even the neo-antiquity of the controversy of the Reformation era. On the other hand many, when they heard him, said, "That is the kind of Catholic I am, and the only kind it is easy for me to be." Non-Catholics, earnest men and women, were often heard to say, "*If I were quite sure that Hecker is a genuine Roman Catholic* I think that I could be one myself"; and this some of them did not hesitate to publish in the newspapers, so that Father Hecker might have said with Job: "The ear that heard me blessed me, and the eye that saw me gave witness to me."

Father Hecker felt that he was a pioneer in thus dealing with rationalized Protestants. His eye was quick to see the signs of the breaking up of dogmatic Protestantism, and he was early out among the vast intellectual wreckage, endeavoring to catch and tow into port what fragments he could of a system founded on doubt and on the denial of human virtue and human intelligence. "I want," he said on one occasion in private, "to open the way to the Church to rationalists. It seems to me to be now closed up. I feel that I am a pioneer in opening and leading the way. *I smuggled myself into the Church*, and so did Brownson." And now he wanted to abolish the custom-house, and open the harbor wide and clear for the entrance into the Church of all men who had been forced back on reason alone for guidance. The words above italicised were uttered with powerful emphasis and with much feeling. He quoted the following saying of Ozanam with emphatic approval: "What the age needs is an intellectual crusade"; and he affirmed that Leo XIII. had done very much to aid us in preaching it, and that Pius IX, rightly understood, had led the way to it. "The Catholics I would help with my left hand, the Protestants with my right hand," he once said. And non-Catholics, all but the bigots, liked him, for he was frank and true by every test. He was neither an exotic nor a hybrid, and they felt at home with him. He much resembled the best type of public men in America who have achieved fame at the bar or in politics; indeed, as we have already intimated, he really belonged to that type, for all his studies and all his training in the Catholic schools and convents, which had given him more and more of truth, more and more of the grace of God, had not changed the kind or type of man to which he belonged. He was the same character as when he harangued the Seventh Ward voters, or discussed the Divine Transcendence at Brook Farm. Scholastic truth sank deep into his soul, but scholastic methods stuck on the surface and then dropped away. " And David having girded his sword upon his armor began to try if he could walk in armor, for he was not accustomed to it. And David said to Saul, I cannot go thus, for I am not used to it. And he laid them off. And he took his staff which he had always in his hands, and chose him five smooth stones out of the brook."

If his duties in the Paulist community and parish had allowed, Father Hecker could have lectured to large audiences during the greater part of the year, and been well paid for his labor. He soon became the foremost exponent of Catholicity on the public platform in the United States. From the close of the war till his health gave way in 1872 he was much sought after for lectures, and spoke in the different cities and very many of the large towns, besides being obliged to refuse numerous applications, constantly coming in from all parts of the Union and from all sorts of societies, secular, Catholic, and even distinctly Protestant. Meantime he was frequently called on to preach on such occasions as the laying of corner-stones of churches and their dedications. He also gave one of the sermons preached before the Second Plenary Council of Baltimore.

The following is the introductory paragraph of a long character sketch of Father Hecker from the pen of James Parton, the historian. It is taken from an article entitled " Our Roman Catholic Brethren," published in the *Atlantic Monthly* for April and May, 1868. The entire article is full of admiration for the Catholic Church and of yearning towards her, though written by a typical sceptic of this era :

" As usual with them [Catholics] it is one man who is working this new and most effective idea [the Catholic Publication Society] ; but, as usual with them also, this one man is working by and through an *organization* which multiplies his force one hundred times and constitutes him a person of national importance. Readers who take note of the really important things transpiring around them will know at once that the individual referred to is Father Hecker, Superior of the Community of the Paulists, in New York. . . . It is he [Father Hecker] who is putting American machinery into the ancient ark and getting ready to run her by steam. Here, for once, is a happy man—happy in his faith and in his work—*sure* that in spreading abroad the knowledge of the true Catholic doctrine he is doing the best thing possible for his native land. A tall, healthy-looking, robust, handsome, cheerful gentleman of forty-five, endowed with a particular talent for winning confidence and regard, which talent has been improved by many years of active exercise. It is a particular pleasure to meet with any one, at such a time as this, whose work perfectly satisfies his conscience, his benevolence, and his pride, and who is doing that work in the most favorable circumstances, and with the best co-operation. Imagine a benevolent physician in a populous hospital, who has in his office the medicine which he is *perfectly certain* will cure or mitigate every case, provided only he can get it taken, and who is surrounded with a corps of able and zealous assistants to aid him in persuading the patients to take it!"

Mr. Parton having given us a picture of Father Hecker as he appeared to Protestants, the following exhibits him as Catholics saw him. It is an extract from Father Lockhart's clever book, *The Old Religion;* the original of Father Dilke is Father Hecker:

"The day after our last conversation, having an introduction to the Superior of the —— Fathers in New York, my friends agreed to accompany me. I was particularly glad of this because Father Dilke was one of the most remarkable men of our Church in the States. Himself a convert, and a man of large views and great sympathies, no one was better able to enter into the scruples and difficulties of religious Protestants on their first contact with Catholic doctrines and Catholic worship.

"On sending in our names we had not long to wait in the guest-room before the good father made his appearance. There was a stamp of originality about him; tall in stature, not exactly what we are used to call clerical in appearance, with a thoroughly American type of face, and with the national peaked beard instead of being closely shaven as is the custom with our clergy generally. I had met him before, without his clerical [religious] garb, on a journey on board a steamboat. At first, I remember, I had set him down as a Yankee skipper or trader of some sort; but when by chance we got into conversation, I found him a hard-headed man, shrewd, original, and earnest in his remarks; but when our conversation turned to religious topics, and got animated, I shall never forget how all that was common and national in his physique disappeared. And when he spoke of the mystery of God's love for man, his countenance seemed as it were transfigured, so that I felt that an artist would not wish for a better living model from which to paint a St. Francis Xavier, making himself all things to all men amidst his shipmates on his voyage to the Indies."

From what has been said of Father Hecker's aptitude to win non-Catholics to hear and believe him, it should not be thought that in order to do so he was obliged to leave off any sign of his priestly character. He was distinctly priestly in his demeanor, though, as already observed, not exactly what one would call a thorough "ecclesiastic." He ever dressed soberly. When he arrived at a town on a lecture tour he always put up at the house of the resident priest, if there was one, and, if he stayed over Sunday, preached for him at High Mass. He invariably corresponded beforehand with the pastor of the town to which he was invited by a secular lecture society, requesting him to send complimentary tickets to the leading men of the place—lawyers, doctors, ministers, merchants, and politicians. And when he appeared on the platform it was always in company with the priest. He loved priests with all his might and was ever at home in their company. It is not very singular, therefore, that some of his most devoted friends and most ard entadmirers were priests, secular and religious, born and bred in the Old World—among them some of• the most prominent clergymen in the country.

Father Hecker often met non-Catholics in private, being sought out by prominent radicals, sceptics, unbelievers, and humanitarians. What they had heard from him in public lectures, or read of him in the press, drew them to him, or they were brought to see him by mutual friends. And here he was indeed powerful, overbearing resistance by the strength of conviction and the simple exhibition of Catholic truth. The sight of a man anywhere, whom he could but suspect of aptitude for his views, was the signal for his emphatic affirmation of them, sometimes leading him to controversy bordering on the vociferous on cars and steamboats. In such circumstances, and in all his other dealings with men, you saw his prompt intelligence, his fine sensibility, his lofty spirit, his forceful and occasionally imperious will to hold you to the point; but the quality which, both in public and private discourse, outshone all, or rather gave all light and direction, was an immense love of truth joined to an equal admiration for virtue.

CHAPTER XXX.

THE APOSTOLATE OF THE PRESS.

ONE Sunday forenoon, happening to cross Broadway near a fashionable Protestant church, we saw the curb on both sides of the street lined with carriages, and the coachmen and footmen all reading the morning papers. The rich master and his family were in the softly-cushioned pews indoors, while their servants studied the news of the world and worshipped at the shrine of the Press outside: a spectacle suggestive of many things to the social reformer. But to a religious mind it was an invitation to the *Apostolate of the Press.* The Philips of our day can evangelize the rough charioteer by means of the written word as easily as they can his cultured master.

To Father Hecker the Press was the highest opportunity for religion. The only term of comparison for it is some element of nature like sunlight or the atmosphere. In the Press civilized man lives and breathes. Father Hecker was as alive to the injury done to humanity by bad reading as a skilful physician is to the malaria which he can smell and fairly taste in an infected atmosphere; and he ever strove to make the Press a means of enlightenment and virtue. He began to write for publication almost immediately after his arrival in America as a Redemptorist missionary; the *Questions of the Soul* and the *Aspirations of Nature* were composed amidst most absorbing occupations between 1853 and 1858. Throughout life he was ever asking himself and others how the Press could be cleansed, and how its Apostolate could be inaugurated. To this end he was ready to devote all his efforts, and expend all his resources and those of the community of which he was the founder. It is true that no man of his time was better aware of the power of the spoken word, and few were more competent to use it, the natural and Pentecostal vehicle of the Holy Spirit to men's souls. But he also felt that the providence of God, in making the Press of our day an artificial medium of human intercourse more universal than the living voice itself, had pointed it out as a necessary adjunct to the oral preaching of the truth. He was convinced that religion should make the Press its own. He would not look upon it as an extraordinary aid, but maintained that the ordinary provision of Christian instruction for the people should ever be two-fold, by speech and by print: neither the Preacher without the Press nor the Press without the Preacher. He was heard to say that in reading Montalembert's *Monks of the West* he had been struck with the author's eloquent apostrophe to the spade, the instrument of civilization and Christianity for the wild hordes of the early middle ages. Much rather, he said, should we worship the Press as the medium of the light of God to all mankind. He felt that the Apostolate of the Press might well absorb the external vocation of the most active friends of religion.

In the Press he found a distinct suggestion from above of a change of methods for elevating men to truth and virtue. In the spring of 1870, while on his way home from the Vatican Council, he wrote to Father Deshon from Assisi:

"I felt as if I would like to have peopled that grand and empty convent with inspired men and printing-presses. For evidently the special battle-field of attack and defence of truth for half a century to come is the printing-press."

He believed in types as he believed in pulpits. He believed that the printing-office was necessary to the convent. To him the Apostolate of the Press meant the largest amount of truth to the greatest number of people. By its means a small band of powerful men could reach an entire nation and elevate its religious life.

This being understood, one is not surprised at the extent of his plans for this Apostolate. He was never able to carry them out fully. Not till some years after the founding of the community could he make a fair beginning, although the first volume of the Paulist Sermons appeared in 1861. Delays were inevitable from the difficulties incident to the opening of the house and church in Fifty-ninth Street, and these were aggravated by the war, which for over four years bred such intense excitement as to interfere with any strong general interest in matters other than political. But the very month it ended, in April, 1865, Father Hecker started *The Catholic World*. Its purpose was to speak for religion in high-grade periodical literature. The year following he founded The Catholic Publication Society, with the purpose of directing the entire resources of the Press into a missionary apostolate. In 1870 he began *The Young Catholic*.

In literary merit and in illustrations it equalled any of the juvenile publications of that period, and was the pioneer of all the Catholic journals in the United States intended for children. And finally, in 1871, he projected the establishment of a first-class Catholic daily, securing within a year subscriptions for more than half the money necessary for the purpose, when the work was arrested by the final breaking down of his health.

The Catholic World was considered a hazardous venture. At the time it was proposed, such modest attempts at Catholic monthlies as had struggled into life had long ceased to exist. The public for such a magazine seemed to be small. The priesthood had little leisure for reading, being hardly sufficient in number for their most essential duties; the educated laymen were not numerous, nor remarkable for activity of mind in matters of religion; nearly the entire Church of America was foreign by birth or parentage, and belonged to the toiling masses of the people: "not many rich, not many noble." And, Father Hecker was asked, whom are you going to get to write for the magazine? How many Catholic literary men and women do you know of? Prudence, therefore, stood sponsor to courage. The cautious policy of an eclectic was adopted, and for more than a year the magazine, with the exception of its book reviews, was made up of selections and translations from foreign periodicals. The late John R. G. Hassard, who had already succeeded as a journalist, was chosen by Father Hecker as his assistant in the editorial work. Efforts were at once made to secure original articles; but before the magazine was filled by them three or four years were spent in urgent soliciting, in very elaborate sub-editing of MSS., and in reliance on the steady assistance of the pens of the Paulist Fathers. As a compensation, *The Catholic World* has introduced to the public many of our best writers, and first and last has brought our ablest minds on both sides of the water into contact with the most intelligent Catholics in the United States. All through its career it has represented Catholic truth before the American public in such wise as to command respect, and has brought about the conversion of many of its non-Catholic readers. Since its beginning it has been forced to hold its own against the claims of not unwelcome rivals, and against the almost overwhelming attractions of the great illustrated secular monthlies, to say nothing of the vicissitudes of the business world; and it has succeeded in doing so.

Father Hecker's purpose in establishing it has been realized, for it has ever been a first-rate Catholic monthly of general literature, holding an equal place with similar publications in the world of letters. He was its editor-in-chief till the time of his death, except during three years of illness and absence in Europe. He conducted it so as to occupy much of the field open to the Apostolate of the Press, giving solid doctrine in form of controversy, and discussing such religious truths as were of current interest. He kept its readers informed of the changeful moods of non-Catholic thought, and furnished them with short studies of instructive eras and personages in history. These graver topics have been floated along by contributions of a lighter kind, by good fiction and conscientious literary criticism. Meantime, the social problems which had perplexed Father Hecker himself in his early life, have caught the attention of the slower minds of average men, or rather have been thrust upon them ; and their consideration, ever in his own sympathetic spirit, now forms a prominent feature of *The Catholic World.*

The Young Catholic was an enterprise dear to his heart. His interest in it was constant and minute, and some of the articles most popular with its young constituency were from his own pen. It has always been edited by Mrs. George V. Hecker, assisted by a small circle of zealous and enlightened writers. It has held its way, but has had to encounter the not unusual fate of bold pioneers. It created its own rivals by demonstrating the possibilities of juvenile Catholic journalism, calling into existence more than a score of claimants for the support which it alone at first solicited. The lowest estimate of juvenile publications of a purely secular tone yearly sold in America carries the figure far into the millions. Some of these, and it is well to know that they are the most widely sold, are first-rate in a literary point of view and employ the best artists for the pictures. To say that they are secular but feebly expresses the totally unmoral influence they for the most part exert. They are the extension of the unreligious school into the homes of the people. When Father Hecker and Mrs. George V. Hecker and their associates began *The Young Catholic*, this vast mirage of the desert of life had but glimmered upon the distant horizon ; they saw it coming and they did their best to point Catholic youth away from it and lead it to the real oasis of God, with its grateful shade, its delicious fruits, and its ever-flowing springs of the waters of life.

As already said, The Catholic Publication Society was begun a year after *The Catholic World* was started, its aim being to turn to the good of religion, and especially to the conversion of non-Catholics, all the uses the press is capable of. It was a missionary work in the broadest sense seeking to enlist not only the clergy but especially the laity in an organized Apostolate of the Press, to enlighten the faith of Catholics and to spread it among their Protestant fellow-citizens. Its first work was to be the issuing of tracts and pamphlets telling the plain truth about the Catholic religion. Local societies, to be established throughout the country, were to buy these publications at a price less than cost, and distribute them gratis to all classes likely to be benefited. To catch the eye of the American people, to affect their hearts, to supply their religious wants with Catholic truth, were objects kept in view in preparing the tracts. Although some of them were addressed to Catholics, enforcing important religious duties, nearly all of them were controversial. More than seventy different tracts were printed first and last, and many hundreds of thousands, indeed several millions, of them distributed in all parts of the country, public, charitable, and penal institutions being, of course, fair field for this work. They were all very brief, few of them covering more than four small-sized pages. "Three pages of truth have before now overturned a life-time of error," said Father Hecker. The tract *Is it Honest?* though only four pages of large type, or about twelve hundred words, created a sensation everywhere, and was answered by a Protestant minister with over fifty pages of printed matter, or about fifteen times more than the tract itself. One hundred thousand copies of this tract were distributed in New York City alone. It is printed herewith as a specimen, both as to style and matter, of what one may call the aggressive-defensive tactics in Catholic controversy:

Is it Honest

To say that the Catholic Church prohibits the use of the Bible—

When anybody who chooses can buy as many as he likes at any Catholic bookstore, and can see on the first page of any one of them the approbation of the Bishops of the Catholic Church, with the Pope at their head, encouraging Catholics to read the Bible, in these words: "The faithful should be excited to the reading of the Holy Scriptures," and that not only for the Catholics of the United States, but also for those of the whole world besides?

Is it Honest

To say that Catholics believe that man by his own power can forgive sin—

When the priest is regarded by the Catholic Church only as the agent of our Lord Jesus Christ, acting by the power delegated to him, according to these words, " Whose sins you shall forgive, they are forgiven them ; and whose sins you shall retain, they are retained ? " (St. John xx. 23).

Is it Honest

To repeat over and over again that Catholics pay the priest to pardon their sins—

When such a thing is unheard of anywhere in the Catholic Church—

When any transaction of the kind is stigmatized as a grievous sin, and ranked along with murder, adultery, blasphemy, etc., in every catechism and work on Catholic theology ?

Is it Honest

To persist in saying that Catholics believe their sins are forgiven merely by the confession of them to the priest, without a true sorrow for them, or a true purpose to quit them—

When every child finds the contrary distinctly and clearly stated in the catechism, which he is obliged to learn before he can be admitted to the sacraments ? Any honest man can verify this statement by examining any Catholic catechism.

Is it Honest

To assert that the Catholic Church grants any indulgence or permission to commit sin—

When an "indulgence," according to her universally received doctrine, was never dreamed of by Catholics to imply, in any case whatever, any permission to commit the least sin ; and when an indulgence has no application whatever to sin until after sin has been repented of and pardoned ?

Is it Honest

To accuse Catholics of putting the Blessed Virgin or the Saints in the place of God or the Lord Jesus Christ—

When the Council of Trent declares that it is simply useful to ask their intercession in order to obtain favor from God, through his Son, Jesus Christ our Lord, who alone is our Saviour and Redeemer—

When " asking their prayers and influence with God " is exactly of the same nature as when Christians ask the pious prayers of one another ?

Is it Honest

To accuse Catholics of paying divine worship to images or pictures, as the heathen do—

When every Catholic indignantly repudiates any idea of the kind, and when the Council of Trent distinctly declares the doctrine of the Catholic Church in regard to them to be, " that there is no divinity or virtue in them which should appear to claim the tribute of one's veneration "; but that " all the honor which is paid to them shall be referred to the originals whom they are designed to represent ? " (Sess. 25).

Is it Honest

To make these and many other similar charges against Catholics—

When they detest and abhor such false doctrines more than those do who make them, and make them, too, without ever having read a Catholic book, or taken any honest means of ascertaining the doctrines which the Catholic Church really teaches?

Remember the commandment of God, which says: "Thou shalt not bear false witness against thy neighbor."

Reader, would you be honest, and do no injustice? Then examine the doctrines of the Catholic Church; read the works of Catholics. See both sides. Examine, and be fair; for AMERICANS LOVE FAIR PLAY.

In preparing these little messengers of truth every style of writing was used, narrative, allegory, dialogue, and positive argument. They are as good reading to-day as when first issued, and the volume which they form may be placed in an inquirer's hands with excellent effect. To keep them agoing Father Hecker laid all his friends of any literary ability under contribution, the series being opened by Archbishop Spalding with a tract on *Religious Indifferentism.* Did space permit, an entire list of the subjects dealt with might be given, and the reader could the better see how they embrace the entire controversy between Catholics and Protestants and infidels, many of the tracts being masterpieces of popular argumentation.

As to the business side of these enterprises, Father Hecker confided it to Mr. Lawrence Kehoe, who was publisher of *The Catholic World* and of *The Young Catholic* from their beginning until the Paulists became their own publishers, shortly before Mr. Kehoe's death. He was placed in charge of the Publication Society as manager when it was started, and so continued until the formation of the present firm, remaining then the active partner in its management. No more ardent advocate of a good cause could be desired than Lawrence Kehoe. Father Hecker cherished him as a friend, and he was his zealous and efficient agent in his entire Apostolate of the Press.

The purpose of the Publication Society was missionary, and the intention was that its books, tracts, and pamphlets should be either given away or sold at cost price, or below it. Therefore it was necessary to secure funds for the running expenses. The reader has seen that this was to have been done by the contributions of subsidiary societies. To aid in the formation of these and to solicit contributions in money, circulars were sent to all the clergy of the United States. Only a few made any practical response. But the meeting of the Second Plenary Council of Baltimore in 1866, the same year the Society was founded, was opportune. The bishops were induced to take the matter up, and a decree, of which the following is a translation, was enacted. After speaking of the need of supplying Catholic literature at a low price the Council proceeds:

" Since a society with this object in view, known as The Catholic Publication Society, has been founded in New York, and has been so far conducted with commendable diligence and with notable success, we therefore consider it to be entirely worthy of the favor and assistance of prelates and priests, as well as of the Catholic people in general. That the whole country may the better and more certainly share in its advantages, we advise and exhort the bishops to establish branches of this Society in their dioceses, by means of whose officers the publications of the Society may be distributed. But as without great expenditure of money these societies cannot be kept up and must fail of success, the bishops shall therefore appoint a yearly collection for their support, to be taken up in all the principal churches, or shall make other provision for the same purpose according to their best judgment " (Con. Plen. Balt., § 500).

From the Pastoral Letter of the same Council we extract the following:

" In connection with this matter [the Catholic Press] we earnestly recommend to the faithful of our charge The Catholic Publication Society, lately established in the city of New York by a zealous and devoted clergyman. Besides the issuing of short tracts with which this Society has begun, and which may be usefully employed to arrest the attention of many whom neither inclination nor leisure will allow to read larger works, this Society contemplates the publication of Catholic books, according as circumstances may permit and the interests of religion appear to require. From the judgment and good taste evinced in the composition and selection of such tracts and books as have already been issued by this Society, we are encouraged to hope that it will be eminently effective in making known the truths of our holy religion, and dispelling the prejudices which are mainly owing to want of information on the part of so many of our fellow-citizens. For this it is necessary that a generous co-operation be given both by clergy and laity to the undertaking, which is second to none in importance among the subsidiary aids which the inventions of modern times supply to our ministry for the diffusion of Catholic truth."

How elated Father Hecker was by this action of the Council, and how over-sanguine, as the event proved, of the future of the Society, is shown by the following extracts from letters to a friend :

" My efforts in the recent Council were completely successful, owing to the many prayers offered to God—yours not the least. Could you have seen the letters from different quarters, from good pious nuns, and persons loving and serving and fearing God in the world, written to me, and their writers all praying and doing works of mercy and mortification for the purposes I had in view, you could not wonder at my success. God did it. What is more, I was fully conscious of the fact, and it is this that made my great joy.

" The Catholic Publication Society has the unanimous consent, and sympathy, and co-operation of the entire episcopate and clergy. Every year there is a collection to be taken up in the principal churches for its support. I have drawn an elephant, but I do not feel like the man who did not know what to do with him after he had got him."

" It is good in God to place me in a position in which I can act efficiently. The disposition towards me is, I know, most pleasant and favorable. I have been placed where I shall be at liberty to act and direct action. Quietly pray for me as the Holy Spirit may suggest. On my part I will also seek the same guidance. How good God is to give it ! "

The Council had hardly adjourned when it began to be plain that in legislating for The Catholic Publication Society the prelates had been over-stimulated by the zeal of Archbishop Spalding and the personal influence of Father Hecker himself, who was present in his capacity of Superior of the Paulists. He went among the bishops and pleaded for the Apostolate of the Press with characteristic vigor, and with his usual success. Aided by the archbishop, he lifted the Fathers of the Council for a moment above what in their sober senses they deemed the exclusive duty of the hour. This was to provide churches and priests, and schools and school-teachers, for the people. Already far too numerous for their clergy, the Catholic people were increasing by immigration alone at the rate of more than a quarter of a million a year. Every effort must be concentrated, it was thought, and every penny spent, in the vast work of housing and feeding the wandering flocks of the Lord. And certainly the magnitude of the task and the success attained in performing it can excuse the indifference shown to the Apostolate of the Press, if anything can excuse it. But it seemed otherwise to Father Hecker, as it does now to us. For the Catholic people could have been better and earlier cared for in their spiritual concerns if furnished with the abundant supply of good reading which the carrying out of Father Hecker's plan would have given them, and that at no great expense. What substitute for a priest is equal to a good book? What vocation to the priesthood has not found its origin in the pages of a good book, or at any rate been fostered by its devout lessons? And all history as well as experience proves that the best guarantee of the faith of a Catholic, moving amidst kindly-disposed non-Catholic neighbors, is the aggressive force of missionary zeal. The Publication Society, if brought into active play, would have done much to create this zeal, and would have supplied its best arms of attack and defence by an abundance of free Catholic reading. It would have helped on every good work by auxiliary forces drawn from intelligent faith and instructed zeal.

A closer view of the case shows that antecedents of a racial and social character among the people had something to do with the apathy we have been considering. To a great degree it still rests upon us, though such organized efforts as the Catholic Truth Society of St. Paul, Minnesota, and the Holy Ghost Society of New Orleans indicate a change for the better.

Had Father Hecker continued in good health there is a chance, though a desperate one, that he might have overcome all obstacles. Many zealous souls would have followed his lead. As a specimen we may name the Vicar-General of San Francisco, Father Prendergast, who, with the help of a few earnest friends, raised several thousand dollars in gold in that diocese alone. But in 1871 Father Hecker's strength began to fail, and in the following year his active life was done. As already shown, it had been the intention to establish branch societies everywhere, whose delegates would regularly meet and control the entire work, giving the Church in America an approved, powerful auxiliary dominantly made up of laymen. In that sense the Society never was so much as organized, the number of branch societies not at any time warranting such a step as a general meeting of their representatives. The money actually collected

was all spent in printing and circulating the tracts and other
publications given away or sold below cost, Father Hecker
and the Paulists managing the entire work. When the
collections gave out, Mr. George V. Hecker contributed a
large sum for continuing the undertaking. The result was
his finding himself in the publishing business, which he was
compelled to place as far as possible on a basis to meet the current outlay. The Society, as far as its name went, thus became
a Catholic publishing firm, with Mr. Hecker mainly involved
financially and Mr. Kehoe in charge of the business. Mr.
Hecker sunk a small fortune in the Apostolate of the Press,
much of it during the hard times between 1873 and 1876. The
history of the whole affair is as curious as it is instructive, and
hence we have given a pretty full account of it. It weighed
heavy on Father Hecker's heart, though he astonished his friends
by the equanimity with which he accepted its failure. His work,
if it did not perish in a night like the prophet's gourd, withered
quickly into very singular form and narrow proportions. The
amazement of Protestant bigots at the appearance of the Catholic tracts, speechless and clamorous by turns; the quaker guns
of the Second Plenary Council, and the bright dreams of a vigorous attack upon the enemy all along the line and by all classes
of clergy and laity—how Father Hecker did in after years discuss these topics, and how he did inspire all about him with his
own enthusiastic hopes of a future and more successful effort!
When he went to Europe in 1873, too feeble to hope for recovery, leaving the enterprise behind him in the same condition as
his own broken health, how unmurmuring was his submission to
the Divine and human wills which had brought all to naught!

Not more than a few words need be said of his undertaking
to buy a New York daily paper. It happened that in 1871 a
prominent journal, a member of the Associated Press, could be
bought for three hundred thousand dollars. In an instant, as it
seems, Father Hecker grasped the opportunity. By personal appeals to the rich men of the city more than half the sum required was subscribed, Archbishop McCloskey heading the list
with a large amount. But soon the doctors had to be called in,
and the enterprise went no further.

How Father Hecker appeared to men when advocating the
Apostolate of the Press, and how he spread the forceful majesty
of Catholicity over his personal surroundings, is shown by Mr.

Father Hecker in 1873.

(From a photograph.)

James Parton's words in the article in the *Atlantic Monthly* already quoted from: "The special work of this [the Paulist] community is to bring the steam printing-press to bear upon the spread of the Catholic religion in the United States." The resistless missionary power *latent* in the Church is thus spoken of by the same writer:

"What a powerful engine is this! Suppose the six ablest and highest Americans were living thus, freed from all worldly cares, in an agreeable, secluded abode, yet near the centre of things, with twelve zealous, gifted young men to help and cheer them, a thousand organizations in the country to aid in distributing their writings, and in every town a spacious edifice and an eager audience to hang upon their lips. What could they *not* effect in a lifetime of well-directed work?"

What follows, taken from a letter of Father Hecker's while sick in Europe in 1874, shows one of his aims in the Apostolate of the Press. It is suggestive of a result since attained, at least partially, in more than one religious community in America:

"Monsignor Mermillod desired, early in the fall, that I should see Canon Schorderet, of this place [Fribourg in Switzerland], as he was engaged zealously with the press. This was one of my principal reasons for visiting this place. My surprise has been most gratifying in finding that he has organized, or rather begun, an association of girls to set types, etc., who live in community and labor for the love of God in the Apostolate of the Press. He publishes several newspapers and journals. The house in which the members live is also the store and the publishing house. Each girl has her own room. They are under the patronage of St. Paul. The canon is filled with the idea of St. Paul as the great patron of the Press, *the first Christian journalist.* What has long been my dream of a movement of this nature has found here an incipient realization. Our views in regard to the mission of the press, and the necessity of running it for the spread and defence of the faith as a form of Christian sacrifice in our day, are identical. You can easily fancy what interest and consolation our meeting and conversation must be to each other. His movement is the completion of The Catholic Publication Society of New York."

As there may be some curiosity about Father Hecker's principles as a public writer, in point of view of ecclesiastical authority, we give the following from a letter written just before the Vatican Council:

"1. Absolute and unswerving loyalty to the authority of the Church, wherever and however expressed, as God's authority upon earth and for all time.

"2. To seek in the same dispositions the true spirit of the Church, and be unreservedly governed by it as the wisdom of the Most High.

"3. To keep my mind and heart free from all attachments to schools, parties, or persons in the Church, Hecker included, so that nothing within me may hinder the light and direction of the Holy Spirit.

"4. In case any conflict arises concerning what Hecker may have spoken or written, or any work or movement in which he may be engaged, to re-examine. If wrong, make him retract at once. If not, then ask: Is the question of that importance that it requires defence, and the upsetting of attacks? If not of this importance, then not to delay and perhaps jeopardize the progress of other works, and condemn Hecker to simple silence.

"5. In the midst of the imperfections, abuses, scandals, etc., of the human side of the Church, never to allow myself to think or to express a word which might seem to place a truth of the Catholic faith in doubt, or to savor of the spirit of disobedience.

"6. With all this in view, to be the most earnest and ardent friend of all true progress, and to work with all my might for its promotion through existing organizations and authorities."

IN 1867 Father Hecker visited Europe in company with Father Hewit for the purpose of opening business relations between The Catholic Publication Society and English, Irish, and Continental publishers, as well as to attend the Catholic Congress of Malines held in the summer of that year. The latter purpose was the chief inducement for the journey. The Archbishop of New York favored the project of holding a Catholic Congress in America, and encouraged Father Hecker to study the proceedings at Malines with this end in view. Their stay at Malines was full of instruction, as they heard there the renowned orators, Dupanloup and Montalembert, as well as others of note. The Catholic Congress of American laymen held in Baltimore a few years ago, and whose good effects are still felt, would have been assembled twenty years earlier if Father Hecker could have brought it about. These meetings were part of his scheme for that *moral* organization of Catholic forces which he knew to be so necessary for the fruitful working of the *official* unity of the Church.

In the early part of the year 1869 Pius IX. wrote Father Hecker an autograph letter commending the various religious works which he and his community were engaged in, especially the Apostolate of the Press, and giving them all his blessing.

"I have good news to tell you," he wrote to a friend. "The Holy Father has written me the 'tallest' kind of a letter, endorsing every good work in which I am engaged. Hurrah for Catholicity at Fifty-ninth Street! My private opinion is that the Holy Father has gone too far in his endorsement of Hecker. He has made me feel ashamed of myself and humiliated."

When Pius IX. called together the Council of the Vatican Father Hecker was urged by friends, among them several bishops, to go to Rome for the occasion. The late Bishop Rosecrans, of Columbus, Ohio, not being able to attend himself, appointed Father Hecker his Procurator, or proxy. Before his departure he preached a sermon on the Council in the Paulist Church, which was printed in *The Catholic World* for December, 1869. He devoted the greater part of it to quieting the wild forebodings of timid Catholics and combating the prognostics of outright anti-Catholics. He concluded by asking the people to pray that the hopes of a new and brighter era for religion, to date from this great event, might be fulfilled; for it was commonly believed and expressly intended that the entire state of the Church should be considered and legislated upon at the Council. The breaking out of the Franco-Prussian war, as is well known, together with the seizure of Rome by the Piedmontese, frustrated these hopes as to all but the very first part of the work laid out for the Council.

Father Hecker arrived in Rome on the 26th of November, 1869. When the preliminary business of organization had been finished it was announced that the procurators of absent bishops would not be admitted to the Council, as the number of prelates present in person was exceedingly large. But, he writes home:

"The Archbishop of Baltimore has made me his theologian of his own accord. This gives me the privilege of reading all the documents of the Council, of knowing all that takes place in it, its discussions, etc. As his theologian I take part in the meetings and deliberations of the American hierarchy, which is, as it were, a permanent council concerning the interests of the Church in the United States, in which I feel a strong and special interest."

Father Hecker had ever been a firm believer in the doctrine of papal infallibility, as was the case with all American Catholics, prelates, priests, and people. Shortly before leaving for the Council we heard him say: "I have always heard the voice of Rome as that of truth itself." This he also showed very plainly in his farewell sermon. Speaking of the dread of undue papal influence over the bishops in the Council, he exclaimed: "All I have to say is, that if the Roman Court prevail [in the deliberations of the Council], it is the Holy Ghost who prevails through the Roman Court." But the tone of the controversy on the subject of papal infallibility, which soon deafened the world, was too sharp for his nerves, and he abstained from mingling in it. As a matter of fact he determined to get away from Rome early in the spring of 1870. If the reader would know what we deem to have been Father Hecker's frame of mind about the proceedings of the Council we refer him to Bishop J. L. Spalding's excellent life of his uncle, the then Archbishop of Baltimore, whose views of both doctrine and policy were, as far as we can judge, shared by Father Hecker, who was his intimate and beloved friend.

But his stay in the Eternal City, at this time more than ever before the focus of all religious truth, as well as the object of all human expectancy, had not been uneventful. Very much against his will he preached one of the sermons of the course given during the octave of the Epiphany, in the Church of San Andrea della Valle, and later on another, on an important occasion, in place of Archbishop Spalding, who had fallen ill. Much of his time he spent with the American bishops and the distinguished priests who were with them ; he renewed the old-time friendships of his stay in Rome twelve years before, seeing a good deal of Archbishop Connolly, of Halifax, N. S.; he made new friends, too, among whom he names especially Mrs. Craven, the author of the *Récit d'une Sœur ;* and he formed acquaintance with leading men and women of all nationalities.

"There is not a day passes," he wrote home, "that I do not make the acquaintance of persons of great importance, or acquire the knowledge of matters equally important for me to know; and I gain more in a day than one could in years at other times. For we may say that the intelligence, the science and sanctity of the Church are now gathered into this one city. Yet my heart is in my work at home."

He had two private audiences with Pius IX., which, though of course brief, were very interesting ; the Pope remembered him, and expressed his interest in him and his work in America. The following extracts from letters to his brother George, written very soon after reaching Rome, recall an old friend:

"I do not know whether I told you of my interview with Cardinal Barnabo. He received me literally with open arms. After an hour's conversation on several matters he ended by saying : 'The affection and esteem which I had for you when you were here before has been increased by your labors since then, and my door is always open for you, and I shall always be glad to see you.' He entertains a high idea of the importance of *The Catholic World.*"

" I had a most pleasant interview a few evenings since with Cardinal Barnabo," he writes in April, 1870, shortly before leaving. "Among other things he said : ' You ought to be grateful to God for three reasons : first, He drew you out of heresy ; second, He saved you from shipwreck in Rome ; third, He has given you talents, etc., to do great things for His Church in your country.' He takes great interest in the Paulists."

Not alone in Rome did he meet with friends, but what follows, written home in December, 1869, tells that his name and his vocation had been made familiar to many observant persons in Europe :

" It surprises me to find my name familiar everywhere I have been on my travels. But magazines, newspapers, telegrams, and what-not have turned the world into a whispering gallery. But the less a man is known to men the more he knows of God ; so it seems to me, as a rule. Yet great activity may flow as a consequence of intimate union with Him whom theologians call *Actus Purissimus.* From the fact of his being known, I entertain no better idea of Father Hecker than I ever did ; and could I get him again in the United States, he will be more devoted than ever to his work."

Father Hecker gave his view of the bearing of the Vatican Council on the future of religion in a letter which will be found below. It concerns what we have already spoken of at some length and what we shall again refer to, namely, the relation between the inner and outer action of the Holy Ghost as factors in the soul's sanctification. We heard Father Hecker several times affirm that he received special illumination from God on this subject while in Rome during the Council, and that something like the very words in which properly to express himself were then given to him. It was written in the summer of 1872, but we quote it here before bidding adieu to Rome and accompanying him in his short pilgrimage among the great shrines of Italy :

" These two months past I have been driven away from home to one place and another by poor health. . . . The definition of the Vatican Council completes and fixes for ever the external authority of the Church against the heresies and errors

of the last three centuries. . . . None but the declared enemies of the Church and misdirected Catholics can fail to see
in this the directing influence of the Holy Ghost.

" The Vatican Council has placed the Church in battle array,
unmasked the concealed batteries of her enemies ; the conflict
will be on a fair and open field, and it will be decisive. The
recent hostility of the governments of Europe, and especially of
Italy, against the Church, has shown the wisdom of the Vatican
Council in preparing the Church to meet the crisis. The definition leaves no longer any doubt in regard to the authority of
the Chief of the Church.

" For my part I sincerely thank the Jesuits for their influence
in bringing it about, even though that were as great as some
people would have us believe. . . . This had to be done
before the Church could resume her normal course of action.
What is that ? Why, the divine external authority of the
Church completed, fixed beyond all controversy, her attention
and that of all her children can now be turned more directly to
the divine and interior authority of the Holy Ghost in the soul.
The whole Church giving her attention to the interior inspirations of the Holy Spirit, will give birth to her renewal, and
enable her to reconquer her place and true position in Europe
and the whole world. For we must never forget that the immediate means of Christian perfection is the interior direction
of the Holy Spirit, while the *test* of our being directed by the
Holy Spirit and not by our fancies and prejudices, is our filial
obedience to the divine external authority of the Church.

" If for three centuries the most influential schools in the
Church gave a preponderance in their teaching and spiritual
direction to those virtues which are in direct relation to the external authority of the Church, it must be remembered that the
heresies of that period all aimed at the destruction of this authority. The character of this teaching, therefore, was a necessity. There was no other way of preserving the children of the
Church from the danger of this infection. If the effect of this
teaching made Catholics childlike, less manly and active than
others, this was under the circumstances inevitable.

" The definition of the Vatican Council, thanks to the Jesuits,
now gives us freedom to turn our attention in another direction,
and to cultivating other virtues. If one infidel was equal to two
Catholics in courage and action in the past, in the future one

Catholic, moved by the Holy Spirit, will be equal to half-a-dozen or a thousand infidels and heretics.

"The stupid Döllingerites do not see or understand that what they pretend to desire—the renewal of the Church—can only be accomplished by the reign of the Holy Spirit throughout the Church, and that this can only be brought about by a filial submission to her divine external authority. Instead of their insane opposition to the definition of the Vatican Council and to the Jesuits, whose influence they have exaggerated beyond all measure, they ought to embrace both with enthusiasm, as opening the door to the renewal of the Church and a brighter and more glorious future. . . . To my view there is no other way or hope for such a future."

He left Rome and his many warm friends there early in the spring of 1870, and, as he thought, for the last time. He was full of courage, he was conscious of not only perfect agreement with every credential of orthodoxy, but of interior impulses of a marvellously inspiring kind. In a very familiar letter to his brother's family he says that just before his departure, while standing in one of the great piazzas, looking at the concourse of representatives of all nations passing back and forth, gathered to take counsel with the Vicar of Christ for the well-being of the human race, he was so exhilarated that he could hardly refrain from calling out, "*Three cheers for Paradise, and one for the United States!*"

"I return with new hope and fresher energy," he writes, "for that better future for the Church and humanity which is in store for both in the United States. This is the conviction of all intelligent and hopeful minds in Europe. They look to the other side of the Atlantic not only with great interest, but to catch the light which will solve the problems of Europe. Our course is surely fraught with the interests, hopes, and happiness of the race. I never felt so much like acquitting myself as a Christian and a man. The convictions which have hitherto directed my course have been deepened, confirmed, and strengthened by recent experience here, and I return to my country a better Catholic and more an American than ever."

That he might say Mass daily and at convenient hours while in Rome, crowded as it was at the time with bishops and priests,

he obtained leave to do so in his own rooms. He made little
pilgrimages to the great shrines of the Holy City, especially
those of the Apostles and the typical martyrs, not forgetting, of
course, his favorite modern saints, Philip Neri and Ignatius
Loyola. The following are extracts from letters home telling of
his celebration of St. Paul's Conversion and of the martyrdom
of St. Agnes. The reader will remember that the "association
of women" here mentioned was one of his earliest ideas, and
one of the many whose realization Providence has given over,
let us hope, to some souls especially favored by Father Hecker's
gifts :

"I pray much for each member of the community, and for
light to guide it in the way of God. Within a short period
much light has been given to me, and the importance of our
work and its greatness have impressed me greatly, more than
ever before. Yesterday I went to the Basilica of St. Paul, being
the feast of his conversion, especially to invoke his aid. I felt
that my visit was not in vain. . . . I forgot no one of our
dear community. . . . On the 21st I said Mass in the catacombs of St. Agnes ; it was the day of her feast. More than
twenty persons were present, friends and acquaintances. I gave
eleven communions, and made a little discourse at the close of
the Holy Sacrifice. The scene was most solemn and affecting.

"What did I pray for? [during my Mass in St. Agnes's Cata-
comb]. For you all, especially for the future. What future?
How shall I name it ? The association of women in our country to aid the work of God through the Holy Church for its
conversion. My convictions become fixed, and my determination
to begin the enterprise consecrated.

"At the close of the Mass I made a short discourse. Think
of it, preaching once more in the Catacombs, surrounded with
the tombs where the martyrs are laid and where the voice of
the martyrs had spoken ! You can imagine that the impression
was profound and solemn on us all. It was a piece of fool-
hardiness on my part to open my lips and speak, when everything around us spoke so impressively and solemnly to our
hearts. I will attempt to interpret this speech : In the days of
Agnes, Christians were called upon to resist and conquer physical persecution. In our day we are called upon to overcome
intellectual and social opposition. They conquered ! We shall

conquer! Agnes tells us there is no excuse for cowardice. Agnes was young, Agnes was weak, Agnes was a girl, and she conquered! One Agnes can conquer the opposition of the nineteenth century. Such in substance was my discourse. The whole scene caused every one to be bathed in tears."

After leaving Rome he went straight to Assisi, for whose saint he had ever felt a very powerful attraction. He thus describes his impressions:

"The people that I have seen about here have a milder countenance and a more cheerful look, more refined and human than the Italians around Rome. They are to the other Italians what the Swabians are to the other Germans. It is easy for the Minnesinger of the human, to become the Minnesinger of Divine love.

"I could have kissed the stones of the streets of the town when I remembered that St. Francis had trodden these same streets, and the love and heroism which beat in his heart. . . . I said Holy Mass at the tomb of St. Francis, and in presence of his body this morning—a votive Mass of the Saint. It seems I could linger weeks and weeks around this holy spot. . . . What St. Francis did for his age one might do for one's own. He touched the chords of feeling and of aspiration in the hearts of the men and women of his time and organized them for action. St. Dominic did the same for the intellectual wants of the time. Why not do this for our age? Who shall so touch the springs of men's hearts and reach their minds as to lead them to the desire of united action, and organize them so as to bring forth great results? There is no doubt that the age wants this. Who is there that is inspired from a higher sphere of life, and sees into the future, so as to be able to speak to men and to invite them to do the work of God in our day? Who takes all humanity into his heart, and with the past and present at once in his mind can inspire men to live and act for the divine future?"

He also visited the Holy House at Loretto, and, passing through Venice and Milan to see the great churches of these cities, "the despair of all modern church-builders," as he says, he came finally to Genoa.

" I turned my steps," he writes, " to the general hospital ; and why ? Because the interest of my heart was there, and has been there for upward of twenty years. It is the spot where St. Catherine of Genoa labored for the miserable, loved God, and sanctified her soul. Her body is in a crystal case, uncorrupted, withered in appearance but not unpleasant to the sight. When the curtain was withdrawn and I could see her face and her feet, which were uncovered, I could not help exclaiming with the Psalmist, ' God is wonderful in His saints ! ' I cannot express what an attraction I have always felt for St. Catherine of Genoa. She knew how to reconcile the greatest fidelity to the interior attrait and guidance of the Holy Spirit with perfect filial obedience to the external and divine authority of the Holy Church. She knew how to reconcile the highest degree of divine contemplation with the greatest extent of works of external charity. She was a heroic lover of God, for she resisted His gifts, lest she might forget the Giver in them, and be hindered the entire possession of Him, and the complete union of her soul with Him. As a virgin she was pure, a model as a wife, and as a widow a saint ! Her writings on the spiritual life are masterpieces, and though a woman, no man has surpassed, if any has equalled, the eloquence of her pen."

He procured an excellent copy of St. Catherine's portrait preserved at the hospital, and brought it home with him. He had done the same for Sts. Philip and Ignatius before leaving Rome. St. Catherine's picture represents a handsome face, earnest, simple, and joyful ; she is dressed plainly as a devout woman living in the world, lovely to look upon and inspiring love of God and man in the beholder.

Father Hecker's stay in Europe during the winter of 1869–70 and the following spring awakened in his soul aspirations towards a wide and enduring religious movement in the Old World, similar to that which he had started in the New. At the time he did not anticipate any personal share in it other than encouragement and direction from America. The reader will learn in the sequel that these aspirations were again felt, and that with renewed force, when he returned to Europe in ill health three years later.

What follows is from a pocket diary, and from a letter home :

" The work that Divine Providence has called us to do in our own country, were its spirit extended throughout Europe, would be the focus of new light and an element of regeneration. Our country has a providential position in our century in relation to Europe, and our efforts to Catholicize and sanctify it give it an importance, in a religious aspect, of a most interesting and significant character."

" I do not wish to cross the Atlantic ever again, and therefore would like to finish with Europe and Italy. As for the notable men of the day, I have seen many of them—enough of them. My present experience in one way and another seems to have prepared me to lay a foundation for action which will be suitable not only for the present but for centuries to come. No one of my previous convictions have been disturbed, but much strengthened and enlarged and settled. I see nothing, practically, in which I am engaged, that, were it in my power, I would now wish to alter or abandon. I shall return with the resolution to continue them with more confidence, more zeal, more energy."

He arrived in New York in June, 1870.

WE have now arrived at the last period of Father Hecker's life, the long illness which completed his meed of suffering and of merit, and gradually drew him down to the grave. It will not be expected that we shall treat extensively of this subject; nor can one who writes in the beginning of the '90s about the closing scenes of a life which ended late in the '80s go very much into detail without bringing in the living. As to Father Hecker's latter days in this world, it may be said that his joy and courage and buoyancy of spirits, as well as his hopeful outlook upon men and things, were all tried in the furnace of extreme bodily suffering as well as of the most excruciating mental agony.

Four distinct epochs divide Father Hecker's life: one when in early days he was driven from home and business and ultimately into the Church by aspirations towards a higher life; another marks the extraordinary dealings of God with his soul during his novitiate and time of studies; the third was the struggle in Rome which produced the Paulist community; the fourth and last was the illness which we are now to consider. The closing scenes of his life are scattered over more than sixteen years, filled with almost every form of pain of body and darkness of soul.

From severe colds, acute headaches, and weakness of the digestive organs Father Hecker was a frequent sufferer. But towards the end of the year 1871 his headaches became much more painful, his appetite left him, and sleeplessness and excitability of the nervous system were added to his other ailments. Remedies of every kind were tried, but without permanent relief, and, although he lectured and preached and did his other work all winter and most of the following spring, his weakness increased, until by the summer of 1872 he was wholly incapacitated. The winter of 1872-3 was spent in the South without notable improvement, and early in the following summer, acting upon the advice of physicians, he went to Europe. "Look upon me as a dead man," he said with tears as he bade the community farewell; "God is trying me severely in soul and body, and I must have the courage to suffer crucifixion." He also assured us that whatever action should be taken in adopting the Constitutions, then under consideration, had his hearty approval beforehand. He was accompanied to Europe by Father Deshon, from whom he parted with deep emotion at Ragatz, a health resort in Switzerland.

Father Hecker remained more than two years in Europe, trying every change of climate and scene, and every other remedy advised by physicians, and returned to New York in October, 1875, with unimproved health. He had derived most benefit from a journey up the Nile in the winter of 1873–4, and a short visit to the Holy Land in the following spring. While in Europe his mind was busy, and he managed to meet many of his old friends there, and formed new and important acquaintances. In February, 1875, he published his pamphlet, *An Exposition of the Church in View of the Present Needs of the Age*, which contains his estimate of the evils of our times, especially in Europe, and the adequate remedy for them. On his return to New York he was too weak to bear the routine of the house in Fifty-ninth Street and lived with his brother George till the fall of 1879, when he removed to the convent, remaining with the community till his death nine years afterwards.

As to the physical sufferings of those last sixteen years, they were never such as to impair Father Hecker's mental soundness. He never had softening of the brain, as the state of his nerves before going to Europe seemed to indicate; nor had he heart disease, as was for a time suspected. His mental powers were intact from first to last, though his organs of speech were sometimes too slow for his thoughts. His digestion had been impaired by excessive abstinence in early manhood, dating back to a time before he was a Catholic, and his nervous system, also, had been injured by that means, as well as by the pressure of excessive work in later life. Gradual impoverishment of the blood was the result, and the dropping down of nervous force, till at last the body struck work altogether. Four or five years before his death Father Hecker became subject to frequent attacks of angina pectoris, said to be the most painful of all diseases. During the sixteen years of illness every symptom of bodily illness was aggravated by the least attention to community affairs or business matters, and also by interior trials which will presently be described.

He was not unwilling to trace his breaking down to exces-

sive austerity in former years. Once when asked for advice
about corporal mortification he answered : " Don't go too fast.
Remember St. Bernard's regret for having gone too far with
such things in his youth. For my part, for many years I prac
tised frightful penances, and now I fear that much of my physical helplessness is due to that cause." His state was not one
of utter debility, though that quickly resulted if watchfulness
were relaxed, or from application to responsible duties. But his
strength never was " much to speak of," " only so, so," to use his
own expressions, which signified a very small amount of the
power of exertion or endurance in the muscles and nerves.

" What about my health? " he wrote from Europe. " There
are days when I feel quite myself, and then others when I sink
down to the bottom. My condition of mind and body often
perplexes me, and there is nothing left me but to abandon all
into the hands of Divine Providence. The end of it all is entirely in the dark, and were there not parallel epochs in my past
life, and similar things in the lives of some others which I have
read, my perplexity would be greater."

And again, from Ragatz, in the summer of 1875 :

" My state of health is much the same. I found last week
that my pulse was bounding in a few hours from the sixties
into the nineties without any apparent cause. Yesterday I determined to consult the leading physician here. He examined
me, and, like all others, attributes everything to my nerves, resulting from impoverished blood. I say to myself: 1st, How long
will the machine keep working in this style? 2d, There will be
a smash-up some day. 3d, Or perhaps I shall be able to get
up more steam and run it a while longer. Who knows?"

And in another letter from the same place :

" Even here, freed from all [labors]; it often seems to me
that a good breeze, if it struck me in the right place, would
drive the soul out of my body, so lightly is it connected with
it, so slightly do they hold together."

As already said, his trip to Egypt had given him a temporary
relief, and this was due, so he supposed, to utter change of
scene and to solitude. When it was over he wrote as follows:

"This trip has been in every respect much more to my benefit than my most sanguine expectations led me to hope. It seems to me almost like an inspiration, such have been its beneficial effects to my mind and body. In Nubia there reigned profound silence and repose, and in lower Egypt, although there is more activity and evidence of modern life, still it is quiet and tranquil. I feel somewhat like one who has been in solitude for three or four months."

"My daily régime," he writes to his brother and Mrs. Hecker, from Italy, "has not changed these two years which I have spent in Europe. If I rise before nine I feel it the whole day. In the morning I awake about seven for good, and take a cup of tea with some bread and butter. I then read; sometimes, not often, I write a note in bed, and rise about nine or ten. I take a lunch at twelve and dine at six. My appetite is not much at any time. My sleep, so so. [All through his illness he went to bed at nine or shortly after.] I feel for the most part like a man balancing whether he will keep on swimming or go under the water. Sometimes I take a nap two or three times a day—if I can get it. There are weeks when I do not and cannot put my pen to paper. To write a note is a great effort. . . . Though my strength is so little my mind is not unoccupied, and I keep up some reading."

Just in what way his spiritual difficulties accelerated his bodily decline it is hard to say, for he was generally extremely reticent as to his interior life. A few words dropped unawares and at long intervals, and carefully taken down at the time, give fleeting glimpses into a soul which was a dark chamber of sorrow, though it was sometimes peaceful sorrow. To this we can fortunately add some sentences written in an unusually confidential mood in letters from Europe. Before his illness he was over-joyful, or so it seemed to some to whom this trait of his was a temptation. "Why," it was said, "religion seems to have no penitential side to Father Hecker at all." From the day of his ordination until his illness began he might have made the Psalmist's words his own: "There be many that say, Who shall show us any good? Lord, Thou hast set upon us the light of Thy countenance, Thou hast put gladness in my heart." But now the light of that radiant joy had faded away, and the face of God, though as present as ever before, loomed over him dark. threatening, and majestic. He had studied spiritual doctrine too well not to be ready for this trial, nor had it been sent to him without warning. Nevertheless the sensible presence of God's love had been so vivid and constant that he could alternate the joy of labor with that of prayer with the greatest ease. And now it was an alternation, not of choice but of dire compulsion, between bitter, helpless inaction, and a state of prayer which was a mere dread of an all-too-near Judge. It seemed to him as if he had boasted, "I said in my abundance I shall not be moved for ever," and now he must end the inspired sentence, "Thou hast turned away Thy face from me and I became troubled." When this obscuration of the Divine Love first grew upon him the misery of it was intolerable and was borne with extreme difficulty. The pain was lessened at intervals as time passed on, and before a year had elapsed, his letters from Europe, though they did not before complain of desolation, now show its previous existence by hailing the advent of seasons of interior peace. But from beginning to end of this entire period of his life we have not found a word of his speaking of joy. And again, even the peace would go and the desolation return; the face of God, not any time smiling, had lost its calm regard and was once more bent frowning upon him. The following extracts from letters written from Switzerland in the autumn of 1874, and within a month of each other, tell of these alternations of storm and calm :

"As to my health these last ten days I cannot say much. My interior trials have been such that it would be impossible that my health should improve under them. As long as they last I must expect to suffer. I see nothing before me but darkness, and there is nothing within my soul but desolation and bitterness. Cut off from all that formerly interested me, banished as it were from home and country, isolated from everything, the doors of heaven shut, I feel overwhelmed with misery and crushed to atoms. My being away from my former duties is a negative relief ; it frees me from the additional burden and trouble which would necessarily fall upon me if I were within reach."

"There remains nothing for me but to confide in, to follow, and abandon myself to that Guide who has directed me from the beginning. I read Job, Jeremias, and Thomas à Kempis, and meditate on the sufferings of Our Lord and the character of His death. I recall to mind what I have read on these matters in spiritual writers and the Lives of the Saints. I reflect how from the very nature of the purification of the soul this darkness, bitterness, and desolation must be; but not a drop of consolation is distilled into my soul. The only words which come to my lips are "My soul is sad unto death," and these I repeat and repeat again. At all times, in rising and in going to bed, in company and at my meals, I whisper them to myself, while to others I appear cheerful and join in the talk. At the most I can but die; this is the lot of all, and no one can tell the moment when.

"Withal, I try to have patience, resignation, endurance, and trust in God, waiting on His guidance and leaving all in His hands."

"Since my last I have had some relief from my interior trials, and no sooner does this take place than my body recovers some of its strength. It would not have been possible for me to have borne much longer the desolation which filled my soul. Each new trial, when passed, leaves me more quiet and tranquil. Past periods of my life give me hope that this trial will also come to an end. What will that be? How will it happen? and when? God alone knows. He that has led me so many years still guides me, and resistance to His will is worse than vain. Judging from that same past, my expectations to return to my former labors are not sanguine. It seems to me sometimes that I am cut off from these to be prepared for a deeper and broader basis for future action. But whether this will be so or not, is in the hands of God. Whatever He wills me to do, I must do it. My own will has become null, and all that is left for me to do is to wait on His good pleasure and His own time. To act or not to act, to suffer or not to suffer, to speak or to keep silence, to return to my former labors or never to return, to live on or die, all have become indifferent to me. I am in God's hands, with no will of my own; for He has taken it, and it is for Him to do with me whatever He pleases. If this be a source of pain to others, none but God knows what it has cost me. There is nothing, therefore, left but to wait in trust on God's will and His mercy and good pleasure."

And again the darkened heavens are above him:

"Death invited, alas! will not come. What a relief it would be from a continuous and prolonged death!"

The obscurity of the drawing of the Holy Ghost, as well as of God's designs, and his incessant fretting against this, partly involuntary and, as he confesses, partly voluntary also, "disturbs my health and reduces my strength."

Next to the evil self-company of an unforgiven sinner there is no loneliness so sad as that of the invalid. He needs company most who is worst company for himself. Yet Father Hecker has not left a single word which would suggest that during more than two years of absence from all his life associates in religion, as well as from his blood kindred, whom he loved with a powerful love, he felt the lack of human companionship. One reason for this was his contemplative nature, and this was the main reason. He was born to be a hermit, and was an active liver only by being born again for a special vocation. Another reason was that his mind was so constituted that, when subjected to trial, it rested better when quite out of sight of everybody and everything associated with past responsibilities. He bade adieu to Father Deshon when the latter left him at Ragatz with sorrow, but without reluctance; and when a year afterwards it was suggested that one of the community should come to Europe and keep him company, he refused without hesitation, saying that his companion would be burdened with a sick man's infirmities, or the sick man distressed by his companion's inactivity on his account. But towards the very end of his life there were times when he felt the need of congenial company and was extremely grateful for it. But this did not happen often, and when it did it was because the waves of despondency which submerged him were heavier and darker than usual.

The following extract from a letter shows this state of mind:

"As I get somewhat more accustomed to my separation from all that was so dear to me, the strangeness of my position seems to me more and more inexplicable. All the things which are going on in Fifty-ninth Street were once all to me, and nothing appeared beyond. To be separated from all; to look upon one's past as a dream; to become a stranger to one's self, wandering from city to city, from country to country, ever in a strange land and among strangers; to be attached to nothing; to see no definite future; to be an enigma to one's self; to find no light in any one to guide me, isolated from all except God—who will explain what all this means? where it will end? and how soon? As I become resigned to this state of things my health suffers less. Occasionally my interior trials and struggles are almost insupportable, but less so than if I were surrounded by those who have an affection for me. To worry others without their being able to give me any relief would only increase my suffering, and finally become unbearable. All is for the best! God's will be done!"

What he wrote to a friend suffering from illness he applied to himself; he made spiritual profit, as best he might, from separation from the men and the vocation he loved so well:

"I can sympathize with you more completely in your sickness being myself not well. To be shut off from the world, and cut off from human activity—and this is what it means to be sick—gives the soul the best conditions to love God alone, and this is Paradise upon earth. Blessed sickness! which detaches the soul from all creatures and unites it to its sovereign Good. But one's duties and responsibilities, what of these in the meantime? We must give them all up one day, and why not now? We think ourselves necessary, and others try to make us believe the same; there is but little truth and much self-love in this. 'What else do I require of thee,' says our Lord in Thomas à Kempis, 'than that thou shouldst resign thyself integrally to Me.' This is what our Lord is fighting for in our souls."

Yet in having his life-work torn away from him he was like a man whose leg has been crushed and then amputated, the phantom of the lost limb aching in every muscle, bone, and nerve. This was partly the secret of his pain while in Europe, at the mere thought of his former active life; it haunted him with memories of its lost opportunities, its shortcomings in motive or achievement, or what he fancied to be such, in view of the Divine justice, now always reckoning with him.

He was ever cheerful in word, even when the pallor of his face and the blazing of his eyes betrayed his bodily and spiritual pain. "The end of religion is joy, joy here no less than

joy hereafter," he once insisted, and he argued long and energetically for the proposition ; but meantime he was racked with
inner agony and was too feeble to walk alone. In his letters
and diaries he speaks of his illness and of its symptoms as of
those of another person of whom he was giving news.

His wanderings in Europe were like gropings after the
Divine will in the midst of the spirit's night, often in anguish,
often in tranquillity, never in his former bounding joy, always
with submission, beforehand, at the moment, and afterwards.
Although the Divine Will gave a cold welcome, he sought no
other refuge.

" There are a thousand things," he writes, " that would worry
me if I would only let them, but with God's help I keep them
off at arm's length. His grace suffices, or in His presence all
the things of this world disappear. God alone has been always
the whole desire of my heart, and what else can I wish than
that His will may be wholly fulfilled in me. Having rooted
everything else out of my heart, and cut me off from all
things, what other desire can I have than that He who has
begun the work should finish it according to His design. It
is not important that I should know what that design is; it is
enough that I am in His hands, to do with me whatever He
pleases. To be and to live in His presence is all."

And again :

" The mind quiet both as to the past and the future, contented with the present moment : as to the past, leaving it
out of sight ; as to the future, unsolicitous. As to the present,
satisfied to be outwardly homeless, cut off from all past friendships and relations. The present gives me all the conditions
required for preparation for the future. Any time these two
years past I would have made an entire renunciation of all relations to my past labors and position, but waited as a dictate
of prudence. Now I feel ready to make it with calmness and
in view of all its consequences."

" No sooner do I set my mind to pray than God fills it with
Himself," Father Hecker was once heard to say. And this
power of prayer by no means left him after 1872; only that the
God who filled him was no longer revealed as the Supreme

Love, but as the Supreme Majesty. "There was once a priest," he said, speaking of himself, "who had been very active for God, until at last God gave him a knowledge of the Divine Majesty. After seeing the Majesty of God that priest felt very strange and was much humbled, and knew how little a thing he was in comparison with God." Comparison with God! It was this that gave him, as it did Job, a terror of the Divine justice beyond words to express, and impressed that air of spiritual dejection upon him which struck his old friends as so strongly in contrast with his former happy and vivacious manners. "You will never know," he once said, while being helped into bed after a very sad day, "how much I have suffered till you are in heaven." Meantime this awful Deity, so prompt to enter Father Hecker's mind, coming at times like a withering blast from the desert, was still the only attraction of his soul, the only object of his love. He could no more keep his mind off God now than he could before, and now God killed him, and then He made him alive. The ideas of the Divine goodness, patience, mercy, and love which formerly welled up in abundant floods at the thought of God, at the same thought now were dried up and disappeared. "Oh!" he once exclaimed, "if I could only be sure that I shall not be damned!" This was said unawares while listening to the life of a saint. The reader will, therefore, understand that Father Hecker's inner trouble was not a state of mere aridity, a difficulty of concentration of mind on spiritual things, or a vagrancy of thought; it was a perpetual facing of his Divine Accuser and Judge, a trembling woe at the sight of Infinite Majesty on the part of one for whom the Divine love was the one necessary of life for soul and body. Yet he knew that this was really a higher form of prayer than any he had yet enjoyed, that it steadily purified his understanding by compelling ceaselessly repeated acts of faith in God's love, purified his will by constant resignation of every joy except God alone—God received by any mode in which it might please the Divine Majesty to reveal Himself. He was, therefore, willing, nay, in a true sense, glad thus to walk by mere faith and live by painful love. "I should deem it a misfortune if God should cure me of my infirmities and restore me to active usefulness, so much have I learned to appreciate the value of my passive condition of soul." This he said less than three years before his death.

And about the same time, to a very intimate friend: "God revealed to me in my novitiate that at some future time I should suffer the crucifixion. I have always longed for it; but oh, now that it has come it is hard, oh, it is terrible!" And this he said weeping.

One aspect of the Divine Majesty which threatened for years to overpower him was the Last Judgment. "God has given me to see the terrors of the day of judgment," he once said, "and it has tried me with dreadful severity; but it is a wonderfully great privilege." Humility grew upon him day by day. No one who knew him well in his day of greatest power could think him a proud man, but his confidence in his vocation, and in himself as God's representative, had been immense. The following, from a memorandum, shows how he ended:

"I told him how courageous I felt. *Answer:* That is the way I used to feel. I used to say, O Lord! I feel as if I had the whole world on my shoulders; and all I've got to say is, O Lord! I am sorry you've given me such small potatoes to carry on my back. But now—well, when a mosquito comes in I say, Mosquito, have you any good to do me? Yes? Then I thank you, for I am glad to get good from a mosquito."

It will thus be seen that whatever diseases may have enfeebled Father Hecker's body, his spirit suffered from a malady known only to great souls—thirst for God. This gave him rest neither day nor night, or allowed him intervals of peace only to return with renewed force. Some men love gold too much for their peace of mind, some love women too much, and some power; men like Father Hecker love the Infinite Good too much to be happy in soul or sound in body unless He be revealed to them as a loving father. And this knowledge of God once possessed and lost again, although it breeds a purer, a more perfectly disinterested love, leaves both soul and body in a state of acute distress. "My *soul* thirsteth for Thee, my *flesh* longeth for Thee, in a dry and desert land without water."

Tried by these visitations, he was free to acknowledge that in past times he had been favored above others:

"Oh! there was a time," he said, "when I was borne along high above nature by the grace of God, and I feared that I should die without being subject to nature, and should never feel the need of the supernatural. But for many years now I have been left by God to my natural weakness and get nothing whatever except what I earn."

The following words of his indicate the cleansing process of these divine influences; it is from memoranda:

"He said to me once, after he had been for nine or ten years subject to almost unceasing desolation of spirit, 'All this suffering, though it has been excruciating, has greatly purified me and was of the last necessity to me. Oh, how proud I was! how vain I was! And these long years of abandonment by God have healed me.' I think this was the only time I ever knew him to connect his sufferings with fault. What he said may have referred to the mere temper and frame of his mind rather than to particular, specific faults. He undoubtedly thought more highly of human nature before that desolation began than he did at the end of it."

Meantime he used every aid for the assuagement of his interior sufferings, just as he conscientiously tried every means for the restoration of his bodily health. Good books helped him greatly. He recited his Breviary as he would read a new and interesting book, underlining here and there, and noting on the margins. But during most of his time of illness his infirmities made the Divine Office impossible. Every day he read or had read to him some parts of the Scriptures in English. "Without the Book of Job," he used to say, "I would have broken down completely." Lallemant, St. John of the Cross, St. Teresa, St. Catherine of Genoa, and other authors of a mystical tendency he frequently used. But next to the Scriptures no book served him so well during his illness as *Abandonment, or Entire Surrender to Divine Providence*, a small posthumous treatise of Father P. J. Caussade, S.J., edited and published by Father H. Ramière, S.J., with a strong defence of the author's doctrine by way of preface. At Father Hecker's suggestion it was translated into English by Miss Ella McMahon, and has already soothed many hearts in difficulties of every kind. It is an ingenious compendium of all spiritual wisdom, but it seemed to Father Hecker that submission to the Divine Will is taught in its pages as it has never been done since the time of the Apostles. The little French copy which he used is thumbed all to pieces. He used it incessantly when in great trouble of mind and knew it almost by heart. As he read its sentences or heard them read he would ejaculate, "Ah, how sweet that is!" "Oh, what a great truth!" "Oh, that is a most consoling doctrine!" just as a man exhausted with thirst and covered with dust, as he drinks and bathes at a gushing fountain in the desert, calls out and sighs and smiles.

Did he not find men here and there in his travels with whom he would take counsel and who could comfort him? There is little trace of it, though he never lacked sympathetic friends for his bodily ailments. In truth he tried to maintain a cheerful exterior, though occasionally he failed in his attempts to do so. Only once do we find by his letters and diaries that he opened his mind freely on his interior difficulties while in Europe, and that was to Cardinal Deschamps, who gave him, he writes, very great comfort.

No part of his sojourn in the Old World pleased and profited him so much as his trip up the Nile in the winter of 1873-4.

"In information of most various kinds," he writes, "it has been the richest four months of my whole life. The value intellectually and religiously as well as physically is incalculable. Given but one trip, it would puzzle me to name any which can compare with that up the Nile to Wady-Halfa. Nubia must be included. It has something of its own which you can find neither in Egypt nor elsewhere: silence, repose, almost total solitude, and its own peculiar people."

His companions were few in number and congenial in tastes, the climate mild and equable, and the people and country altogether novel. The journey, which extended into Nubia, was made in a flat-boat, the *Sittina Miriam el Adra—Our Lady Mary the Virgin*—the sail propelling them when the wind was fair, the crew towing them in calm weather; when the wind was contrary they tied up to the bank. The progress was, of course, slow, and yet his diary, the only one written during his illness with ample entries, shows that every day gave new enjoyment. He was provided with letters which enabled him to say Mass at the missionary stations along the river. The wonderful ruins of the ancient cities of Egypt gave him much entertainment. But his mind dwelt fondly on thoughts of Abraham, Joseph, and the chosen people, and especially upon the Holy Family, as well as the monks of the desert. He was much interested in the Mohammedan natives; their open practice of prayer, the instinctive readiness with which the idea of God and of eternity was welcomed to their thoughts, and, withal, their utter religious stagnation, which he traced to their ignorance of the Trinity, filled his mind with questions. How to convert these sluggish contemplatives, what type of Catholicity would be likely to flourish in the East, and how it could be reconciled with the stirring traits of the West, busied his mind. He often recalls his distant friends and contrasts new America with old Egypt. He wrote home when opportunity served, as thus to Father Hewit :

"With the hope that this note will reach you in due season, I greet you from this land from which Moses taught, and which our infant Saviour trod, with a right merry Christmas and a happy New Year to yourself and all the members of the community, all in the house, and the parishioners of St. Paul's. In my prayers all have a share and in the Holy Sacrifice of the altar. My heart and its affections are present with you. Could I realize its desire, I would shed a continuous flow of blessings on each one of you like a great river Nile—the river which Abraham saw and whose banks were hallowed by the footsteps of Jesus, Mary, and Joseph. Remember me especially in all your prayers on these great festivals. Offer up a Mass for my special intention on each of them."

The excursion to Nubia and back did him so much good physically, and left his mind with a peace which seemed so settled, that for a time he had strong hopes of recovery; but he was soon undeceived.

On the 15th of April Father Hecker left Cairo for Jerusalem, and spent some weeks in the Holy Land, continuing to enjoy an interval of spiritual relief. He writes :

"In reciting the Gloria and the Credo, after having been in the localities where the great mysteries which they express took place, one is impressed in a wonderful manner with their actuality. The truths of our holy faith seem to saturate one's blood, enter into one's flesh, and penetrate even to the marrow of one's bones."

The first greeting which he sent from the holy places was a letter to his mother, full of expressions of the most tender affection and gratitude, as well as of ardent religious emotions produced by moving among the scenes of our Lord's life. He enclosed a little bunch of wild flowers plucked from Mount Sion. He soon returned to Europe to escape the hot summer of Palestine, and began his round of visits to health resorts, shrines, and occasionally to a friend of more than usual attraction. His brother John died about this time, and this news drew from him a letter of encouragement and condolence to their mother. To George Hecker and his wife he wrote often, his letters being full of affection, of entire submission to the Divine Will, and of religious sentiments.

The following may be of interest as indicating the return of his disconsolate frame of mind:

"I have taken to writing fables. Here is one: Once upon a time a bird was caught in a snare. The more it struggled to free itself, the more it got entangled. Exhausted, it resolved to wait with the vain hope that the fowler, when he came, would set it at liberty. His appearance, however, was not the signal for its restoration to smiling fields and fond companions, but the forerunner of death at his hands. Foolish bird! why did you go into the snare? Poor thing; it could not find food anywhere, and it was famishing with hunger; the seed was so attractive, and he who had baited the trap knew it full well, and that the bird could not resist its appetite. The fowler is our Lord. The bait is Divine Love. The bird is the soul. O skilful catcher of souls! O irresistible bait of Divine Love! O pitiable victim! but most blessed soul; for in the hands of our Lord the soul only dies to self to be transformed into God."

In all his journeyings in search of beneficial change of air or for the use of medicinal waters, he endeavored to take in the famous shrines; as for places noted in profane history, or the usual resorts of tourists, there is not the least mention of them in his letters, unless an exception be made in favor of those in Egypt and some art galleries in Europe. But, "attracted by St. Catherine," he went back to her relics at Genoa once more. Drawn by St. Francis de Sales, he made a visit to Annecy which had a soothing effect upon him, for that saint was another of his favorites. He often went out of his way to see a friend, or to seek the acquaintance of some man or woman of reputation in religious circles, and he was himself surprised at the number of those who had heard of him and wished to know him. He readily formed acquaintances, and American, English, and French fellow-travellers could easily have his conversation and company on condition that they would converse on religious matters, or on the graver social and racial topics. It was not a little singular that, although suffering from weakness of the nervous system, he could talk abstruse philosophy by the hour without mental fatigue. Discussing such points as the different movements of nature and grace, the various theories of apprehending the existence of God, or how to bring about conviction in the minds of non-Catholics on the claims of the Church, he could tire the strong brain of a well man. It was the things below which tired *him*. He illustrated his conversation by gleams of light reflected from his past experience. When circumstances condemn such generous souls as Father Hecker to inactivity, a favorite solace is picking up fragments of work or recalling high ideas from the crowded memory of their former zeal, often with much profit to those who listen. And this was no idle-minded or boastful trait in him, as we see from the following:

"Be assured I shall not follow my own will if I can help it. Every dictate of prudence and wisdom will be my guide. Until the clouds clear away I shall be quiet, waiting, watching and praying, seeking for light wherever there is a reasonable prospect of obtaining it. In the meanwhile my time is not misspent. The journeys which I have made, the persons whom I have met on my way—these and a thousand other things incident to my present way of life are the best of educators for improving one's mind, for correcting one's judgments, and for giving greater breadth to one's thoughts. . . . It seems to me that I almost see visibly and feel palpably the blessing of divine grace on the work of the community, in its harmony, in the success of its missions, in the special graces to its members, in their cheerfulness and zeal: all this, too, in my absence. My absence, therefore, cannot be displeasing to the Divine Will; rather these things seem to indicate the contrary, and they awake in my soul an inexpressible consolation."

But he said to one of his brethren afterwards: "Oh, father!

I was sad all the time that I was in Europe. Why so? Well, it was because I was away from home, away from my work, away from my companions. And that was why I attached myself while there to those persons who felt as we did, and were of like views, and participated in our aims and purposes."

How he felt about his chances of recovery is shown by the following:

"I have nothing further to say about my health than that I have none. Were I twelve hours, or six, in my former state of health, my conscience would give me no moment of peace in my present position. It would worry me and set me to work. As it is I am tranquil, at peace, and doing nothing except willingly bearing feebleness and inertia."

From Paris, June 2, 1874, he writes to George and Josephine Hecker of a visit to Cardinal Deschamps in Brussels, where he met his old director, Father de Buggenoms. He expressed himself fully to them about the state of religion in Europe, and, although both were his admirers and warm friends, it was only on the third day that he made himself fully understood, and disabused their minds of reserves and suspicions. But before leaving "a complete understanding, warm sympathy, and entire approval" was the result. In one of the earlier chapters of this Life we have adverted to Father Hecker's difficulty in making himself understood. On this occasion he suffered much pain, for which, he says, the joy of the final agreement amply repaid him.

He formed an intimate friendship with the Abbé Xavier Dufresne, a devout and enlightened priest of Geneva, and with his father, Doctor Dufresne, well known as the mainstay of all the works of charity and religion in that city. The Abbé Dufresne became much attached to Father · Hecker. "The Almighty knows," he wrote to him, "how ardently I wish to see you again, for no one can feel more than I the want of your conversation, it was so greatly to my improvement." We have received from the Abbé Dufresne a memorial of Father Hecker, which is valuable as independent contemporary testimony. It is so appreciative and so instructive that we shall give the greater part of it as an appendix, together with two letters from Cardinal Newman written after Father Hecker's death.

The following is from a letter from Mrs. Craven, written early in 1875:

"That we have thought of you very often I need not tell you, nor yet that we have thought and talked of and pondered over the many and the great subjects which have been discussed during this week of delightful repose and solitude (though certainly not of silence). Let me, for one, tell you that many words of yours will be deeply and gratefully and usefully remembered, and that I feel as if all you explained to us in particular concerning the inward life which alone gives meaning and usefulness to outward signs and symbols (let them be ever so sacred), and the ways and means of quickening that inward life, all come home to me as a clear expression of my own thoughts by one who had read them better than myself."

Such was a devout and intellectual Frenchwoman's way of describing an influence similarly felt by men and women of all classes, and of the most diverse schools of thought, whom Father Hecker met in Europe.

This was written on hearing news of the community:

"It is consoling to see all these good works progressing [in the Paulist community]. To me they sound more like an echo of my past than the actual present. Before going up the Nile I used to say to some of my friends, that I once knew a man whose name was Hecker, but had lost his acquaintance, and I was going up the Nile to find him. Perhaps I would overtake him at Wady-Halfa in Nubia! But I didn't. Sometimes I think the search is in vain, and that I shall have to resign myself to his loss and begin a new life. Tuesday of this week my intention is to go to Milan and stop some days. I find friends in almost every city. Friday last I dined with the Archbishop of Turin, and have made the acquaintance of one or two priests here. Occasionally I visit museums, picture galleries, etc.; and thus time is outwardly passing by, until it pleases God to shed more light on my soul, and to impart more strength to my body, and make clear my path."

Here are his impressions of Rome after its occupation by the Italians, together with an account of an audience with the Holy Father:

"Rome is indeed changed, not so much outwardly, materially, as in spiritual atmosphere. It has lost its Christian exorcism and returned to its former pagan condition. The modern spirit, too, has entered it with activity in the material order. The old order, I fear, is never to return ; that is to say, as it was : if it returns at all it will be on another basis. The last citadel has given way to the invasion of modern activity and push. Who would have dreamed of this twenty years ago? The charm of Rome is gone, even to non-Catholics, for they felt raised above themselves into a more congenial and spiritual atmosphere while here, and their souls enjoyed it, though their intellectual prejudices were opposed to the principles. The charm they were conscious of forced them back again to Rome in spite of themselves. But that charm has in a great measure gone."

" The other evening I had a very pleasant private audience with the Holy Father. Among other matters I showed him *The Young Catholic,* which pleased him very much. He was struck with the size of the jackass in the picture of Ober-Ammergau, and asked if they grew so large in that country. I replied : ' Holy Father, asses nowadays grow large everywhere.' He laughed heartily and said, ' *Bene trovato.* ' "

Father Hecker was in Rome when, in March, 1875, his old friend and patron and first spiritual adviser, Archbishop McCloskey, was made Cardinal. He was much rejoiced, and sent the Cardinal a rich silk cassock, and gave a public banquet to Monsignor Roncetti and Doctor Ubaldi, who were to carry the insignia of the cardinalate to New York. We are indebted to the kindness of Archbishop Corrigan for a copy of Father Hecker's letter of congratulation, the principal parts of which we subjoin. The view of public policy concerning the College of Cardinals expressed in this letter was developed at length in an article published by Father Hecker in *The Catholic World* when Cardinal Gibbons was appointed ; it will also be found in his latest volume, *The Church and the Age :*

" The choice of the Supreme Pontiff in making you the first Cardinal of the hierarchy of the United States gives great satisfaction here to all your friends. For as honors and dignities in the Church proceed by way of distinguished merit and abilities, the qualities which they have always recognized and esteemed in you are by the event made known to the whole world.

" This elevation to the cardinalate of an American prelate is a cheering sign that the dignities of the Church are open to men of merit of all nations, and it is to be hoped that every nation will be represented in the College of Cardinals in proportion to its importance, and in that way the Holy See will represent by its advisers the entire world, and render its universality more complete. The Church will be a gainer, and the world too ; and I have no doubt that your appointment to this office in the Church will be, from this point of view, popular with the American people."

His continued and insensibly increasing weakness of body, as well as what seemed an unconquerable mental aversion to attempting even partially to resume his former career in the United States, seemed to settle negatively the question of his early return home. He began to think that it was God's will that he should permanently transfer his influence to the Old World. His mind was full of the religious problems of Europe, and the notion of Paulists for Europe, differing in details from American Paulists but identical in spirit, soon occupied his thoughts. The reader will remember Father Hecker's conviction, expressed when leaving Rome after the Vatican Council, that the condition of things in the Old World invited the apostolate of a free community of wholly sanctified men, such as he would have the Paulists to be. He now became persuaded, or almost so, that God meant his illness to be the means of practically inaugurating such a movement. By it the dim outlines of men's yearnings for a religious awakening, which he everywhere met with among the European nations, could be brought out distinctly and realized by an adaptation of the essentials of community life to changed European conditions. He thought he could select the leading spirits for the work, and, without overtaxing his strength, teach them the principles and inspire them with the spirit necessary to success. All this is brought forward in his letters and discussed. But it was not to be in his time.

The following entries in his journal, made during the Lent of 1875, have this European, or rather universal, apostolate in view :

"The Holy Spirit is preparing the Church for an increased infusion of Himself in the hearts of the faithful. This increased action of the Holy Spirit will renew the whole face of the earth, in religion and in society. Souls will be inspired by Him to assist in bringing about this end.

"The question is *how* shall such souls co-operate with Him in preparation for this extraordinary outpouring of divine grace? The law of all extensive and effectual work is that of association. The inspiration and desire and strength to co-operate and associate in facilitating this preparation for the Holy Spirit must come to each soul from the Holy Spirit Himself.

"What will be the *nature* of this association and the *special character* of its work? The end to be had in view will be to set on foot a means of co-operation with the Church in the conquest of the whole world to Christ, the renewal of the Apostolic spirit and life. For unity, activity, and choice of means reliance should be had upon the bond of charity in the Holy Spirit and upon His inspirations.

"The central truth to actuate the members should be the Kingdom of Heaven within the soul, which should be made the burden of all sermons, explaining how it is to be gained now.

"Men will be called for who have that universal synthesis of truth which will solve the problems, eliminate the antagonisms, and meet the great needs of the age; men who will defend and uphold the Church against the attacks which threaten her destruction, with weapons suitable to the times; men who will turn all the genuine aspirations of the age, in science, in social ism, in politics, in spiritism, in religion, which are now perverted against the Church, into means of her defence and universal triumph.

"If it be asked, therefore, in what way the co-operation with the new phase of the Church in the increase of intensity and expansion of her divine life in the souls of men is to be instituted, the answer is as follows: By a movement . . . springing from the synthesis of the most exalted faith with all the good and true in the elements now placed in antagonism to the Church, thus eliminating antagonisms and vacating controversies. . . ."

"Can a certain number of souls be found who are actuated by the instinct of the Holy Spirit, the genius of grace, to form an associative effort in the special work of the present time? If there be such a work, and an associative effort be necessary, will not the Holy Spirit produce in souls, certain ones at least, such a vocation? Is not the bond of unity in the Holy Spirit which will unite such souls all that is needed in the present state of things to do this work?"

CHAPTER XXXIII.

"THE EXPOSITION OF THE CHURCH."

WHILE in Europe God opened Father Hecker's soul to the cries of the nations. He was profoundly interested in the state of religion there, and the persecutions suffered by Catholics in Germany, in Switzerland, and in Italy during his stay, while it aroused his sympathies, increased his desire to find a remedy, and a fundamental one, for the evils from which the Church suffered. The peoples of the Old World, with their differing tendencies, were incessantly disputing in his mind. They were always displaying over against each other their diverse traits of race and tradition, at the same time that they were actually passing before his eyes in his constant journeyings in search of health.

What amazed and no less irritated Father Hecker was the political apathy of Catholics. All the active spirits seemed to hate religion. A small minority of anti-Christians was allowed entire control of Italy and France, and exhibited in the government of those foremost Catholic commonwealths a pagan ferocity against everything sacred; and this was met by "timid listlessness" on the part of the Catholic majority. These latter evaded the accusation of criminal cowardice by an extravagant display of devotional religion. To account for this anomaly and to offer a remedy for it, Father Hecker in the winter of 1875 published a pamphlet of some fifty pages, entitled *An Exposition of the Church in View of Recent Difficulties and Controversies and the Present Needs of the Age*. It is a brief outline of his views, held more or less distinctly since his case in Rome in 1857–8, but fully unfolded in his mind at the Vatican Council and matured during his present sojourn in Europe; the reader has already been given a summary of them in a letter treating of the providential meaning of the Vatican decrees.

What is the matter with Catholics, that they allow their national life, in education, in art, in literature, in general politics, to be paganized by petty cliques of unbelievers? How account for this weakness of character in Catholics? The answer is that the devotional and ascetical type on which they are formed is one calculated to repress individual activity, a quality essential to political success in our day. Energy in the world of modern politics is not the product of the devotional spirit dominant on the continent of Europe. That spirit in its time saved the Church, for it fostered submission when the temptation was to revolt.

" The exaggeration," says the Exposition, "of personal authority on the part of Protestants brought about in the Church its greater restraint, in order that her divine authority might have its legitimate exercise and exert its salutary influence. The errors and evils of the times [the Reformation era] sprang from an unbridled personal independence, which could only be counteracted by habits of increased personal dependence. *Contraria contrariis curantur.* The defence of the Church and the salvation of the soul were [under these circumstances] ordinarily secured at the expense, necessarily, of those virtues which properly go to make up the strength of Christian manhood. The gain was the maintenance and victory of divine truth, and the salvation of the soul. The loss was a certain falling off in energy, resulting in decreased action in the natural order. The former was a permanent and inestimable gain. The latter was a temporary and not irreparable loss."

The passive virtues, fostered under an overruling Providence for the defence of threatened external authority in religion, and producing admirable effects of uniformity, discipline, and obedience, served well in the politics of the Reformation and post-Reformation eras, when nearly all governments were absolute monarchies; but the present governments are republics or constitutional monarchies, and are supposed to be ruled by the citizens themselves. This demands individual initiative, active personal exertion and direct interference in public affairs. Vigilant and courageous voters rule the nations. Therefore, without injury to entire obedience, the active virtues in both the natural and supernatural orders must be mainly cultivated ; in the first order everything that makes for self-reliance, and in the second the interior guidance of the Holy Spirit in the individual soul. This, the Exposition maintains, is the way out of present difficulties. That it is the Providential way out, is shown by most striking evidence : the diversion of the anti-Catholic forces from the attack against authority to one against the most elementary principles of religion—God, conscience, and immortality; the drift of Anglo-Saxon and Teutonic minds of a religious cast towards the Church, calling for spiritual attractions in accordance with the independence of character peculiar to those races; the hopeless failure of the post-Reformation methods to meet the needs of the hour; and especially the Vatican decrees, which have set at rest all controversy on authority among Catholics. The needs of the times, therefore, call for virtues among Catholics which shall display the personal force of Catholic life no less than that which is organic. These must all centre around the cultivation of the Holy Spirit in the individual soul.

"The light the age requires for its renewal," says the Exposition, "can only come from the same source. The renewal of the age depends on the renewal of religion. The renewal of religion depends upon the greater effusion of the creative and renewing power of the Holy Spirit. The greater effusion of. the Holy Spirit depends on the giving of increased attention to His movements and inspirations in the soul. The radical and adequate remedy for all the evils of our age, and the source of all true progress, consist in increased attention and fidelity to the action of the Holy Spirit in the soul. 'Thou shalt send forth Thy Spirit and they shall be created: and Thou shalt renew the face of the earth.'"

The following extract gives the synthesis of the twofold action of the Holy Spirit, showing how external authority and obedience to it are amply secured by the interior virtues:

"The Holy Spirit in the external authority of the Church acts as the infallible interpreter and criterion of divine revelation. The Holy Spirit in the soul acts as the Divine Life-giver and Sanctifier. It is of the highest importance that these two distinct offices of the Holy Spirit should not be confounded. The supposition that there can be any opposition, or contradiction, between the action of the Holy Spirit in the supreme decisions of the authority of the Church, and the inspirations of the Holy Spirit in the soul, can never enter the mind of an enlightened and sincere Christian. The Holy Spirit, which through the authority of the Church teaches divine truth, is the same Spirit which prompts the soul to receive the divine truths which He teaches. The measure of our love for the Holy Spirit is the measure of our obedience to the authority of the Church. . . . There is one Spirit, which acts in two different offices concurring to the same end, the regeneration and sanctification of the soul.

"In case of obscurity or doubt concerning what is the divinely revealed truth, or whether what prompts the soul is or is not an inspiration of the Holy Spirit, recourse must be had to the Divine Teacher or criterion, the authority of the Church. For it must be borne in mind that to the Church, as represented in the first instance by St. Peter, and subsequently by his successors, was made the promise of her Divine Founder, that 'the gates of hell should never prevail against her.' No such promise was ever made by Christ to each individual believer. 'The Church of the living God, the pillar and ground of Truth.' The test, therefore, of a truly enlightened and sincere Christian will be, in case of uncertainty, the promptitude of his obedience to the voice of the Church.

"From the above plain truths the following practical rule of conduct may be drawn: The Holy Spirit is the immediate guide of the soul in the way of salvation and sanctification; and the criterion, or test, that the soul is guided by the Holy Spirit, is its ready obedience to the authority of the Church. This rule removes all danger whatever, and with it the soul can walk, run, or fly, if it chooses, in the greatest safety and with perfect liberty, in the ways of sanctity."

"The practical aim of all true religion is to bring each individual soul under the immediate guidance of the Divine Spirit. The Divine Spirit communicates Himself to the soul by means of the sacraments of the Church. The Divine Spirit acts as the interpreter and criterion of revealed truth by the authority of the Church. The Divine Spirit acts as the principle of regeneration and sanctification in each Christian soul.

"Such an exposition of Christianity, the union of the internal with the external notes of credibility, is calculated to produce a more enlightened and intense conviction of its divine truth in the faithful, to stimulate them to a more energetic personal action; and, what is more, it would open the door to many straying but not altogether lost children, for their return to the fold of the Church. The increased action of the Holy Spirit, with a more vigorous co-operation on the part of the faithful, which is in process of realization, will elevate the human personality to an intensity of force and grandeur productive of a new era in the Church and to society; an era difficult for the imagination to grasp, and still more difficult to describe in words, unless we have recourse to the prophetic language of the inspired Scriptures."

It is thus made plain that Father Hecker does not deny the harmony between the devotional spirit and practices prevalent in different ages of the Church; but he calls attention to the fact that the dominant note of one age is not always the same as that in another. And in using the words criterion and test, descriptive of the Church, he would convey their full meaning: not merely a plumb-line for the rising wall but divine accuracy itself made external. His outer criterion is to the inner life what articulate speech is to the human voice.

"The Exposition is nothing else," he writes home, "than a general outline of a movement from without to within; as in the sixteenth century the movement was one from within to without. This was occasioned by the nature of the attack of Protestantism. The Church having with increased [external] agencies protected what was assaulted, can return to her normal course with increased action. I give an indication of the nature of this movement:

"An increased action of the Holy Spirit in the soul in consequence of this greater attention directed to the interior life, and a more perfect explanation of the same. An exposition of the relation of the external to the internal in the Church. The action of the Holy Spirit in the soul and His gifts are the remedies for the evils of our times. The development of the intelligible side of the mysteries of faith, and the intrinsic reasons of the truths of divine revelation. Such a movement will open the door for the return of the Saxon races. The Latin-Celts in relation to the development of the hierarchy, discipline, worship, and æsthetics of the Church are considered. Causes of Protestantism—antagonism and jealousy of races; present persecutions. The Saxon idea of the Catholic Church. Reason for it—they see only the outward and human side of the Church. Return of the Saxons in consequence of the new phase of development—the display of the inward and the divine to their intelligence. The transition of races; in the future the Saxon will supernaturalize the natural, the Latin-Celts will naturalize the supernatural. The plan and suggestions given are the way to escape the extermination of Christianity by the Saxons, and the denial of Christianity by the apostasy of the Latins. The union of these races in the Church, with their civilization and force, is the means of spreading Christianity rapidly over the whole world.

"In the Exposition I follow simply the footsteps of the Church as indicated in her history, in the Encyclicals of Pius IX., and the Vatican Council. The Church is God acting directly on the human race, guiding it to its true destiny, the road of all *true* progress."

The Exposition, as already said, had been talked to all comers by Father Hecker, and in various parts of Europe, but was put into shape in the autumn of 1874, while he was in the north of Italy. He took it to Rome and offered it to the Propaganda Press. No fault was found with it; many high dignitaries, some of them members of the Congregation of the Sacred Palace, which has charge of the censorship, heartily approved of it and would have it published at once; but at the last moment this was decided by the authorities to be inexpedient. It was then sent to London, and Pickering brought it out anonymously, and it was at once put into French by Mrs. Craven. It was published as a leader in *The Catholic World* about the same time, and in 1887 formed the first chapter of *The Church and the Age*, a compilation of Father Hecker's more important later essays.

The Exposition contributes to the solution of the race problem as it affects religion. A glance at Europe shows the radical difference which is symbolized by the terms Transalpine and Cisalpine, Latin and Teutonic. The one group of races most readily clings to the interior virtues of religion, the other to external institutions. The problem is how to reconcile them, how to bring both into unity. Father Hecker believed that the Latin race had crowned its work in the Vatican Council and done it gloriously, and that the time had arrived to invite the Teutonic race to develop its force in the interior life of the Church. There are passages in the following letter which indicate the weight of this racial problem to him, as well as the supernatural earnestness which he brought to the study of it. It serves to explain a remark he once made: "I wrote the Exposition while I was having very many lights about the Holy Ghost—I couldn't help but write it."

"DEAR GEORGE AND JOSEPHINE: There is not much for me to add to my letter of the third of this month. My preparations are made to go to Mayence during the Catholic Assembly, which commences on the fifteenth and lasts three days. There I shall meet several persons whom I am interested in and wish to see. Besides, ecclesiastical affairs in the German Empire are in a very critical state, and this must add to the interest of the Assembly. Meeting, as I frequently do, the leading minds of Europe, enables me to compare views, appreciate difficulties, and hear objections.

"It is just as difficult to get the Celtic [and Latin] mind to conceive and appreciate the internal notes of the Church, and the character of her divine interior life, as it is to get the Teutonic mind to conceive and appreciate the divine external constitution of the Church, the importance, and essential importance, of her authority, discipline, and liturgy. But the weakness of the former, and the persecutions now permitted by Divine Providence to be visited on the latter, are teaching them both the lessons they need to learn. To complete the development of the truth; of the Church, each needs the other; and Divine Providence is shaping things so that in spite of all obstacles, natural and induced, a synthesis of them both is forming in the bosom of the Church. The work is slow but certain, concealed from ordinary observation because divine; but exceedingly beautiful. Underneath all the persecutions, the oppression, the false action, the whole outwardly critical condition of the Church and society, there is an overpowering, counteracting, divine current, leading to an all-embracing, most complete, and triumphant unity in the Church. To see how all things—wicked men as well as the good, for God reigns over *all*—contribute to this end and are made to serve it, gives peace to the mind, repose to the soul, and excites admiration and adoration of the Divine action in the world.

"To have a conception of this all-embracing and direct action of God in the affairs of this world, and by the light of faith to see that the Church is the dwelling place of His holiness, majesty, mercy, and power, and is the medium of this action, at first stupefies, overwhelms, and, as it were, reduces the soul to nothing. By degrees and imperceptibly it is raised from its nothingness;

timidly the soul opens its eyes and ventures to cast a glance, and then to contemplate the Divinity which everywhere surrounds it, as air and light do our bodies. The contemplation of the Divine action becomes its only occupation and it is an irresistible one. All the life, mind, and strength of the soul is involuntarily absorbed in this direction, leaving the body scarcely sufficient strength to continue its ordinary functions.

"How far will the body regain its former strength? What will be the relation of the soul with its former occupations? Will this additional light require other conditions? Was this light given for another and wider field of labor? These and many other questions must arise in the soul, which in due season will be answered. Its present duty is to practise conformity to God's will, patience, detachment, discretion, and confidence."

There is hardly any part of this Life which does not assist one in understanding the Exposition, especially the chapters on the idea of a religious community and that giving his spiritual doctrine. Many leading spirits hailed it with joy, among them Margotti, the editor of the *Unita Cattolica* of Turin, and Cardinal Deschamps. The former made Father Hecker's acquaintance during a visit to Turin, and became a warm admirer of him and his views. He compelled him to leave the hotel and lodge at his house during his stay in that city. When the Exposition came out he gave it two long and highly commendatory notices in his journal, at the time the most influential Catholic one in Italy, and published three chapters entire.

We have a copy of the Exposition annotated, at Father Hecker's request, by the late distinguished Jesuit, Father H. Ramière. These comments are valuable and suggestive. While modifying Father Hecker's judgment as to the causes of the deterioration of Catholic manliness, Father Ramière recognizes the fact. The remedies receive his emphatic approval, as also the author's explanation of the synthesis of the inner and outer action of the Holy Ghost in the Church.

When *The Church and the Age* appeared the English Jesuit magazine, *The Month*, in its issue of July, 1888, gave the book a very full and favorable review, endorsing all the principles of the Exposition. After saying that the Vatican decrees mark a special epoch in the evolution of Christianity, and close a period of attack—one of the sharpest which the Church has ever sustained —upon her external authority, the reviewer continues:

"It completed the Church's defence, and left her free to continue unimpeded her normal course of internal development. . . . The author displays remarkable breadth of thought, and the book contains many passages which are not only eloquent as a defence of Catholicity, but which cannot fail to impart instruction to the reflecting reader. We think it deserving of a wide circulation among both clergy and laity, and it is with a desire to further such a result that we propose to explain at some length the views which we have already touched upon. . . . We want a Catholic individualism, which necessarily requires a clear and recognized authority as a safeguard against the errors to which individualism exposes itself, but which, on the other hand, can never be begotten by the mere principle of authority as such."

The *Literarischer Handweiser*, a German Catholic critical review, published in Münster, having a high character and wide circulation, gave an equally favorable estimate of Father Hecker's views in a notice of *The Church and the Age.*

The following extracts from letters will close our consideration of the Exposition, which we have thought worthy of so careful and full a study because it is the remedial application of Father Hecker's spiritual doctrines to the evils of European Catholicity :

"It is consoling to see men of different opinions and of opposite parties in the Church regarding my pamphlet as the programme of a common ground on which they can meet and agree."

"I have had several interviews with Cardinal Deschamps. He invited me to spend the evenings with him, as we are old and very close friends. On all points, main points, our views are one. And it is singular how the same precise ideas and views have presented themselves at the same time to the minds of us both. In matters which regard my personal direction, I have consulted him several times, and fully. He has always taken a special interest in my welfare in every sense. His counsel has given me great relief, increased tranquillity, and will be of great service. He remains here eight or ten days longer, and I will see him as often during that period as I can."

A distinguished Swiss orator and prelate, since made cardinal, told Father Hecker of a devout priest who gave a large number of retreats to the clergy : "'When I saw him last,' said Monsignor ———— to me, 'he said that since we had met he had given retreats to seven hundred or eight hundred priests, and that he had read to them the Exposition of the Church which I gave him at my last interview with him.'"

"It will take time to understand the ideas in the Exposition. It will take still longer time to see their bearing, application, and results. Few at first will seize their import; by degrees they will take in a wider circle. The difficulties of the times, the anguish of many souls in the midst of the present persecutions, etc., will draw attention to any project or plan or system that offers a better future."

CHAPTER XXXIV.

IN THE SHADOW OF DEATH.

"I LOOK back," wrote Father Hecker in the summer of 1875, "on these three years as one continuous and dreadful interior struggle." This shows that the shadows were too deep and broad for the intervals of peace, which we know from his letters he had now and then enjoyed, to banish the impression of constant gloom. And Father Hecker's readiness to return home upon positive request will be the better appreciated when we remember how very painful to him was the very thought of his past occupations. Nor was his bodily health in a hopeful condition. While at Ragatz in the month of June, 1875, he met a distinguished physician from Paris, an excellent Catholic, whom he had been strongly advised to consult before. Glad of the chance, he submitted to a thorough examination, and received from him a written statement to the effect that it would be dangerous to take up any steady occupation, and that he should be entirely free from care for at least a year; otherwise a final break-down was to be expected. This seemed effectually to bar all thoughts of return. And such was his own settled conviction, as is shown by the following, written about the end of June:

"Where could I find repose? Not in the community; not at my brother's: nowhere else to go. Then, again, I would be constantly required to give opinions and counsel in the affairs of the community, which would require an application beyond my strength. There is no other way than for me to remain contented in Europe, with my feebleness and obscurity, in the hands of God."

But on July 29 he received a letter which compelled him to decide between tranquillity of spirit and bodily comfort—perhaps life itself—on the one hand, and the call of his brethren on the other. He decided without a moment's hesitation and with the utmost equanimity. We quote from a letter to George Hecker:

"Three days ago a letter from Father Hewit reached me urging my immediate return in such strong language and with such considerations that I wrote a reply expressing my readiness to return at once. On re-reading the letter I found its tone so urgent that I sent a telegram to the above effect. . . . In God's hands are my being, my soul, and all my faculties, to do with them and direct them as He pleases. To return to the United States and there arrange things to His pleasure, or to leave me here. I am indifferent, quiet, entirely ready either not to act or to act."

And so in October, 1875, Father Hecker was again in New York. He begged the Fathers to allow him to stay with his brother for the present, "for my nerves could not stand the noise, the routine, and the excitement of the house in Fifty-ninth Street." And when he did return to the convent to live, which was four years afterwards, he was quite sure that his end was at hand, though it did not come till nine years later.

During all the thirteen years between Father Hecker's return to America and his death, his daily order of life was pretty much the same as he described it in one of his letters from Europe, already given to the reader. He did not resort any longer to change of place or climate as a means of recovery; he had tried that long enough. His physician, the one who served the community, assisted him constantly with advice and remedies, and once or twice he tried a sanitarium; he was apt to try anything suggested, being credulous about such matters. But his strength of body slowly faded away. He was more disturbed than surprised at this, and fought for life every inch of the way.

"If I were a Celt," he once said with a smile, "I should more readily resign myself to die, but I am of a race that clings fast to the earth." His persistent struggle was sometimes calm, but was generally sharpened by a horrible dread of death, which fastened on his soul like a vampire, and gave a stern aspect to his self-defence. His patience in suffering was most admirable, though seldom clothed in the usual formalities. "Perhaps, after all," he would sometimes say, "God will give me back my health, for I have a work to do."

Though anything but an ill-tempered man, Father Hecker was yet by nature ardent and irascible and quickly provoked by opposition, but God gave him such a horror of dissension that he would not quarrel, though it was often plain that his peaceful words cost him a hard struggle. Occasionally he lost his temper for a little while, and this was when compelled to attend to business under stress of great bodily or mental pain. We do not think that he was ever known to attempt to move men by anger, or even sternness. "If you ever tell any one about me," he said, "say that I believed in praising men more than in condemning them, and that I valued praise as a higher form of influence than any kind of threatening or compulsion." Nor did he resort to the formalities of obedience to secure his end. "Why don't you put me under obedience to do this?" asked a father who did not exactly approve of a proposal Father Hecker had made to him. The answer was given with a good deal of heat: "I have never done such a thing in my life, and I am not going to begin now!" Nor had he any use for bitter speech even in cold blood. "One thing," he said in a letter, "I will now correct; a sneer—intentionally or consciously—is a thing that, so far as my memory serves, I am as innocent of as a little babe." Yet he could be sarcastic, as the following memorandum shows: "Cardinal Cullen once said to me, after I had made a journey through Ireland, 'Well, Father Hecker, what do you think of Ireland?' I answered: 'Your Eminence, my thoughts about Ireland are such that I will get out of the country as soon as I can; for if I expressed my sentiments I should soon be put into jail for Fenianism!' This was in 1867 while Fenianism was rampant. Of course he did not approve of it, but the sights he saw taught him its awful provocation. And once when unduly pressed with the dictum of an author whose range of power was not high enough to overcome Father Hecker's objections, he said: "I am not content to live to be the echo of dead men's thoughts." But it was not by skill in the thrust and parry of argumentative fence that Father Hecker won his way in a discussion, but by the hard drive of a great principle. The following memorandum describes the effect of this on an ordinary man:

"It is rather amusing when Father Hecker asks me some of his stunning questions on the deepest topics of the divine sciences. I look blank at him, I ask him to explain, I fish up some stale commonplace from the memory of my studies—and he then gives me his own original, his luminous answer."

And both his choice of subjects in conversation and his natural manner were according to his temperament, which was meditative. This gave his countenance when at rest a peaceful cast until within a few years of the end, when "death's pale flag" cast upon it a shade of foreboding. We have a photograph of him taken when he was about forty-five and in average good health, showing a tranquil face, full of thought and with eyes cast down; to the writer's mind it is the typical Isaac Hecker. But this expression changed in conversation, when not only his words but his gestures and his glances challenged a friendly but energetic conflict of opinion.

If it be asked, how did Father Hecker recreate himself during those mournful years, the answer is that recreation in the sense of a pleasurable relaxation seemed contrary to his nature whether in sickness or in health. It was once said to him, "Easter week is always a lazy time." "No, it is not," he answered. "I never have known a time, not a moment, in my whole life, when I felt lazy or was in an idle mood." He found himself obliged, however, to get out of the house and take exercise, walking in the park leaning on the arm of one of the community, or, if he was more than usually weak, being driven in his brother's carriage. There were occasions when to kill time was for him to kill care—to call his mind away from thoughts of death and of the judgment, the dread of which fell upon him like eternal doom. Then he would try to get some one to talk to, or to go with him and look at pictures and statues; or he would work at mending old clocks, a pretty well mended collection of which he kept in his room against such occasions. In the park he would often go and look at the beasts in the menagerie, and he spoke of them affectionately. "They bring to my mind the power and beauty of God," he said. He came to meals with the community, at least to dinner, until five or six years before his death, when his appetite became so unreliable that he took what food he could, and when he could, in his room. He also attended the community recreations after meals until a few years before the end; but it was often noticed that the process of humiliation he was undergoing caused him to creep away into a corner, sit awhile with a very dejected look, and then wearily go upstairs to his room. When he was urged not to do this, "I cannot help it to save my life," was all the answer he could give. He finally gave up the recreations almost entirely.

But he hated laziness. "I am so weak," he once said, "and my brain is so easily tired out that I am forced to read a great deal to recreate myself. That's why you see me reading so much." The book in which he was at the moment seeking recreation was a ponderous work on metaphysics by a prolix Scotchman, treating in many dreary chapters of such amusing topics as the unity of the act of perception with the object perceived! As may be supposed of such a man, whose illness forbade action and whose interior trials made contemplation an agony, he chafed sometimes at his enforced inactivity, though he was never heard, as far as we can get evidence, openly to complain of it.

Time and stagnation of bodily forces did not alter his progressive ideas.

"Is it not wiser," he said, "to give one's thought and energy to prepare the way for the future success and triumph of religion than to labor to continue the present [state of things], which must be and is being supplanted? Such an attitude may not be understood and may be misinterpreted, and be one of trial and suffering; still it is the only one which, consistently with a sense of duty, can be taken and maintained."

A bishop on his way to Rome once called on Father Hecker. "Tell the Holy Father," he said to him, "that there are three things which will greatly advance religion: First, to place the whole Church in a missionary attitude—make the Propaganda the right arm of the Church. Second, choose the cardinals from the Catholics of all nations, so that they shall be a senate representing all Christendom. Third, make full use of modern appliances and methods for transacting the business of the Holy See." Sometimes he discussed the activity of modern commerce as teaching religious men a lesson. He once said:

"When Father Hecker is dead one thing may be laid to his credit: that he always protested that it is a shame and an outrage that men of the world do more for money than religious men will do for the service of God."

No glutton ever devoured a feast more eagerly than Father Hecker read a sermon, a lecture, or an editorial showing the trend of non-Catholic thought. After his death his desk was found littered with innumerable clippings of the sort, many of them pencilled with underlinings and with notes. These fur-

nished much of the matter of his conversation, and doubtless of
his prayers. Once he wrote to a friend :

" Nobody is necessary to God and to the accomplishment of
his designs. Yet at times I wish that I had the virtue that
some creatures have ; when cut into pieces each piece becomes
a new complete individual of the same species. I should cut myself into at least a dozen pieces to meet the demands made
upon me. What a splendid thing it is to think of our Lord going about doing wonders, eternal and infinite things, and all the
time seeming to be unoccupied. The truly simple soul reduces
all occupations to one, and in that one accomplishes all."

And his organizing faculty would busy itself in various
schemes, which, if they could not cure his weak body, could re-
lax with a fancied activity his tired soul. Thus in a letter he
said :

" Why should we not form a league for the cause of our
Lord, to whom we owe all ? Unreserved devotion to His cause
with patience, perseverance, humility, and sweetness, are weapons
that no man or woman or thing can withstand. Our Lord has
promised that if we believe in Him we shall do greater works
than He did. Let us believe in Him, and clothe ourselves
through faith in Him with His virtues, and who shall resist us ?

" The first of all successes is Christ's triumph in our souls.
Everything that leads to this, humiliations, afflictions, calumnies,
contempt, mortifications, all work for us a glory exceeding the
imagination of man. To suffer for Christ's sake is the short-cut
in the way of becoming Christ-like."

The following anecdote of his missionary days shows Father
Hecker's contempt for lazy devotion. Once, when upon a mission, a young priest just returned home from Rome, where he had
made his studies, expressed his desire to get back again to Italy
as soon as possible, saying, " I find no time here to pray." Father
Hecker felt indignant, for it did not seem to him that the young
man was very much occupied. " Don't be such a baby," said he.
" Look around and see how much work there is to be done
here. Is it not better to make some return to God—here in
your own country—for what He has done for you, rather than
to be sucking your thumbs abroad ? What kind of piety do you
call that ? "

He took a personal interest in all the members of the community, and this was greatly heightened if any one fell sick. We
remember his excitement when it was announced that one of
the Fathers, who had been sent to a hospital for a surgical
operation, had grown worse and was in danger of death. He
began to pace his room, to question sharply about doctors and
nurses, and immediately ordered Masses to be said and special
prayers by the community ; and this father he had seen very
little of and hardly knew from the others. "I cannot tell," he
wrote to a friend at the time of Father Tillotson's illness, "I
dare not express, how much I love him, what he is to me."
Always tender-hearted, the nearer he came to the end and the
more he suffered the more gentle were his feelings towards
all, the more kindly grew his looks, but also the more sad
and weary. He was always careful to express thanks for
favors, small or great. The following is from a letter to a
friend :   .

"Your last note contained at the end a kind invitation.
Don't be troubled ; I'm not coming ! Do you know that sometimes I am tempted to think that I am necessary? Sometimes
the thought has come to me that I might run away from home
a week or so. Then I have driven the thought away as I
would a temptation. But I wished to thank you none the less
for your invitation, though I should never see you again. *I
have an uncontrollable horror of ingratitude.*"

During his long years of illness Father Hecker's reading continued upon the lines he had ever followed, the Scriptures holding, of course, the first place. Besides reading or having read to
him certain parts adapted to the spiritual probation he was undergoing, such as Job, the Passion of our Lord, and chapters of
the sapiential books, he also took the entire Scriptures in course,
going slowly through them from cover to cover and insisting on
every word being read, genealogies and all. He would sometimes interrupt the reader to make comments and ask questions.
The last words that he listened to at night were the words of
Scripture, read to him after he had got into bed. He declared
that they soothed him and settled his mind and calmed its disturbance, and this was easily seen by his looks and manner.
Some who knew him well thought from his comments that God

gave him infused knowledge of a rare order about the sense of Scripture. Once he said:

" When you were reading Ezechiel last night, oh, you cannot understand what thoughts I had! During the past six months I have learned how to understand him. I say within myself: ' O Ezechiel! Ezechiel! no one understands, no one understands you in this world, except one here and there.' "

Next to Scripture came St. Thomas and St. John of the Cross, the one for dogmatic and philosophical, the other for devotional uses. It must have been soon after returning to America as a Redemptorist that he procured a copy of Alagona's Compendium of St. Thomas, submitted it to Bishop Neumann, whose learning was in high repute, and obtained his assurance of its accuracy. That little book is a curiosity of underlining and various other forms of emphasizing. It was with him till death. From it he referred to the full works of St. Thomas for complete statements, but he loved to ponder the brief summary of the abridgment and work the principles out in his own way. St. John of the Cross and Lallemant, as already stated, were his hand-books of mysticism and ascetic principles. The former he caused to be read to him in regular course over and over again, enjoying every syllable with fresh relish. In later days the *Life of Mary Ward*, by Mary Catherine Chambers, and *The Glories of Divine Grace*, by Scheeben, afforded him special pleasure. Books which told of the religious tendencies of minds outside the Church were sure to interest him. He studied them as Columbus inspected the drifting weeds and the wild birds encountered on his voyage of discovery. Those who served him as readers sometimes found this kind of literature pretty dry, just as Columbus's crew doubtless found it idle work to fish up the floating weeds of the sea. The following sentences occur in a diary written while in Europe in 1875. It is a statement of his opinion of the objective points at which Catholic teachers and writers of our day should aim:

" In dogmatic theology, when treating of the doctrine of the fall of man keep in view the value of human nature and the necessity of divine grace preceding every act of Christian life.

" In moral theology, stimulate the sense of personal responsibility.

"In ascetic theology, fidelity to the Holy Spirit.

"In polemic theology, develop the intrinsic notes of the Church."

As to novels, he fully appreciated their power over minds, but we believe that he did not read half a dozen in his whole life, and these he treated as he did graver works: he studied them. "To read is one thing, to study is another," says Cardinal Manning; but all reading was study to Father Hecker. We remember one novel which he read, slowly and most carefully, underlining much of it and filling the margins of every page with notes. "Why don't you read novels, as other people do?" he was asked. "Because life is more novel than any fiction, for fiction is but an attempt to paint life," he answered. No printed matter of any kind, much less a book, ever could be a plaything to Isaac Hecker. He often made more of the sentences on a scrap of newspaper, and studied them far harder, than the writer of them himself had done. A man whose play and work are in such problems as, how God is known, how the Trinity subsists, what beatitude is, how God's being is mirrored in man's activity, has too real a life within him and about him to tarry long in fiction or in any of the by-roads of literature. Poetry, however, in its higher forms, or with a strong ethical tendency, he was very fond of. Perhaps his favorite among the poets was Coventry Patmore.

After returning to New York Father Hecker, besides supervising the editorial work of *The Catholic World*, wrote an occasional article for its pages. The more important of these, twelve in number, with the Exposition as a leader, were published in a volume already mentioned, *The Church and the Age*. This book appeared in 1887, and contains his views of the religious problems in Europe and America, and also some controversial writings against orthodox Protestantism and Unitarianism. These are well-written, clean-cut, and aggressive pieces of polemical writing, whether against the errors of Protestants or of infidels. *The Church and the Age* is the best exhibit of the author's opinions and principles on topics of religious interest and those of race and epoch having a religious bearing. He has left a considerable amount of unpublished matter, notably some essays on how God is known, the reality of ideas, and the Trinity, together with much on spiritual subjects. Let us hope that these and more of his unpublished writings will some day be given to the public. He always found difficulty in preparing matter for the press. Using a pencil and a rubber eraser, he often positively wore the paper through with writing, correcting, and writing again. He seemed scrupulous about such matters, and in these circumstances he lacked the immediate expression of his thoughts which came to him so spontaneously in his letters and diaries, as well as in his public speaking. But he dictated readily, and with a result of reaching quickly the form of words he would finally be content with. By this means he prepared his articles on Doctor Brownson, which appeared in *The Catholic World* between April and November, 1887.

His intercourse with the members of the community was naturally much interfered with by his illness. But he loved to listen to them speaking of their work, was greatly interested in the building and decorating of the new church, and when the missionaries came home was eager to hear them tell of their success. He would invariably suggest that we should study how to extend our preaching outside the regular missions, so as to take in non-Catholics. He was also alive to opportunities for stimulating others, in and out of the community, to do literary work. At Lake George, where he spent his summers with the community, he was able to have a familiar contact with us all, especially the students, whom he enlisted in working about the grounds or the house, helping as best he could. But after his illness began he ever showed a certain constraint of manner when the conversation took a grave turn, a kind of shyness, which a judge of character might interpret as meaning, "I am afraid you'll misunderstand me; I am afraid you'll think I am a visionary."

CHAPTER XXXV.

CONCLUSION.

FATHER HECKER'S prayer during all these years was a state of what seemed almost uninterrupted contemplation of varied intensity. He attended the evening meditation of the community as long as he had strength to do so, frequently giving a commentary on the points read out at the beginning, simple, direct, and fervent. He was exceedingly fond of assisting at High Mass on Sundays and feast days, and he had a small oratory built between the house and the new church, from which, by passing a few steps from his room, he could hear the music and see the function through a window opening into the sanctuary. This often overpowered him with emotion, which was sometimes so strong as to drive him back to his room and into bed. Once a week and on the more solemn festivals was as often as he could say Mass, or even hear it, on account of his extreme weakness in the mornings. For the last three or four years of his life to say Mass at all became a struggle which was as curious as it was distressing to witness. Those who had often read of such things in the lives of the servants of God were nevertheless amazed at the sight of them in Father Hecker. The following is from a memorandum:

"*Father Hecker:* Do you know what it is to be in spontaneous relations with God—where the Divine Object works upon the soul spontaneously? It is that which prevents me from saying Mass, because I make a fool of myself. At any point I am apt to be so influenced by God as to be utterly deprived of physical force, to sink down helpless. At my brother's house they expect it and get me a chair. A few moments on a chair, and I am ready to go on. Now, if I yield to this I know that I shall be thrown into a clean helpless state, and I have a practical work to do. *Question:* Does this effect come at receiving Communion? *Answer:* I don't know, as I have never yet received Communion out of Mass. But I am afraid of it. Any such thing is apt to throw me off, and I am afraid. *Question:* But suppose it to be God's will that you should say Mass notwithstanding this difficulty? *Answer:* Then let Him bring it about."

At one time several months passed, months of very low

vitality in body and awful darkness of soul, during which he neither said Mass nor received Communion. The following memorandum describes how this period, perhaps the most painful of his life, was ended:

"*Christmas*, 1885.—For the first time since early summer Father Hecker undertook to say Mass: I assisted him, and a stormy time we had of it. It was at five in the morning and in the oratory. He wanted to have the door locked, but there was no key. 'Don't speak a word to me,' he said while he was dressing in his room. Arrived in the oratory, he sank down upon a bench as if some one had struck him; he threw his birettum down on the floor, and began to weep and cry in a very mournful way and aloud. But he quickly recovered, and rested as if he were preparing to be hanged. I supported him over to the altar, and as he began the *Judica* he blubbered out the words like a school-boy being whipped. Most of the Mass he said out loud, hardly holding in his sobs anywhere except from the *hanc igitur* till near the *Pater Noster*. His calmest time was during that most solemn part, and at his Communion. Three or four times he was forced to sit down on a chair I had provided for him on the predella. At the *Memento* for the living he was deeply affected and patted the floor with his foot, sobbing aloud and acting like a child with an unendurable toothache. He was afraid of the *Pater Noster* and asked me to say it with him, which I did; also various words and sentences in other parts of the Mass. I have heard him say that the *Pater Noster* is a prayer which breaks him down. After he was through he insisted on trying to say the Pope's prayers. We said the Hail Marys and the Hail, Holy Queen, together, and I recited the prayer for him. I had to take off his vestments the best I could while he sat, and when I got him down to his room and into bed, he was in a state of nearly complete unconsciousness. After saying my three Masses, I saw him again at about 8.30, found him up and dressed and very bright, and he has been particularly so all day."

What follows is from a letter dated early in 1886, and seems to refer to the occasion above described. He speaks of himself in the third person:

"And he [Father Hecker] was never so occupied as now,

although he is doing nothing and has been in that condition for months. Though he does hear Mass, he does not, because he cannot, say it—without showing what a *big fool* he is. However he has begun again to say it. If it had not been for human respect he would not have said it last Sunday; he was too feeble. God is killing him by slow fire, by inches. He dies terribly hard."

If Father Hecker had had an unimpaired physical system when his interior trials came, he might have resisted the nervous depression which they caused, at least well enough to maintain an active part in his undertakings. Or if his bodily weakness, resulting from his early austerities, had been accompanied with interior equanimity, he might have held up. A rickety ship can, with care and skill, get into port if the engine is sound, and so can a sound ship with a broken-down engine sail home, however slowly. But with both a rickety ship and a disabled engine the port should be near at hand or there is danger of shipwreck. That Father Hecker did not die long before he did, was due, apart from God's special designs, to the extraordinary skill and care of Doctor James Begen, who was also an attached friend. Mr. Anthony Ellis, one of his former penitents, served him in his sick-room out of pure love from 1879 until his death, which preceded Father Hecker's by about a year. He had a kind-hearted successor in Mr. Patrick McCann.

Father Hecker's beloved brother George died on February 14, 1888. He had been ailing for some time and Father Hecker went to see him frequently. "George and I," he once said, "were united in a way no words can describe. Our union was something extremely spiritual and divine." The following memorandum tells how Father Hecker received the news:

"George Hecker died about nine o'clock last night, and when I informed Father Hecker of it this morning he was deeply moved. 'Don't say a word to me!' he cried, 'not a word. Read something! Read something quick!' I stepped over to the table and took the Scriptures and began to read the thirteenth chapter of St. John, read it through, and another chapter. By that time he calmed down. He only wept twice, except a few little sobs, and went out riding as usual this afternoon. He is profoundly moved. 'I knew it,' he said this morning; 'I saw it, I saw it last night—it seemed to me that I saw it. I came

near coming to your room at half-past ten, but concluded not
to do so.' Another time to-day he said: ' If God enables me to
bear this I hope I shall be able to do my allotted work.' "

He bore it well, but it added very much to a burden already
too heavy. For some weeks afterwards he now and then
moaned and wept for his brother, and this happened occasionally
till summer came. Those who attended Father Hecker could
not but be convinced, from what they saw and heard, that God
allowed George to visit his brother more than once after his
death, and these supernatural interviews were productive of
mingled consolation of soul and pain of body to the survivor.
George Hecker was worthy of his brother's love. He was a
noble character, full of that sort of religion nowadays most
needed. His piety flourished in the withering atmosphere of
wealth and in the turmoil of commercial life. Industry, thrift,
enterprise, quick perception of opportunities, determination, a
keen sense of his rights and a bold hand to defend them,
manly frankness, were conspicuous traits in him and made
him a rich merchant. But all these qualities served him as
well for high spiritual ends. He was essentially and dominantly a spiritual man, fond of prayer, regular in all religious duties. He was as honest as the day, and all for conscience' sake and the love of God. His understanding was wide
and clear, his heart tender, simple, and courageous. He loved
his wife and children, he loved his brother Isaac, with an absorbing devotedness, and these loves were blended and mingled into
one with the love of God. His charities are known to the
reader, but they should be understood as the result not merely
of affection for his brother, or even of faith in his apostolate,
but also from his own perception of the intrinsic worth of the
undertakings themselves. We know not what quality could be
added to George Hecker to make him a model Christian of our
day.

His death had a serious effect on Father Hecker's state of
body and mind. But from the previous autumn and during the
winter following he had failed rapidly. In fact, he had requested and received the last Sacraments from Father Hewit on
September 15, 1887; but this was on account of an alarming
irregularity of the heart's action, which was but temporary. He
had no long distance to drop at any time to get to the bot-

tom, and it became evident in the summer of 1888 that the end was not far off. He could not stand the strong air of Lake George that summer, and came home after being there but a couple of weeks. He tried the sea-side with even worse success; and the short journeys he made were extremely painful. The paroxysms of angina pectoris became more frequent and daily left their victim less able to rally. Patience strained to the uttermost by physical suffering, the mind distressed, fits of despondency and of indescribable gloom, the weight of a body of death —all this he had borne for sixteen years, with only occasional intervals of peace. There was little left to suffer except death. His bodily resistance grew weaker towards the end of his last summer on earth, and he lost flesh rapidly. The fulness of his face was gone by autumn, and a wan look, as of decaying force, was stamped upon it. He suffered in literally every member of his body, by turns or simultaneously. We find the following memorandum:

"*Question:* What's the matter with the back of your head? [he was rubbing it with extract of witch hazel]. *Answer:* It is sore, it hurts me. *Q.* Well! As soon as one part is better another gets out of order? etc. *A.* Do you know it was all revealed to me and foretold [beginning to weep]. *Q.* When? In your novitiate? *A.* Yes. *Q.* But not all the details of your sufferings? *A.* Yes, all the details. But I will not say another word about it. *Q.* But you ought to, etc. [He refused to say more.]"

Little by little during the latter years Father Hecker's visitors had become very few. An occasional call was received from an old friend, lay or cleric, and this was not apt to be repeated, so painful was the contrast between the former Father Hecker and the present one. Instead of the active and powerful man, of contagious courage and hopefulness, they saw a tall, wan old man bending with the weight of years and of suffering, but still majestic in his look and bearing, with a white beard, and soft, attractive eyes. The quick movement, the joyous greeting, even the smiling serenity, had passed away, and instead an air of sadness had come, or of enforced cheerfulness.

The following memorandum, taken over two years before his death, tells of a relief which he hoped would be permanent; but such was not to be the case:

" Father Hecker said to-day: 'Only within the last three days has God released me from the sensation that I might die any instant. Oh! how I have suffered from that feeling for ten years. I did not know whether I should ever be delivered from it. Now, little by little God is lifting it off from my soul. For ten years I have been under this cloud. Oh, how terrible a suffering it has been!' This he said, his hands covering his face; he had interrupted me to say it while I was reading St. John of the Cross. 'Oh!' he added, 'how I could weep for my sins,' and so on for a few more words."

The clouds soon settled down again. The following was noted a little over a month after the above:

" Father Hecker said to me to-day: 'There was a time when I seemed to know God so clearly and to be so conscious of His attraction that my whole thought and wish was death; to break the chain of life to be united to God in Paradise. Now it is altogether different; nothing but darkness and depression.'"

Here is another memorandum, taken some time before the above:

" Father Hecker said: 'God is now visiting me with the profoundest desolation of spirit. I have the most deadly terror of death; if I yielded to it I should tremble from head to foot. Yet there is a spell on me which makes me wish that I may die without sensible faith and deprived of every present spiritual comfort. . . .' He also said many things about his continued and unbroken desolation of spirit these several years back. 'Yet,' said he, 'I never knew that God would permit me to come so near to Him and see so much of Him as I have.' Then he made me read to him the first chapter of the Book of Job. . . . After he had gone to bed I read to him part of an article in *The Month* on the indwelling of the Holy Spirit, and he discoursed meantime to me most profoundly on that topic. And he added: 'One reason why I have always been so much interested in the doctrine of the Holy Ghost acting in the soul is a practical one, because I myself have never had any other director, though I have more than once opened my mind entirely to others and profited by their advice, but none was or could be really my director. Hence, too, I am so much attracted to saints who have had to struggle on alone like St. Catherine of Genoa, who was without a director for twenty-five years.'"

Towards the close of October, 1888, two months before death. Doctor Begen saw that the end was approaching. This was evident from a sudden and general failure of strength, the appetite, not much at any time, seeming now to vanish quite away, although Father Hecker's strong will forced down a little nourishment. This loss of strength caused the heart to work badly and to give an occasional sudden alarm. Internal congestions followed, relaxing the bowels and causing much bodily annoyance. Meantime he was hardly ever out of his room and many days he spent entirely in bed. His fits of depression of spirits were more frequent than usual and more saddening. He no longer rested at all, what sleep he got being produced by drugs and serving but to pass the time unconsciously. From the beginning of December he was apt to fall into a semi-comatose state, though generally in full use of his faculties. Some days before he died he seemed to realize that the long struggle was nearly over, and he no longer talked to the doctor or others of the medicines or of his bodily ailments, nor did he seem to think of them; and his mind appeared to have suddenly grown peaceful. The Scriptures as well as other books were read to him, as usual, up to the very evening before he died. On the night of the 20th of December, two days after his sixty-ninth birthday, the last sacraments were administered, Father Hecker receiving them without visible emotion but in full consciousness. During the following day he was quiet and apparently free from acute pain, the benumbed body refusing to suffer more; but the mind calm and attentive. When the morning of the 22d came all could see that his time was near at hand. In the middle of the forenoon the members of the community were gathered at the bedside, the prayers for the dying were read and the indulgence was given. As this was over the doctor arrived, and Father Hecker, who had gradually lost advertence to all around him, was roused by him into full consciousness, and gave the community his blessing, feebly raising his hand to make the sign of the cross and uttering the words in a light whisper. Then he sank away into unconsciousness and in an hour ceased to breathe.

And so Father Hecker died. Our beloved teacher and

father, so blameless and brave, so gentle and daring, so full of
God and of humanity, entered into his eternal beatitude.

Dying on Saturday, and so near Christmas, the funeral was
delayed till Wednesday, the feast of St. Stephen, the body being
embalmed. Christmas afternoon it was placed in the church
and was visited and venerated by great throngs of people. A
vast concourse attended the Requiem Mass the next morning,
which was sung by Archbishop Corrigan surrounded by many
priests, an eloquent sermon being preached by Father T. J.
Campbell, the Provincial of the Jesuits. The body was placed in
the vaults of the old cathedral.

The life we have been following is a harmonious whole from
beginning to end. The child tells of the youth, the youth
promises a noble man, and the promise is more than fulfilled.
He was guileless; no dark ways of forbidden pleasure ever
heard the sound of his footstep. There was no barter of conscience for ambition's prize. He was fearless; from beginning to
end there was no halt from want of courage. Nor did he rush
forward before the light came to show the road, though he often
chafed and panted to hear the word of Divine command; he
never moved at any other. But when the voice of God bade
him forward he never flinched at any obstacle. The ever-recurring persuasion that there were so few who saw God's will as
he saw it cut him to the heart, and the mystery of the Divine
times and moments grew upon him with fatal force till the end,
until he drooped and pined away with grief that he could but
taste the first-fruits. Yet he was ever submissive to the Divine
Will, to live, to die, to begin, to end the work, to be alone or
to be of many brethren, to lead or to follow. Though a most
active spirit, he was yet contemplative, and to unite the manifestation of the Holy Spirit in the inner and outer life was the
end he always kept in view; but he was distinctively an interior
man.

Few men since the Apostles have felt a quicker pulse than
Isaac Hecker when the name of God was heard, or that of
Jesus Christ or the Holy Spirit. Few men have had a nobler
pride in the Church of Christ, or felt more one with her honor.
Few men have grown into closer kinship with all the family of
God, from Mary the great mother and the holy angels down to
the simplest Catholic, than Isaac Hecker. But his peculiar trait

was fidelity to the inner voice. " There are some," he once said, " for whom the predominant influence is the external one, authority, example, etc.; others in whose lives the interior action of the Holy Spirit predominates. In my case, from my childhood, God influenced me by an interior light and by the interior touch of his Holy Spirit." The desperate demand of Philip, " Lord, show us the Father and it is enough," was Father Hecker's cry all through early life. After the founding of his community, in 1858, his life was like an arctic year. From that date till 1872 there was no set of sun. The unclouded heavens bent over him ever smiling with God's glorious light ; and its golden tints lit up all humanity with hope and joy. Then the sun went down to rise no more. The heavens were dark and silent, or rent asunder with wrathful storms, only a transient flash of the aurora relieving the gloom. When the light dawned again it was to beam upon his soul in the ecstasies of Paradise.

We know not what to say of his faults, nor can we think that he had any that were not to be traced to his eager love of God's cause, such as his overpowering men with pleading for God in their souls ; or too easily crediting unworthy men who prated to him of liberty and the Holy Spirit ; or over-fondness during his illness for playing in the lists of fancy at an apostolate denied him in the battle of active life ; he repined at being forced to plan great battles in a sick-room. He could not help betraying a heart heaving with a pent-up ocean of zeal, while he was creeping about helplessly, often too feeble to speak above his breath. A lover of liberty, its only boon to him at last was liberty to accept and rivet upon himself the chain of patient love.

Some may say " Hecker was before his time." But no man is before his time if, having a divine message, he can get but one other to accept it, can arrest men's attention, can cause them to ponder, to ask why or why not, whether this be the day or only its vigil. The sower is not before his time though he dies before the harvest ; there is a time to sow and a time to reap.

And now the tree is dead, but its ripe fruits are in our bosoms bearing living seeds, which will spring up in their time and give fruit again each according to its kind.

The life of Father Hecker is a strong invitation to the men of these times to become followers of God the Holy Ghost, to fit their souls by prayer and penance in union with Christ and his Church, for the consecration of liberty and intelligence to the elevation of the human race to union with God. We do not bid him farewell, for this age, and especially this nation, will hail him and his teachings with greater and greater acclaim as time goes on. As God guides His Church to seek her Aposto late mainly in developing men's aspirations for better things into fulness of Catholic truth and virtue, Isaac Hecker will be found to have taught the principles and given the methods which will lead most surely to success.

THE END.

PRINTED AT THE COLUMBUS PRESS, 120-122 W. 60TH ST., N.Y.

APPENDIX.

LETTERS FROM CARDINAL NEWMAN.

I.

THE ORATORY, BIRMINGHAM, February 28, 1889.

MY DEAR FATHER HEWIT: I was very sorrowful at hearing of Father Hecker's death. I have ever felt that there was this sort of unity in our lives—that we had both begun a work of the same kind, he in America and I in England, and I know how zealous he was in promoting it. It is not many months since I received a vigorous and striking proof of it in the book he sent me [*The Church and the Age*]. Now I am left with one friend less, and it remains with me to convey through you my best condolement to all the members of your society.

Hoping that you do not forget me in your prayers,

I am, dear Father Hewit,

most truly yours,

JOHN H. CARD. NEWMAN.

II.

THE ORATORY, BIRMINGHAM, March 15, 1890.

DEAR FATHER HEWIT: In answer to your letter I am glad to be told what is so interesting to me, viz., that the Life of Father Hecker is in preparation. I had a great affection and reverence towards him, and felt that which so many good Catholics must have felt with me on hearing of his illness and death. I wish, as you ask me, that I could say something more definite than this of his life and writings, but my own correspondence with friends, and especially the infirmities of my age, burden me and make it impossible for me to venture upon it. This, alas! is all that I have left me now by my years towards the fulfilment of welcome duties to the grateful memory of an effective Catholic writer (I do not forget his work in England) and a Benefactor, if I may use the term, to the Catholic Religion, whose name will ever be held in honor by the Catholic Church.

Yours most truly,

J. H. N.

RECOLLECTIONS OF FATHER HECKER BY THE ABBÉ XAVIER DUFRESNE, OF GENEVA.

I.

I first knew Father Hecker in 1873, meeting him at a Catholic Congress held at Ferney and presided over by Monsignor Mermillod. Father Hecker visited Geneva several times after that, living in the closest intimacy with our family.

He spent several weeks on a visit with my father, Dr. Dufresne, at a châlet situated on Salîne mountain above Geneva, being at the time in feeble health and seeking recovery by a prolonged sojourn in Europe. For this enforced inactivity he recompensed himself by continual and earnest conversations, for the purpose of gaining to his ideas all whom he believed capable of understanding them, whether Protestants or Catholics. There was about him an indescribable charm which mysteriously drew one to him and penetrated one with his influence. Although he did not know French thoroughly and preferred to use English, yet he spoke with such power, elevation, exuberance, and depth of thought that he captivated his hearers.

When I made Father Hecker's acquaintance I had just lost my eyesight, being at the end of my ecclesiastical studies, and not yet ordained. He did my soul much good by teaching me a kind of holiness which was joined to lively intelligence and the most energetic activity. Father Hecker remains to me not only the type of an American* priest, but of the modern one, the kind needed by the Church for the recovery of the ground lost as a result of Protestantism and infidelity, as well as to enable her to start anew in her divine mission.

II.

The principal impression produced by Father Hecker on those who came in contact with him was one of sanctity. In his company one felt his whole being influenced as if by something venerable and supernatural, and a constant inclination to correspond to the action of the Holy Spirit and submit the human will to the divine. In conversing with him about spiritual things one was transported into a higher region, the heart growing warmer and the conscience more sensitive. Father Hecker plainly inclined by habit to the type of character given us by Jesus Christ. He suffered much, both physically from weakness of nerves and morally on account of enforced inactivity, yet he not only never complained but was always cheerful. This was the greater merit in him because he seemed by nature impatient of opposition and contradiction. He had a sagacious mind and easily discovered the faults of others, but, although he spoke of men and affairs with openness and candor, he yet ever sought for favorable interpretations. Like St. Francis de Sales, he knew how to judge of people and yet remain full of charity for his neighbor. Profoundly individual, and profoundly attached to his ideas, like all Anglo-Saxons, and in fact like all who have acquired the Protestant habit of free inquiry, he nevertheless had for the Church a docility almost naive and infantile; and this was because he recognized in her the authority and the action of the Holy Spirit.

It may be said of him without exaggeration that he was every moment ready, if it became necessary, to bear witness to the divinity of the Church by martyrdom, and in fact he often made that declaration. In him the most heroic virtue was faith. He had come into the Catholic Church in spite of the most extreme natural repugnance, and he remained in it, overcoming the perpetual objection of Protestants that Catholicity could not be the truth because Catholic countries had become the least powerful and the least prosperous in the civilized world. On this point he loved to expound the text of Scripture which says that it is better to lose an eye and an arm and enter into the kingdom of heaven, than to save both, and fall into hell. His piety was wholly interior. It consisted in the perpetual exercise of the presence of God. He had a natural disinclination for devotional practices as they are in vogue among the southern races.

His tendency was to spiritualize as much as possible all the devotions in use in the Church. His own principal one was to the Holy Ghost and His divine Gifts. He never spoke of the Incarnation and the Eucharist without deep emotion and a contagious love. As to devotion to the Blessed Virgin, he explained it in a most elevated manner, ever showing, and with great dignity and nobility of manner, how it flowed from the principle of the divine maternity. The last book he sent me was one on the Blessed Virgin written by an American priest. Since Father Hecker's death I have never failed a single day to invoke him in my prayers, and to his intercession I attribute many graces obtained, some of them very important.

III.

Father Hecker had a marvellous openness of heart. I heard him relate several times the story of his life, his conversion, his joining the Redemptorists, his case before the Roman Congregations, and the founding of the Paulist community. I can still recall the banks of the Lake of Geneva at the Villa Bartoloni, where Father Hecker, walking with a friend and myself, told us of his leaving the Redemptorist order. It was the way in which he talked of so delicate a matter that enabled me to appreciate that the man was a saint. He liked to repeat, while on this subject, what Cardinal Deschamps had said of him: "Here is a man who has been able to leave our Congregation of the Most Holy Redeemer without committing even a venial sin."

In my opinion, Father Hecker was, after Père Lacordaire, the most remarkable sacred orator of the century. This does not apply to his writings, for his ideas lost much of their force in the process of getting into print. Like all natural orators his chief quality was a power of drawing and persuading, which, to use an expression often applied to Père Lacordaire, had something magnetic about it. He had a prodigious gift of showing his Protestant or infidel hearers that their own hearts and their own reason aspired by instinct towards the Catholic truth which he was teaching them. In that way he drew his hearers to discover the truth in their own minds instead of receiving it by force of argument or any extrinsic authority. To acquire this power he had made a great study of the Gospel, and, sustained by Divine grace, he went about the exposition of the truth as Jesus Christ did. One of the most original aspects of his mind was that he joined the practical sense of the American to the taste and aptitude of the European for speculation. He had not been able to make a complete course of studies because he had spent several years in commercial life, but he had great natural gifts for metaphysics, theology, and above all mysticism.

Unlike the English converts of the Oxford school, he had reached Catholicity by way of liberal Protestantism, which he had renounced because it could not satisfy the religious aspirations of his nature. It would be interesting to study his case in connection with those of Newman and Manning, for it shows that souls are led to Catholicity by all roads, even the most opposite, and that minds most inclined to rationalize can be drawn to the Church as easily as those of a conservative or traditional temperament.

IV.

But I wish to dwell especially on what preoccupied Father Hecker's mind and formed the fundamental theme of his eloquent words. We were just on the morrow of the Vatican Council, of the defeat of France by Prussia, and in the first agonies of the Culturkampf in Germany and Italy. Now, if one remembers that Father Hecker was of an American family originally from the town of Elberfeld, Prussia, he can better understand the gravity of the problem which weighed upon his mind, as upon that of so many others. Must we admit, it was asked, that the Council of the Vatican has affixed its seal upon the decadence of Catholicity, binding the Church to the failing fortunes of the Latin races ? Must Protestantism finally triumph with the Saxon races ? And here Father Hecker's faith did not halt an instant, but grasped the difficulty in all its terrible magnitude. His solution may be questioned by some, but I believe that no one will dispute that the mind which conceived it was of the first order.

Father Hecker remarked, as did many others, that, starting from the sixteenth century, the Church, although ever exerting a considerable influence, no longer appeared at the head of the world's activity. This was in contrast with what she had done in the era of the conversion of the Roman Empire, during that of the invasion of the barbarians, and amid the immense religious movement which characterized the apogee of the Middle Ages. Father Hecker discovered the cause of this lessening influence in the fact that since the sixteenth century the Church had been compelled to stand upon the defensive. This had greatly paralyzed her power of initiation and her liberty. As a consequence of the Protestant heresy, which threatened the utter destruction of the principle of authority, the Church had been forced to concentrate on that side of her fortress all her means of defence. In order to protect herself from the excesses of the principle of individuality and free inquiry, she had been obliged to resort to a multitude of restrictive measures, which were conceived in a very different spirit from that which animated her in previous centuries. In the sixteenth century the Church placed before everything else the idea of authority. She sacrificed the development of personality to fostering the association of men whose wills were absolutely merged by discipline in one powerful body. It can be seen at a glance how intimately and profoundly the spirit of the dominant religious orders of the later era differs from that of the great orders of the Middle Ages, in respect to the expansion of nature and the development of individuality. The needs of the sixteenth century were altogether different from those of the ages preceding it, and to meet those needs God inspired St. Ignatius with the idea of a different type of Christian character. The result was the triumphant repulse of Protestantism from all the southern nations. But the victory was gained at the price of real sacrifices ; the Catholics of the recent centuries have not displayed the puissant individuality of those of the Middle Ages, the types of which are St. Bernard, St. Gregory VII., Innocent III., St. Thomas Aquinas. The Divine Spirit often exacts the sacrifice of certain human qualities for the preservation of the faith ; and it is in this sense that we should interpret the mysterious words of Jesus Christ, that it is better to lose an eye and an arm and not fall into hell, than to save an eye and an arm and be lost eternally.

The Council of the Vatican, Father Hecker maintained, by giving to the principle of authority its dogmatic completion, has placed it above all attacks, and consequently has brought to a close the historical period in which it was necessary to devote all efforts to its defence. A new period now opens to the Church. She has been engaged during three centuries in perfecting her external organism, and securing to authority the place it should have in working out her divine life; she will now undertake quite another part of her providential mission. It is now to be the individuality, the personality of souls, their free and vigorous initiative under the direct guidance of the Holy Spirit dwelling within them, which shall become the distinctive Catholic form of acting in these times. And this will all be done under the control of her divine supreme authority in the external order preventing error, eccentricity, and rashness.

The Latin races were fitted by nature to be the principal instruments of the Holy Spirit during the period just passed. In the new one the Anglo-Saxon and Teutonic races, of a nature strongly individual and independent, will take their turn as instruments of Divine Providence. This is not saying that the development of the Church is the result of the natural aptitudes of races, but that God, who has created these aptitudes, takes them one after the other, and at the hours He chooses, and causes them to serve as instruments for carrying out His designs. It was thus, from the fourth to the seventh century, that He made use of the metaphysical subtilty implanted by Him in the Greek genius, issuing in all those great definitions which have fixed not only the substance but the verbal form of Catholic dogma. Hence the first general councils were all held in the East.

Father Hecker cherished hopes for the conversion of the Teutonic and Anglo-Saxon races. Doubtless God could convert them suddenly, but considering the way heretofore followed that conversion will be brought about insensibly and by the two following instrumentalities: On the one hand, the new development of individuality in souls within the Church will create a sympathetic attraction towards her on the part of Protestants, who will discover affinities with her of which they were wholly unaware. On the other hand, the more the Protestant races expand, the more they will find the dwarfed Christianity which they profess falling short of their aspirations, and by that means they will be inclined towards Catholicity. It is not a little remarkable that Father Hecker expressed himself thus during the last years of the pontificate of Pius IX., at a moment when such ideas seemed to be least in favor in high Catholic circles. But soon afterwards the pontificate of Leo XIII. began, and with it a movement in the spirit indicated by the American priest, and in a manner so strikingly in accord with his views that Father Hecker seemed to have been enlightened from above in his presages of the future.

Father Hecker developed a grand theological synthesis of what he called the, exterior and interior mission of the Holy Spirit in the Church. He has explained it in a pamphlet; but how much more impressive it was when he expounded it in person! We had the privilege of hearing him do so in a long conversation with the most celebrated Protestant minister of French-speaking countries, the illustrious philosopher and orator, Ernest Naville. Father Hecker said that the antipathy of Protestants for the Church arose from the fact that they imagined that Catholicity reduced all religion to obedience to external authority. Protestants, on the other hand, pretend to place all religion in the interior life, directly generated in souls by the Holy Spirit, and it is for this reason that Catholicity impresses them as a tyrannical usurpation and a stupid formalism. In this they are deceived, as a close acquaintance with Catholics and with such writings as those of St.

Francis de Sales and St. Teresa soon proves to them. So, also, when they fancy that the authority of the Church is not necessary to the preservation of the action of the Holy Spirit in the soul. As a matter of fact, the innumerable divisions of Protestants among themselves plainly show that the interior action of the Holy Ghost does not extend to making each individual infallible. To safeguard souls against deception, scepticism or illuminism, there is need of another action of the Holy Spirit which shall be conservative of the interior life. That other action is exterior, and is exercised by means of the authority of the Church. The Holy Spirit cannot be brought into contradiction with Himself. By His action in the exterior authority of the Church He can never interfere in the least degree with the fulness or the spontaneity of His own interior action in souls.

The exterior action is one of control and of verification, to hinder souls from being lost in the depths of illusion and in the deceits of pride. But besides this, humility, obedience, self-abnegation, virtues dear by excellence to the heart of Jesus Christ, are impossible without due submission to the external authority. When one believes only in himself, he obeys only himself, and hence has never practised complete renunciation nor complete humility.

Father Hecker also maintained that the direction of souls in confession should be made to strengthen and develop individual life. We do not need blood-letting, he said, as if we suffered from plethora, but rather we need a course of tonics, sea-baths, and the invigorating air of the mountains. We should not hold our penitents in leading-strings, but should teach them to live a self-reliant life under the direction of the Holy Spirit. Souls tempered by that process would render the Church a thousand times more service than they do now.

No doubt such souls may sometimes run the risk of pride and of temptation to revolt. But in such cases the Church is so provided with power by the dogma of infallibility, as proclaimed by the Vatican Council, as to be able to counteract this danger without serious loss, as was proved in the case of Dollinger and the Old Catholics.

The Holy Spirit, preparing for a great development of individual life, has made provision beforehand that the Church should be armed with power sufficient to repress all waywardness, and this was done by the Vatican Council. Some had feared that the definition of infallibility would introduce an extravagant use of authority, and lead to a diminution of reasonable liberty and individuality in the Church even greater than before. But the very contrary has been the result.

With reference to the interior life, I can affirm that Father Hecker's was full and rich. Having spent the greater part of his life in a devouring activity, at its close he lived as a true contemplative. He was a genuine mystic. We heard him discourse with marvellous beauty on the Trinity, the Incarnation, the Eucharist, expounding these great truths in a way not only to enrapture one with their splendor, but utterly to refute deism, pantheism, and materialism. The latter error, he said, owed its introduction partly to the fact that Protestantism had refused to the senses their legitimate place in divine worship, this excessive spiritualizing having brought about a reaction.

V.

Father Hecker often spoke of the future reserved for Catholicity in the United States, saying that it was there that the union of the Church with democracy would first take place. In that nation the prejudice against the Church is not so strong as in Europe, and her position is free from the embarrassments of traditional difficulties. Catholicity is there valued for its immediate effect upon human nature, and the rancor born of historical recollections is not in such full control of men's minds; hence conversions are more easily made. Furthermore, Father Hecker believed that it would finally be discovered that the Protestant spirit is contrary to the political spirit of the American Republic. America has based her Constitution on the fact that man is born free, reasonable, and capable of self-government. The Protestant Reformers, on the contrary, never ceased to teach that original sin deprived man of his free will and made him incapable of performing virtuous acts; and if Protestants seek to escape from this whirlpool of fatalism, they fall into infidelity. The day will come when Americans will admit that if they are to be at once religious and reasonable, they must become Catholics. Therefore, whether it be acknowledged or not, every development of political liberty in the United States contributes to the advance of Catholicity. The Constitution of the United States has formulated the political principles most conformable to the Canons of the Council of Trent.

www.ingramcontent.com/pod-product-compliance
Lightning Source LLC
Chambersburg PA
CBHW020857130726
47900CB00014B/939